INFRACTION

Yvonne Zipter

Rattling Good Yarns Press
33490 Date Palm Drive 3065
Cathedral City CA 92235
USA
www.rattlinggoodyarns.com

Cover Design: Rattling Good Yarns Press
Cover Image: *Tea* by Mary Cassatt

Library of Congress Control Number: 2021932855
ISBN: 978-1-7341464-8-6

First Edition

Also by Yvonne Zipter

Kissing the Long Face of the Greyhound, poetry collection (Terrapin Books, 2020)

Like Some Bookie God, poetry chapbook (Pudding House Publications, 2006)

Ransacking the Closet, essay collection (Spinsters Ink, 1995)

The Patience of Metal, poetry collection (Hutchinson House, 1990)

Diamonds Are a Dyke's Best Friend: Reflections, Reminiscences, and Reports from the Field on the Lesbian National Pastime (Firebrand Books, 1989)

For my mother, Elaine, whose love of *Doctor Zhivago*
planted a seed

Author's Note

Infraction is based on the true story of a lesbian who lived in late nineteenth-century Russia. The central facts of her case were recorded by a gynecologist and are translated in Laura Engelstein's "Archives: Lesbian Vignettes: A Russian Triptych from the 1890s," but the embellishments bringing her story to life are my own, including the invention of a fictional girls boarding school, the St. Petersburg Institute for Girls.

A Word about Russian Names

Russian gentry of the period in this book used—both when addressing somebody formally and when among friends—not only a first name but also a patronymic. (A patronymic is a personal name based on the name of one's father.) Because these long Russian names can be confusing for someone unused to them, I have opted to dispense with patronymics almost entirely, using only first and last names, as well as nicknames, to make for easier reading.

Primary Characters

Marya Zhukova, also known as Masha or Mashenka (nicknames) and sometimes Misha (normally a boy's nickname, meant, therefore, to be pejorative)

Lidia Zhukova (Marya's aunt), also known as Lida or Lidochka

Ilya (servant), also known as Ilyusha

Nadezhda (servant), also known as Nadya

Vera Dashkova (girlfriend of Marya), also known as Verochka

Aleksandra Kobiakova (writer [in historical reality] and friend [fictionally] of Vera and Marya), also known as Sasha

Sergei Trepov (Marya's suitor), also known as Seryozha

Liudmilla (servant), also known as Liuda

Grigorii Rostovtsev (Marya's math instructor), also known as Grisha or Grishka (derogatory)

Filipp Trepov (Sergei's cousin), also known as Filya

Nikolai Trepov (Sergei's brother), also known as Kolya

Irina (Lidia's childhood friend), also known as Irochka or Irushka

Olga Levitskaya (Lidia's friend), also known as Olya

Anna Karmazinova (Lidia's friend), also known as Anya

Mikhail Feoktistov (Lidia's fiancé), also known as Misha

Ilya Bunin (Sergei's friend/coworker), also known as Ilyusha

Lev Nekrasov (Sergei's childhood friend), also known as Lyova

Pavel Solovyov (Vera's student), also known as Pasha

Varvara Solovyov (Vera's student), also known as Varya

Where does such tenderness come from?
These aren't the first curls
I've wound around my finger—
I've kissed lips darker than yours.

The sky is washed and dark
(where does such tenderness come from?)
Other eyes have known
and shifted away from my eyes.

But I've never heard words like this
in the night
(where does such tenderness come from?)
With my head on your chest, rest.

Where does this tenderness come from?
And what shall I do with it? Young
stranger, poet, wandering through town,
You and your eyelashes—longer than anyone's.

—Translation from Russian Ilya Kaminsky and Jean Valentine

MARINA TSVETAEVA

Part I

We arrive at truth not by reason only
but also by the heart.

~Blaise Pascal~

1
Marya

The wood of Marya's desk wore a skin of dust and was littered with an untidy heap of papers, worn pencils, a circular brass logarithmic scale, a pen with an ink-crusted nib, a protractor, and broken bits of eraser, all also covered in dust. During the many months of her long depression, she had neglected her work, leaving her desk to stand lonely as a grave marker.

If you put so much as a pair of mittens on an already heavy cart, you will notice it immediately, thought Marya, shaking her head sadly.

$$\text{loss} + \text{loss} + \text{loss}^{n} = \text{too much to bear}$$

Marya automatically translated the old proverb into a mathematical equation of sorts in her head. The deaths of her mother, then brothers, and finally her father—those had been true agonies to withstand. And they had, indeed, brought her to her knees. Yet each time, she forced herself to rise again, to move forward, to carry on with life.

But when it came to Katya—her departure was the additional weight on the already heavy cart.

The ensuing depression into which Marya plunged was like a bottomless well. She had grown weak, unkempt, listless.

And this is the result, she thought, brushing some dust from the desk, then lifting a sheet of paper to blow the dust off of it.

How her aunt had tried to rouse her! Lidia had devised all manner of distractions and outings for her. And when none of them worked, she began inviting gentleman callers to their home for twice-weekly salons, insisting Marya attend.

"The best and brightest St. Petersburg has to offer," her aunt had said.

Marya shook her head at the memory.

Week after week, she had at remained entrenched in her lethargy. But the vapidity of these gentlemen callers!

Oh, she'd been roused, alright! But perhaps not in the way her aunt had been hoping. The polite prattle of these so-called gentlemen threatened to numb her brain like a draught of absinthe, and she found herself itching, again, to challenge her mind.

She sat down, now, at her desk for the first time in months, dismayed at the disarray but determined to impose a sense of order so that she might again resume some measure of mathematical study. Among the scattered tools and mathematical scribblings, Marya found a draft of a letter she had written to Grisha, her mathematics instructor at the St. Petersburg Institute for Girls. She was dismayed at how pitiful she sounded, even to herself, and how transparent her protestations in that missive seemed. She couldn't recall, now, whether she had in fact posted a copy of this letter but hoped that, if so, her final version excluded the sort of cheerless formalist musings she found upon the page before her.

"Mathematics!" she read. "The symbols are quite as meaningless as the entirety of life. We move the symbols around as though with reason, but it's naught but a game. Grisha, how is it you persist, when your livelihood is bereft of meaning? You and I, we should do honest work, Grisha—fashion leather into humble boots or till the fields. Even selling kvas upon the streets would be more honest, for don't people need to drink and wash away their sorrows?"

She groaned aloud as she scanned further the contents of the letter, praying she hadn't sent the letter in any version. "The rules! How arbitrary are the rules? Can I not as easily tell you π = 2,004 or 0.11 as 3.14? We have assigned a certain meaning to π that allows us to play games in which we say, 'Here the size of this circle' or 'The way across, from this side to the other, is so many units,' much as we have assigned the name 'shoe' to the leather article that houses a foot. If we had given it, instead, the name, 'dog,' then each day I would be hooking closed the buttons of my dog!" Here she couldn't quite suppress a little chortle, confronted with this comical image. But no such humor seemed to have seized her, it would seem, the day of the letter's writing, for she went on there in quite a sour vein: "And then what have we proved, Grisha? I'm at pains to understand how such games played with symbols—meaningless marks created by whom?—once gave me solace."

Looking at these words, Marya's face showed the strain of trying to reach, again, whatever place she'd been in that would bring her to say such unfeeling things about something so vital, so primal, as mathematics. *Meaningless?* All of human progress had ridden on the backs of numbers! *Games with symbols?* Bridges, houses, the huffing engine of a train—none would be present across the globe were it not for mathematics. A house might be built with no reckoning of units, but the many-sized walls would wobble in the fierce winds that shriek across the Gulf of Finland or beneath winter's heavy white cap of snow. And soon such a house must surely topple to the ground. *What conceit!* she thought, to believe that she, or any human, might, of a whim or fancy, *invent* mathematics. The elements of mathematics were like a vein of gold, waiting only to be tapped, or like trees, which are there whether one looks upon them or no. Unable—happily so—to regain that dark point that would have spawned the sort of despair that would cause one to deny the existence, the pure fact, the supremacy of mathematical knowledge caused Marya to shake her head in sad wonder. What manner of misery would deny the importance of a factorial? She was incredulous at her own audacity, hardly believing it was she who had written such scurrilous words.

Again she prayed she had not sent such a hateful letter to someone like Grisha who alone, among all her limited circle, revered the power of mathematical inquiry. Marya tore the letter in fourths and placed the pieces into the ceramic stove, pausing before closing the door in order to watch them turn to ash.

2
Lidia

Seated at her desk near the window in her bedroom, Lidia was transfixed by a tiny tuft of feathers stuck to the windowpane. She watched as it trembled in the cold breeze, moved up and down and side to side but didn't blow away. How can something so insignificant cling so tightly to what it knows? She didn't pause to ask herself why a tuft of feathers should want to take root upon her window nor what calamity might have brought the feathers to rest there in the first place. She pondered only their tenacity. With a structure so tender, how did they withstand the tugging and pummeling of a force so much mightier and more eternal than they?

She felt a tingling in her veins from the blood coursing through but avoided the question of whether this could be good for her wasting health. Since Marya had come to stay with her, this hot coursing had become a familiar sensation. If it wasn't good for her, she didn't want to know: it was the most alive she'd felt in years. *Irony*, she thought wryly, *is wasted on the dying.*

With Marya came a surfeit of questions. This, no doubt, was what was at the root of her routinely surging blood. Why was Marya behaving so indecorously with those fine young men? Did she mean to embarrass her aunt? But why?—when Lidia had never been anything but kind to her. But then, just the same—why drive them away, the most handsome and eligible men of Petersburg? Could her loyalty to Katya run so deep she dared not sully it and so shunned all others? Lidia remembered how it had been for her when she had learned of her childhood friend Irina's betrothal and the changes that signified. At first when Irina said she was to marry the dark-eyed Andrei

Khlebnikov, Lidia had squealed excitedly, and the two girls clasped arms and jumped and spun in a circle like leaves caught in an eddy of wind. But the realization that Irina would be moving to Moscow after her wedding had been like a stone on her heart.

Still, she found it improbable that it was Marya's fondness for Katya that was preventing her from pressing onward with her life. Though Lidia didn't ultimately fare well in transferring her own affections from Irina to a young man of her set was beside the point. Propriety must always prevail over passion among people of their social standing.

No, it must be some other thing distancing her niece from such fine gentlemen. Perhaps Marya has been damaged by the endless talk, so prominent these days, about the rights of women? Or was it possible Masha was simply fundamentally unable to play the coquette, and nothing more? *She has the face of a beauty, but only hell likes her temper*, thought Lidia.

Ultimately, Lidia decided the answers to these questions were not important; that Masha was engaged once again with *life*—that was the important thing. Lidia would have been the first to admit the salons hadn't been quite what she'd envisioned. Nevertheless, it was clear to her there was nothing to do but continue to entice the eligible men of Petersburg to her doorstep. If Lidia wouldn't behold the blushes and flirtations forthcoming from her niece as she'd hoped, then smirks and flashes of fire in her eyes would have to do. Perhaps Marya would come round in the end, and if not, the vitality returned to her grief-drained face made the experiment worthwhile. Furthermore, Lidia reminded herself, she had no other plan.

When she had begun hunting for a mate for Marya, it was for Marya's sake she had risen to the challenge, but now, strangely, she was even more noticeably infused with vitality than Marya. It was she—who was, in fact, slowly dying—who now felt more vibrant than she had in years.

One morning, however, found Lidia sitting at the edge of her bed. She held a white handkerchief bordered with silvery lace. At its center: an irregular splash of color. She stared at this splotch of color as it turned from shiny crimson to a dull rust. She had begun to cough up blood.

"Certainly that's a handkerchief ruined," she said to herself, refusing to think any more deeply about the matter, but even then, she couldn't bring herself to put the handkerchief down. *So this is my blood*, she thought. She had watched it seep from a cut in her hand, on her foot, or a dozen other places on her body, of course, in her long life, but this blood, the blood now holding her attention, had come from a place she couldn't see and was anything but regular. This blood was mystical, mesmerizing, unstoppable. How can you stop something you can't even see, can never touch the source of? She sensed her life was leaving her—could ascertain as much from the dark stain on her handkerchief—and she could do nothing about it, no matter how much work she had yet to do on Marya's behalf.

At the same time, she reminded herself, so much had already been accomplished: in spite of Marya's inhospitable style of entertaining, the twice-weekly gatherings Lidia had engineered had clearly been good for her. Not since Katya had left had Lidia sensed such keenness in her niece's face, such flash in her eyes, such joy in her smile.

"Aunt," Marya announced one night at dinner, "I believe I shall attend the Alarchin courses." So eager was she to relate this plan, she let a trickle of borscht dribble down her chin. She frowned and wiped the soup away. "Yes," she continued, and hurriedly spooned up the last of the soup in the bowl. "I began thinking about it shortly after you started inviting those dreadful young men to our house."

Lidia opened her mouth to defend either the young men or herself—she had not quite decided which—when Nadezhda came in to clear the soup things.

"Thank you, Nadya," Lidia said instead.

"You must admit, Lidia, for you can't fail to have noticed, I'm just as bright as they are, even if *they* are generally too pompous to realize it. I do owe them a debt of gratitude, though. Their inane conversations about horses and gambling and tobacco and their trite perceptions concerning literature have made me yearn for something more intellectually stimulating. I long, dear Lidia, to converse with equals, to be challenged to think deeply and clearly. Such fellows as those we've entertained here only present me with the challenge not to slap their self-assured faces! The prigs. Why do you insist on tormenting me this way, aunt?"

Marya scowled.

Lidia meant to ask how it was she found her way to the drawing room each Tuesday and Thursday evening, given her obvious antipathy, but Marya rushed on before Lidia could put forth her question.

"Yes, aunt, I'm thinking the evening lectures would be just the thing. I'll be among women there, who are as a rule a more charming race than men. It appalls me now to think on how much I adored the male sex as a child and shames me to realize how indifferent I was to my own kind. But really, I don't think the fault was mine." She paused to sample a morsel of the smoked goose Nadya had brought out, pinching a piece directly from the bird on the platter. She licked the grease from her fingers, then continued. "Some transformation takes place, I think"—she paused to chew the piece of goose she had in her mouth—"that turns little boys into gloating dullards and at the same time turns simpering little girls into great companions." She frowned and took another bit of goose, this time with a fork from the piece on her own plate. "Yes, I think that's it! What do you think, Lidia, dear?"

"Well, yes, Masha, I do count among my dearest friends many women, but—"

"I wonder what those boys I played with back home at Khrupkaya Luna are like now." She didn't seem to notice she had interrupted. "Do you suppose it's only among the gentry that men grow so stupid? Maybe men of the lower classes are of a finer cut—do you suppose that's true, aunt? Think of Ilya—you don't find him babbling on only to hear himself talk. My math instructor at the institute, Grigorii Rostovtsev, seems clear thinking as well. One won't, at any rate, find him holding the opinion he is cleverer than any of his fellows, nor even than his students."

Lidia had given up any hope of interjecting her own thoughts into the conversation, as Marya effervesced for the remainder of the meal. But what a pleasant music by which to eat, she thought to herself: the animated voice of her niece.

3
Marya

"It's important for you to learn how to be a lady in all parts of society, my dear. Your 'Alarchin courses' will be of no help in that regard," her aunt had said. There was no mistaking her aunt's disdain for the lecture courses that Marya had proposed to attend.

And with those words, Marya had been compelled by her aunt to dine with her and her cronies, Anna Karmazinova and Olga Levitskaya.

Marya thought to protest, of course. If she found the conversation of the gentlemen that called on them tedious, how much more tiresome the nattering of a gathering of old society women? But given that her aunt would almost certainly have been unable to make her way to the carriage on her own, Marya relented. And when her aunt leaned heavily both on her on one side and on her long-time servant Ilya on the other, Marya suspected her aunt's insistence on her company served another purpose beyond the one stated.

At Anna's house, Marya, mute as a fish, sat at the ornately outfitted table along with the three others—four, if one were to count Anna's little Italian greyhound, Kalach, who sat on his mistress's lap. His soulful brown eyes looked huge and bulging on his slender white head. Marya found him a queer creature—somewhere between cat and canine—when compared to the borzois and wolfhounds she'd grown up with at Khrupkaya Luna, her family's estate.

When Anna was paying no attention, the little beast would purloin paper-thin slices of smoked elk tongue from her plate. "Naughty boy," Anna would say when she chanced to notice his pilfering, then stroke him tenderly. "Give mama a kiss."

Ordinarily, Marya would have found this droll, but on this occasion, she instead watched the scene with the detached interest of a theatergoer at a second-rate play, brooding about the time she had lost during her mourning over Katya—and now to suffer through this frivolousness? She could be reading a math text! Even reading a novel by Tolstoy would be better than sitting among these rattlebrains.

"Here, darling," Anna said, as she deposited the miniature greyhound in Marya's lap. "Would you be a dear and hold Kalach while I ask cook to prepare the sweetmeats? Where is that serving girl?"

The world of lapdogs was truly peculiar to Marya. A dog should be used for hunting, Marya thought—that was a true dog, a dog with dignity. With purpose. Nevertheless, she couldn't help but be charmed by Kalach, who sat on her lap without complaint, his comically small head on her breast. His ear flickered and tickled Marya's chin, and she absently fingered his collar, where she found a small gold plaque attached. She turned it over and discovered that a short verse had been inscribed there: "I promise no largesse / To the person who finds me. / Whoever returns me to my mistress / Will be rewarded—he will see her." Marya frowned.

"There. Now that's settled." Anna glided back into the room like a fragrant breeze.

Marya was about to lift Kalach to return him to Anna, but as Anna seemed not to notice either of them in the least, Marya was content to let the little warm creature curl in her lap again and idly rested her hand on his haunch. Though the thought wasn't conscious, Marya felt some measure of peace from the warmth and life of him pressed against her.

"Now, my dears," Anna said, while sliding as fluidly back into her chair as she did the conversation, "you haven't found yourself so swayed, have you, by those among us who fancy themselves reformers that you won't plan this winter's charity ball?" She fussed with the edging of lace along the neckline of her dress.

"Please!" said Olga with a wave of her left hand, while with her right, she snared a piece of honey cake from the plate the serving girl was setting on the table. "People these days—they worry far too much." She took a small bite of honey cake. "Why should it be of concern if we spend a few rubles on flowers, ribbons, and pearls?" She paused briefly to push back a small bit of cake that threatened to tumble from her mouth. "Why shouldn't we enjoy ourselves while we raise money for those poor unfortunates? What is the harm, after all?" She licked the honey from her fingers, then dusted a few crumbs from her bosom.

"Yes," said Anna, "I quite agree with that writer in the *Stock Exchange News*—a charity ball is but inoffensive vanity (if vanity you find it), and it has benefited many useful social causes." She leaned forward toward the plate of cakes and lifted a piece to her own plate with the silver server. She smoothed the napkin on her lap, then delicately raised her fork, as if moving too quickly might frighten the cake away.

Marya sighed. Their endless talk grated on her. She pinched the bridge of her nose. Kalach growled softly in his sleep and nestled more deeply into her lap. She ran her fingers along his neck, finding his relative stillness preferable to the prattling of her aunt and friends.

"What I can't bear," said Lidia, "are those who find our philanthropic work not 'scientific' and condemn almsgiving as an encouragement to beg. Our own Jesus Christ, after all, was a beggar! And all the saints as well! Were I less wedded to my comforts and were I again unencumbered ..." Lidia silently indicated her niece with a movement from her eyes. "I should be tempted to give all I own to the poor and roam the streets myself, like Blessed Ksenia. No doubt I should be adjudged insane as she was—her whom they called a 'fool-for-Christ.' Giving succor to others—how is that madness? I tell you, she that has no money needs no purse."

Lidia poked a bony finger at the air. "How things would be simplified, if money were of no concern. That woman will be canonized someday, mark my words." It had been almost a hundred years since Ksenia Petrova had become a widow, given away her husband's fortune, and taken to the streets in his military uniform. Yet so famous had her story become that Anna and Olga both gave involuntary shudders at the thought of their friend following her lead and sleeping in fields on the outskirts of town, relying on handouts from strangers for her sustenance.

"Oh, really now, Lida—this is all going too far. I can't picture you wandering the streets of Petersburg in nothing but a ragged gown. What would the good in that be? The poor are better served with you here among us." Anna reached across the table and patted Lidia's hand.

"Yes," chimed in Olga. "You must remember the old saying, 'The beggar is fed by the rich man, and the rich man is saved by the beggar's prayer.' It's our spiritual duty to take up charity work! If the reformers—"

"The reformers! Bah!" Lidia shook her head. "They treat poverty as though it were a problem one could solve, when Christ himself said, 'You always have the poor with you.' Too much change. All the time change. Why do people wish always to alter the world?"

"I don't see the need." Anna flew from her chair, made an imperceptible adjustment to a frame upon the wall behind Marya, and was quite settled again before the breath of her last word had fully cleared her lip. "Why, the tsar himself," she continued, "has given his blessing to the work we do! Have you not witnessed charitable societies like ours grow to life everywhere? What we do isn't frivolous, my dear friends: it's our *duty* to relieve the suffering of the poor. It's like saying there is a science to loving. What did the pamphlet on charity say? The best person … Oh, what was it now?" Anna smoothed her dress at the waistline.

"The best person is the one who … who loves people the most," Olga filled in, "and who … who brings them the most assistance. Or something of the sort. I think, ladies, it's clear to which group we belong. We have tradition, God, and the tsar on our side; let the reformers say what they will. Now enough of that—let us turn our thoughts to our charity ball."

And on they went in like vein, until Marya joined Kalach in a nap, there on her chair, and ceased listening. Marya had certainly been little tamed by her time at the Institute where matters of civility and deportment were concerned. She had never cared much for tradition, perhaps owing to her father's delight in her mischief and his having taught her to hunt—about which he'd had loud disagreements with her mother. But never had she cared less about tradition than now, so soon after she had lost her beloved Katya to the senseless tradition of arranged marriage.

To Marya, tradition was a null set, made of nothing—notions and empty words and pointless acts. Tradition, she believed, existed but to justify those things that are done the same, year in and year out, each decade, even across the centuries. Making the sign of the cross over a baby before it sleeps, welcoming visitors with a round loaf on which a saltcellar rests, waiting for the first star to appear in the sky before beginning the Christmas Eve meal—each no more than tradition. Each based on nothing more compelling than superstition and repetition, near as Marya could discern.

But perhaps the most inane and degrading convention of all, to her way of thinking, was the one that promised a woman to a man she had not herself chosen. If one were searching for an example of a degenerate iterative process, one would need look no further than the custom of choosing husbands for women! Why, she wondered, would a woman submit to such degradation? A man might just as well choose a woman's shoes each day, decide the flavor of her kvas, the herbs with which she scents her bath, or the number of bites into which she cuts her meat!

These were the thoughts that occupied her mind during the carriage ride home, while Lidia let it be known that her behavior had been unbecoming—much as it was with the gentleman callers, she'd added.

"Your father, it seems, wasted his money! You learned nothing about how to comport yourself in society at that St. Petersburg Institute for Girls!"

"Yes, aunt." Marya sighed. All her life, she had heard similar complaints about her unruly nature—from her mother, her nanny, her teachers. *One can't wash a black dog until it turns white*, she thought, trying to comfort herself about her inability to be a lady. Was there anywhere she'd ever fit in?

After she and Ilya had gotten Lidia up to her room, where she collapsed on her bed, exhausted from their short excursion, Marya left her aunt in the caring hands of Nadezhda and Liudmilla and retired to her own room.

The windows of that room, in the apartment at no. 112 on the Moika, overlooked Novaya Gollandia—the naval yard on the far side of the canal, from which no sound could be heard but the clatter of timber and the occasional shout of a navy man as planks for ships were stacked behind the porous screen of trees. Such sounds of labor and the most common of men would have been far preferable to the jabbering of the society people with whom her aunt wished she would more seamlessly blend.

The promise of the Alarchin courses threaded through her thoughts as Marya fell asleep with a copy of the *Historical Herald* next to her on the bed.

4
Vera's Journal

5 November 1875

Years hence, when all I may remember of the Alarchin courses is the startling woman I met the first night I attended, will it matter what brought me there at the start? It seems unlikely any save myself (and perhaps not even I) shall concern themselves with my hope to preserve my position as tutor to the Solovyov children to ensure they don't quickly outstrip the meager education granted by the pedagogical course. Tonight, to be sure (though I can't speak for the future), my only care is for how a simple smile might come to send a river of emotion flooding through me and overrun my breath.

For that's what happened when I sat beside the woman with a mop of chestnut brown hair, which she wore brushed back (cut à la mouzhik, as they say), when she turned to me and smiled, though I dare say I should have noticed the smile regardless because it was such a contrast to her slightly melancholy, rather pensive face—like a ray of light piercing a cloudy sky. I returned her smile, of course—how could I not?—but that the lecture then began is all to the good as I felt distinctly peculiar. Throughout the lecture my heart beat erratically.

I cast sidelong glances to determine what force was tugging at my heart in this way, which only made my state worsen, especially when my glance was met with that disarming smile. I must have blushed a half dozen times or more during the course of the lecture, certainly at least in part because she was dressed so queerly, her clothes plain and dark. A Narodnik? This thought but inflamed my curiosity and my enthrallment the more, for I had never met in person a socialist or populist or whatever it was they stood for. In consequence, I applied myself more diligently to the pretense of note-taking at each such occurrence to try to hide my discomfiture.

And when, after the lecture, Marya—for such is her name: Marya Iuryevna Zhukova—spoke to me, I could hardly hear her words, there was such an insistent buzz—nay: a roaring—in my head. I thought for a moment I was becoming ill, but the sensations I was feeling were much too pleasant for that. I did manage to calm myself, at last, and joined Marya in conversation. I was impressed immediately by her sharpness of mind, her earnestness, her attentiveness. It seemed perfectly natural then, when she invited me to attend the meeting to which she intended to go, to accompany her. As we strolled to a nearby apartment, she linked her arm through mine, and we walked together like old friends.

We arrived at our destination at the very moment several other women did, and the lot of us joined the ten or fifteen women already assembled. In an instant, one could sense this wasn't a typical gathering of young women, giggling and gossiping and primping. Small groups of three or four women were scattered round the room, each of which was engaged in quiet, ardent discussion. The air was so thick with cigarette smoke, I found it difficult at first to breathe. After our coats had been taken by a servant and we had found our way to the samovar, one woman clanked her spoon at the edge of her cup and we all found seats.

"The Alarchin courses are a means to an end," she began. "Ultimately, what we are trying to do is free ourselves from the stagnant past, from 'tradition,' a tradition of family and marital authority that has served to make slaves of us, that has kept us from the larger goals of self-development and, especially, of working for the betterment of our society as a whole."

"Yes," interjected a second woman. "Personal relationships are an obstacle to women doing real work in the world. I've no intention of marrying and subverting all of my energies into bearing child after child. Into running a household!"

"Yes."

"I agree."

"Exactly right."

Voices of assent rose up around the room, while other women merely nodded their agreement.

"But then, are we choosing to leave children—and husbands—completely out of our lives? Is there not also pleasure in being a member of a family?" This bold question brought a hush over the room, and I strained to see who might have asked it.

"There is plenty of time for that later! Marry when you are thirty, then, if you must. For now, we must arm ourselves with knowledge. Knowledge is the key to our independence, to our ability to act freely in the interests of society, to the proper path of action."

"Yes! Knowledge!" shouted several women, and the energy in the room caused the assembled women to once again splinter into smaller groups. Marya and I suddenly found ourselves between two women arguing about whether it was better to keep men's and women's circles separate or bring them together. A tall and stately woman insisted there was no reason to keep them separate.

"We are all working toward the same goals, are we not?" she added.

"Men?" said another. Smoke from her cigarette curled in front of her face but didn't hide her smirk. "You know quite as well as I that we wouldn't meet with them as equals when they yet believe 'as chicken is not a bird, woman is not a human being.'"

"That's unfair! Types like that—they aren't those who would frequent groups such as ours." The tall woman held her hands up in a gesture of bewilderment.

"Even those working toward the same goals, however," said a short, stocky blonde, "would dominate, with their greater educational achievements, and make it difficult for women to think for themselves. In the end, to include them would be harmful."

"I agree," joined in Marya. "I'm not intimidated by the male mind, but I've observed how they try to commandeer every conversation. Many women are too polite or too meek to assert themselves, in spite of their possibly superior intellects."

I listened quietly, too shy yet to speak up, and too excited by all of these new ideas even to really know my own mind hitherto. We stayed for an hour more, the conversation rising in angry waves before falling again into constructive discussion of how to proceed to reach their goals—or "ours," I suppose—of greater equality and freedom. At last, Marya, noticing my stifled yawn, asked if I should like to go.

On the street once again, Marya signaled to a coachman. He grabbed the reins and, speaking sweetly to his horses, pulled the carriage up alongside us, his full beard settling, as he came to a stop, on his long blue kaftan, the Circassian belt cinched around his ample waist just beyond the beard's lengthy reach.

Marya asked where I lived, then called out the address to the coachman. Once inside the carriage, Marya asked whether I frequented the Alarchin courses and whether she could hope to see me there again.

"Yes," I said, only half a lie, for while I had never been before this evening, I knew without doubt, now, that certainly I would attend again.

We talked for a while, then, as we bumped amiably along Petersburg's rutted streets, about the meeting we had been to. Upon hearing my opinions on various matters, Marya encouraged me to speak up more the next time.

"That is," she added, "if you'd like to join me again?" And we both blushed—I think: it was hard to tell in the dark cab. Well I, at any rate, felt heat rise in my cheeks.

"Oh yes!" I replied. Then, with a bit more decorum, blushing once again: "Yes, I should like that very much indeed."

We arrived, much too quickly it seemed, here at the house where I board, and reluctantly, I said good evening to the young woman who had stirred me in a pleasant yet unnerving way. She kissed my cheeks in the proper manner, though I find myself surprised to confess I wished she might linger there longer, her breath warm on my skin, in my ear.

I stepped from the carriage, confused by but enchanted with the evening's direction. I waved goodbye, turned toward the door, and tripped upon the first stair. It seems I had become slightly unmoored from the specifics of space and time.

5
Marya

Not for the first time, Marya reflected that the men who attended the gatherings Lidia had designed for her were, to a one, boors. The mere thought of their inexhaustible blather, which they delivered as though what they had to say was of great import, caused Marya to vow that when next they assembled she would remind the whole pack of louts that rope is good when it's long, while speech is better when it's short.

Irrespective of Marya's irritation with these foolish salons, she recognized that she owed a debt of gratitude to Lidia, for it was the fatuity of the gatherings that had stirred her to explore the Alarchin courses. Further, had she not gone to the Alarchin School, she would likely never have met Vera Dashkova, whose comely demeanor had stirred her at the outset, despite her reticence to give her heart again after having had it broken so recently. But how resist those eyes, blue as the Gulf of Finland in June, cheekbones of architectural majesty, hair the color of a wheat field in autumn? How indeed!

But Marya did try to resist. Once she had greeted the woman in the seat beside her in the lecture hall, she thought there was an end to it. She had set her focus to Gonchorov's lecture on anatomy. But then the ghostly touch of another's gaze would trail across the flesh of her neck, compelling her to turn toward that illusory caress. Upon finding its source, each time, Marya couldn't prevent her face melting into a smile.

In the days that followed that first encounter, Marya tried to distract herself from the thought of Vera lest she let herself cross into territory she wished to avoid. But each book she tried to read—whether Riemann's *Basis for a General Theory of Functions* or Turgenev's *Smoke*—fell slowly into her lap, the pages obscured by the vision of the girl's face filling her mind. Even to hold a conversation with her aunt proved a challenge as she felt again, in memory, the feathered glance of scrutiny from those icy blue eyes.

By the evening of the next lecture at the Alarchin School, Marya could think of nothing but seeing Vera again. She attempted to fool herself into believing it was the anticipation of gaining further education that had her excited. But the multiple changes of gown, the desire to achieve precisely the right effect, belied her true interest. Though no doubt Lidia would have found every one of Marya's gowns as dreary as the next, for Marya each portrayed her in a shade different light: this one serious, that one solemn, a third stern, and another sincere. In the end, she settled on a black skirt, white shirt with stiff collar, and narrow black tie. Though she took special care with her hair, as well, in the end she was dissatisfied and ran her fingers through it and wouldn't let herself examine it again. For by then she had all but convinced herself that likely Vera wouldn't appear again anyway and, further, that Vera's presence or absence would be of no interest to her regardless.

But the moment Marya saw Vera beside the Alarchin Bridge that evening, her heart leapt and her wish for indifference had become a futility. Vera, peering down Angliisky Avenue, didn't notice Marya on the bridge. Marya stood, hands in the pockets of her peacoat, attempting to decide whether to risk the pain of loss again or whether it would be better to bypass Vera altogether and find a place in the lecture hall far from her, off in a corner, where she might go unnoticed. She chewed her lip, trying to ignore the sensation of pleasure she got simply from gazing at this woman who had last time smiled at her so kindly and with whom she had conversed so amiably.

The faint odor of water and decay drifted up from the Ekaterininsky Canal on the damp evening air, and she brushed rapidly at the sleeves of her jacket as if she might whisk away any trace of deterioration. Then she ran her fingers through her hair and, with a smile unstoppably blooming on her face, approached Vera.

"Good evening, Vera Dashkova."

"Oh! You startled me." Vera raised her gloved hand to her collarbone to form a V at the base of her neck. Marya thought fleetingly of how those fingers, thus arrayed, resembled the symbol for vector space, how like arrows Vera's forefinger and thumb were, and how they might describe the sum of the forces at work as her gaze fell into the hollow that dipped between the fine bones that crowned Vera's chest. Vera's hand closed more closely around her neck in an unconscious protective gesture against the intensity of Marya's fixed stare. Vera cleared her throat.

"Good … good evening, Marya." Her gaze dropped to the muddy road.

"Shall we go in?" Marya gestured toward the door.

Vera nodded assent and took the arm Marya offered.

The two women found a place in the lecture hall among the many others. There were women of every class and manner of dress, but Marya was aware only of Vera. Her skin tingled from the nearness of Vera, causing an involuntary shudder. Normally, a phrase such as "numerical sequence" would have pulled her attention like a charged particle to the speaker of these words. But the faint fragrance of lilacs emanating from Vera exerted a far greater pull. And though Marya's eyes were, for the most part, dutifully fixed on the man delivering that evening's lecture, she hardly noticed the long tresses that sprang frenziedly from his receding hairline, or the generous beard that rambled from his chin, or the rough cut of his coarse-looking jacket. And in those moments when the sensation of finding Vera so near to her that she was overpowered, Marya would chance a look, as if to reassure herself that she had not conjured a phantom to appease her longings. And if their eyes happened to meet, Marya was unable to suppress a glad smile. The color would then rise across Vera's cheeks, and immediately she would avert her eyes.

So distracted were Vera and Marya on that evening, they would perhaps have been unaware the lecture had concluded if not for those around them rising to their feet and collecting their things. Marya cleared her throat and opened her mouth to speak, but Vera looked away shyly. They walked in silence to the door, though Marya's thoughts were anything but quiet. She didn't know what Vera might be feeling, but she understood all too well her own feelings. Again, Marya struggled with whether to hold herself safe from harm and say goodnight as they exited the door or relent to the insistent prodding of her yearnings.

The crowd of eager students dispersed along Angliisky and Ekateringofsky Avenues and across the Alarchin Bridge as Marya and Vera stepped out into the brisk November night. Marya could not bear simply to turn her heart away from Vera, and so devised, on the spot, a test: she would offer Vera her hand to shake. If Vera seemed to disdain this gesture as too masculine, then the decision would be made for her. As Marya reached her hand out, she felt as though the very blood in her veins fell still, waiting.

Vera reached with hesitation for Marya's hand. Marya squeezed Vera's hand lightly. Thinking, *I can't bear the torment again*, she did not wait for a response but said, "Good-bye, then." With that, she turned to walk away.

"Marya!" Vera called out.

Marya pressed her eyes shut against the pain of hearing her name on Vera's lips. Certain she should walk away, Marya turned anyway to Vera, telling herself it would be discourteous not to hear what she might say.

"I, that is to say," Vera began, "would you care to come back to my rooms for some tea?" She pulled her lower lip between her teeth and pierced Marya with her eyes as though she meant to consider Marya as a specimen for her Kunstkammer—her cabinet of curiosities.

"Thank you, Vera, for your kind invitation." Marya bowed, fully intending to decline, but heard herself say, instead, "Yes, I should very much like that." Then, before she should regain her reason, Marya hailed a coachman.

When they arrived at the house where Vera took rooms, Marya helped Vera from the coach, then followed her up the stairs. The two climbed the stairs in silence. Once or twice Vera glanced nervously over her shoulder. The creak of the stairs and the swish of Vera's gown were being inscribed on Marya's memory like a simple equation.

When finally Vera stopped beside a door, she paused with her hand upon the knob and turned to Marya. Her eyes moved about Marya's face, as if deciphering a coded text, and each place Vera's eyes landed, Marya felt a sensation delicate as an eyelash falling.

"My rooms ... my rooms are spartan," Vera said, and cleared her throat. "But ... but I hope ... I hope you will find them comfortable. Nonetheless."

Marya said nothing but strode in directly after Vera. Marya's eyes roamed over all, from the gouged wooden table and chairs, tarnished samovar, worn velvet chairs, and small writing table that made up the modest sitting area to the bed, closet, and washstand that she glimpsed in the adjoining room. Marya feared that she appeared to be taking inventory, perhaps even judging, but in truth, her scrutiny was a tactic to provide her with time to decide what next she should say or do. Marya paused beside the writing table near the doorway to the next room and absently ran her fingertips across its glossy but scarred surface, noting, without thinking about it, the odor of cooked cabbage that had followed them in from elsewhere in the large rooming house.

Marya noticed Vera was yet standing in her own doorway, watching as this stranger took in the details of her life. Marya knew it would be a kindness to say something of what she saw but was for once unable to find even the simplest of words. She turned, then, toward Vera, hoping for rescue.

"Excuse my rudeness!" Vera said, springing again to life. "May I take your coat?"

Marya slipped her heavy peacoat from off her arms and shoulders and handed it to Vera, who brushed past Marya to get to the closet in the cramped bedroom area. Marya, having noticed some photographs on the wall, leaned across the writing table to get a closer look.

"My mother," Vera said, observing the direction of Marya's gaze as she left the bedroom. "And my father. Let me put water on to boil."

Marya managed a smile but, still mute with trepidation, could produce naught but a raised eyebrow and a gesture of the hand, meant to inquire whether she might sit down.

"Oh!" Vera said. "Yes. Please, sit down. Do forgive me. I don't know where my manners are tonight."

Vera pulled a white linen cloth from the cupboard and spread it across the little dining table, where Marya pulled out a chair for herself. The scrape of the chair on the wood floor resounded in the sparsely furnished room. Seated, Marya busied herself with smoothing nonexistent creases in her skirt and adjusting the sleeves of her blouse to no purpose. She wasn't so engaged with these "tasks," however, that she didn't perceive herself being observed. This caused her to again tug at the cuff of her blouse.

Aware as she was of Vera's eyes taking her in, Marya was nevertheless startled when Vera cleared her throat. She looked at Vera, then, for the first time, truly, since she'd entered these rooms.

"Perhaps …" Vera cleared her throat again. "I mean, if you have thought better of coming here—for tea—to have tea—you could, I mean, if you'd like to … I would understand if you … shall I—"

"What? Oh, goodness, no!" Marya jumped up so abruptly the chair nearly tumbled over, but Marya was able to catch it, just. "Oh! No. No! If I gave you the impression … no, Vera. It's only that I … I'm happy to … Tea. Is the tea yet …? Oh, then I shall sit again, until …"

During this jumble of fragmented remarks, Marya had taken the few steps required to reach Vera and, without thinking, had wrapped her hand around Vera's upper arm from behind it. The instant she was sensible of where her hand had come to rest, she released her grasp as though a flame had risen up the wick of Vera's arm to burn her palm. Marya returned to her seat, the chair scraping inharmoniously again, producing in her a slight shiver.

Finally, the tea was ready. Vera brought all they might need for their light refreshment on an enameled tray and sat opposite Marya. Self-consciously, they each prepared their tea, exchanging an awkward smile from time to time.

Vera then placed her spoon poorly at the edge of the table and it dropped to the floor. Both women bent to pick it up and bumped their heads together. They laughed.

This unexpected contact apparently put them at ease, for they began to talk, at last, and talked, in fact, for several hours about their lives, their families, their studies, their opinions on this matter and that. The time flew by quickly on their amiable talk and easy laughter, and Marya silently noted with a mixture of fear and delight that she was all the more enchanted with Vera. She found Vera's voice warm and sweet, her mouth altogether pretty. And she was all but captive to those blue and piercing eyes.

As tender feelings began to well up in Marya, she felt she must go, apprehensive of what she might do were she to stay a moment longer, certain she could not bear it if she were mistaking Vera's kindness for something more.

"Thank you for a lovely evening, Vera." Marya abruptly pushed back her chair and stood.

"Oh, you are … yes, I suppose it's rather late." Vera then went to retrieve Marya's coat, while Marya closed her eyes and tried to think about nothing more than her breathing.

When Vera returned, Marya searched Vera's eyes as she handed Marya her coat. Vera answered her gaze, but soon reddened, and looked down, brushing at an imaginary crumb on her skirt.

When Marya leaned to kiss Vera's cheeks, she ached to kiss her lips instead and savored the brush of Vera's cheek on her own. But she cautioned herself not to be like the woman in the proverb who had no trouble and so bought a piglet. Marya took care to put literal space between herself and Vera, hoping to lessen Vera's gravitational pull. She placed her hands on Vera's arms near her shoulders, but this seemed a too-forward gesture as well. She swiftly withdrew her hands and took another step away.

"I won't, uh, I won't be at the lecture tomorrow evening," Marya said. "I have … another engagement." She slipped her now empty hands into the pockets of her peacoat lest Vera see how they trembled. "Good-bye, then. Until Wednesday?"

Marya turned with reluctance to leave. Since no hand moved to stop her, she walked out onto the landing.

Descending, she heard a faint "good-bye." Or imagined it? She didn't check to see which. For she felt certain that, were she to look upon Vera one more time, she might find answers to questions she wasn't yet ready to ask.

6
Lidia

Increasingly, Lidia found herself too weak to leave the house, although shortly after Marya had declared her intention to attend the Alarchin courses, Lidia had a good day and felt well enough to accept an invitation to join Olga Levitskaya for tea at her apartment.

Remarking the two women together, one might presume to know the disposition of Lidia's mislaid robustness: where Lidia was frail, Olga was plump; where Lidia's voice was soft, Olga's was booming; where Lidia merely picked at the assortment of cakes set before them, Olga devoured hers with obvious relish, sometimes pausing, after a mouthful, with eyes closed as if she had been transported into a rapture.

"Tell me now, Lidia, how is your health?" Olga slurped some tea in a rather common fashion, then reached a fleshy hand over and clasped her old friend's bony fingers. Her pale blue eyes, averted temporarily from the dessert plate, searched Lidia's face with genuine concern.

"Oh, you know." Lidia waved her free hand as if the question weren't even worth answering. At a raised eyebrow from Olga, she elaborated. "The coughing spells are more frequent. There's more blood. I would say in all, Olya, it isn't good. It gets harder to hide it, but I don't wish to worry Masha."

"How *is* your niece? I hear she has been attending those courses at the Alarchin School." Olga gave Lidia's hand a gentle squeeze and reached for another cake. She seemed casual enough, but Lidia could tell she was relieved to have an opportunity to change the subject. Why did people not trust her, then, when she attempted to avoid their questions? She didn't doubt they cared, but no one knew what to say to The Dying, for that was the class to which she now assumed primary membership. Just the same, she was herself perfectly happy to change the subject, so why did she find fault? Who wants to face their own mortality every minute of the day in any event?

"Yes, most evenings Ilya takes her by sledge to the Alarchin High School. And there she sits, from six in the evening until nine, listening to lectures of some sort—delivered, she tells me, by 'distinguished' professors. But this does not impress me as I think she hopes it might."

"Uhhhn." Olga grunted her agreement as she chewed.

"Why do you suppose, Olga, there is this sudden need among women to 'improve their minds'?" Lidia daintily broke off a piece of cake with her fork and brought it to her lips.

"The woman question." Olga punctuated the last two words with two jabs of her fork to the air. "That's precisely when all this foolishness began."

"Why do people always need to stir things up? The serfs, educational reform, rights for women—why not leave things as they were. I was happy—weren't you happy Olya?"

The other woman nodded her assent.

"Then leave things be. Improving their minds! My mind has never needed any improvement. It's just fine as God gave—" Lidia's passionate delivery caused her to be overtaken by a fit of coughing. Olga jumped up to offer help, knocking her fork from her plate to the table with a clatter. But at a sign from Lidia, she returned to her chair. Olga busied herself with brushing the crumbs from the table, and Lidia tried not to notice each time her friend cast a glance her way to reassess her state. How self-conscious she felt, to be wracked by coughs in this way while another looked on and tried to guess the outcome. At last the coughing tapered to a halt.

Olga poured a fresh cup of tea for Lidia.

"Thank you." Lidia's voice was a hoarse whisper. After a sip of tea, she continued as if there had been no interruption.

"In my day, young ladies didn't roam around town unaccompanied, attending lectures and meetings and—"

"Meetings?"

Lidia tried to express with her eyes the gratitude she felt toward her old friend for going along with the charade that nothing of import had happened only a moment ago. She tucked her blood-spotted handkerchief out of sight in her sleeve.

"Yes, meetings—she goes sometimes to gatherings at an apartment following the lecture. For 'discussion,' she says. No men are allowed at these either, she has given me to understand. Now I ask you, Olya, is that sensible? How does she ever expect to meet a suitor under circumstances like those?"

"But there are still the gatherings at your apartment on Tuesdays and Thursdays, yes?"

"Fortunately, that's so. I think had I not been resolute, though, she would go to those abominable lectures every night of the week. Honestly, Olya, I don't understand young women these days."

Later that day, at home, as if Lidia's earlier conversation with her friend had made its way to Marya's ears, Marya once again brought up the subject of attending the lectures daily.

"I'm missing important lectures on those evenings, aunt." She looked at Lidia imploringly.

"You will get along just fine without two additional lectures a week. Moreover, I've heard *radicals* are trying to recruit young women at those lectures. It won't do for you to associate yourself with that type."

"Aunt Lidia! Wherever did you hear such a thing?"

"I hear things. I have many friends. With connections." Lidia omitted that this considered opinion came via the nephew of a cousin-in-law of Olga's who worked as an underling in Dmitrii Tolstoy's office of the ministry of education. Not quite from the lips of the tsar himself, but still.

"A pig will find mud anywhere, aunt! No one is there to recruit anyone to any such group. All of the women there want to broaden their *intellects*, just as I do. Because there was rioting in sixty-nine doesn't mean such forces are at work among students everywhere. We want to learn, and that's all. Really, aunt!" Marya shook her head disdainfully.

Why do women of her generation insist on wearing such dark clothing? Lidia thought, irritated. Then she coughed sharply a few times and felt her lungs constrict. Dizzy, she closed her eyes a moment and put her hand on her gaunt chest, as if she could calm the spasms thus.

"Aunt Lidia! Are you all right?"

Lidia held up her palm and nodded.

"Can I help you to your bed, aunt? Should I send Ilyusha for the doctor?"

When Lidia opened her eyes again, she became aware of Marya's intense gaze, a deep crease between her eyebrows. Lidia closed her eyes again, held up her palm, and shook her head no.

Marya sighed.

"Fine, Aunt Lidia. Yes. I will arrange to be home on those evenings, just as you ask."

Her voice was quiet, soothing.

Lidia tentatively withdrew her hand from her chest, too preoccupied with whether she had, in fact, held off another fit of coughing to notice her ill-health had won the argument for her.

"But I do so wish you didn't disapprove of the Alarchin courses." Marya scowled. "It's such a *splendid* sight to observe so many women gathered together—the daughters of noblemen and those of merchants and civil servants and priests—all of us joined together for the plain purpose of learning more about the world around us. And what women, aunt! I've never before seen so many incredible women! Quite brilliant. Strong-willed. I sit there in the evening, aunt, surrounded by a hundred or more women, and I think to myself, 'At last: I've found mates to my own soul.'

"I feel full of the possibilities of life again, Aunt Lidia!"

Lidia, still weak from coughing, managed a feeble smile.

"Thank you," Marya added then, and dipped her head, sheepishly returning her gaze to the periodical opened on her lap.

7
Grigorii

Wednesday, 10 November 1875

Dear Masha,

What sadness I felt on hearing you had indeed been ill, but I'm pleased to know you have grown weary of neither mathematics nor me. Of all the ailments known to humankind, sorrow is perhaps the hardest to cure. For our men of science have yet to find a medicine that will ameliorate melancholy. Just the thought! Can you imagine, Masha! A pill or tonic that would master gloom!

But no doubt there are many things to come we have yet to imagine. Did little Mamochka, sitting in her hut, taking care not to prick her finger on a needle while pressing it through the fabric of her daughter's wedding costume, ever dream there would one day be a machine that could sew? Did Potemkin on the battleground in the Crimea imagine one day something called a telegraph could print out his words of love to Catherine, far away in St. Petersburg? And surely General Kutuzov—even if he'd been blessed with two eyes—could never have foreseen that one day the Russian army's troops could be gathered in mere weeks rather than months. Why, had the railroad spanned the countryside in 1812 as it does now, perhaps Napoleon would never have stood atop the Ivan Bell Tower and watched as Count Rostopchin set aflame all of Moscow's shops, all the houses of the nobility, all the merchants' warehouses in his effort to leave the French with nothing but the scorched earth where once a vibrant city stood!

But you see to what fancies I'm given, left to my own thoughts and the insubstantiality of my reluctant students, day in and day out. It isn't a bad entertainment of itself, this musing, but when I should be expressing my sympathy for the departure of your friend Katya, it's unpardonable. Please trust I don't mean to diminish the importance of her leave-taking. I know how dear she was to you. I'm delighted to hear, however, you have enrolled in the Alarchin courses and have set about finding new friends.

Do you not suspect, though, it's this selfsame randomness of social interaction, this unpredictability in our relations with our fellows, that has factored into our indecent affection for mathematics? Is it not precisely the case, given a particular set of constraints, a theorem isn't just sometimes true but, rather, is true always, as you've said? In mathematics, it's possible to make unequivocal statements. For instance, once we have all agreed the number seven is the number seven, that does not change, and what you call seven, I also call seven. There is, to be sure, comfort in this immutability. For in nature, in life, there are frequently anomalies. There is naught, in biology, in art, in social interchange that's one hundred percent true. And this is why we, you and I, have sought refuge in mathematics. No doubt this is a weakness in our characters, a failure to adapt to change or something of the sort—I would wager that you, as I, have been accused of being less than flexible. If pressed, I will admit to there being some kernel of fact in that accusation. But, too, isn't being a mathematician like being a god? For should an exception seem to arise, we have methods for exerting control over it, so its exceptionality is but an illusion.

Ah, Marya, how it delights me to have a companion with whom I can share my ramblings about numbers and mathematics, to marvel at how it allows us to play the bear trainer, making unruly integers do tricks at the whip crack of its orderly demands. But it isn't without guilt I engage you in these ramblings, which are fine for me—in my teaching post, I'm occupied at what may be the peak of my possible achievement. But you—you ought to have a project, some manner of focus. I haven't got your talent, but if you set about working on something, I have the capacity to be an appreciative audience and, perhaps, to offer a comment here and there. Do you have a subject in mind? Or shall I suggest one? Of course, it may be you don't seek a project, and this is for you to decide, but I will grieve if you choose other than to pursue some course of mathematical endeavor. I long to witness the mind I helped nurture reach full bloom. And how, I ask you, can a man be blamed for a desire such as that?

How sad, you may say, a man of thirty-and-two has put such stock in a young woman scarcely past girlhood. Were I more brilliant or ambitious or better born, there might be a more dazzling life for me elsewhere. But you know what they say: if you knew where you were going to fall, you could first spread some straw. The life of a teacher isn't such a bad one, though. Every ember of mathematical curiosity I blow to life in a student's mind counterweighs a dozen others that gutter out. A conflagration like yours, my dearest Marya, is the event of a lifetime.

It isn't my intention to anticipate your reply in the affirmative concerning my proposal about a mathematical project, but I tell you now: I will spend my spare moments exploring my mathematical texts and periodicals in search of a puzzle deserving of your attention.

At your service,

Grisha

"A true mathematician who is not also something of a poet will never be a perfect mathematician." —Karl Weierstrass (repeated here in defense of the many metaphors with which I've filled this letter!)

8
Lidia

In the midst of composing a note to her attorney, Lidia was seized by a violent fit of coughing. A thin jumpy trail of ink formed across the sheet of paper. When her coughing subsided, Lidia stared at the jagged line of ink, transfixed. A chill ran up her arms, and she pulled her shawl closer around her. She had the eerie and unshakable feeling the line was her lifeline, though she couldn't fathom how to read it. She couldn't bring herself, either, to throw the spoiled sheet away, afraid of what the effect of doing so might be—superstitious about it now that she had imagined the vein of ink a lifeline. She set this page to the side while she reached for another sheet. All the while she wrote then, after, she found her eyes drifting toward the ruined page.

"Don't be a ninny," she said at last, and let the flawed sheet drift from her hand to the wastebasket, though she couldn't yet bear to tear or crumple or otherwise deface the line she had taken for her life.

Such moroseness had been creeping into her consciousness with greater frequency, though she tried to distract herself, first, with Marya's depression and, of late, with finding, for her young niece, both happiness and a suitable match. She wondered at the sense of responsibility she felt for this young woman who had but recently come into her life, but the girl was, after all, her flesh and blood. And it was good to focus on something other than her health, someone other than herself. She was making certain all of her affairs were in order so Marya would have no financial worries when she passed on. *Poor child.* Scarely two months before she was to leave the Institute, she had received news that her beloved Papa—Lidia's only sibling—had died of an apoplectic stroke. All who had been dearest to the girl in her childhood home at Khrupkaya Luna—the home where Lidia herself had summered as a youngster—had been lost to her. First Marya's mother had passed on, then her young brothers Timosha and Mitya, and finally her Papa, whom Marya had adored. So. Marya would inherit not only Khrupkaya Luna, but Lidia's apartment as well. If she could but secure Marya's marital well-being, Lidia could die in some peace, if not, to be sure, happily. How could she possibly be resigned to death now, when there was so much possibility? Marya was a challenge, a delight, a lesson. So complex, her feelings for this girl, who made her think, made her wish not to think, made her itchy with irritation and wonder.

Some two weeks after Marya began attending the Alarchin courses, she seemed more thoughtful than usual over dinner. Lidia—who was once again, as all too often of late, feeling enormously exhausted—poked her fork at the pullet with juniper berries and tried to convince herself she should eat a bit of it to keep up her strength. Without Marya's usual monologue, then, about either the previous evening's lecture or the insufferableness of the preceding evening's gentleman callers, depending on the day, it was quiet but for the scrape of utensils on their plates. Or rather, on Marya's plate, for Lidia's ineffectual prodding of the pullet made barely a sound.

"Aunt Lidia."

Though Marya had not spoken loudly, her voice coming out of the silence, as it did, startled the older woman. "Sorry, aunt—I didn't mean to cause you disquiet. But Lidia, the most wonderful thing has happened. She set her fork down on her plate and leaned toward her aunt, touching her lightly on the arm. "I've met someone." Her voice was almost a whisper, and at first Lidia thought she might have misheard her.

"Why, Mashenka, my dove, that *is* good news. What's his name, dear, if I might ask? It may be I know his family." A lightness crept under Lidia's skin, into her lungs, and she felt a small surge of energy.

"No, aunt. It isn't a man I met but an extraordinary young woman. Vera Dashkova."

Lidia could feel her niece's eyes scouring her face, so she was careful to show no disappointment but couldn't help but think of Katya and the disastrous outcome of *that* friendship. And yet it was hard to take exception to the elation Masha so clearly felt. Too, at least her heart was no longer sealed off, and if Vera Dashkova could begin to enter there, so could another.

"I'm pleased for you, dear niece." Lidia reached her hand for that of her niece, still resting on her left arm, and gave it a gentle squeeze. "Why do you not invite her to dine with us Friday evening? It's been quite some time since you and I've dined with anyone but one another. It will be lovely to have company for dinner again."

"Are you sure, aunt?" Her eyes took in her aunt's visage. "I mean, are you sure you will be equal to it? You have been …"

"Child, child! I will be fine. I will rest during the afternoon. Don't concern yourself."

Lidia made an effort to appear robust, sitting up straighter in her chair and taking a bite of her pullet but was relieved when Marya excused herself. Alone, Lidia let herself sink into her chair and close her eyes.

On Friday, just as she had said she would, Lidia took a long nap. Nevertheless, it had been an effort to put on her shoes and make her way downstairs. When Ilyusha went to answer the chime at the door to the apartment, Lidia was reclining on the chaise lounge in the drawing room. The chaise, beside the ceramic stove, was well placed for her optimum warmth. Barely had Ilyusha taken the visitor's name when Marya bounded down the stairs, oblivious to any semblance of decorum. Lidia smiled ruefully at her niece's unbridled zest.

"Vera," she heard then, from her seat in the drawing room, "you've come!" There was the rustle of fabric against fabric.

"Oh. Thank you, Ilya." Marya seemed to notice, finally, that Ilyusha was still there, uncertain whether his services were yet needed. "You may go," she said, and Lidia saw her niece give his arm an excited squeeze, then give him a quick peck on the cheek. He turned to go with a bow, a warm smile crossing his face.

"Did you have trouble finding us here?" Marya was breathless.

"No, the driver knew the way well and found the address without difficulty."

"Come. I shall introduce you to my aunt."

Lidia struggled to pull herself into a more dignified sitting position as Marya entered the room, her hand clasped to that of a beautiful young woman draped in a shimmering emerald gown.

"No, please." Vera dropped Marya's hand when she saw Lidia straining to sit up and rushed to her. "Please: don't rise on my account. You look so comfortable there by the stove. May I?" she asked, and pointed to the blanket that lay askew at Lidia's ankles. With barely a nod from the older woman, Vera bent to pull the blanket into place and tucked it around her feet. She turned then to Marya.

"Oh!" said Marya. "Yes. Lidia, this is Vera Dashkova."

Vera smiled warmly at Lidia and pulled a chair next to the chaise.

"It's a great pleasure to meet you, Lidia. Ever since I met Marya, a week and some days ago, I've been anxious to meet the woman who has the strength and good will to harbor this firebrand. She is quite an amazing woman, you know."

Lidia stifled a momentary irritation at this stranger telling her about her niece—her niece over whom she had worried and had labored to return to health these past months. *The girl is but making polite small talk*, Lidia reminded herself.

"Yes, I'm quite aware of her unique qualities," she said in a way she hoped wouldn't betray her passing irritation. Or hoped it would. She wasn't entirely sure of her motivations. The two turned, then, to the subject of their conversation, which caused Marya to scowl. This embarrassment, Lidia knew, wasn't on her account, and she felt an unaccustomed pang of jealousy. She was too drained, however, to tease out whether she was jealous of Marya's attention to another (and after all Lidia's hard work!) or whether she was jealous of the easy flirtatiousness of their manner together. While the two younger women tried to suppress their smiles, she thought in passing again, as she so often had since Marya came to live with her, of Irochka. She thought of her friend's soft brown hair and how it fell in adamant ringlets around her brow, no matter what efforts she took to restrain it, of her irrepressible spirit, her infectious laugh. Two years Irochka's junior, Lidia had been quite in love with her. But that's the way it is with girls, always getting crushes on one another, she thought, and sighed.

"Lidia?" Her niece's voice broke into her reverie then. "Are you unwell?" She had half-risen from her chair.

"What? Oh—no, I'm fine. It's just so lovely to have company," she said. She turned to smile at their guest. Just then, Ilya called them to dinner, and Lidia let Vera help her to her feet and hold her arm as they made their way to the table.

Over dinner, Lidia asked about their guest's family. She learned Vera was the only child of Lev Dashkov, a low-level bureaucrat who had always been thin and always ailing and had died of inflammation of the lungs when Vera was barely more than a child. Her mother, Aleksandra Dashkova, was stouter and a generally healthy individual, but she too succumbed—of a liver ailment—not more than a year ago, when Vera had just turned seventeen. Poor child, Lidia thought to herself: she, like Masha, has been left orphaned; perhaps that's what draws them to one another.

Whatever peevishness she might feel concerning Vera, Lidia couldn't help but marvel over her effect on Masha. She watched as Masha self-consciously smoothed her hair into place, as her eyes flickered with animation, as her hands were in constant flight, riding the currents of her conversation with Vera. Now this, thought Lidia, is someone who will appeal to men. And then, in an instant, she was caught up in the playfulness of their talk, though she couldn't follow much of their teasing, which had to do with geography and physics—the stuff of the lectures they attended together—and the meetings to which they went.

Ultimately, Lidia was transported by their easy banter back to her own youth. Fifty years, and Irochka still dwelled like a sliver of glass in her heart, she thought. Though the sliver had long been buried, it had become impossible to ignore it now, with Marya in her house. It wasn't simply the pain of loss that made her want to forget, to keep that shard of memory interred. There was also the uncomfortable feeling that perhaps her love had been more than a schoolgirl crush. She had told herself, these many years, that was purely false—and what sort of sense did it make anyway? What sort of romance would that have been, between two women? And yet she was sometimes tormented by the thought that Irina occupied a firmer place in her heart than did Mikhail, Lidia's fiancé, who had perished in a duel after an illicit liaison. But time and again, she had dismissed that also as ridiculous: if she had not loved Mikhail fiercely, why had she never married after his death? The facts were the facts, she argued with herself: the past is no moon, to wax and wane in the night sky of memory. It is a fixed point, a distant star that never changed. What was the purpose of all this silly speculation on her part, in which she now engaged all too often, like the old ninny she'd turned into? This is what comes, she thought, of so much idleness. She hadn't been so daft when she'd been able to keep herself busy.

She wondered where Irina was now, if she was still alive. They had corresponded for some years, after Irina first married, but their lives had taken such different paths—Irochka's filled with children and nannies and society events, her own with charity work and a devotion to the theatrical arts. If they had lived in the same city, perhaps … But it was painful enough, the letters, and to occupy so little of Irochka's thoughts in them—how dreadful it would have been to be near her, to smile and talk as if her heart wasn't breaking for a tender embrace.

Lidia was glad to have such thoughts interrupted by Masha and Vera, as they excused themselves to hurry off to their lecture.

Masha leaned in to give her aunt a kiss and whispered, "You look tired, Lidia, dear—why do you not take yourself to bed early tonight, get some rest?"

"I'm fine, Masha. Thank you." Then she called out, as Vera went to take her coat from Ilya, who was holding it out to her in the foyer, "Please, Vera, won't you join us for dinner again?"

Vera turned as she reached for her coat.

"Thank you, Lidia. Thank you for your hospitality. Yes, I should be delighted."

"Good-bye, Aunt Lidia!" Marya called back over her shoulder. Then she whirled and walked backward from the room as she said in a loud whisper, "Remember what I said, Aunt Lidia." She wagged her finger at her aunt playfully before she spun around again toward the door.

Then they were gone, and Lidia sat alone amid the clutter of the table and her thoughts. How nice to see Masha happy again, she thought, then frowned, though she couldn't quite remember why. She pressed her thumb and finger to either side of the bridge of her nose, overcome suddenly with a numbing fatigue. She considered calling for Nadezhda to help her to bed but decided to be alone with her confusion of emotions and made her way up slowly with the help of her cane. She could sort it all out tomorrow.

9
Vera's Journal

Friday, 19 November 1875

Dinner with Marya and her aunt a week ago was like peering into an Imperial Glass Works Easter egg to see the wax cradle in which a cherub sleeps. It was a glimpse into a world not my own but one which I now long to enter. How I should enter this egg and what my place in it might be, I don't know. I know only that Lidia is a woman of incredible grace, still beautiful despite her illness, and I can't help but wonder why it is she never married. As for Marya—why, she is like a bright sun (or like the orange-yellow yolk of an egg, should I choose to amuse myself and carry my egg image to its absurd extension), and I ache to set aside my lonely life. What a strange tug Marya exerts on me—peculiar, but not unpleasant.

The lecture this Wednesday night past, however, exerted a pull of its own on me, enough to divert my attention from Marya, albeit briefly. For out upon the stage came a wiry man, tall, his bones nearly poking through his wrinkled suit: Dmitrii Kaigorodov, the naturalist. His hands flew about like startled birds at every word he spoke, while his dark stringy hair fell again and again across his forehead, though he pushed it many times away.

"You will not," he said, with hands held out at his side, fingers splayed, "see a skull upon the stage here beside me, nor skeleton, nor pickled in a jar of alcohol some poor creature, pale as this lamplight, floating about like a beet or herring. An animal isn't a mere collection of bones and skin and hair.

You there!" He called out to a young woman in the first row, startling her. "Say what makes an animal." He paused before her, his hands for once at rest, folded before him on his suit jacket. His face wasn't unkind, but the intensity of his gaze was such that I, many rows back, nearly winced from it.

"An … an animal? What sort of animal?" Her voice was barely above a whisper.

"Any sort of animal. If I were to put before you a … a …" He paced as he contemplated. "The alley cat that lounges about at the fish market—if I were to put it here, before you on the stage, how would you know it to be an animal?"

"Well … because he moves?"

"Yes! Quite right! Exactly. Go on."

"Because it breathes and has legs and—"

"Stop!" He held his hand up. "And what of fish? Snakes? Are these less animals for lack of legs?"

"Oh," she said. Her head dropped forward.

"No, of course not," he continued, "but this is the point I wish to impress on you: you can't know an animal without knowing its role in wild nature. To know its components—legs, fin, tail, fur, ribcage, feathers—is to know nothing of the animal. Only when we have joined together nature itself with natural history will we be able to behold and understand the beauty and poetry of nature.

"You shall hear from me tonight no mention of the artificial boundaries between separate kingdoms of nature: nothing of botany or zoology, no mineralogy but, instead, I shall speak of a natural history that's *united and borderless*, of a nature encompassing its component parts, each of which makes something of a whole on its own—forest, meadow, steppe, pond, marsh, and so forth. I encourage you to think of each as living places for different plants and animals, places where they will *interact* with one another and with inorganic nature—the soil and shores, the rocks—and with the different seasons.

"But here, in this confined space, where we sit amid dust and the smell of candle wax—this no place to talk about nature. We should be out among the trees and stars, feeling the bite of the air and observing the clouds as they labor to bring us the season's first snows. That's where talk of nature should be! How else appreciate it? But it's with my words, alas, you shall have to content yourself this evening."

And then he spoke of the many systems of nature and how they interlock like a puzzle—a living puzzle. With what passion he spoke! And how it kindled in me an old interest, long forgotten, from when I was a child and the great ardor I held for nature. I so loved to stand beside my mother and tend the garden, then wait and watch for the first green shoots to come heaving their way through the soil. Such patience I learned from this. And for such rewards.

Even more, I loved the animals, the goats we kept for milk, the tabby cat that lazed on the windowsill, licking the tiny pads of her feet with her rough tongue, the mice that scurried about, searching for seeds. Suddenly, quite in the middle of Kaigorodov's lecture, I remembered a book I'd had as a child, a much-loved book Mama had given to me one year at Christmas. All in English, to help me better master that tongue. It had many parts to it: needlework designs, stories, poems, short biographies. The part I loved best, though—and why I should happen to recall this book just as Kaigorodov spoke of how we must embrace nature if we are to be fully healthy—was on birds and how to keep them.

With what great fit of nostalgia I longed to hold that book again. Surely, I couldn't have discarded such a cherished book. I must, I told myself, ask Kovalev, at the first chance, to help me pull my trunk from the storage so I may rummage through it. Kovalev isn't worth much as a landlord—perhaps he can make himself useful in other ways!

When the lecture was over, we made our way to the aisle, upon which, Marya took my arm, which pleased me. We walked readily together from the hall, and my words bubbled forth as though I were indeed a child who had, for the first time, seen a bear dancing in the public square.

"Are you not ready, now, to step outside and watch as the trees sweep the night sky with their bare branches, as if they were conducting the wind in performance of Tchaikovsky's *Winter Dreams*!"

Marya turned and scrutinized me as though surprised to discover with whom she had linked arms. I suddenly felt self-conscious in the beam of her frank appraisal.

"Forgive me," I said. "It's only, I found Kaigorodov's words so moving I felt a longing to gaze upon a field of something other than tall rows of buildings popping their heads out of the earth."

"You have the sensibilities of a poet."

"Rather, I think, of a peasant! I would as soon sit upon a stool in the open air and milk a goat than confine myself to a theater, even to hear the greatest of operas."

"You are a vessel of many wonders. I shouldn't be surprised to discover you might hold my attention for many a year, so many layers there seem to be yet to encounter, Mademoiselle Dashkova."

"Well, then, Mademoiselle Zhukova," I said, "perhaps we should begin to find out—shall we return to my rooms for some tea?"

How bold I had grown! Could I be flirting with her, a woman? This exchange only added to the disorder of my thoughts and feelings since meeting Marya.

"Yes, I should very much like to," she said, running the fingers of her free hand through her hair, a habit I had begun to find unreasonably charming.

At my rooms, we sat for a while and drank tea and considered whether Kaigorodov was right that there should be no division of nature into different fields of study or whether such divisions might have some merit. All too soon, it was time again for her to go. And again she stirred me, both with her very nearness as she kissed my cheeks goodbye, letting her palms linger the length of my arms until her hands rested in my own, and with her parting words.

"I shall not be at the lecture on Thursday, but I would be pleased to meet you again on Friday. Will you be there?" I nodded and saw her to the door, discontented, wanting I knew not quite what—more time or … I couldn't have said what.

Tonight, then, I waited near the doors of the lecture hall, stricken with the fear Marya wouldn't remember our engagement for the evening. I had no reason for this fear—always, before, when she said she would come, she had—except that I so longed to see her, I felt certain I must be destined for disappointment.

I nodded and said good evening to several women as they entered the hall in small groups or pairs, a few walking in singly. I didn't know them, but their faces, over the last week or two, had become familiar to me as mine had apparently become to them. I turned from one such greeting to scan the street anxiously, as if I could ensure Marya's appearance with nothing more than my gaze. I was encouraged in this belief, then, by the open smile directed at me.

"Good evening, Vera." Marya approached, bowed deeply before me, and kissed my hand.

While pleased by her attentions, I glanced nervously about, worried someone had noticed this unseemly display of gentlemanly behavior on Marya's part and think us both peculiar. But my genuine affection for this uncommon woman overtook my concerns for propriety, and I let myself get caught up in her good humor.

With a quick curtsey, I replied, "Yes, good evening to you, Marya Iuryevich," addressing her as if she were both her father's daughter and son and took her arm to walk into the lecture hall. She let drop my arm and whirled to face me, clearly taken aback. I think she was ready to be angry with me, if I mocked her, but she sensed my playfulness, smiled, and took my arm again.

"Come, let us go in. I don't wish to be late, tonight of all nights."

"My, but you are in a buoyant mood tonight, Marya." And indeed, excitement danced about the corners of her eyes and lips; there was an eagerness to her walk.

"Yes, I'm quite excited about this evening's lecture. And you?"

"To be sure," I responded, too embarrassed to admit I was quite ignorant of the evening's topic, my main concern having been to secure Marya's company again.

"Alexander Strannoliubsky is one of the premier teachers of mathematics in this country," she rhapsodized as she led me uncustomarily to a bench at the front of the hall. "He's just thirty-one, you know, but quite brilliant." And though I had heard Marya speak with passion before, there was a near-reverent quality to her voice on this occasion that was new to me.

We settled ourselves on the bench. A hush replaced the low hum of voices in the hall, and a strikingly handsome man with piercing eyes walked across the stage.

"Good evening, ladies," he began. "I am Strannoliubsky. Our topic this evening will be analytical geometry."

These were among the last words of his I understood. But Marya furiously made notes throughout the lecture and often nodded her head in understanding or appreciation. "Ah!" she even exclaimed quietly from time to time, or whispered, "Yes. Wonderful!"

My admiration for her now blossomed fully, and I considered her with awe, wondering at the depth of her interest and intelligence.

"Amazing!" Marya beamed as we readied ourselves to leave. "Wasn't that simply fascinating?" she enthused.

"Well, yes ...," I said, "but it was a bit ... beyond me. In parts."

"Hmm." She looked at me appraisingly, as if surprised by this admission. "Hmm," she murmured again. I nervously chewed the inside of my lip, afraid I had disappointed her. At last she said, "Well, mathematics isn't everyone's cup of tea. There is to be a discussion this evening," she continued, without missing a beat, "on how to achieve equality of the sexes. I believe I might go. Will you join me?"

"Yes, I should like that very much."

We left the lecture hall and approached the Alarchin Bridge. I could hear the water gently lapping at the banks of the Ekaterininsky Canal. The sound suffused me with a sense of well-being, and we walked for a time in silence, arms linked, content as young lovers. (What a strange choice of words! Ah, well—best leave them now than turn the page into rubbish by blacking them out and choosing others.)

At last, we were at the building where our hostess, whom I had not yet met, had an apartment. We walked to the second floor and knocked on the door.

When we entered the large room to which our hostess had shown us, the air, as it had been at the previous meeting we had attended, was so thick with cigarette smoke I felt I might suffocate. I willed myself not to cough, lest Marya find such a vocalization a sign of weakness or criticism.

"It's rather smoky in here, isn't it?" she said. A smile played on her lips as she regarded me, and I felt utterly transparent.

"No, no—well, yes, it's smoky, but I don't mind," I lied.

"Come," she said. "There seem to be fewer smokers in the far corner." Again a hint of a smile grazed her lips.

We approached a tight circle of a half dozen or so women, all of them perched at the edges of their chairs in heated conversation. Several had rather short haircuts and all of them wore austere, dark clothing. Much like Marya, I noted.

"No!" cried one woman, her eyes hidden behind blue glasses. Her finger poked the air rather viciously. "There you are wrong. We must fight for the rights of women. Education is all well and good, but if a woman secures a medical degree yet is still not allowed to get something as simple as a passport on her own, then what shall we have accomplished?" Her thick black ringlets quivered atop her head with every gesticulation.

"Yes, but don't you see?" responded another of the women, leaning even farther into the circle. "It's all connected. It's our lack of education they use as the excuse to exclude us from attaining equal rights. Men speak openly of our inferiority—use that supposed inferiority in order not to allow us to determine our own fates, but at the same time deny us access to the means to better ourselves. It's a circle! There is no way out." She leaned back.

"Yes! Yes, there is a way out. Revolution! That's the answer." The speaker of this bold statement was a petite brunette. Her green eyes were speckled with gold, like flashes of fire.

"To be sure!" offered yet another woman. "You have heard, I suppose, what it is Bakunin says? No? Education, he says, will only increase the gap between the privileged and the people. If we are to serve the revolution, we must leave our schools and go to live among the people."

"That's a fine thing for a man to say, for have men had to fight for higher education as we have? I? Give up education? Why, it's education that will free us, all of us, from material and intellectual enslavement!"

"No! The writers of this pamphlet, *To Women from the Russian Revolutionary Society*, lay it out quite plainly." The little brunette with green eyes pulled a battered pamphlet from her coat pocket and thumped it with her forefinger for emphasis. "It's men who create civil law, and they do so with only their own interests in mind. They leave to women only positions such as whore or cook."

"Yes, we all know that already, Olga," said the woman with blue glasses, clearly exasperated.

"Those in power are nothing but exploiters," Olga went on, ignoring the interruption. "Only social revolution will provide an enduring solution, will allow us to free ourselves from tradition and oppression. Listen. Here is what they say: 'Only a revolution that abolishes exploitation will give you a chance for *human* existence.'" She paused to ascertain what effect her emphasis had had on the others. "*Your cause is indissolubly linked to that of the working class.*" She pursed her lips, a dare to us to refute the logic of this statement.

"I've read that pamphlet." Marya spoke for the first time from where we stood at the edge of the circle. All heads turned to the new speaker. "No doubt a federative government would have much to offer the working classes. But what of us? What of women? The writers of this pamphlet have nothing to say on the subject of how such a revolution would benefit women. They say nothing about employment or training for women, nothing about the oppressive nature of marriage."

"She's right."

"That's true."

Murmurs rose up around the circle.

"That's why education is the key," I said, taking courage from Marya's successful entry into the debate. "Just this evening we were at the Alarchin courses where—"

"Oh, the Alarchin courses." Olga waved her hand in dismissal, as if these lectures weren't worthy of her wasting her words to list their demerits.

"No, no—I agree with her entirely," said the woman who had first suggested the value of education. "I'm tired of the old saying 'The hair is long but the mind is short' being brandished against us!"

"Well, Avdotia, I don't think you need to worry about anyone saying that of you." The woman with blue glasses tousled Avdotia's close-cropped hair, and everyone laughed.

"Always the wit, Aleksandra. But you know what I mean…." The conversation resumed, but I lost its thread as Marya began whispering to me then.

"Shall we leave? The smoke in the room is beginning to overwhelm me."

"Yes," I agreed, hoping this didn't mean the evening was at an end.

"Please—before you go." The woman with blue glasses grasped our arms lightly in each hand. "Aleksandra Kobiakova."

She shook my hand, then Marya's. Twice in one night, to shake another woman's hand. How unexpected life can be.

"You—"

"Marya Zhukova."

"Pleased to make your acquaintance." She bowed her head briefly, recovering, for a moment, her social graces. "You spoke of the oppressiveness of marriage. It's a topic of much interest to me, and I hoped we might continue discussing it."

Up close, I realized she was much older than I had at first guessed. The blue glasses, I suppose, gave her the air of a young revolutionary. In fact, though, she was much older than us, perhaps in her fifties, which gave me a shock, set against her drollness and the spiritedness with which she joined the meeting's conversations.

"Well." Marya glanced in my direction. "We were just about to leave—"

"If not now, perhaps at some other time?" Aleksandra interrupted. "Both of you? I'm sorry—your name was …?" She shifted her attention to me. I told her my name and she clasped my hand. I could feel the many cracks and calluses in her skin. "Lovely!" she said. "I apologize for my boldness, but you know how it is with these meetings—the participants change more rapidly than the costumes of a minor player in a ballet. I feared if I didn't speak to you now, I might not encounter you again, and as you have experienced, we aren't all of a similar mind here."

"Vera?" Marya queried.

"I should enjoy that."

"It's settled, then!" Aleksandra once again grasped our arms. "When and where shall we meet?"

"Perhaps Saturday next? The twenty-seventh of November?" Aleksandra and I both nodded assent. "Will Leiner's suit you? At no. 18, Nevsky Prospect? It's but a delicatessen with sawdust on the floor, as you know if you have been there, nonetheless it's cozy and favorable to conversation."

"It's agreed, then!" Aleksandra gave each of our arms a light squeeze. "I shall look forward with eagerness to advancing our exchange. And now I must go throw myself back into the fray, for who shall tease them and keep them plain, if not I?" I detected the twinkle in her eye, even behind the blue glasses.

When Marya and I stepped out onto the walkway, I stopped a moment and filled my lungs with the fresh air. I closed my eyes to savor it. When I opened them, Marya appeared bemused.

"I was only now doing the very same thing," she said, and we erupted into laughter.

"Oh, Marya. I've never met anyone quite like you."

"Yes. I've heard *that* before." We laughed again.

"Marya, would you—would you like to come for tea again before you return home?" I felt suddenly shy, in spite of the warm and easy moments we had just shared. I chewed my lip.

"That would be a distinct pleasure, Vera."

Then we walked with linked arms until Marya spied a carriage and flagged it down. We sat side by side on the carriage seat, our two knees touching, my hand wrapped in hers. We didn't speak. I don't know why Marya was still, but as for me, I felt I was under a spell I didn't wish to break.

"Come. We are here." Marya spoke in a whisper, her voice cracking after sitting unused the last minutes.

"Oh. Yes, we are." The spell slipped from me, and I stepped from the carriage to Marya's waiting hand. We climbed the stairs of the boarding house then, once again in silence—the doors along the stairway are far too thin and the walls too cheerless to inspire any ease of conversation.

In my rooms, I offered to take Marya's coat. As she undid the buttons, I noticed a short strand of her hair slipping toward her eye, and without thinking what a forward act it was, I went to move it back in place. When my hand touched her cheek, Marya closed her eyes and sharply drew a breath, as if I had affronted her or caused her pain.

"Oh! Forgive me, Marya. I didn't mean to be so brazen." As I spoke, I attempted to withdraw my hand, but Marya grasped it and held it in place with her own. Her breathing seemed to require concentration and she didn't speak for a moment.

"No, oh please no, Vera. Never apologize for tenderness." She released me and let her fingers trail over my hand. Then she turned away from me.

I was puzzled but drawn more than ever to this enigmatic woman. I stood quietly for a moment, unsure what to do.

"Here," said Marya. She turned toward me again and slid her coat off. "You asked for my coat. Can I help prepare the tea?"

"Oh no. Please—just have a seat. I will prepare the samovar." But I was aware, the whole time, of her eyes following me, and I wondered if it might not have been a better idea to give her something else to do.

But at last we were both seated at my makeshift table, a steaming cup of tea before each of us. Marya asked if I might pass the sugar cubes.

I handed her the sugar bowl. As she took it, her hand partially cupped over mine, and we froze there for an instant. I studied the sight of her hand clasped over mine and decided I liked it. I could feel her eyes on me and met her gaze. She was smiling. I returned her smile tentatively.

"Thank you." She reached her other hand to support fully the sugar bowl and withdrew both her hand and the bowl from me. I wrapped my hands around my teacup to give them something to do. Then I watched as Marya chased the sugar cube around her teacup with a spoon, the handle clutched between forefinger and thumb while her middle finger coaxed the spoon into rapid circles. But I felt unaccountably embarrassed all of a sudden and focused on bringing my cup to my mouth.

"You have lovely fingers, Verochka." She spoke softly. I thrilled at her calling me Verochka, noting the change. Her eyes held me in a warm embrace.

"Thank you … Mashenka." We both gazed at my left hand where it now rested on the table. Mashenka stroked her fingers across the back of my hand and traced their tips along mine. Then she placed her hand over mine before turning my hand palm up, resting it in hers. I watched my hand as if it were not a part of me, but when she took the fingers of her other hand and traced the lines in my palm and let her fingers glide over every crease on each finger, the impulses that danced through my arm and into my chest made it quite clear the hand was indeed mine. My mouth felt suddenly dry, but not for one minute did I consider lifting my cooling cup of tea.

I was aware of her appraisal and held her eyes with my own. She slipped her fingers between mine and held them together there in the cup of her other hand. I glanced at our hands entwined so. Her eyes again sought mine. I couldn't speak, but I offered a soft smile. She smiled in return and began to stroke my top finger with her thumb. I sat spellbound until Mashenka slowly released my hand and bumped the handle of her teacup. The brief clatter roused me.

I cleared my throat.

"Your tea must be quite cold by now." I rose to get her some more tea.

"Oh no, please." She grasped my wrist in her hand. I wanted to place my hand over hers but stupidly stood there, unable to move. "I must go," she said.

"Yes," I said, and turned my back to her to hide my disappointment. "Yes, I suppose it's late." I fussed absentmindedly with the tea canister, closing it up, and brushing aside a few stray leaves.

"I've had a wonderful time … Verochka."

Marya's hand lightly clasped my upper arm, and without thinking, I began to lean back a little into her. Her hand slid down my arm, and soon I could feel her breath right behind my ear. We stood that way for a minute or so, until Mashenka raised her other hand to give my shoulder a gentle squeeze.

"I have to go," she whispered. She moved away from me, and I became sensible enough to go retrieve her coat for her. I longed to beg her to stay.

"Marya—Mashenka—I …"

"Yes?"

"Have a safe journey home."

"Thank you." She kissed my cheeks, lingering a tantalizing beat over each. She slid her hands from my shoulders down my arms as she had before, but this time I caught her hands lightly in mine until she pulled away and walked toward the door. She opened the door and turned.

"Au revoir, Verochka," she whispered, then deftly swung the door closed behind her.

"Au revoir, Mashenka," I whispered to the door.

10
Marya

A project! Marya, having just reread her old math instructor's letter from earlier in the month, found herself overwhelmed by his confidence in her ability. She was, to be sure, flattered by his encouraging words and excited at the prospect of beginning some sort of mathematical project, but she hardly knew where to start.

Although she attended the Alarchin courses, Marya's time and studies were, at best, ill-defined after she'd left the rigors of the St. Petersburg Institute for Girls, amounting to little more than reworking problems from old algebraic texts she had kept. The thought of having an actual project to which she could apply herself was a welcome thought, and she wondered why she had not conceived this idea on her own.

But no matter. The question now confronting her was, which project? It occurred to Marya that a trip to the Imperial Library would probably be the best plan, so that she could consult some additional texts, beyond those she already owned, and perhaps also some of the latest mathematics periodicals.

She took a droshky to Nevsky Prospect and Sadovaya Street, pausing on the street before entering the Library. She was struck by the absurdity that only now would she be visiting this Mecca for book lovers for the first time. Certainly, there were a number of perfectly good reasons this was so—from how cloistered her life had been at the Institute to her utter collapse at Katya's departure—but it was nevertheless dismaying to her that she had heretofore ignored the Library's siren song.

Walking into the Library was akin to a religious experience for Marya. Her gait was uncharacteristically deliberate, as though she were endeavoring to remember the feel of every stair against the soles of her boots as she unconsciously registered the momentousness of this occasion. She was so very grateful for the Alarchin courses, but how much sweeter to guide her own trajectory, choose her own fate, read as chance and the book spines might lead her.

After she had secured a permit, she found her way to the mathematical texts. She felt like a child choosing among jams and honeys during Pancake Week before Lent. She pulled down several books that seemed to hold promise, but she was unsure how to select wisely among the hundreds of books lining floor to ceiling and into the balcony above her head. She took the books she'd selected to a nearby table. When her chair scraped the floor, a number of men glanced up from their studies, but she didn't generate a second glance from them, which inattention she welcomed.

She opened the first book but found herself too excited to focus on its pages just yet. Much else at first called her notice: the low hiss of the gas jets in the lights hanging overhead, the stale smell of old paper and leather, and, above all, the other people. At one table, several students from secondary schools or universities; there, an old man wearing his military medals; farther down, several peasants in traditional garb with long flowing beards; and even a member of the Imperial Guard.

She turned her attention, finally, to the books she had set on the table, scanned the contents of one, set it aside, opened another, flipped through its pages, opened another, and finally came back to the first. She tried to read, and she did manage to jot a few notes for herself, but at each shuffle of a nearby foot, at each cough or whisper, she found herself distracted again. *Another time,* she thought, and sighed. *It's only I must accustom myself to the idea of being a scholar again in earnest*, she told herself, and planned to return the next day.

Regardless of her intentions, however, Marya didn't return to the Library the next day, as she'd planned, or for some time after. First, there was the anticipation of a Friday-night lecture, where, among other things, she knew she would find Vera. But the topic of the lecture was also of interest. A professor from Novorossysk University, Ivan Sechenov, spoke about his theory that activity in the brain is associated with some manner of energy stream. Marya had not spent a lot of time contemplating the brain, but the differing abilities and interests of every person did cause her to be curious about its inner workings. However, with Vera sitting beside her, feelings took precedence over thoughts, and at the conclusion of the lecture, she had learned less than she'd anticipated.

Marya was eager to leave with Vera—desire being a delicious sort of torment to court—but as they made their way out, a woman began to walk in lockstep with them.

"We have met, yes?" She looked directly at Vera and Marya as if to reassure herself she wasn't in error. "At the rooms of Varvara Kuznetsova. On Kanonerskya Street?"

"Ah! Yes," Marya said, remembering at last why her face looked familiar. "Your name … your name is …"

"Avdotia," she grinned. "You will join us this evening? Vera Filippova is meant to come to speak of her plans to study medicine in Zurich. She is certain to be an inspiration. You will be there?"

Marya stole a look at Vera, hoping to see what her wish might be, but at once decided it was of no concern since Marya could no longer bear to stand beside Vera and pretend that every particle of her being didn't ache for her. Though Marya hadn't made a conscious plan, she realized that she'd hoped to discover that very evening what Vera held in her heart for her. If Marya were to find that they were to be but comrades in education, she would school herself never to think of touching Vera's face with her hand, kissing her lips—

"Yes, I suppose it will be a topic that will provoke much discussion," Marya said, breaking short her own perilous train of thought. "But … I have other plans this evening. I can't attend."

"And you?" Their would-be companion turned to Vera.

"Well … I …"

Marya raised an eyebrow at her.

"Oh. Well. Yes, but … I. No, I mean yes, I have a prior engagement as well." She knit her forehead.

"Ah, such a pity. You will join us some other time then, I hope. Yes?"

"Oh, yes."

"Of course. Yes."

Vera and Marya offered quick assurances and bid farewell to Avdotia as she made her way across the Alarchin Bridge. Then they turned their attention to each other.

"Well. Goodnight, then." Vera said to Marya, with the air of a question.

"Wait! I, ah, I had hoped those plans, um, were with you." An atypical shyness made Marya stumble over her words.

Even beneath the gauzy glow of the streetlamp, Marya could see Vera's face open into a smile. Then Vera ducked her head timidly and said, "I should like that." The snorting horses of a passing troika nearly overran her softly spoken words, but Marya heard them and grinned.

When at last they had made their way to Vera's rooms and the samovar was gaily burbling, Marya longed to reach across the table and know the feel of Vera's face beneath her fingers. Marya felt this yearning so intensely there was a physical ache in her chest. To distract herself, Marya sought to direct the conversation away from herself.

"Are you sorry, then, Vera, not to be in attendance now with Avdotia and Vera Filippova? I hope I did not cause you an unwelcome change of plans."

"I like them, the meetings, well enough. And the discussion seems to be quite lively among those in attendance. But I do find …"

"Yes?"

"Oh, it's naught. No more than rude curiosity."

"Then you *must* share! If it's 'rude' it's sure to be of interest to me." Marya smiled to think what unladylike remark someone so tender as Vera might have in mind to share.

"Avdotia—do you find her … do you like her hair?"

"I haven't thought much about her hair!"

"It's so short."

"Is that not a new style?" Marya, having paid scant attention to fashion, spoke with genuine ignorance.

"Of … among a certain sort."

"I don't grasp your meaning."

Vera cleared her throat.

"I wanted to ask you … I wondered …"

Vera was clearly nervous, which in turn made Marya nervous. What was it that was distressing Vera so?

Vera waved her hand, as though at an irksome fly. "No, no. It's nothing of concern. It's nothing. I should have left it be."

Vera's voice trailed off, as she spoke, and she began to busy herself with a few grains of sugar on the table, clustering them together.

"Vera." Marya leaned forward on her arms, closing the distance between them. "If there is aught troubling—"

"Troubling? Oh, no. I wouldn't say tr— Why do you dress as you do, Marya?"

"And how is it I dress?" Marya withdrew her arms from the table and sat tall in her chair. *Shall I be nervous? Angry? Disappointed?* Marya decided to defer making a decision until Vera had offered more as to her meaning.

"Your skirts … plain … they are … um … short … Plain and short. Dark colored. It's nothing," she mumbled and blushed furiously. "I mean no offense," she said, then looked Marya in the eye. "I just mean to understand. Are you a Narodnik? It matters not. To me. I just wish to know with whom I take tea." Her manner had turned bold, and Marya was equal parts amused and affected.

"No, Vera. I am no revolutionary. I do sympathize with the way their lot wish to break with tradition in many spheres. And I find them, therefore, interesting to converse with as they have a tendency to *think*—not merely to accept all manner of traditions and 'values' precisely as they have been presented to us. But I prefer more solitary pursuits. I'm not the sort to find my place in a flock."

"But then—"

"Why do I dress thus? Practicality, merely. No—practicality and on the grounds of health."

"Health reasons!"

"Yes. Have you never noticed how your corset prevents you from breathing properly, from bending at your waist, the way your long skirt sweeps up all manner of filth—dirt and mud, cigar ends, bits of fallen food, the spit of coachmen along the roadway? And the weight—the weight of all that excess fabric, the petticoats—do you not grow tired hauling that about with you, everywhere you go, day in and day out?"

"But that's—"

"What? The fashion? What is expected? I must move freely, Vera! How can one move or even think, so burdened? What must lashing oneself up in a corset to the point of altering your body's shape—what must that do to one's internal organs? It cannot—cannot!—be good, Vera."

"I've never thought of it thus."

They sat quietly, then, each with her own thoughts. Marya worried over what might come of such talk, fearing Vera's overconcern for convention wouldn't bode well in the long term. She cast a sidelong glance across the table but found no clue as to what Vera might be pondering.

"Do you not worry," Vera said moments later, "what others—"

"What others think? I don't give a fig for the opinion of anyone who would question such a sensible approach to clothing one's person! I'm not some man's object, or anyone's, for that matter, to be decorated with frills and ribbons and ruffles. I care not. And you, Vera, what think you?"

"I? Surely you can't care what I think."

Was there bitterness in her tone? Dismay? Marya didn't yet know how to decipher Vera's hidden meanings. And perhaps, now, she never would. Marya frowned.

"But I do care, Vera. What you think matters a great deal just now."

Vera narrowed her eyes but said nothing at first. Marya had an impulse to fidget, to shake the table—shake, even, Vera, maybe—so anxious was she for an answer. Instead, she held herself rigid.

"But how do you bear the contempt? The … the stares of reproach?"

"A goose is not a pig's friend, Vera. I concern myself little with how the ignorant, the fools, perceive me. But … this is a concern … of yours? It troubles you … to be seen with such a one as me?"

"No! That isn't what I … what I mean … my only concern … well, I do wonder … There are times when I feel eyes set upon us—you—unkindly."

Marya's chair grated against the floor, then clattered down as she rose abruptly.

"I thought you weren't like the others, the shallow ones who care only—I shall take my leave now, Vera Dashkova."

Marya hurriedly retrieved her coat, anxious to exit as hastily as possible so as not to allow Vera to see how misery had deformed her face.

"No, Marya. Don't leave! Let us not part so. I meant no offense. I wish only to understand … to … to …"

She, also, had risen quickly and reached for Marya's sleeve, but Marya shook her off.

"Enough! I won't be humiliated. I need neither your judgment nor your pity."

Marya closed the door sharply and ran from those rooms of regret as swiftly as her feet would carry her, hardly pausing long enough to touch each stair. When she reached the street, she leaned back against the building, her breast heaving as much from sentiment as exertion. She pounded her fists upon the stone wall behind her until the outer edge of each palm was lacerated. And much as Vera had asserted, passersby did indeed cast curious glances Marya's way.

10.5
Marya

When returning in thought to that night, Marya sought to hew the next events from her memory, but the apparatus of this faculty she likened to a Möbius strip: wherever you begin to follow its chain, no matter its twists or turns, in time you will find yourself traversing the same worn path again and again; there is no avoiding its integrity.

Scraped raw from little finger to wrist on each hand, still pressed to cold stone, Marya found herself manipulating her sense of what had so freshly transpired—dividing and multiplying and carelessly adding to it—until she could find no way to resolve the equation with reason. After some moments, she bounded up the stairs, often taking two at a time. Though she could no longer ascertain what it was she felt, she was determined to tell Vera, regardless. She banged open the door to Vera's rooms, and Vera turned toward the sound of it with a small scream of fright. In Marya's state of agitation, she mistook Vera's alarm to be revulsion, which tormented her all the more.

Marya grabbed Vera roughly at the shoulders and shook her.

"I embarrass you? You don't wish to be seen with me?"

"Marya! No, that isn't at all—"

Vera tried to grab Marya's wrists, but Marya shoved her away.

"I shall save you from that ordeal! You won't find me at your side again."

Marya lurched toward the door, but Vera clutched the back of her coat.

"Marya! Please not like—"

Marya yanked the coat, hoping to wrest it from Vera's grasp. Vera held fast, however, transforming Marya's coat into a whip. Vera was whirled into a corner of the table. Crying out in pain, she released Marya's jacket. Though Marya had no intention of concerning herself further with Vera, she couldn't resist directing a final look of disdain at the woman who had so abused her heart.

Her searing look, however, was wasted on Vera, who had covered her eyes with her hands and wept. Something of Vera's posture—the bowed shoulders, her arms raised in neither defense nor aggression—caused Marya to regain her senses. In that instant, she realized how foolish she was to have doubted Vera. Could such a being as Vera ever bear anyone ill? Marya considered that perhaps she was now as hasty to view Vera in a positive light as she'd had previously been to interpret her concerns in a negative fashion. But how abject Vera was! And to think she, Marya, was the cause! Though Marya was ofttimes rough-edged, certainly she wasn't devoid of compassion.

"Verochka." Marya's voice broke as she reached to remove Vera's hands from her face. Vera flinched at her touch. Marya's chin fell to her chest in her shame. She closed her eyes a moment against the pain of her humiliation. She thought perhaps it would be best to leave. But her horror at how Vera must think of her now—what picture she must carry now forever in her mind—caused Marya to try to right things.

"Darling," she whispered and haltingly reached for Vera's hair. Vera had turned from Marya and started to raise her hands to her tear-stained cheeks, but perhaps sensing Marya's movement near her, she instead froze like a rabbit wishing to escape notice by the wolf, keeping her hands like shields before her eyes.

Marya held her own hands up before her, palms outward, in a gesture of submission, though Vera could not see her. Marya's fingers curled into fists as she dropped her hands to her chest, as though her heart might not stay in her breast without the weight of them there.

"Forgive me, Verochka. I don't deserve it, but please—please!—forgive me."

Marya fell to her knees, then, and wrapped her arms about Vera's thighs, laid her head against Vera's hipbone. Vera shuddered, then tentatively let her hand drop to Marya's shoulder, only to snatch it away again. Marya could feel Vera's body strain against her embrace. Marya vowed not to hurt her again, but she couldn't—not yet—let there be space between them. She held to Vera gently but firmly. And like a wild thing lulled by stillness, Vera gradually relaxed into Marya.

Vera turned to look at Marya and pulled gently at the arms encircling her.

"Come," she said. "Come: off your knees, now."

Marya was reluctant to see her ignominy reflected in Vera's eyes, but at last she rose.

"Verochka." Marya took that tear-stained face between her hands and their eyes locked in exploration. But for Vera's streaked face, Marya felt she could almost have forgotten that there had been trouble between them.

"Verochka." Marya leaned forward, moving toward Vera by no right but only desire, made weak and vulnerable by her spent emotion. Without thought, Marya leaned toward Vera and let her lips press to Vera's mouth while she cupped the frame of Vera's face in her hands. Vera neither resisted nor reciprocated, and though Marya perceived this inequality, in that moment, she did not care. Then, however, her awareness of what must seem like a vile trespass to the woman she had so recently mistreated made her draw back, ready to blurt out yet another apology. But to her surprise, Vera brought her arms up along Marya's sides, and with her hands pressed to Marya's back, wrapped Marya more tightly to her. Vera lifted her head, then, and returned the kiss she had moments before passively received.

Marya savored the moment, closed her eyes, let any hint of her defenses fall aside. But her eyes flew open again as Vera wrenched her mouth away. Vera averted her gaze but pressed her right hand to Marya's shoulder—a connection, still, but one that mapped a distance between them.

"Oh! Mashenka! Forgive me. I don't know what possessed me to … to—"

"Hush. Hush now. It's fine."

Marya reached for the hand at her shoulder and clasped it in her own.

"You are shivering," she observed.

Marya led Vera to the bed, then, and lifted back the heavy quilts. Marya sat at the bed's edge and began to slide in beneath the quilts, pulling Vera toward her, willing her to climb beneath the bedclothes as well.

"Wait!" Vera cried and withdrew her hand.

Now it was Marya's turn to freeze in place. She tried to gird herself against whatever recrimination might be coming.

"Our shoes," said Vera, then knelt beside Marya whose feet weren't quite hidden beneath the quilt yet and unlaced her shoes, which she gently slipped off and placed neatly at bedside.

Without a word, afraid to break the spell that surely they were under, Marya moved to let Vera sit beside her on the bed as she undid her own footwear. Vera pulled off first one, then the other shoe, but did not immediately set the second shoe down, hesitant, perhaps, to see what uncommon thing might occur next.

Marya raised herself to her elbow and rested a hand on Vera's hip. The shoe slid from Vera's hand, landing with a soft thud on the floorboards, and Marya began to work herself farther onto the bed, the weight of the covers pulling like gravity against her clothes. Vera soon slipped beside her, her skirts rustling and twisting as she did so.

The whole while, in the dim light afforded by the oil lamp yet burning in the other room, Marya fixed her eyes on Vera as if that fine thread of union might suffice to tug the other woman in her wake.

When the two were settled, Vera rose on one elbow and gazed at Marya's face. With her free hand, Vera traced the line of Marya's jaw.

When Vera's fingers began to drift from Marya's face, Marya grasped them and held Vera's palm to her lips. In that moment, Marya felt she lacked for nothing. She wanted to consider no other thing, to know nothing more than the feel of this woman's flesh against her starved mouth, to catch the faint scent of Vera's lavender soap beneath her nose. Marya lost herself momentarily in the perfection, but a thought soon bubbled to the surface: Vera had not pulled away. Vera had allowed her hand to be pressed to Marya's lips. Marya turned to look at Vera and loosed her fingers from Vera's. Marya wanted to say something. Felt, indeed, that something ought be said. But when Vera took her newly freed fingers and let them drift down Marya's temple, her cheek, her jaw, Marya could not imagine a single thing to say.

"Verochka." Marya's voice came at last in a husky whisper. Marya then reached to touch the wonder of the lovely face so near her own and marveled at that proximity and that this face remained focused on her and had not turned away. Marya felt a shiver travel through Vera.

"Are you cold? Come: close the space between us."

Vera slid deeper under the covers and inched closer to Marya, who ran her hand deliberately the length of Vera's forearm, any and all ill feeling from earlier categorically set aside. Marya let her hand drift to the topmost part of Vera's leg. Vera sighed, her breath warm on Marya's cheek.

"Vera," Marya choked through a catch in my throat. "Vera Lvovna Dashkova, you are utterly lovely. I never hoped to meet anyone … like … again in this lifetime." Marya lifted her hand to trace the edge of Vera's ear.

"Marya—Masha. I—" Vera abruptly stopped speaking. Marya continued to stroke her face, waiting until Vera could find the words for which she sought. "Marya," Vera said again, her voice cracking. But this time, whatever she might say was silenced by a kiss from Marya. It was a careful kiss, soft enough, Marya thought, she could deny the desire behind it if Vera didn't respond agreeably. Marya withdrew from the kiss and tried to gauge Vera's reaction. Vera silently put her hand to Marya's face, and once more, Marya took that hand within her own and brought it to her lips, only this time kissing it quite deliberately, many times. All at once, then, each woman threw an arm around the other, and Marya pulled Vera into a tight embrace. A small gasp from Vera fell warmly on Marya's ear.

"Verochka," Marya whispered, and covered Vera's neck with light but hungry kisses. Vera's breath became ragged, and she gently but firmly pushed Marya away. Marya, crestfallen, turned away from Vera. Not wishing Vera to see her misery, Marya was about to take her leave when Vera turned Marya's face toward her own and pressed her forehead to Marya's so that the tips of their noses touched and they could feel the other's breath lightly graze their lips.

Before long, Vera lifted her head and brought her fingers lightly, tentatively to Marya's hair, then let her fingers mingle among the hairs before letting her hand glide down the side of Marya's head, encountering, along the way, her ear.

"Your ear," she said, speaking in a whisper. "It's so tiny." Marya gently pulled Vera's arm aside and kissed her mouth again, more firmly this time and with great intensity. Then, her breath ragged with desire, Marya let her cheek rest atop Vera's, hoping her struggle for restraint was not evident. She willed herself to take control of her breathing, of her overwhelming emotions, which was not a simple task with this other body so near beside her—this body, this woman who stirred her, who was even now allowing herself to be held.

"Verochka," Marya said when she had succeeded in calming herself. "I must go. I must go, or my aunt will worry, though I long to stay here in the comfort of your arms."

"Masha—I … I'm moved by you beyond reason. I—" But Vera had lost the words again.

"Verochka. Darling." Marya tenderly ran her fingers along Vera's cheekbone and jaw, then down her neck. "You are an angel. A radiant and wonderful angel. How ever could I have doubted you?"

Marya turned aside the quilt and rose from the side of the bed opposite Vera, going to the nearby chair to lace up her shoes. She shook her head, chagrined once more by her earlier irrational fury.

Though the light was dim, Marya saw Vera shiver as she put aside the quilt before drawing it around her shoulders.

"Marya, I … I …"

"Shhh," Marya said soothingly. Finished with her shoes, she rose and walked toward the bed. "What troubles you? Are you frightened? There is no longer a need to be frightened. I've becalmed myself, and you are in no danger from me. I vow, Verochka, that never, never again shall I do anything to harm you." Marya tilted Vera's head up and tenderly kissed her forehead. She stood back then to memorize her before turning to go.

When Marya closed the door behind her, she paused before descending the stairs, thinking how, though it might not yet have been love she saw, gazing back at her, she was fairly certain that neither was it dread.

11
Vera's Journal

Monday, 29 November 1875

What a great deal there is to write! Yet no question where to begin: What does it mean, the time I spent with Marya this Friday past? It's a question I've pondered at every opportunity in the days since. If I haven't committed my thoughts to paper before this night, it's because I've felt rather foolish, as if I had a schoolgirl crush. Also, there is the uncomfortable business of the confrontation between us. I meant no offense when I inquired about her unconventional style of dress, but there can be no doubt offense was taken. The more I come to know her, the more I see that Marya is not a glass through which one can peer and observe all. She seems rather more like a prism, such that one's line of sight bends here and there at the odd angle and one's viewpoint of her is never quite straightforward.

To be sure, the depth of her anger affrighted me—especially when I had been all innocence in my inquiring. But how genuine her remorse! And the tenderness she showed me when we had set aside the ill feelings all but wiped away the moments of misunderstanding.

I ask myself whether I should nevertheless decline the company of Mlle Zhukova henceforth, but when I contemplate the solitary life I'd been leading before she turned my life upon its head like a twirling top—I cannot tolerate the thought of a return to such barren stillness. What does it matter if the ride may sometimes be bumpy as a wooden-wheeled cart on a cobblestone thoroughfare? It's nevertheless desirable to see where this liaison might transport me. For such a trifling amount of happiness is secured in the sum of a life—best enjoy it while I can.

So I tell myself now, but on Saturday evening, when we were to meet Aleksandra Kobiakova, I felt most peculiar in Marya's presence. When I stepped from the carriage at no. 18, Nevsky Prospect, she was waiting there upon the walkway to greet me. I couldn't meet her eyes. How does one interact with a woman with whom one has shared unexpected passion and whispered endearments? I fear my formalness with her caused her some pain, but there wasn't time to explore this concern, for Aleksandra immediately joined us, and we entered Leiner's. When we had been seated, Aleksandra ordered tea, while Marya and I each ordered the zakuska. When we returned from filling our plates—Black Sea oysters, smoked sturgeon, mayonnaise, caviar, dried salmon, cured ham, thin slices of aromatic cheeses, and the most delectable pickled mushrooms—we found Aleksandra already sipping her tea. On the table were two thimbles of vodka that the waiter had left for us.

Aleksandra, with those blue glasses perched on the end of her nose, was dressed in a dark gown, and I spotted several places where the shapeless heavy material had been mended. Despite the bulkiness of her garments, it was easy enough to conclude she was thin as a rail. Her eyes, above the blue glasses, were tired.

"Will you not have some of my zakuska, Aleksandra? I fear I've taken more than I can eat; it all smelled so delicious." I set the plate between us and hoped she wouldn't take offense. It was clear, though, she was a woman of no great means.

"Thank you for this kindness." She speared a slice of ham, put it on her plate, and fell to eating. "What lovely flavor! It reminds me of my mother."

I smiled, nearly giggled, at the thought of smoked pig reminding her of her mother, but turned my amusement to a cough, aware we didn't know each other well enough for me to share my puerile wit with her. Evidently, however, I was none too expert at hiding my merriment.

"Ah!" she said. Her eyes twinkled as she went on. "But of course I don't mean that the *pig* has reminded me of my mother—it's the flavor—how she—didn't your mothers vie with the neighboring wives to perfect their recipes for smoking bacon and ham? *No*? Ah, mine was like a sorceress, or a ... a chemist!—carefully calculating the proportions of juniper, the bundles of aromatic herbs and pine twigs, the dried fern leaves, to give the exact flavor she desired, until the year she felt satisfied none should best her ham for taste." Aleksandra took another bite of ham and closed her eyes in pleasure as she savored the juice and the texture of the smoky meat.

Marya exchanged a brief glance with me, then pressed her plate on Aleksandra as well.

"You must try the mushrooms," she said. "I fear I, too, have taken more than I dare eat, and the mushrooms are *not* to be wasted."

As we shared our food, we began the pleasant work of getting to know one another better.

"Have you frequented the women's meetings like the one where we met you the other night?" I inquired. I shifted in my chair and my foot brushed against Marya's. I quickly tucked my leg back, grateful the dim lighting would hide my embarrassment.

"Yes," she said, "I go as often as I can spare the time from my needlework and writing. I've witnessed enough of the hardships of women, here in St. Petersburg and in the town of Kostroma where I grew up, that I feel a fury to wrest us from the darkness which shades our futures."

"You are a writer?"

"Do you still have family in Kostroma?"

Marya and I spoke at once, and Aleksandra let forth a laugh, in which we joined.

"Well," she said. "It's apparent we must share our autobiographies, in this intimate setting, before we begin to examine larger questions of rights and paths. Very well. I shall start.

"I come from a merchant family. My father and his brothers kept a small shop where they sold books, paints, icons, and the like. My uncles and father are wholly old-fashioned, with long beards and kaftans, and would be appalled to discover me in a place such as this, drinking *tea*."

"Tea!" I said, interrupting. "Whatever for?"

"To drink tea, as well as spirits," she said, eyes flicking from my thimble of vodka to Marya's, "is considered sinful by them. They also condemn course language. I should think they wouldn't find much to approve in the meetings we attend!"

"But you—" I let the thought hang.

"No, I haven't adhered to their beliefs." She fingered the handle of her teacup and seemed lost for a moment in reverie. Then she took up her story again.

"My mother tried to teach me the Slavonic alphabet when I was quite young, but I rebelled against such rigor. I grew up with three boys—my brothers Ivan and Vasily and my cousin Evgeny—and I much preferred running about in the yard with them than playing with dolls."

"I, too!" said Marya. She lightly touched Aleksandra's wrist, as though to emphasize the connection. "How I despised those dolls, all in a line upon my shelf, where they collected dust and followed me with their reproachful eyes! But how did you come to write, then?"

"It was a long time in coming," she went on. "At last, they subdued me and settled me into a sedentary life of needlework. Once they no longer forced me to read, I began to steal away the books my father occasionally brought home from the store for himself and tried to read them during the night by the light of candle ends I had purloined from the kitchen.

"When I was thirteen, the local deacon began teaching my brothers to write, and I copied what they wrote, though my handwriting remains quite awful to this day. I was altogether enamored of historical novels, the way they bring the past to life right before one's eyes, and I read them whenever I might encounter the chance. My mother, herself strangled by the stagnant, poisonous life of a small-town merchant's wife, encouraged my reading. Her main wish for me, however, was to marry a government official so I might escape her fate.

"When I was fifteen, a young local townsman, who planned to study medicine, took an interest in me, brought me books, and declared to my mother he intended one day to become her son-in-law. I didn't love him, but I cared deeply for him, and we remained close even after he went to the Medical Surgical Academy in Moscow. But something changed within him and he became bitter and unkind—and in the meantime, will you believe, I rejected another suitor to remain faithful to him! But when we at last broke it off, I felt empty of heart and head. To occupy my thoughts with something other than Pavel, I took an interest in my grandmother's stories of the old days. Her tales caught my fancy to the extent that I filled out the characters of her tales, ordered the events chronologically, and within three weeks, I had easily and with immense pleasure composed my first novel, *The Last Execution*, though it would be many years and much hardship before I found a willing publisher."

"I know that book!" Marya said. "Now I know the author, I must locate it and read it again."

"Oh please, no." She grasped Marya's wrist and released it in a quick squeeze. "You will find, I think, *A Woman in Everyday Merchant Life* to be a much finer work. And quite coincidentally, I assure you, it takes as its theme the ruinous effects of marriage on a woman." She laughed gaily and with one hand pushed up her blue glasses and with the other speared a mushroom with her fork. We laughed, too, and I fell captive to her warmth and easy manner.

We asked several questions about the novel, particularly about Aniuta, the main character, and her brutal merchant husband, and then fell into a comfortable rhythm of weaving together our own small histories and the large theme of how to secure, for women, basic rights. We shared among us several more thimbles of vodka, and the discussion grew the livelier in proportion. When several gentlemen raised their eyes from the papers over which they were laboring, we felt a flush of embarrassment and bid farewell to one another—with both relief and regret, on my part, when it came to taking leave of Marya.

For though the normalcy of chatting amiably in a public place—aided, no doubt, by the draughts of vodka—had eased my awkwardness at being with Masha after our time of ardent embraces, my previous discomfort refreshed itself with the chill of the night air. Previous, I may say, but it's not a thing that has ceased to be, though still I feel a flutter when I think about our eyes meeting, and still I ache to be folded in her arms. And still I find such feelings peculiar though not entirely unpleasant.

We left each by her own carriage, but I sensed a sad longing in Masha's eyes so that, had the driver not already coaxed the horse to movement, I might well have pressed myself to her, in front of all, there on the Nevsky Prospect. I won't claim peace, in this short space of time, and "resignation" sounds too close a cousin to "dread." Perhaps it's that I've resigned myself to be happy and forget all else.

Such a tremendous surge of—I know not what!—I have felt these past weeks. New people, new ideas, new feelings—I shouldn't wonder it spilled over into my teaching. With what zest did I approach my morning together, today, with Pasha and Varya!

As I entered the Solovyov household this morning, I bade the driver of my carriage wait. Loaded in the carriage were a copy of *The Girl's Own Treasury*—that cherished book from my childhood, which on Sunday I had found in my trunk with the help of Kovalev, my languid bear of a landlord—

a birdcage, and some items suggested for the catching of birds. What a marvel, to open the trunk—all manner of things about which I'd forgotten! The ribbons and childish drawings, a poem my childhood friend Anya had written for me, a letter from a man I thought I loved once, a doll, an icon—well, I'm afield now from what I meant to record.

"Come," I said, to Pasha and Varya, "put on your outdoor things; we are going to the Summer Garden for our lessons this morning."

We drove along Dvortsovaya Embankment to the garden. Along the way, I told them about the purpose of our excursion and answered their many questions. When we arrived, the driver helped unload our things, and we carried them into the garden.

"Where shall we go? To the Fontanka Embankment?" Pasha skipped backwards before me on the path, the cage, which he carried, bumping against him.

"Pasha!" I called, as a corpsman and his friend quickly stepped aside. "Sorry!" The men gave me an amused look.

"Pasha, dear, I know you are excited, but you must be more contained, or you shall do injury to yourself or someone else. Now come; please walk facing forward. Let us go to the Krylov statue, where there are many bushes and trees in which a bird might rest, and we can then talk about Krylov's fables as well."

"Who is Krylov?"

"What is a fable?" the children asked at once.

"Ah!" I said. "Let us start our lesson, then, as we walk. A fable, my darlings, is a tale in which animals can talk like humans. The actions of the animals are meant to teach us something."

"Teach us what?" asked Varya.

"Hm. Let me see whether I can remember a tale to tell you. Ah! There is the tale of the monkey and the mirror. A monkey one day sees himself in the mirror and nudges his friend the bear, saying, 'Look at that silly creature! What grimaces he makes and how he skips about. I should hang myself from irritation if I were like that.'"

"But it's he!" cried, Varya. "He is looking at himself!"

"Yes, Varya, darling, but you see, he does not realize it, never having seen himself in a mirror before."

"What happens then, Mademoiselle? Does the monkey hang himself?" Pasha, I thought, sounded a bit too eager over such an outcome, but I let it pass.

"No, Pasha. Now listen. The monkey then says to the bear, 'But let's be honest, Mishka, do we not have among our friends many who grimace so?' And the bear replies, 'But why search among our friends? Would it not be better to look at yourself?' But the monkey pays him no heed."

"Then what do the bear and monkey do, Mademoiselle?" Varya's words kept company with small puffs of vapor.

"That's the end of the tale, my doves."

"That's a silly story! Nothing happens."

"Yes, perhaps. It isn't meant to be a tale of adventure or great drama. It's meant to tell us about human nature."

"Human nature?"

"Yes, about people. For instance, in the tale of the monkey and the bear, Krylov means us to understand that while it's simple to find others' faults, it isn't so simple to notice our own."

"Look! Birds! Let us catch some, Mademoiselle Dashkova!" Pasha pointed, then spun to face me, nearly hitting me in the shins with the birdcage.

"Shh, Pasha. You will scare them all off. We aren't yet ready in any case. I must gather up the necessary items we need and find the best spot to coax a bird to come join us. Let me see … Ah! There, near the stand of trees. Beneath it lies a leafy hedge where we may set our bait. Now—"

I rummaged about in the bag I had packed with what I thought I might need, according to the section on birds in my girls' treasury. Pasha and Varya both stood on tiptoe, trying to peer in.

"Be patient, please. I shall explain it all to you. Here we go. First, we shall find a twig that stands a bit clear from the others."

"Will this one do?" Varya wrested a twig from the hedge and handed it to me.

"Ah, Varya. No—it must be a twig still attached to the hedge so our bird may land on it."

“Like this, Mademoiselle?” Pasha took hold of my hand and pulled me several paces along the hedge and placed his hand beneath a twig around which the other branches were mostly bare.

“Yes, Pasha. Excellent.” I cupped the top of his head a moment beneath my hand. “Now, we must put a paste upon the twig so when the bird lands, its feet will stick to the twig and we can then grasp it and place it gently in our cage. The paste, my dears, is called birdlime, and there are several ways one can make it. I have some here, already made, in this jar.” The children sniffed at it and wrinkled their noses.

“Had I the time, I should have made it from unripe mistletoe berries, dried, crushed, soaked in water, and their skins removed. I didn’t want to delay our excursion today for fear the weather would become inclement. So. What I have, instead, is a mix of spruce resin—the sticky sap from a spruce tree—and some linseed oil. Varya, darling, do you still have the stick you showed to me? Splendid! I shall use it to spread some birdlime on the twig Pasha found for us. There we go. Now how shall we get a bird to land upon our stick? Do you know, Varya?”

“Here, birdies.” Her voice rang out in the crisp air and the few people strolling the paths turned toward the sound.

“I fear, my darling, that will frighten them off, rather than call them to us. Do you have an idea Pasha?”

He screwed up his face in thought.

“When you’ve been out playing in the cold air and I want you to return to your studies, what is the surest way to get you to return?”

“Ah!” His face lit up. “Shall we put tea and some cracknels out for them?”

“That’s the idea, Pasha, but you must think like a bird. What do birds like to eat?”

“Worms?”

“Yes. What else?”

“Seeds?”

“Yes. And?”

“Berries!” Varya’s face lit up at being able to contribute.

“Yes, Varya. Very good. Seeds, worms, and berries would make a sumptuous banquet for a bird. Worms, however, aren’t to be found this time of year; they have burrowed far into the earth where they may sleep until the spring air warms them. And seeds aren't so easy for a bird to notice from afar, so we shall use berries."

I pulled a branch with some juicy, red currants on it and nestled it near the limed twig and pulled the other branches away so as not to offer another landing site for our bird.

"Now, children, we must wait quietly."

I spread a blanket out some yards away from the limed branch, and we all three sat upon it. I unwrapped some oatmeal cakes for the children. We spoke in whispers for a while as I told them about the different birds we might encounter—the linnet, the grosbeak, the storm thrush, or any of various finches—until their heads nodded, and I let them lean against me and drowse. I pulled the blanket up around us to keep us a bit warmer. Then I, too, began to nod into sleep—until I heard a frantic flutter of wings.

"Children," I whispered. "We have a visitor: a bullfinch has taken a liking to our berries. Shh," I cautioned, then, as I saw their blossoming excitement. "He is frightened, does not understand why he can't fly away," I whispered. "We must keep our quiet so as not to further frighten him and cause him to do injury to himself. Sit here; I shall go to him."

I took the birdcage and, with barely a sound, crept to the hedge. The finch was flapping its wings, in a frenzy to be free of the branch to which it was stuck. I feared it would indeed harm itself and felt a pang of regret. Was I being merely selfish, wanting only the sport or satisfying a wish for companionship? Was I wrong to have fallen in line with those who think it a kindness to a bird to provide a safe haven for the winter? Too late to argue the point with myself now, I reasoned—now while the poor thing is beating its wings against the branch and dried leaves.

"Shh, my darling," I whispered to the frightened bird, as I edged ever closer. "Quiet, love. I mean you no harm." And on I continued with sweet phrases of reassurance.

"We have caught a bird!" Varya's voice rose like a pure bell.

I cast her a stern glance, and she bit her lip.

Inches from the bullfinch, I stood as still as possible for a minute or more, continuing to whisper sweetly to it. I moved my hand in short increments toward it and with the other lifted the cage so the open door would be near.

"There, my love. Nothing to fear." I clasped my hand around the trembling body and gently pulled to unstick first one, then the other foot and released it into the cage. I shut the door, and the poor dear beat against the bars looking for escape. I cooed to it and carried the cage toward the children.

"Gently, Pasha, Varya. He is very frightened. You may look at him a moment, and then I will cover him with the blanket to help calm him."

We gathered our things, then, and made our way to the street, where we hailed a carriage and made our way back to the Solovyovs. As we jostled along the embankment, I answered their questions about birds and trees and the like. I left them, soon after, to their nanny and bade them think about the events of the day, as tomorrow I would have them write a composition about it.

And now, here I sit at my desk, in the company of Zubilo, as I've named the bird, who wields his beak at his birdseed like a chisel. I had thought to leave him—discovered to be thus (a *him*) by the red tinge upon his breast—with the Solovyov children, but their parents didn't want the bother of caring for him. In truth, I'm glad, for I do welcome his company. Though he is silent now, under his cover, I feel like a young child, anticipating the sight of his rotund form and glossy plumage, his melancholy song, come morning.

12
Lidia

Lidia was roused by the sound of loud, urgent whispers just at the bottom of the stairs. At first, the muffled voices all pulped together like grains of cooked kasha. But then, above the others, she distinctly heard the robust voice of her friend Olga.

"Please let me through! I *will* see her. I don't comprehend how a visit from her oldest, dearest friend could possibly have a debilitating effect on her health!"

As Lidia tried to pull herself up on the pillows and push her hair into something she hoped might look more civilized, the door to her room flew open, and in lurched Olya.

Liuda raced in after her, breathless.

"Forgive me, Lidia—"

"These dreadful serving people of yours, they tried—only doing their jobs, yes, yes, pish—and I your closest—Lida, my dear, how *are* you?"

Liuda, who had uselessly tried to address Olga's complaints, bowed her head and left the room as Lidia had weakly signaled with her fingers.

"Ah, Olya! How good of you to come. What a fright I must look. I was but resting a b—"

"No need, no need."

Olya pulled a chair bedside, dropped heavily down to it, then stood at once to remove her overcoat, which she draped over the foot of the bedstead, talking all the while.

"Anya and I've been sick with worry, we haven't—how are you, dearest?—we have tried on more than one occasion to come see—but they wouldn't—we have missed you."

Seated once again, Olya reached across the bedclothes and draped her large palm atop Lidia's dry hand.

Lidia shook her head from side to side on the pillow where it lay, afraid to attempt to speak lest it precipitate another coughing spell. It was one thing for her to see her own handkerchiefs become darkly spotted each time she coughed, now, but to have another witness it was unseemly. But not to speak also seemed rude.

"I'm," she rasped softly. "I've been—"

"Tut, tut, Lida. You must save your strength. I shall talk for the both of us. My, it's warm in here." Olga pulled a fan from her handbag. "Don't know why," she muttered. "Why am I so flustered?" A shiver visibly passed over her.

"Ah," she said, as she put away her fan. "Well. We have made progress on the ball. We have secured a date at the Hall of Nobility and made arrangements for the velvet draperies to be brushed freshly clean just before then and, as well, to have the old wax cleared from the candelabra and the brass polished.

"The young ladies are clamoring to help with the charity bazaar, making of it a contest to see who can raise the most money for the Society for the Improvement of the Lodgings of the Laboring Population. Natalya Palovna says that as it's a festive occasion, all will want champagne, and therefore she shall sell the most for our cause. But Elena Grigorievna says that though a glass of champagne may make the occasion the more merry, the dancing will make everyone thirsty and so she will sell tea enough to furnish an entire lodging hall. Sophia Vladimirovna—you know, the Korovin girl? Yes! You must know—her mother was at—no? Well, anyway, she vows to best them both, for since all shall no doubt be cold from their travels to the hall, they will want most of all to buy the brandy she will sell." Olga paused to chuckle.

"I don't suppose your Marya—no? Mmmm." Lidia's raised brow over her too-bright eyes, almost lost now in their sockets, told her the folly of her question. "I do so hope you will have recovered your health by then."

Lidia made a sour face and closed her eyes.

"You don't know, Lida! You don't know God's plan for you. And I—and Anya—are praying for you and I have—I have something for you."

Olga looked into her handbag, moving items aside, until she had found what she was seeking.

"Here: you must take this."

Olga put a ball of something wrapped in a scrap of white linen and tied with a black ribbon onto the bedclothes. Lidia looked at her quizzically, then with great effort reached for the little package on her lap. She fumbled with the ribbon before her old friend clasped both her skeletal hands in a single grasp.

"No, no, Lida. Don't untie it. It's ... it's dirt from Blessed Ksenia's grave. I had Afonya—do you recall my coachman? I had him drive me to Vasilievsky Island, to the Smolensky Cemetery. The wooded grounds, the Smolenka River—it's so peaceful there, Lida. You should—yes. Peaceful.

"I ... I had Afonya pull beside the, ah, the, um, the grave, and with a small shovel, he took a clot ... a ... a sample ... of earth for me in a coarse sack. At home, I bound it for you so you might hold it or ... or put it beneath your pillow. So many miracles, Lida! How many have been healed or borne a child with Ksenia's intercession? If the doctors can do nothing—solutions of alcohol and iodine or tannins—bah! What good have they done you, Lida? Ksenia. And my prayers. We will ... we will. Forgive me, Lida. I must go. I'm late for ... for—"

Olga rose quickly and quickly exited the room, sweeping her coat from the end of the bed as she did so. But not before a small sob escaped her, betraying the lie behind the need for her leave-taking.

13
Vera's Journal

Wednesday, 1 December 1875

I met Marya this evening for a lecture about John Stuart Mill's *Principles of Political Economy*, which considers how the use of wealth must be *taught* and espouses an appreciation for those things which wealth can't buy. Most rousing! Never have I thought about monetary comfort in such a way—never having had an excess of such resources at hand, I suppose, but I can see the value of such education for those who find themselves in a circumstance in which they have time to pursue thoughts beyond how to secure a simple loaf of black bread or what lesson to impart to one's charges. Now, of course, I begin to seek such mental stimulation myself, being in a more secure position with the Solovyovs.

Afterward, we decided once again to attend a discussion group. We took a carriage to the residence where the meeting was already underway. The discussion was the most heated we'd yet been to.

We noticed, straightaway, a short brunette with blue-gray eyes who was speaking animatedly to a small group of women gathered around her, and we walked to the edge of the group.

"Yes, of course! Certainly, Elizaveta—our talks exclusive of men have been of critical importance. I'm not—no one is—denying that. Such talks have indeed freed us from the static past, much as we have hoped. But now what, eh? Now we are free, what is it we do with our freedom?"

"What do you mean, 'what do we do with our freedom'? We do what anyone would do! Enjoy it." A number of women chuckled.

"Oh, then, so you say our responsibilities are at an end? The others, whatever their terrible condition—the factory workers, the peasants, the women still enslaved by family despotism—they should all be left to find their own way, if they can find it at all?"

"Now, Evgenia, you twist my meaning. With our freedom, we enjoy its benefits—to study, to learn many things, among them how to achieve the betterment of others."

"But do you not understand, Elizaveta, these things—working toward improvement of the lives of working people, of peasants, of our Russian way of life—are already being done among the men? Why not join them? Together, we will be twice as strong. We will have double the influence, double the intellect applied to these problems!"

"It isn't so simple! What have we won yet?" Marya said. The circle widened out to include her. Faces turned toward her. I recognized Avdotia from our last meeting, and Aleksandra was there as well, with those blue glasses! "Can a woman get her own passport yet?" continued Marya. "Can I yet attend classes at the university? What is it we have gained?" A few women nodded their heads in agreement.

"What you say is true—I'm sorry, but I don't know your name," replied Evgenia.

"Marya Zhukova."

"What you say may be true, Marya, but can you not grasp how we will achieve progress faster if we present a united front, men and women together? The important thing is we are no longer subservient to men. If we remain separate, we will simply cut ourselves off from efforts by male students who, like us, are organizing. Together, we can organize around those issues that concern *both* sexes."

"No, Evgenia—I think to expect men to treat us now as peers is to divide the skin of an unkilled bear. Men are … men are … well, *men.*"

Many of the women gave an appreciative laugh. Evgenia, however, kept her fine lips tightly closed.

"Men," Masha continued, "are so long used to being in control, even the most well-intentioned can't break this habit. They must always be the directors, the instigators. You will discover, Evgenia—if you become a member of a group with men, you will not be an equal member."

Avdotia, Elizaveta, a few others, and I nodded our agreement with this assessment.

Evgenia shook her head sadly.

"You insult me, Marya." She spoke softly but with intensity. "You insult all of us here." With a sweeping gesture, she indicated the room. "You don't give me credit for knowing my own mind, for having control of my will. Once, what you say may have been true. But we are no longer ignorant of the disadvantages we have faced as women—that's the difference. If we join with men now, we join with our eyes fully open."

"Yes, but what of the men—are their eyes open?" a dark-haired woman countered defiantly. Everyone turned to Evgenia, then, to judge her response.

She threw up her hands. "Ack! We are just scratching our tongues here. You may stay and continue in this idle chatter if you like, but I know of a group of male students eager to have any of us who wishes join their ranks. Those of you who are tired of talking solely for the sake of talking, you are welcome to accompany me."

As she stormed from the room, she shook her head in disgust. Several women rose and followed her, and then, after a discussion in heated whispers, a few more rose to go as well, though whether to follow Evgenia or simply to leave wasn't clear. What was left of our group broke into smaller units, but we didn't stay, any of us, much longer. It had been a contentious meeting, and we were all rather tired. When Marya suggested we ourselves leave, I agreed. We said goodbye to Aleksandra and pledged to dine together again one day soon.

Marya took my arm, and we walked a few blocks until we spotted a carriage we could flag down. The driver was about to descend from his perch to help us into the carriage, but Marya waved him off and handed me up to the seat herself, then climbed aboard, too.

"Well," she said, "you were most quiet, as you often are at these meetings. Now that it's but the two of us, what do you think of the issue of separate versus joined groups, an issue that seems to divide women more greatly, even, than before?" She linked her arm through mine, convivially.

"Well," I said, "I'm not entirely sure what to think. What Evgenia says makes some sense." With that, Marya let a small explosion of air issue from her lips. "No," I continued, "I think she is right that there are many things we could accomplish together that we women couldn't readily do by ourselves. *But*," I said, cutting short Masha's objection, "but I also recognize how easily women's voices are crushed by the bigger voices—and larger self-image—of men."

"Yes, now that's something I can tell you about from my own experience!"

"Yes?"

"Every Tuesday and Thursday evening, my dear aunt insists on inviting 'the finest men Petersburg has to offer,' and I must tell you, thus far I'm at a loss to discover how they have come to be perceived as our finest."

"Ah! So that's what takes you from the Alarchin lectures on those evenings."

Marya turned to me, appraising. I felt that I had revealed something too much of myself, though it was no secret I enjoyed her company.

"But why does she have them come?" I asked, to divert her attention from myself. "The men."

"Why? She says it's for the company and to introduce me into society, but I suspect she is hoping to find me a husband. What a great disappointment these gatherings must be to her as well in that case, since I can rarely abide their boastful and ingratiating conversation long enough to discover their names most evenings! What nonsense they talk. And they have no insight into literature whatever. They are complete boors."

"Oh ho! Now I understand more clearly the genesis of your argument at the meeting just now."

"Yes, but I don't let myself be bullied by them, of course. I merely can't grasp how it could be useful to work with such prigs as these. Besides, women have their own demands and aspirations. I will grant there is much wrong with the world generally that might benefit from mending, but until women are allowed access to a decent education and certain basic freedoms, I'm of the impression we are unlikely in a position to help anyone else. Let Evgenia and her kind go off and save the world. I'm too thirsty for knowledge to give up drinking just yet and turn my attention to other matters."

During this monologue, Marya let go my arm to punctuate her agitation with her hands. I was stirred by what she said, but I had to smile, as well, at the tumult of her passion.

When the carriage pulled to a halt outside my door—much too soon, as always—I bid Marya a good evening. We leaned in to kiss each other's cheeks, and my nose was met with the faint odor of rosemary, a clean, woodsy smell that made me wish to linger and press my face to her neck.

Instead, I stepped from the droshky. I might have stood right where I stepped to the ground, in such a dream state I seemed to be, had I not heard Marya command the driver wait. I knew she waited for me to be safe inside my doorway, and so I compelled myself to move counter to whatever force begged me draw nearer to her.

I closed the door of the boarding house behind me and rested my forehead on its cool wood, listening to the sound of horse hooves growing fainter while a smile took hold on my face. Only when I could hear the clop of hooves no more did I turn to the stairs, shaking my head in wonder.

Surely some mischievous fate had been winking at me the day I first sat beside Marya Zhukova at the Alarchin courses.

14
Marya

One remarkable evening, Marya and Vera attended a lecture on physiology—though it wasn't the lecture that formed a vivid memory for Marya.

As the two left the lecture hall, Vera tucked her arm in Marya's, and they walked while they sought out a carriage to hail.

"Had you *any* idea the body was so complicated?" Vera asked.

"Mmm," was Marya's vague reply.

Vera glanced furtively at Marya, puzzled by such uncharacteristic impassivity. What if Marya found her comment naive? The last thing Vera wished to appear before this woman was dull-witted, having long since sensed that Marya had little patience for vapidity. She chewed her lip, trying to decide whether to offer further comment on the lecture or let Marya speak next. She reminded herself that a word is not a sparrow: once it has flown out, you won't catch it.

The women walked on, then, silently for a while. At last, uneasy with the silence, Vera squeezed Marya's arm tightly to her body.

"Shall we … would you like to come … have tea in my quarters? Or would you … would you as soon go home and rest? The lectures do make for long days."

"What?" Marya said. "Oh no, I'm fine. Fine. Just ... I got lost in my thoughts—pondering a thorny mathematical problem I had encountered the other day, something Weierstrass has written about Abelian functions."

"Oh."

After a pause, Vera asked, "And who is Weierstrass?"

"Sorry," Marya said, smiling. "I forget you don't share my passion for mathematical expression. Karl Weierstrass has done extensive work on functions, especially elliptical and Abelian functions. We didn't get so advanced in our mathematical studies at the Institute, but Grigorii Rostovtsev, the mathematical instructor there, encouraged me greatly, and I've learned much from reading on my own. And I correspond with Grisha still, from time to time." She smiled to herself, thinking of Grisha's most recent letter and its comical closing, then went on, anticipating what would likely be Vera's next question, "A function has to do with how two variables—that is, unknown quantities in mathematics—relate to one another, how their values are dependent on one another. It's rather complicated ...," Marya said, trying to sense whether Vera wished more explanation.

"Oh, no—that's fine," Vera said, giving a light laugh. "A carriage is coming—up ahead there?—and I don't think you will have time to catch me up to where you are before the carriage arrives! Unless you would like to have that tea, after all?"

"Yes," Marya said, also laughing, "tea sounds lovely. But no more talk of mathematics. It's too late at night for that, except for the truly obsessed!"

In the carriage, though, Verochka came back to the topic.

"Mashenka ..."

"Yes?"

"Have you considered pursuing the study of mathematics further? With your enthusiasm, you would make a wonderful teacher."

"Bah! And where would I study? Who would let me teach something so weighty as mathematics? Even at girls' schools, the science and mathematics courses are taught by men!"

"Well, but is that not one of the things we are working toward in the discussion groups we attend—greater educational opportunities for women?"

"Yes, of course, that's the goal. But as has been remarked, we aren't there yet, or why would so many of us run to the Alarchin courses each night, where we can't even get a degree!"

"But what about the Technological Institute? I've heard rumors it might be possible for a woman to enroll in the engineering division and study mathematics there? Or there is always Switzerland—I've heard talk of a regular *colony* of Russian women who have gone to Zurich to study."

"Zurich can't even be considered—I couldn't leave my aunt now. You've borne witness to her failing health. I know Nadya and Ilyusha would care for her, were I to leave, but she is the last of my family—how could I be away from her now, in her final days of life? As for the Technological Institute, there is support for women among the faculty, to be sure. But I overheard not long ago that when Mendeleyev tried to sneak a woman through the back door into the lecture hall, she was discovered, and the male students nearly provoked a riot. How is one to learn, even could I get in, when one is under attack?" Worried her reply might have sounded harsh, she added, "I'm touched by your thoughtfulness, though, Vera, to consider my interests." Marya took Vera's hand, then, and kissed it softly.

"It's a shame, Marya, that your talent should simply be wasted. But what can I expect of a country that for so long kept its own citizens utterly enslaved? They have freed the serfs, but when will women be free?" Vera threw her hands up in exasperation. "What is the justification for denying knowledge to women? It's all about power, I tell you, Marya." Indignation flashed in her eyes.

"Power, yes—and men are determined to keep it from us," Marya said, falling back against the seat of the carriage, brooding. Vera seemed similarly disposed and stared vacantly out of the carriage. They rode on in silence.

As the boarding house came into view, Vera spoke again.

"I'm sorry, Mashenka. I didn't mean to sadden you." She took Marya's hand between her own. "Will you still take tea, with me?"

"Yes, of course. A steaming cup of tea is exactly what I need, right now—and your good company. As well, it's certainly not *you* who has saddened me." Marya withdrew her hand and ran it the length of Vera's forearm as the carriage came to a halt. Marya paid the driver, and they ascended to Vera's rooms rather somberly, the mood of their conversation yet clinging to them.

They set aside their cloaks, and Marya rested her palm on Vera's cheek, wishing to press upon Vera her sincerity.

"Thank you again for your belief in my—"

A melancholy call from a bird startled Marya with a sound of intense loneliness.

"Vera, do you have a … is there a … don't tell me you have windows open in this chill weather!"

"Are you cold?" Vera rubbed her hands down the length of Marya's arms.

No, Marya thought, *I am most certainly not cold.*

"Here," Vera said, "let me get you a shawl."

As she turned toward the bedroom, Marya took hold of her wrist.

"No—the bird. Did you not hear it?"

"What? Oh," she laughed. "You mean Zubilo!"

"Zubilo?"

"Forgive me! I quite forgot I had not yet told you of him. Come."

Taking Marya's hand, Vera led her into the bedroom, where beside the desk on a chair sat a birdcage with a stout little bullfinch inside.

"But—" Marya said.

"Pasha and Varya and I caught him several days ago in the Summer Garden. The lecture by Kaigorodov inspired me to introduce the children better to nature. I thought to leave this spry young fellow with the children, but their parents didn't want the burden of caring for him. So now he is my most frequent companion." She bent and clucked her tongue, and the bird fluttered a bit on its perch. Standing, she said, "But only until the spring, when I shall release him again into the open air. Let me feed him, and then we will find where our conversation unraveled."

She slipped into the other room and, after some rummaging, returned with some seeds and nuts, which she emptied into a small feeding tray inside the cage.

"He is very comely," Marya said and bent to look at him more closely.

"Do you think so? I also find him graceful, dignified even. I think I may begin to train him soon. You didn't come, though, to visit with a bird. I shall go light the samovar."

"No," Marya said and held lightly to Vera's wrist. "Wait. I wanted to say … that is, I meant to tell you …"

Marya could feel the heat of Vera under her fingertips, where they rested on her small wrist, and whatever it was she had intended to say was lost. Without prelude, Marya leaned in to kiss Vera, and they relaxed into each other's arms. Marya pressed Vera close, overcome with some blend of gratitude and longing.

After what seemed like both an eternity and an instant, Marya held Vera at arm's length to drink her in with her eyes. But within seconds, the two were once again feverishly kissing.

"Verochka." Marya spoke in a hoarse whisper. "I love you with all of my heart."

"And I, I love you as well."

A feeling of tenderness surged in Marya even toward the catch in Vera's voice.

"No—no tears, my darling. There is no reason for tears," Marya said, and bent to kiss the tears on Vera's cheeks, then brushed them away with her thumbs. "I dream of nothing, day and night, but holding you."

Marya kissed Vera's cheek and neck. Then, with her fingers poised at the buttons of Vera's blouse, she inquired, "May I?"

"Yes." Vera's reply was barely audible. Marya didn't stop to think whether that whispered reply was an indication of reserve or desire and took it only for what she wished.

Hurriedly, Marya unbuttoned Vera's blouse, her fingers feeling clumsy to the task. When she had undone enough of the buttons to allow it, Marya reverently pulled Vera's blouse aside and placed her lips upon the rise of one breast peeping above Vera's corset.

"Oh!" Vera cried. "Oh!" She grasped Marya then and held her face tightly to her chest.

"Mashenka! Please. Please!" Vera pressed the heels of her hands to Marya's shoulders and pushed her away. Marya feared she had been mistaken—had made a mistake—but Vera began yanking free the buttons of Marya's blouse from their holes.

"Oh, Masha."

Vera kissed Marya's chest, placing her lips first one place, then another. Then, with a gentle fury, Vera pulled Marya to her so that their every inch was pressed to another. In the next instant, Vera wildly wrenched Marya's skirt from her.

At the same time, Marya pulled Vera's blouse from her. She tried to wrestle Vera's skirt to the ground, but their arms were often tangled as they tore the clothing from one another so the task was performed awkwardly at best. The whole while, they each pressed their lips hungrily to whatever flesh they encountered.

"Masha, Masha," Vera whispered again and again.

At last, with no layer of cloth between them, they pressed bare skin to bare skin—each with an arm holding tightly to the other.

"Under the covers," Marya whispered, then. "We should get—." Marya, skin pricked with cold, finished the thought not with words but with a turning to the bed, clasping Vera's hand and gently drawing her along.

In Vera's bed, they became a maze of limbs, Vera's hands and lips everywhere, and Marya reciprocating. In the days and weeks that would follow, Marya searched for the words to describe the sensations she felt that night—and felt often since, though perhaps not with quite that pitch of intensity. But there seemed no words to express adequately the sense of feeling at once euphoric and unsettled and full to bursting.

"Verochka," Marya said when they at last lay exhausted in one another's arms. "Verochka. Verochka. Come—come live with us, with my Aunt Lidia and me."

"You are too droll, Mashenka."

Vera, a smiling playing on her lips, twined her fingers with Marya's, then slipped them slowly away so that their tips traced the back of Marya's hand and rode lightly across the knuckles of Marya's fingers.

"I do not jest, Verochka! I am quite serious—please leave this dreary place—made lovely only by your presence here—and come join our little household at no. 112 on the Moika."

Vera propped herself up on an elbow and let her eyes wander Marya's countenance.

"But … but what will Lidia think?"

"She will think you will make me happy. She will think you will be good company for both of us. She will think there is no reason for you to stay in these cramped rooms when there is ample space for us all in her apartments. She will think you are lovely and kind and a pleasure to have around. Allow me to ask her."

"You don't think she will find me forward? We have only known one another such a short time."

"Say you would like this, that you would like to be by my side always, not merely a few hours each week. Say you are willing to share our home—my … bed," Marya added, "—and I will ask her at the first opportunity."

"How unexpected! I had not thought to leave these rooms so soon." Vera sat up, then, and gazed about the room. Masha took it all in then as well, attempting to experience Vera's surroundings as Vera herself would. Would she focus on, perhaps, the peeling paint? The scratched furniture? Or would she notice the moist smell of beets cooking across the hall, the dry odor of dust? Maybe she would see only that these were her own rooms, with her own things, arranged in her own fashion.

Vera pressed her forehead to Marya's.

"Yes," she said, shortly, pulling back a bit. "Yes, I would like that—if your aunt does truly agree." She leaned in to kiss the outer corner of each of Marya's eyes and the bridge of her nose. "Mashenka. Mashenka."

15
Lidia

Some weeks had passed—Lidia was finding it more difficult to keep track of time as increasing amounts of it were spent abed—and Vera did indeed come for dinner again. Lidia, weaker by the day, mostly sat resting her back against the chair while the two young women chatted gaily about a recent lecture or about this woman or that they had met at their meetings. As she often was these days, Lidia was rather feverish. But still: Could more than a couple of weeks have gone by since they had all been together? There was something, some way they interacted with one another … Perhaps it was simply their ease with one another. Or maybe it was the shameless way they let their eyes fall upon one another as they spoke.

Lidia felt a twinge of anger, then, at how little attention they paid her, flushed and damp in her chair, her meal untouched. All she had done for Masha, and this was the compassion she showed her!

Then, almost as if Lidia had given voice to her thoughts, Marya turned to her.

"Aunt Lidia! How unwell you seem. What can I have been thinking to let you sit like this? Come: we must get you to bed."

"No, no—sit. Please." Lidia's voice was little more than a whisper. Who would have expected that to utter a simple word or two could require such stores of energy? "Please: I'm fine. Let me enjoy the pleasure of your delightful company yet a while. It keeps my mind from my troubles." And having said it, Lidia realized it was true. And what did she want with them fussing over her anyway? Better to let them savor conversing with one another than to have them verify for her she was someone in need of ministering to.

But at last, she asked Marya to summon Ilyusha, and he helped her up the stairs to her bed.

In the week following, Lidia thought of almost nothing else but the joints of her arms and legs, which ached nearly constantly. Dr. Chlenov was called but couldn't offer much at this stage beyond bed rest, though he did prescribe laudanum.

"Not too much," he warned, "or your breathing may worsen." Liudmilla, who had been standing at the door should the doctor need anything, went to find a spoon at his request. The dark brownish-red liquid he offered to Lidia was less than appealing, and she wrinkled her nose at the horribly sweet smell but she sipped it down, eager for any kind of relief.

The laudanum seemed to help the pain and let her sleep less fitfully, and within two days after the doctor's visit, her symptoms had quieted enough to allow a proper conversation with Masha for the first time in many days.

Lidia asked after the household affairs and about Marya's courses, and then she remembered to ask about Vera.

"She is quite well, aunt, and has expressed concern for your health. I have meant, in fact, to tell you I've asked her to join us here, in your apartments, that is, to come live with us. I mean," she continued hastily after a frown from Lidia, "if this plan meets with your approval, of course. It's just that, I thought she might be of some help now that … that is … with you being …"

Lidia closed her eyes tightly and hoped her expression would pass for pain. She reminded herself that a fly won't get into a closed mouth.

"Aunt?"

"Oh! Sorry, my dove. It's my legs. So swollen." She groped at the bedclothes, intending to show her inflamed legs to Marya, but she was ineffectual at even this simple task in her weakened state. Angered by her helplessness, she nearly forgot what they had been talking about.

"I know, aunt. I understand." Marya smoothed the covers back in place, then said, "But … Verochka?"

Lidia kept her eyes closed a moment longer while she chose her words. If she were honest, she didn't wish to share her last weeks—or days?—of life with a near stranger. Neither did she wish to share Masha. Nor was she fond of the solicitousness Vera seemed to show her. Who was this young woman to her? How presumptuous to assume concern for her! Still, she could not entirely discount how her niece's melancholy had been vanquished since Vera had entered her life. In the end, she spoke only half the truth.

"Why, yes, of course, Mashenka. She is a lovely child. And it's clear she makes you happy indeed, which is a happiness to me." She reached across the bedclothes toward her niece, who leaned forward to grasp her aunt's hand so she wouldn't overtax herself. "I'm pleased to see you thus again, dear. You know, I almost despaired, after Katya left, of restoring you from your despondency. But enough of those darker times, lest I weigh down upon your high spirits. Come, give me a kiss, my little dove, then go make whatever arrangements you must with Ilyusha and Nadya for adding another soul to our small household.

"Do you want to have Ilyusha and Nadya clean and air out my father's old study?" Then Lidia answered her own question before Marya had a chance. "No, it's too dark in those rooms, too close to the foyer. No doubt Vera would find it much cozier to room with you. I remember how Irochka and I would snuggle in under the covers and talk into the night when she would come for those long visits."

Marya raised an eyebrow, wondering if there was more to this story, but Lidia looked exhausted, and so Marya left any questions for another time.

"Thank you, Aunt Lidia." She squeezed her aunt's hand tenderly and placed it, again, at her aunt's side. "It will please Vera greatly to depart the dreary boarding house where she now resides." She rose, then, and kissed each of her aunt's hollow cheeks. She stopped briefly, on her way to the door, to say, "She will be a comfort to you, aunt. Thank you!"

Lidia relaxed into her pillow and closed her eyes. While she was indeed pleased to witness her niece's happiness once again, she looked with foreboding on this addition to their household.

Except for on her worst days, however, when her pulse raced and grew weak over and again, like a dragonfly rising then resting, rising then resting, Lidia admitted to herself that, with Vera among them, gone from every corner was the gloom brought on first by Marya's melancholy, then, of late, by her own illness. The despondency that had so long lingered in the apartment on Moika Street had been swept away by the sound of laughter, which had been a stranger to her home for such a great many weeks.

At times, Lidia even felt as though Vera had, as promised, infected her with a new sense of vitality. But just as often, she resented Vera's cheery good nature and, especially, the way her niece doted on her, hanging on her every word and touching her gently when she thought no one was paying them any mind, while she, Lidia, was consumed with coughs and fevers.

There was something vaguely obscene about so much vitality set next to such wasting.

If forced, Lidia would have admitted the young women couldn't reasonably be accused of ignoring her; they were very attentive to her and often sat on either side of her bed while they chatted, when they could have put themselves in a far less dismal milieu. Nevertheless, she couldn't quite conquer the feeling they had let the goat into the kitchen garden when they let that Vera enter their house.

As for the bird, Lidia grumbled from time to time about the noise of the bullfinch in its cage in the drawing room—what had Vera named it? Zuby? Zubilov?—but truth be told, she rather enjoyed, most days, his bright chirping, so reminiscent of spring.

Did she only imagine he courted her, there on the divan, behind the wire walls of his new home? Bowing his head to her, as at the conclusion of a minuet, puffing out his neck, ruffling his feathers until he looked quite the ball of fluff.

It was easy enough to imagine he might mistake her for another bird, so thin she had grown of late! But how it delighted her to see him inflate his brightly tinted chest toward her and sing his series of soft notes.

If she closed her eyes, she could believe, for a short time, she was a young girl again, lounging on a blanket in the wood near Khrupkaya Luna after hunting all the morning for mushrooms and, then, enjoying the lovely lunch prepared by cook. But then her swollen legs would begin to throb or a cough would jolt her, and she would be hurled from her reverie with all the ignominy of being thrown from a headstrong pony.

Notwithstanding the expansion of their small household on the Moika, life there didn't alter much. Most evenings, the girls left Lidia to doze in her chaise lounge by the gleaming tiles of the fireplace while they went off to attend the Alarchin courses—though Tuesdays and Thursdays were still set aside for gatherings with young men, despite Marya's obvious distaste for this project.

"Aunt Lidia, you are much too fragile," she had protested when Lidia mentioned the next gathering after Vera's arrival. "Let me send word our doors shall no longer be open to young visitors on those evenings. We can resume when your health is better," she added quickly, sensing her aunt's imminent objection.

"But Masha," rasped Lidia between coughs, "how else will you find a husband?"

"Aunt Lidia, I don't want—"

And there she stopped after a raised brow from Vera. She sighed deeply.

"Yes, as you please, Aunt Lidia."

She directed a half smile at Vera: matter settled.

But it wasn't settled, to Lidia's mind. She had purposefully designed these gatherings to include only Masha among all the young male guests. And now there would be Vera as well.

She insisted to herself it wasn't that she didn't have faith in her niece, but she was wary of providing distractions from, or an immediate point of comparison to, Masha's unconventional charms. And now, Vera might be that distraction.

What if, she asked herself, Vera were the one to find a husband among the young men and Marya left a spinster still? A prickle ascended her spine at the thought, though it might have been fever. Well, there was nothing to be done about it, she thought. Nevertheless, Lidia contemplated with trepidation the first gathering at which Vera would be present.

At dinner on a Tuesday shortly after Vera had come to live with them, Lidia ate not more than a spoonful or two of her borscht. She had no appetite and was drained from her wracking cough. Nevertheless, she refused to miss the gathering.

She let Vera escort her to the sitting room and ease her to the divan since she could think of no polite way to decline her offer—she might be dying, but that was still no excuse for rudeness—and she was incapable of taking even so few steps on her own any longer.

Lidia glowered at Masha, who settled into a nearby chair with her copy of *Fathers and Sons* and let Vera prop pillows against the arm of the divan to help her recline. If either young woman noticed her sour expression, they didn't comment. Or perhaps they assumed it was the pain of her illness that made her look thus. In any case, Vera simply pulled a blanket over Lidia's feet and legs.

"Ilya!" Vera called, as she passed through the hallway. "Could you please add some firewood so Lidia's feet don't grow cold?" Lidia scowled again: the presumption—ordering the servants around as if they were her own! Even as she thought it, she knew she was merely being truculent, since she was in no condition to call out to Ilyusha on her own.

Ilyusha clattered logs in the ceramic stove, and Vera bent toward Lidia so she could be heard above the din.

"Would you like some tea?"

Lidia shook her head no, not wishing to feel further indebted to Vera. She closed her eyes and listened while Vera prattled on about her young students. Lidia wished Vera would simply keep quiet.

Eventually, though, the rhythm of Vera's words and Zubilo's hushed chirrups carried her off. As she drifted, her ruined strength felt like it might be replenished, or so she hoped, for the visitors that would soon arrive.

After some time, Masha put her hand on Lidia's shoulder. Lidia opened her eyes, which were noticeably sunken in their sockets, she knew, for she had chanced upon a mirror earlier in the day. She preferred not to think about it. She turned her head slightly, and Vera was standing off to the side, smiling benignly at her. Lidia turned back toward her niece.

"Do you need anything, aunt?"

Lidia croaked something approximating the word "no."

"We're going to retire to freshen up for the … gentleman callers."

Lidia smiled at her niece's effort to suppress any sarcasm when she said "gentleman callers."

Marya placed her palm along her aunt's emaciated face but said nothing more.

Though undoubtedly not Marya's intent, this simple gesture frightened Lidia: How dreadful must she look?

She watched as the two young women linked arms and left the room, their heads bent toward one another as they conspired.

She must have dozed off then for a while because the next thing she knew, Ilyusha was lightly touching her arm.

"Lidia, the young men have begun arriving. Shall I show them here into the sitting room now?"

Lidia pulled herself up into a more upright position.

"Yes, Ilyusha." Her mouth was dry and tasted of metal. "Yes, don't let's keep them waiting. But first, Ilyusha, could you bring me a small cup of tea?"

She pushed at her disheveled hair in a half-hearted attempt to make herself more presentable, but she knew once the young ladies entered the room, her presence would hardly be noticed.

"After you show in our callers, could you please knock at Masha's door and tell the young ladies to come down?"

She gratefully folded her icy fingers around the cup of tea Ilyusha handed to her. The steam curled around her face, and she smiled, imagining she had uncorked a small bottle of summer. She savored the damp heat on her ruined skin.

Just then, a small parade of young men began filing into the room in pairs, small groups, and singly, about a dozen or so in all, over the course of fifteen or twenty minutes. They chatted jovially among themselves. Lidia cast an appraising eye over them and wondered which of this group might find himself captivated by Marya.

"Ah, Lidia!" A dashing young man in a splendid suit swept up alongside her and dropped to his knee, immediately taking her now free hand, still warm from the teacup, into his own and kissing it.

"Andrei."

She smiled in spite of herself. Andryusha was the youngest son of an old friend of hers, Elena Ovsyannikova, with whom she had become acquainted during her days with the St. Petersburg Society for the Improvement of the Lodgings of the Laboring Population.

He rose to his feet again, and with a gesture toward Lidia, announced, "Gentleman! Our hostess for the evening, Lidia Zhukova." He turned back toward Lidia. "May I get you some more tea?"

His smile was warm and broad and didn't show so much as a trace of horror at how she knew she looked compared with when last he had seen her.

"Why, yes, thank you, Andryusha."

No sooner had she handed the cup to him than one after the other of the young men approached, introduced themselves, and thanked her for her hospitality. She was glad to have rested after dinner; she could feel some color flow back into her cheeks. She did her best to ignore the ache in her joints; if she took laudanum just then, she would surely find herself asleep.

She sensed a stirring, then, on the other side of the room, and a ripple of bowing began, as if a breeze were bending the fresh heads of wheat with its passing: Marya and Vera had entered the room. Lidia felt a dull pinch of anxiety at the sight of Vera and her bright smile.

But when all were seated except for a few who leaned casually against a wall or doorjamb, drinking their tea, Vera had placed herself at Marya's elbow, deep in a shadow and slightly outside the circle. Nevertheless, thought Lidia, if you throw a glass-apple into the deepest, darkest part of the Fontanka Canal, does it not always rise, glistening, to the surface?

Through some miracle, though, Vera remained at the edge of the proceedings all evening, clearly content with simply watching her friend bring these virile specimens figuratively to their knees. Lidia watched as a bemused smile teased at the edges of Vera's lips. Whether to keep her merriment at bay or to ensure the uninterrupted pleasure of watching Marya turn the once articulate men into sputtering fools, Vera said very little all evening, and Lidia was surprised to find herself grateful to her niece's friend.

Vera's unwitting cooperation aside, the outcome seemed as though it would be the same. Lidia watched as the confidence of each man melted away and they began to tug at their collars, wipe their sweating brows, and clear their throats. At last, one by one, they excused themselves for the evening, unable to bear any longer the lash of Marya's tongue. Lidia supposed even their exams at school couldn't have given them such anxiety as they had experienced that night at the hands of her niece!

When there were but four gentlemen remaining, Nadezhda came to check on whether she would be needing anything, and Lidia took the opportunity to excuse herself. With Nadya's help, she made her way from the room. She thought it likely the evening would draw to a close shortly, but she was too exhausted to stay on for the finale.

The next morning, however, over her breakfast of boiled eggs and reindeer sausages, she learned she was mistaken: one brave soul had actually remained well into the night. She could scarcely hide her astonishment or refrain from asking immediately a hundred and one questions about this clearly special young man.

Fortunately, Vera and Marya were as astonished by him as she was and spoke freely of this rare figure among his fellows. Sergei Trepov was his name, and once they had described him—a slender, serious-looking young man, with very light brown hair, a blond mustache, and brilliant blue eyes, perhaps just slightly older than the rest—Lidia recalled having noticed him, if only just in passing.

For an instant, Lidia felt a spasm of panic at the thought perhaps he had stayed on to get to know Vera better, but almost as if anticipating her worry, the two quickly allayed it: a librarian at the Imperial Public Library, Sergei was, by their account, apparently enchanted with Marya's obvious love of the written word and with her ability to speak so insightfully about what she read.

"And you rolled your eyes when he first joined us!" Vera teased.

"No, it was you who gave the first mocking glance," insisted Marya.

"It was definitely you," said Vera, "but how easily you were won over by his ardent opinions!"

"This was your first gathering, Verochka—you haven't seen what buffoons these men can be! And they have no respect for a woman's opinion, think we are all stupid and shallow. Sergei—now there is a man who knows how to respect women."

She paused to mop up some egg yolk from her plate with a piece of black bread, then bit into the yellowed edge of the bread and laughed. She nearly lost her bite of bread and had to put her hand in front of her mouth.

"Oh, but how *earnest* he looked in his plain black suit! He looked quite the monk now, didn't he?" She looked Lidia's way with a twinkle in her eye, as she brushed crumbs from the bodice of her dark dress.

"Masha!" Lidia's cheeks were flushed ruddy, both from their playful conversation and a spike of fever.

"A monk!" Vera, laughed. "Why, Masha, he doesn't even have a beard! And his hair is closely shorn. Or did you snip off beard and locks as he came through the door, like some Russian Delilah? Perhaps that's how you've rendered him powerless to your charms."

"It would seem there is at least one among us who paid attention during her religion classes!"

Vera made a face, and they all laughed. But the frivolity was cut short by the rattling cough that seized Lidia. Marya rose and gently rubbed Lidia's back. At last, the spasms ceased, and she lightly ran her hands up and down over Lidia's shoulders, easing her back against the chair as she did so, while Lidia discretely tried to hide her blood-spattered handkerchief.

Marya took her seat again and exchanged a worried look with Vera, but then Lidia closed her eyes and saw no more between them. At first, she merely concentrated on breathing, but as she became more relaxed she thought again of Sergei Trepov. She felt a blossoming sense of hope for her niece. She had a dozen more questions, but she understood it was premature to press Marya further on the subject of Sergei Trepov.

"Aunt?" Her niece's querulous voice broke through her musing.

"Oh. I'm fine now, dear. Just fine."

16
Sergei

5 January 1876

Filya, my dear cousin—

I've met the most amazing woman. Yes, yes, she is a genuine beauty—you can see in an instant, for she does not take pains to dramatize her appearance like so many other young women but lets her features impress naturally. But what truly sets her apart is her mind. I've never met anyone like her. She has a way of finding, in any discussion, where the dog is buried—and spares no one her opinion. Such old-fashioned qualities as truth and honesty are of far greater import to her than catching a husband. It's plain, in fact, that finding a husband isn't at all her aim, for rather than a flirt, she is far the opposite. At the gathering where I fell under her spell, many of the other men fled like frightened schoolboys when she behaved the scholar and didn't accept their authority.

But here I am, going on in a rush, with nary a care for propriety and manners, it would seem.

How are things for you there in Italy? Have you quite done with, then, being a Russian? Perhaps you won't even be celebrating Christmas two days hence and have marked the occasion already on the twenty-fifth of December as one not of the Russian Orthodox faith!

Even as a boy, you worshipped the sun, so I understand how you've come to flee our wintry clime. And they say the Mediterranean is a brilliant blue. I'm sure all there captures your painterly sensibilities, and yet I do miss you so terribly—would that you could meet the lovely Marya Zhukova and render your opinion, as I've always valued your estimations. But here—let me at least take a step backward and tell you something of her in a more measured fashion.

How I came to meet her was a stroke of luck, really. Dora Stasova (the wife of Vladimir Stasov—head of my section at the Library, as you may recall) entreated all of us who were neither yet married nor betrothed to attend a salon given by her dear friend Lidia Zhukova. Lidia, she said, had a niece come to live with her, newly graduated from the Petersburg Institute for Girls, whom she was trying to introduce into society. I had a mountain of paperwork to attend to, but it was no use refusing Dora; she would ensure Stasov would excuse me from my work, so I didn't bother to argue and wrote down the time and address like the other few fellows there as yet unspoken for.

I went grudgingly, as I say, but I found myself intrigued and enchanted. Marya is very much a modern girl, Filya, as you may have gathered from the cascade of words with which I opened this letter. She has chestnut brown hair, which she wore cropped rather short, and she seemed to prefer her dark skirt short as well, which she accompanied with an equally somber shirt. But it's her quick mind, as I've said, that truly impresses. She is especially keen on the subjects of literature and mathematics and is a formidable opponent in any debate on those topics. She loves especially Dostoyevsky, and as for mathematics, she leaves *me* far behind—that much I can tell you! Yes, this much I know already, in just one meeting, for I stayed long into the night, so completely under the spell of her words, I hardly knew of the passage of time!

Filya, I tell you: I haven't found myself thus stimulated since—well, since I can't recall when! Her aunt holds these gatherings each Tuesday and Thursday, and you may rest assured I shall be there one night hence so I may give you a fuller report of the lovely Marya Zhukova.

Until then, I remain your cousin, though much enthralled,

Seryozha

17
Lidia

A colorful wooden sled captured midglide down a frosty white hill, the head of the figure upon it bent into an imagined wind; a brown dog below, howling at its approach; and in the distance, the beginnings of a forest, a fat bear lumbering out from among its trunks. Nadezhda had fixed this scene for Lidia to remind her of younger days at Khrupkaya Luna: the trees, bear, dog—all of it carved by peasants from a nearby village. Children's toys, really, but Nadya had set them on the salt poured between the windows to hold back the bite of the winter months, and from her snowy mound of pillows, Lidia viewed the scene with something like happiness.

Even in the face of her worsening health, Lidia felt a measure of contentment. Often, before now, she had fancied it was the chilling breath of death staining the window above Nadya's salt snow. And for months, she had felt not only that her blood was draining away from her but that the Zhukov bloodline was also on the verge of being erased. She had admitted to herself, too, that her worries went beyond the vanity of family pride: she was, in fact, fretful about what would become of Marya—Marya *herself*, beyond her role as the sole Zhukov heir—when she was gone. All her life, Lidia had been haunted by the phrase "not married, not human," and she wanted her niece never to know the pain of such ridicule. And now, at last, it seemed there might be reason to hope.

The previous day, Thursday, Lidia had taken an especially long nap, in anticipation of meeting Sergei Trepov. She had been in such a state of excited anticipation about this one young man who had not only the courage to engage her niece but also the ability actually to do so that she doubted she would have been able to drop off to sleep without the aid of laudanum.

All day Wednesday, after that raucous breakfast with Marya and Vera, Lidia had fretted about whether Sergei had been as enthusiastic about Masha as she'd imagined. Late in the afternoon, after tea, Lidia was feeling uncommonly robust, and since Vera had gone to the Solovyovs to tutor the children, Lidia had Marya all to herself. They played a rare game of whist, during which Lidia guided the conversation with all the finesse of a barge hauler on the Neva.

"What was your young man's name?" Lidia fumbled with her cards in an effort to appear nonchalant. "The one who stayed the other evening with you and Vera?"

"I? A young man? Oh! You mean Sergei Trepov?" Masha played a card.

"Oh, yes! That's right," Lidia said, as if she had not repeated his name to herself a dozen times already since breakfast that morning. "Are you expecting him tomorrow evening?"

Lidia set a card down on the table, careful not to make eye contact with Marya lest she reveal her elation.

"I believe he said he planned to be here."

Lidia peeked at her niece, whose forehead was creased in contemplation of the cards in her hand.

"How nice."

Lidia had been striving for a noncommittal tone, but suspicion instantly flashed across Marya's features.

"Yes, I suppose. If I must continue to endure these salons—not that I'm not grateful, mind you, Aunt Lidia—I welcome his relative lack of narcissism, compared with those other popinjays."

After a short pause, Marya added, "Perhaps it's his somewhat greater age?"

"Oh, he is older, is he?"

Lidia fingered her cards as if there was nothing more crucial to her than finding just the right one.

"Yes. I believe he said he was thirty-six."

"Ah. Not *so* very old then."

"No, I suppose not. Just older than the others."

And so their card game had gone, each of them pretending they didn't know what the conversation was truly about.

But thus reassured he was indeed likely to return, Lidia found her spirits much improved and realized she was able to think of something, for a change, besides her diminishing life. *What a peculiar change of events*, she thought.

For only weeks before, Marya's marriage prospects had tortured her thoughts, while now thoughts of Marya and marriage had, instead, begun providing her respite from more devastating concerns. She reminded herself, though, not to begin making fish soup before a fish had even been caught.

Nevertheless, after her long nap on Thursday, Lidia's level of anticipation climbed steadily again. Interested only in what was to follow the meal, she did little more than push her spoon around the bowl of buckwheat consommé before her on the dinner table. Her appetite had been reduced in general, of late—swallowing was made more difficult by the ulcerations in her throat—and she looked on dispassionately as the girls ate their smoked ham and *pirozhki* of rice and wild mushrooms.

After dinner, she dozed on her chaise, despite her excitement, and then watched the evening's soiree begin like any other: grown men of some stature, eager for a pleasant evening of conversation and flirtation, instead reduced to stuttering or sheepish or ineffectually blustering fools, but fools just the same, who eventually skulked away muttering bitterly to one another after they had excused themselves. Lidia questioned the wisdom of the old adage that proclaimed that fools aren't sown or reaped but instead appear by themselves, for it certainly seemed as though her niece had a hand in their making.

And so, one by one, they all took their leave—all but Sergei, who was the sole guest to seem genuinely interested in an honest exchange with Masha rather than being on a quest to prove himself brighter or wittier or cleverer than any of the assembled. Though Lidia was quite exhausted by then, she elected to stay on yet a while to monitor how the two got on when there were fewer distractions.

She shifted on her chaise, trying to find some level of comfort for her ravaged frame, then watched in awe as Masha dealt Sergei the usual biting comments, to each of which he responded with an amused smile or a quiet joke. Lidia was also pleased to note that Vera seemed, for the most part, content to watch the drama unfold rather than become one of its principal actors.

As though sensing her presence in Lidia's thoughts, Vera rose to tidy Lidia's blanket and asked whether she might like some tea. For her part, Lidia was so distracted by Sergei's interest in her niece, she forgot to be irritated by Vera's solicitousness. After Vera had handed Lidia a steaming cup of tea, she went to sit in the gold brocade chair directly across from Marya, no longer hiding herself in the shadow but now part of the conversation. Yet it hardly seemed to matter to Sergei, who could barely tear his eyes from Marya's face. *Vera and I,* thought Lidia, *might as well be nothing more than faces framed on the wall, for all the notice he pays us!*

"No, no, no," Sergei was saying. "It's clear from the text Nastassya Filippovna was incapable of choosing! She wouldn't have stayed with Rogozhin."

"Then why," Marya asked, breaking into Lidia's thoughts, "did he go with her in the first place, if he already knew this?" Judging from her tone, she was apparently genuinely interested in what Sergei might reply.

"Well, but of course he knew and he didn't know. Do you not see? He was so blind with love for her he hid even from himself his knowledge of her inability to stay true to one man. He believed what he wanted to believe," he said, shrugging his shoulders.

"Yes, of course," interjected Vera. "People often do so."

"I am willing to accept that," responded Masha, then added pensively, "but then why was it necessary for Rogozhin to kill Nastassya Filippovna when he admitted to himself what he knew? Why not just leave her for Myshkin to deal with?"

Both women turned their eyes to Sergei, awaiting his response.

"Because he is mad, of course. He is a madman. He was feverish, completely demented in his love for Nastassya Filippovna, a love he could never claim with certainty as his own. Obviously, the only honorable act in that situation would be for Rogozhin to kill himself. Any other course would have meant loss of face—or insanity, which is the course Dostoyevsky clearly saw for him."

"Bah!" jeered Marya. "That's nothing more than foolish pride. Yes, lost love is like having a fist reach in your chest and wrench from it your heart, but there is no reason for a life to quite literally come to a close because of it. Why can't all the parties go on living and each in his own way come to terms with his grief?"

Their voices continued to rise in their passion, but by this time, Lidia was nearly shaking with exhaustion. She motioned to Vera to come to her.

"Verochka, would you be a dear and ask Nadya if she would come help me to my bed?" Lidia harbored the hope that Vera would decline to get Nadya and simply assist Lidia herself, leaving Sergei and Marya alone to become better acquainted. She didn't pause to ponder her willingness to leave them unchaperoned, so eager was she to hurry along this delicate thing between them.

Vera's attention, however, kept wandering back to the conversation. She patted Lidia's hand distractedly before walking briskly from the room, her skirts swishing around her ankles as she went to fetch Nadezhda.

A few minutes later, Lidia climbed the stairs on Nadya's arm with the sound of the heated and earnest voices of Marya and Sergei entangling together. *Never mind,* she told herself, *that Verochka sits there among them like a tending angel: it's* their *voices that are engaged with one another.*

18
Marya

Though Lidia's health had begun to fail at a pace that alarmed her niece, Lidia suddenly took an interest in life—Marya's life, to be specific. And Marya was quite certain it was no coincidence that her aunt's fresh engagement with living was commensurate with Sergei's regular appearances at the salons in their home. For her part, Marya looked on her aunt's enthusiasm with a good deal of caution, for if Lidia had designs on Sergei becoming Marya's husband—as Marya suspected she did—any such schemes were as likely to be realized as a solution to Riemann's hypothesis.

Nevertheless, Marya was glad that Lidia was unwilling to let life fare without her—even beseeching their little household to celebrate Christmas in the traditional fashion. Though Marya worried it would cost her aunt too much energy to celebrate thus, she was likewise convinced that to do anything else would serve only to plunge them all prematurely into a virtual state of mourning. Fearing that such a time would come only too soon of its own accord, she threw herself into making the holiday as festive as possible.

With the help of Verochka and the servants, Marya set to work. Her first order of holiday business was to send Ilya to buy a fir tree, which Vera and Marya then quietly decorated, careful not to disturb Lidia while she napped. Zubilo hopped to and fro in his cage, excited, perhaps, to see a sign of his former life. Observing him, Marya felt a twinge of sympathy, recalling her own "caging" at the Institute—for thus it felt, after the unfettered freedom and open air at Khrupkaya Luna.

Vera and Marya hung the fragrant branches with fruits, candy, and nuts held with strings, carved wooden figures the size of a finger, tinsel, and a few delicate, colored glass balls. These last Marya handled reverently, for they had been her grandmother's. Having never met either set of grandparents, handling the beautiful baubles gave her a chill, as if she were touching the literal past.

She kept this notion of reaching back into a time gone by to herself, for she worried it would sound peculiar to Vera. But it didn't seem manifestly strange to Marya, for she reasoned that if numbers might continue, all forever in a line, might not time? *Much like numbers,* she thought, *do we not count time as well, the seconds, the hours, the days assembling in more orderly fashion than the Hussar's Guard under review? And what of Plato's heaven of ideas, where reality remains fixed and we may pluck from it?* Though Marya would have been the first to concede that no one grasped the whole of these concepts yet, this was its very lure for people like herself, who were bound to the mysteries of numbers—and to how those numbers build the universe, as surely as a horse is lashed to a carriage, from first light to the twilight of his life.

"Masha."

"Hmmm?" Marya quickly shook the numerals from her head.

"Do you need help with finding a place for that glass ball?" Vera asked, a wry smile on her lips.

"What?"

"You've been standing there, holding it like an egg about to hatch, for some time now!"

"Oh. No. Here. This is a good place for it," Marya said, hanging it hastily on a branch. "I was but musing."

"Let me conjecture: You were lost in a forest of numbers yet again?"

"Yes. In a way. But, come—let us finish, now, so we might surprise Lidia when she rises."

After the tree was decorated, Vera and Marya spread the white cloth on the table, and Marya shook her head to think of the baby Jesus swaddled in it, with its leftover stains and mended tear, but she hadn't been able to find a newer one. Marya put the white candle and Lenten bread in place, and Ilya contributed some hay at the table's center, though Marya thought its presence there would scarce transport them from the warmth of their fine rooms to the humble stable where the poor Christ child was born.

Once the first star of the evening appeared in the sky, they all gathered at the table, the servants included: three simply does not make for a festive party, reasoned Marya, so their numbers alone would have made the servants welcome. Lidia, fresh from her nap, was all but drowning in her green velvet gown, but she appeared quite happy so Marya was pleased with the efforts they'd taken.

Marya said the Lord's Prayer and a prayer of thanksgiving, at which she couldn't resist stealing a glance at Vera. Then they each, in turn, bent down before Lidia so she could draw the cross of blessing with honey upon their foreheads. Following that, they had a bit of bread, dipped first in the honey, then the chopped garlic. Never before had Marya been so keenly aware of the sweetness and bitterness of life represented by the honey and garlic, owing to the ways in which those qualities were embodied at their table that night.

After the blessing, Nadya and Liudmilla went to collect the Holy Supper from the kitchen and brought back with them Iulia, the cook, to join the small party at the table. The bowl of kutya was passed round, thick with wheat berries and dotted with poppy seeds; the steaming porridge infused the air with the smell of the honey drizzled over it. When it was Marya's turn to eat her taste of the porridge from the common bowl—something she'd done with little thought so often in the past—she pondered the symbols of this part of the repast: the unity of their single bowl, the hope symbolized by the grain, the happiness and peace by the honey and poppy seed. She had many hopes of peace and happiness, when her eyes alighted on Vera's serene countenance, but felt far more somber when she gazed upon her aunt's pale and wasted form.

Impulsively, when the kutya had made its way back to Marya, she took another spoonful and, threw it at the ceiling, as any peasant might, to liven the festivities. Lidia, however, glowered, and Marya closed her eyes for a moment while she forced all the air from her lungs, certain she was about to be reprimanded.

Lidia surprised her, though, unsteadily raising her glass of wine and winking.

"Well," she said, in her raspy voice, "we shall have a plentiful harvest this year!"

Everyone laughed, then shouted, "Da svidanya!"

And just that quickly they threw off their worries for the future and were merry, feasting on the baked cod, peas, potatoes, biscuits, kidney beans, nuts, and apricots that the cook had prepared and laid before them all. Even Lidia managed to nibble a little of everything.

Then Ilya and Nadya, made cheerful by the company as much by their draughts of vodka, regaled the assembled household with tales of life in Nizhny Novgorod, where they both grew up.

"The fair!" said Nadya. "The whole region, up and down the Oka and the Volga and as far away as the Tatar desert—we lived for those eight weeks every summer. Fifteenth of July to the tenth of September." She sighed, and on that breath seemed to be carried back in time. "The town would swell to four, maybe five times its usual size for those weeks. It was as though the very rivers and roads had sprung to life, for they were filled to overflowing with a ceaseless stream of barges, tugboats, and steamboats, horses, carts, and carriages. You have been, Lidia—do you recall?"

"Goodness, yes! The air, too, seemed a thing alive, with the constant buzz of a dozen or more languages, the streets filled with, as well, people in every manner of brilliant and strange costume. I felt so queer there, almost as if I were transparent. As though I, who didn't know their many languages, could walk among them somehow unnoticed. Bah!" She lifted her hand in a wan gesture of dismissal. "You must think me daft. I don't explain it well."

"No, no," the others all chorused.

"I think I understand."

"I know just what you mean."

Lidia gave a weak nod.

With a lift of her eyes over Lidia's head, Nadya silently asked Marya whether to continue.

Though torn by concern for Lidia, Marya decided to keep the evening festive and as normal as possible—for her aunt's sake as much as her own, she told herself.

"But who were all these people, Nadya?" Marya asked. "What was at the fair that so many came?"

"Oh, Marya!" Nadya waved her arms back and down in a gesture of disbelief. "Why, everyone, just everyone was there: merchants from China selling tea, Prussians from the Baltic selling amber, and there were curly jet-black lambskins from Karakul. There were outdoor ballets and circuses—why, there were alone lines and lines of merchants selling nothing but trunks! In one store you might buy a portrait of the tsar and in another a box of beetroot sugar or a keg of caviar." The more she spoke, the more animated she became, clearly warming to the task.

"Gypsies sang and danced in the cafés. I would watch everyone come and go—Russians, Germans, Hungarians, Poles—while I refilled the zakuski on the long tables. My fingers were puckered from cutting cucumbers, and the smell of caviar never quite left me!"

"Why do you think I fell in love with you? It was your salty taste." Ilya laughed, and the others joined him.

"Ilya! Shh!" Nadya gave him a scowl, though it was clear she wasn't truly angry.

"And this one," she said, jerking her thumb in Ilya's direction. "How do you think I came to find this one in that crowd of people?"

"How, Nadya?" Vera leaned forward on the table. "It never occurred to me you haven't known each other always, so like two boots in a pair you seem, but of course there must have been such a time."

"Well," Nadya began, inching forward on her chair. "At the inn where I worked, they would often allow performers to entertain the guests, you see. In the summer of my seventeenth year, a chorus of boys in belted red blouses sang. Some played accordions, some tambourines, while others danced to the exciting folk music that was their specialty. The patrons, mostly, seemed to pay them little notice, as they threw back glass after glass of vodka while they snacked on the zakuski, and I had little time to notice them either, for during the fair, it was a rush always to have the table filled, you see. But one young man among them, I couldn't help but notice, for he made it his business to be always whirling in my path. And it didn't matter which route I took from the kitchen! Always he was there. I glared at him, but it did no good."

Marya stole a look over at Ilya who beamed with pride.

"Yes, you may smile now if you like," Nadya said and shook her finger at him. "But you cost me my job with your mischief!"

"I?" he protested. "Not I! That wasn't mischief—it was love!"

"Bah! If Lidia's parents had not hired me on, I don't know what I should have done!"

"Why? What did he do?" Vera asked.

"There I was, an empty pail in my hand, for I had just replenished the caviar, and as I was returning to the kitchen to clean more mushrooms, this one puts his hand to my waist, and spins me toward him. And each time I would try to leave, he would pull me to him and make me part of the dance. 'Nadezhda!' growled my boss like a bear from the door of the kitchen. I hit Ilya—for it was him, of course, with a belly that more easily accepted a belt." She wrinkled her nose at him while he grinned and patted his round belly. "But he wouldn't release me. 'Ack! Why do I hire young girls?' my boss muttered as he returned to the kitchen, then he turned back again. 'After you finish your dance,' he shouted, 'you are free to go!' He raised his hand in a gesture of dismissal. 'And it won't be necessary for you to return!'"

"What did you do then?" Marya asked.

"Well, I hit him!"

"Your boss?"

"No, you silly goose! The same Ilya what you see before you here. Only …" She brought her hands into a gesture of narrowness several times, though whether she couldn't find the words to describe her husband or chose not to, Marya wasn't certain.

Ilyusha merely grinned, then reached across the table to give his wife's chubby cheek a loving pinch.

"Ilyusha! Your manners, mind: we aren't at our own table here."

Marya winked at Ilyusha, charmed by the sweetness of their love.

"And then?" Marya said to Nadya, as she turned in her direction, all the while keeping her eyes on Ilyusha, for his merriment was infectious.

"I beat upon his chest—I couldn't believe the cheek of this stranger, who had now cost me my job with his foolishness—and yet it did no good: he but grabbed my wrists and whirled me about and made me part of his dance again."

"And then?" Vera said, prompting Nadya to continue her story.

Nadya shrugged.

"And then we were married."

"But not as simply as that!" objected Vera, who plainly longed for more story.

"It was a courtship quite like any other; surely you can't be interested in our story."

Nadya seemed to have grown self-conscious about being the center of attention. Ilya, however, didn't seem to share her concerns.

"If you will, miss, Nadya and I have two different tales to tell though we were equally in the same story."

So with another few utterances of "if you will, miss," and several insertions of "by your leave, miss," and much scoffing from Nadya, the tale of their courtship was told, as well as how Ilya, remorseful for his role in Nadya's losing her job, went from fairgoer to fairgoer seeking employment for her until at last Marya's grandfather hired them both.

Though Marya and Vera still had questions for the pair, the servants took their leave so they might attend church services.

Marya, however, couldn't bear to go to church, finding the fire in the drawing room stove and the company of her aunt and Vera more inviting than the weather outside. Marya and Vera left the cluttered table for the servants' return and helped Lidia to her chaise beside the stove. Lidia bade Marya pull the presents from beneath the tree, where she had somehow managed to put gifts for her young niece and Vera.

For Marya, there was an ancient board game that had belonged to her father, Lidia said, which involved a steeplechase and lots of beautifully painted horses; for Vera, a pair of soft leather gloves lined with rabbit fur that Lidia had purchased for herself but had never worn. Lidia entreated Vera to try them on.

Marya watched as Vera slipped her fingers into the silken lining, her pleasure at the feel of them evident in her face.

Without doubt, Marya thought, these gifts were far better than anything Lidia might have had one of the servants shop for.

Marya then gave Lidia some hard, sugared drops on which she might suck to relieve her mouth of its dryness, and Vera gave her a pair of thick wool socks to keep her always chilled feet warm.

Earlier that day, Marya and Vera had decided to wait until later to exchange gifts with one another in private, so with no other gifts to open, Vera knelt down to slip the socks onto Lidia's thin feet. Lidia closed her eyes to savor the sensation and let her head drop back on the chair from equal parts contentment and exhaustion.

And though Marya was anxious as ever to spend time with Vera on her own, none of them could bring themselves to be done with their holiday together. The fire crackled pleasantly, and the tree smell was reminiscent of Marya's summers, where, like a ruffian, she roamed the nearby woods with the servants' children and her brothers. In the distance now, carolers could be heard, making their way down the streets to one another's homes. The three women sat in silence, nearly dozing from their supper.

"Shall I tell the tale of Snegurochka?" Vera broke into the silence. "If I don't talk, I shall fall asleep sitting here in my chair! And yet I don't wish to retire quite yet. I hate for Christmas to end."

"Yes," Marya said. "I always loved that story when I was a girl. Papa would ... Bah! Tell the story, Vera: if I begin reminiscing again, I shall put us all to sleep!"

Vera cleared her throat and began to recite from memory.

"A long time ago, in the forests of Russia, there lived a peasant by the name of Ivan with his wife Marya...."

Marya filled with great tenderness to hear Vera telling the old folk tale, and she relished again, the details, as she had when a child, of how the husband and wife had built a maiden out of snow, how she came to life and delighted them, who had been sadly childless, and how she disappeared—simply melted away—when the first signs of spring began to arrive.

How much more poignant the tale seemed to her now, though, than when Papa used to tell it, for her hard-won understanding of loss had sharpened the moments of sadness in the tale.

When Vera came to the end, in which the snow maiden returned again, come winter, Marya watched the most serene of smiles flicker on Lidia's face as she listened, her body barely creating a bulge under her blanket.

19
Vera's Journal

Saturday, 8 January 1876

Christmas Eve, after Masha and I readied Lidia for bed, we retired to our room. We put on our nightgowns and sat under the covers against the chill air.

"Merry Christmas, my darling," Masha said and leaned in to kiss me, a kiss that made me glad to be abed as I felt I might collapse upon the floor had I not been. She crushed me in an embrace then. "I love you so, my sweet seraph," she whispered. "How blessed I feel. To have you here beside me each night and each morning is a gift. I've no need of further Christmas."

"Ah," I said and kissed her lightly on the forehead, "but more Christmas you shall have!"

I reached behind my pillow and pulled from there two gifts, which I set upon her lap.

"Merry Christmas, my beloved. I count myself lucky the day I chose to visit the Alarchin courses." I kissed her cheek, and then, twisting myself nearly around, I let my lips linger a moment on her neck and breathed in the smell of her skin.

"Now!" she said. "If you continue to kiss me thus, we shall find ourselves opening presents other than these."

"Mashenka!" I pushed affectionately at her shoulders. "What has come over you?"

She raised an eyebrow at me and gave me a sly smile.

"I shall pretend not to understand your meaning. Please, now, will you open a present?"

"Not until I've done this," she replied. With her hand beneath the covers, she leaned until she had reached my bare ankle, then began to slide her hand up my leg beneath my gown.

"Stop, now," I said, and playfully slapped at her hand yet beneath the quilt.

She pretended a pout.

"Go on, then: open one," I insisted.

She unwrapped the first gift, a book.

"It's Aleksandra's book, *A Woman in Everyday Merchant Life*," I blurted out. I turned open the cover. "I made some inquiries and found where she lived and I've had her inscribe it!"

"'For Marya,'" Masha read softly, "'A woman who knows the value of women's rights and is not afraid to pay the price.' What an amazingly thoughtful gift, my darling. So much trouble you went to. Thank you." She kissed me lightly. "Here is one for you." She pulled a small package from behind her own pillow. "Open it."

I could feel her watching as I peeled away the paper. It was a silver brooch studded with amber.

"Do you like it? I could get you another. Or something else. Here—I shall get you something else; you don't like it."

"Masha, no! I love it. It's lovely. Thank you." I wrapped my palm across her cheek and marveled at how someone so self-assured could also be so tentative. "Now," I said. "Open the next."

I bit my lip as she pulled the paper from the small package.

When the burgundy leather case was revealed, she ran her thumb across it and looked a question.

"Go ahead," I said.

She opened the case and lifted the pink-gold cylinder from it.

"It's beautiful, Verochka, but I'm not sure—"

"It's a propelling pencil!" I couldn't contain my excitement. It had been such a coup to find this gift. I grasped its fluted edges and asked, "May I?"

"Oh! Yes!"

"See, if you twist the nozzle, a pencil lead peeks out."

"How ingenious!" She reached for her gift.

"Wait," I said. "This shield shape on the end? This is a seal with your initials on it." She leaned in to view for herself the MIZ. "The stationer said it's bloodstone," I said. "And if you unscrew it …"

"More pencil leads!" She seemed genuinely delighted.

I handed the propelling pencil back to her, and she sat with it in one hand and in the other still held the case. She tipped the case so as to see the gold medallion tacked to the lid.

"Hawley & Son, 289 High Holborn, London." Her English was quite good, I thought.

"Oh, Verochka." She let her hands drop to her lap. "Verochka, it's exquisite. Practical and yet ornate." She held the pencil aloft and slowly turned it between her fingers, then rested it as she might to write. "It's beautiful, Verochka." She blinked back some tears. "It must have cost you a fortune," she whispered. "You will spoil me entirely."

"Ah," I said, "but one can't spoil porridge with butter." She gave me a playful push. "I'm so glad you like your gift, darling." I leaned my head until my ear was resting on her cheek, then I twisted again to the base of her neck, where I lingered with my lips.

A small gasp escaped her.

"No! Wait," she said. She gently pressed me from her. "I've got another gift for you!" She turned right, then left, the pencil yet in one hand, the case in the other. At last, she raised the pencil to her lips, kissed it, placed it in the case, which she carefully closed. She rose from the bed and put the pencil in its case on her pillow, letting her fingers glide along its leather as she stepped away.

I shivered and pulled the quilt around me closer.

I could hear her rummaging in her wardrobe: there was much rustling, some banging about, a few muttered curses. It was beyond imagination what she might have concealed there.

"Masha, what are you—"

"Close your eyes!" she called from behind the wardrobe door.

I did as she bid me.

"You may open them now."

And there stood Mashenka, my lovely savant, with the largest, most gleaming birdcage I had ever seen.

"It's a birdcage. For Zubilo. Of course you can see that with your own eyes! And a book."

She sat beside me on the bed, then, and set the cage in front of me. It was really quite beautiful, the cage, with several perches so Zubilo might not have to sit in one place the day long, and room enough for him to stretch his wings a little. On the floor of the cage lay a book. *Wild Nature Tamed by Kindness.* Perhaps if the English text didn't prove too difficult, the children and I could read some of it together, I mused. But then I put aside all thought of work and all else outside the perimeter of our cozy nest.

"Is this book your autobiography?" I said mischievously.

"Well, it might be," she said. "Thanks to you."

She gave me a long, soft kiss, her hand firmly at the base of my skull. I sighed.

"This is the most wonderful Christmas I've had since I was a child. Thank you, Verochka."

She moved the birdcage to the floor and flipped open the quilt. I heard my brooch ping against the wires of the cage.

"My brooch!"

"Shh," she said. "It does not matter, come again under the quilt so we can get warm and so I may thank you properly. Or perhaps," she added, "'improperly,' would be the truer term."

I pulled back from her so I might look upon her more fully.

"What?" she said, her eyebrows knitting.

"Oh, nothing, darling. It's just you are so … I've never seen you like … you are so—"

"Wicked?" There was a mischievous glint in her eye.

"Mmmm," I said. I leaned in to kiss her and she pulled me into a snug embrace.

"I've been waiting for you all my life—*all my life*," she said into my ear, "and I didn't even know it." She breathed in the scent of my hair, then began to kiss and bite at my neck with hunger until I didn't know whether to hold her tight or push her away.

"Mashenka!" I said huskily. "Oh, dear lord, what a demon you must be to make me feel so reckless, so wanton." And then I could speak no more but only make animal noises, beautiful and base, as she touched me in my secret places.

I surprise myself by even recording this, for though I've never heard anyone speak of such things, I feel instinctively they must, in some way, be untoward. And yet, how so? How could such beauty, such love, be something to feel shame for? And since no eyes but my own shall view this record, I feel free to write it all down. For how do I know whether this feeling, this good fortune, shall last? If it does not, I want to know, years hence, I once could feel such joy. And so our Christmas Eve came to a close, after a day of worry and joy, merriment and tenderness, and a sense of peace that had little to do with commemorating the holiday.

As for Christmas day and the day after, we did little. Lidia, poor darling, kept to her bed, while Masha and I read or dozed by the stove and, for a time on Christmas afternoon, entertained Sergei. He stopped in to wish us a merry Christmas, and we drank tea together and talked of the weather, of Lidia's health, of the ominous direction Tolstoy seemed to be going in the latest installments of *Anna Karenina*.

After Sergei donned his fur cap and winter coat and took his leave, Masha and I attempted to continue the conversation, but we felt entirely lazy, or perhaps content, and let Zubilo dominate with his sweet and meandering song, which fit our mood so well.

"Better I love thy wood-notes wild to hear," I began to recite quietly. "Than all the melodies that art can teach."

"That's lovely," said Masha. "What is it?"

"A poem I learned from that childhood book of mine. I was thinking about how we are letting Zubilo carry the bulk of the conversation for us right now. And the poem goes on to say, 'Those untaught strains, so simple, soft and clear, / Seem ever near akin to human speech.'"

"Mmm," she replied, sleepily. "Lovely. Quite lovely." She gave my hand a squeeze, then let her head fall back upon the chair, a serene smile lighting her countenance.

I studied that face I had come to love so, and smiled. Where others seemed to dread what words of retribution might issue forth from those full red lips, I had come to learn their sweetness. And how much more special did it seem as this sweetness was for me alone. And the way her long nose divided her face seemed a symbol: the two sides of Marya or some such. But I was beginning to write a bad sort of poetry, I suspected, so I ceased my study and let my head, too, fall back upon the chair, and listened to the sizzle and crackle of the wood in the stove and Zubilo's pensive singing and let the toe of my shoe rest familiarly against Masha's.

20
Marya

Whatever charge of energy Lidia had gotten from the excitement of Christmas, it was not enough to sustain her for long. Too ill to join Marya and Vera for meals for several days following Christmas, Lidia had asked Nadya to tell the young women she was not up for visitors. Marya was concerned, of course, but imagined that the festivities had simply tired her aunt and did not read too much into her request for quiet.

So on the first afternoon that Marya and Vera were allowed to visit again, they were shocked to see how emaciated and ashen Lidia looked. They each pulled a chair to the side of her bed and did their best to attempt a light-hearted conversation in hopes of cheering her.

However, the rusty flecks of dried blood on Lidia's lips and on the bib of her nightgown were a constant reminder of her deterioration, and at last they set aside pretense and sought to make Lidia more comfortable. Vera gently ran a brush through her thin hair while Marya plumped her pillows.

When Nadya responded to the bell that Marya had rung, Marya asked her to bring some plain yogurt with honey for Lidia. But when Nadya had brought it, they couldn't convince Lidia to eat. Lidia quickly became fatigued by their concern for her, and she soon sent them away.

When they had shut the door to Lidia's room behind them, Vera whispered, "Mashenka—I'm so—"

"Shh." Marya put her fingers to Vera's lips. "Let us distract ourselves a while. I would as soon not talk about Lid—about … Not just yet."

It was plain to Marya that Lidia's death would likely not be forestalled for long, but she could not bear to think of it. She had grown quite fond of her aunt, to whom she owed a great deal. Furthermore, it was disconcerting to entertain the thought of losing the last of her family. It gave her a queer feeling, like being, perhaps, a boat in Kronstadt Harbor cut adrift or the last Astrakhan grape on a stem.

"Why, yes, of course, my darling," Vera said. "What shall we do? In what manner should we distract ourselves?"

Vera's brow was knit with concern.

"Anything—a game of Your Own Fools or Millers, perhaps," said Marya. "I could get the cards. Or—ah! I know. You've read *The Idiot*? But of course you have. What can I be thinking? You were at my side, discussing it with me and Sergei the other night. Forgive me, Verochka; I'm distraught. But, ah—there is a passage I wanted to share with you alone. Come: I've been reading it now again, and it lies upon my nightstand."

Marya had earlier bent down the page to mark it for easy detection.

The two women sat on the edge of the bed, with the copy of *The Idiot* between them. They read aloud to one another while tracing words with their fingers from the passages about Aglaya and Nastassya that had captured Marya's attention.

"What else can it mean," Marya said, "when Dostoyevsky has Aglaya say of Nastassya, 'She writes me she's in love with me, that every day she looks for an occasion to see me, even from a distance'?"

"How can I not have noticed this passage when I first read it? But of course," Vera added, "I had no idea there could be anyone like you then. If Dostoyevsky has written of this, though, certainly there are others like us? Others, I mean, whose feelings have transcended ordinary schoolgirl crushes or boarding school romances."

"But you've heard of the great statesmen Filipp Vigel, certainly? Everyone knows about his nature. And also the poet Aleksey Apukhtin."

"Yes, yes—those old 'aunties.' The air is thick with gossip about them. And there are also the princes Aleksey Golitsyn and Vladimir Meshchersky. Or such are the whispers I've heard, at any rate. But they are men, Mashenka—what of women, women like us? Do we exist only in the mind of some writer?—not you and I, of course, but I mean other women like us."

She smiled at the unintended foolishness of her question. "Surely Dostoyevsky can't have made us up out of nothing, can he?"

"Literature is purely astonishing! That we can find companionship in a few such passages in a very long book! But how fortunate am I to have not only these names on a page for companions but you, right here beside me."

Marya gave Vera's hand a squeeze, grateful that, for that short span of time, she was able to put her aunt's illness from her mind.

21
Lidia

Lidia dreamed she was set adrift in a cloud and imagined she must have died at last and been cast upward to make her way with the wisps that were the others who were formerly living. When she woke, a short time later, she was disturbed to find herself surrounded by a sea of white and thought perhaps she was yet dreaming—or, worse, that she had, in fact, died. But then she remembered Nadya had made up the bed, the evening before, with a snow-white quilt and bedding. Nevertheless, Lidia scanned her belongings—dressing table, cherrywood desk, the cane leaning on the bedside table—to further reassure herself she was still among the breathing.

Calmed, at last, by the familiarity of her room, Lidia let her thoughts meander, for until someone came to her, there was little else she could do. Thus it had been for several days now—she had lost count of exactly how many. She had been so debilitated by the ravages of consumption it was all she could do, the previous day, to recline in the daybed across the room while Nadya changed the bedding.

Her peripatetic thoughts took her first to Marya, and how alarmed the girl and her friend had looked upon visiting with her for the first time in days. They had tried to hide it, but how corpselike she must appear had been evident in their faces. The dears tried their best to be a comfort to her, but at last she had to send them away. How weary the living made her.

Lying there now, she wondered what day of the week it was, whether Sergei was still courting her Masha. Thinking of Sergei made her think, then, of Mikhail Feoktistov, the fiancé she had lost as a young woman. Such a contrast to Sergei! The thought of Mikhail brought with it, as it always did, even these many years later, a sense of sadness. But for the first time—because she was dying?—she now let herself realize that perhaps this sadness was tinged with something more. She tried to make herself comfortable so she could better settle into her thoughts. She wondered if, as she thought about Mikhail, she might find some nugget of insight she could then impart to Marya.

Mikhail Feoktistov! Lidia remembered setting eyes on him for the first time, well before she knew her parents had arranged for her to marry him. What a dashing figure he cut in his uniform, that of His Majesty's Hussar Guards: the white jacket with high, stiff collar, two rows of flashing gold buttons, the smart-looking epaulettes, and the black pants, tucked neatly into knee-length boots. She remembered thinking he seemed crisp and strangely cool, regardless of those dark flashing eyes. She could yet recall, quite vividly, his lustrous black hair, which he combed back in stiff waves from his high forehead and deep-set eyes. She could envision, as if he were there before her now, his long fine nose and his sensuous lips, nearly hidden by a generous mustache. Flawlessly handsome. At the time, she never forgot the way a chill had run the length of her spine that first time she'd seen him.

He was meticulously polite and charming, and Lidia was in disbelief the day her mother and father told her they had arranged with the Feoktistovs for Mikhail and herself to be married—she, Lidia Zhukova. Again and again she asked them to repeat this news, to verify she had not imagined it. This match was quite a coup, but her happiness was then multiplied by the announcement she was to stay the summer in St. Petersburg with a friend of her father's to get better introduced into the social scene with Mikhail, who was then stationed with his regiment in nearby Tsarskoe Selo, not far from the Catherine Palace.

The one flaw in all this joy, she remembered thinking at the start of that summer, was that Irochka wouldn't be there to share it with her. She still got letters occasionally about Irochka's life in Moscow with Andrei and his family. But dear as those letters were to her, there was little satisfaction in embracing a sheet of paper.

But then, as Lidia remembered with pleasure all the balls and the masquerades she and Mikhail—her Misha—had attended, she on the arm of the handsomest man in the room, her wan face briefly showed signs of life. She had felt like a fairy princess, dancing the mazurka and the quadrille beneath the chandeliers and amid the mirrors of the Sheremetev Palace. Then there were the soirees after the balls—and after the theater and the opera. How she loved the opera! The costumes, the music, those clear angelic voices. And the Bolshoi Kamenny Theater itself! What a spectacle it had been: hundreds and hundreds of people, from the humblest to the highest nobility, all gathered together in the flickering light of the candles to have their eyes and ears and souls filled with something so extraordinarily beautiful.

In the past, the splendor, the grandeur, the laughter, the beauty had been all she dared allow herself remember of Mikhail. But there was more, she knew, to be remembered, and she no longer had the strength or the many distractions of her former life to keep her thoughts from wandering the entire landscape of her past. During that long summer of their courtship, she began to notice Misha's eyes were not fixed adoringly on her alone. She had chastised herself for being silly and jealous, but she couldn't stop the ache when she would catch sight of him leaning in over one woman or another in a way that left no doubt of a prior intimacy between the two. She said nothing, lest she appear the untrusting shrew she believed herself to be. By July, there were other signs Mikhail Feoktistov wasn't the man he appeared: he would vanish for days at a stretch.

Once, he had been gone for nearly a week without a word to Lidia regarding his whereabouts. When he presented himself at last at the home of Vasily Borisovich, with whom she had been staying, she was sitting in the parlor, doing some needlework. Mikhail walked in before Vasily's serving man could even properly announce him. She could see straightaway his face was unshaven, and there was a button missing from his usually pristine uniform.

"Misha! What is wrong? Is something amiss?" She dropped her needlework on the divan and went to embrace him. But when she reached for him, he pushed her away.

"What do you want, you stupid cow?" His bloodshot eyes flashed menacingly, and his breath stank of cigars and alcohol. "Must you always hang yourself upon me like a damp blanket on a line?"

"Mikhail!" Frightened, she turned away from him.

"You little fool! How dare you turn from me." He gripped her arm and spun her around. When they were face to face, he had raised his arm to strike her, but she refused, despite her fear, to let him think she would be an easy target for his bullying, and she glowered at him. "Ack!" he spat out and pushed her away. He turned sharply toward the door, nearly lost his balance, then stumbled from the room. Lidia had collapsed, then, on the divan and wept softly so none of the rest of the household might hear.

When she saw him again the following evening, he was himself, which is to say the perfectly polished gentleman, but the memory of the previous evening was fresh enough she didn't dare ask him what his intended purpose had been when he'd visited the day prior. Lidia set about trying to convince herself that his beastliness was a one-time aberration. He never did threaten her again. Nor did he present himself to her in such a state but for that one time. Thus, she was nearly successful in her effort to delude herself about her fiancé. But then rumors began to reach her that Mikhail had a penchant for drinking and for gambling. At a gathering one evening, in fact, she overheard a whispered exchange, just around the corner, that on the day of his outburst he had actually come hoping to borrow some money from her.

Worse still were the rumors about him ruining the reputations of first one, then another young noble woman.

"People," she remembered having said, when Tatyana took her hands to comfort her, "will say anything to alleviate their boredom." Tatyana's pity was horrifying. While it was painfully clear to her that Misha was a philandering drunkard and gambler, she saw nothing to be gained by letting the world witness her pain. This man, after all, she reasoned, was going to be her husband, and she remained naively optimistic that once they were married, he would settle down. He would change. She said this to herself as if it were a fact.

And she was able to hold closely to this belief for years, for by the end of that summer, Mikhail was dead, killed in a duel, and so her assertion had never been proven wrong. No one wanted to tell her *why* Misha had been involved in a duel, but rumors delicious as those couldn't be kept silent: Misha, it seems, had been found by an officer of the Guard to be sleeping with his wife. When this rumor finally found its way to Lidia, she fled back home to Khrupkaya Luna, broken-hearted and ashamed. At Khrupkaya Luna, Lidia's younger brother Iuri, Marya's father, did his best to comfort her. Her parents had tried to convince her all she needed was to take her mind off of the vile man that had been her fiancé. Go back, they said—go back to St. Petersburg! But Petersburg and all its magnificence were tainted for her. Her parents had pleaded with her, then, to let them invite a party of young people for a visit to Khrupkaya Luna.

And she, in turn, had pleaded to be left in peace. There was no one she wanted to spend time with except, perhaps, Irina, who had vowed in a letter to come and keep her company. But then, it seems, she was pregnant, and her husband didn't want her traveling too far from the excellent doctors there in Moscow. She never came.

Her parents had tried a new tack, then, and suggested she travel abroad: the Mezentsovs were planning a trip, they said, and would love to have her join them. In the end, she said yes, too embarrassed by the humiliation of her engagement to Mikhail, too bereft by her definitive abandonment by Irina, to remain at home.

Thoughts of the past were interrupted in the present when her body was wracked with a sudden fit of coughing. At any minute, it was possible she might hemorrhage out the last spark of her life, and she hoped her last minutes on earth wouldn't have been spent with such sad ruminations. Once she stopped coughing and could focus on something more than breathing, she deliberately recalled her travels with the Mezentsovs—fond memories.

For two years, she traveled: Paris, Zurich, Rome, London. And the longer she traveled and the farther away she was from Russia, the easier it became for her to imagine a life for herself that didn't have Mikhail or Irina in it. It was during this trip she had first fallen in love with London, a love that drew her back many times over her life. When she finally returned to Russia from that trip, she came back to the family apartment in St. Petersburg, old enough to live there year-round, even while her family remained at Khrupkaya Luna, and happy with the solitary life she was just beginning to design for herself.

22
Marya

Months down the road, after things went terribly wrong, Marya would come to realize just exactly how ill she had used Sergei as their lives became increasingly entwined. Though he was never the type to snatch the stars from the sky—a poor librarian at the Imperial Library—he loved dearly to talk about literature, and in that, at least, Marya and Sergei were, as Lidia might have said, "two boots in a pair." But when it was too late to alter things, Marya admitted to herself that he had likely expected something more of her—something more than camaraderie and a shared love of books. In the end, though, she had given him what she could.

In the beginning, however—in the beginning, they took naught but pleasure in one another's company. So many wonderful—impassioned—discussions! About Rogozhin and Nastassya, *Crime and Punishment*, politics, education—they even spoke of childhood, though of course their main intent was never merely to reminisce! No, Marya must put Sergei to the test, always, and then see what might come of it. One night, for instance, when Sergei had been coming to her aunt's salons for a short while—two weeks, perhaps, or maybe three—Marya began her habitual rant about the others' shortcomings after they had taken their leave.

"They won't allow women to study at the universities, here in Russia, but what kind of education have our men received? Perhaps they have studied, at St. Petersburg University, gambling and drinking? Or perhaps these are things they learned at their mother's knee? 'Here, little Petya, let mama instruct you in the varieties of vodka: Passage of the Danube, Bulgaria—see how the ice floats about in the Nordenskold?'" Marya laughed at the picture she painted.

Then seeing Sergei's furrowed brow, she said, "But of course, I don't mean you, Sergei—you are a sensible man."

"You jest, Marya, but these are questions worthy of consideration."

"What is there to consider?" She shrugged. "The woman you find here is but the child with legs quite doubled in length! My sharp tongue? My boldness? Listen, and I will tell you how these things took seed.

"Surely, you had—where is it you grew up, Sergei?"

"Svetliachie Gory is our estate. It's on the Oka River, south of Moscow."

"And you, Verochka, from Petrovsky Island—certainly you must know of ice slides. Yes?"

Vera and Sergei both nodded, Sergei's eyebrow raised, wondering where such a question might take them.

"No doubt it was quite the same when you were a child, but I remember passing through the village square and watching the workmen build the sloping platform of wood, and afterward raising it up and up onto several tall pillars. And when the platform was secured, and after they had set stairs in place to the top of the platform, I would daily see the laborious process of water being hauled from the Donets, handed man to man as they sang: 'One, two, heave-ho! All together! Let us move it! One more time!' The water from one pail and then another was sent cascading down the slide in what seemed an infinite number until the whole surface of the slide was slick and shiny as a mirror.

"Days, it took, to complete the ice slide—do you remember how it was?—and during that time, my excitement grew exponentially in anticipation of the first exhilarating ride down that frozen rise. At last, at holiday time—yes: you remember, too, Seryozha!—the slide would be ready and we each would pull on our warm boots and heaviest overcoats and climb into a wagon loaded with hay, and Papa would drive the horses toward the ice slide."

Marya paused, sighing at the fond memory. But before anyone else could interject, she went on, moving to the edge of her seat in her excitement for the story she was about to tell.

"One year—I was perhaps seven years old, or maybe eight—I leapt over the sides of the wagon before it had entirely come to a stop at the edge of the square. Mama protested that I would hurt myself and called to me that I must wait for her and Papa and the boys, but ignoring her complaints, I raced to the slide, quite red-cheeked already from the cold. They moved far too slowly to suit my high spirits. I wasn't by the slide for the length of a breath before I realized I had forgotten my sled in the wagon and raced back.

"'Papa! Papa,' I shouted. 'My sled, Papa! I need my sled.'

"Mama, to be sure, chastised me for my lack of restraint—did I not say that I, the woman before you, and that child are one? Her chastisement was more gentle than usual, though, and had I been less ebullient, I would have sensed, I think, that she was actually pleased for me to be so happy."

A smile crinkled Marya's eyes.

"I remember so distinctly now, how I stood, bobbing impatiently from side to side while Papa unloaded the sleds from the wagon. As soon as mine was pulled to the ground, I grabbed the rope and raced away, shouting a thank you over my shoulder as my sled thumped and rasped across the snow behind me to the ice slide. My breath came in small wispy white clouds before my face. Ahead, I could hear the joyous and terrified shrieks of the other children mixed in with the giddy cries of the women and the triumphant shouts of the men as all zoomed along the icy surface, going fast as trains.

"Gasping for air, I climbed the stairs. My sled, which Papa had painted with horses on a splendid background of red, the whole bordered in a glittering gold, banged on each stair in my ascent to the top. I imagined I was climbing a mountain. Though our own plain, flat part of Russia had none of them, I had seen them in books. I climbed and climbed, imagining there was danger in every step I took, that I wouldn't give up, wouldn't be afraid, even if I was a girl—you see? I trudged through what I fancied deep drifts of snow, though, in actuality, the stairs had been swept almost clean of any traces of the recent snowfall. At last, I reached the crest of the mountain—or the top of the ice-laden platform—and I gasped to see the glorious scene before me. From where I stood, I could catch sight of the very treetops along the Donets River and the snowy roofs of the peasant huts. People were everywhere, the peasants and servants mingling among the gentry—yes? you remember the same?—they sped away on either side of me, down the glassy face of the platform, mounted the stairs behind me, and lingered on the sidelines of the slide, simply watching or calling out encouragement to those racing by. It was the same for you in your towns, no?"

Marya barely waited for their nods of assent before rushing on.

"After I took in as much as I could bear, I positioned my own sled, then climbed aboard. As I pushed off with my mitten-covered hands, my heart ran headlong, again and again, into the walls of my chest. I closed my eyes for just a moment as the varnished bottom of my sled dipped over onto the polished sheet of ice, but in spite of my terror at hurtling down this homemade hill, I couldn't keep my eyes closed. The wind tugged at the corners of my eyes and pulled a thin line of water from them across my face. The cold pricked my exposed cheeks and swept through my hair, ducking right under my scarf. Suddenly, I began to laugh from sheer joy. I laughed and laughed, hanging on for dear life.

"I leaned a bit to my left to avoid running into the boy beside me on the slide, then hit a small bump in the ice that caused me to lift inches off my sled. My stomach fluttered inside, like a bird rising into flight, and again I laughed aloud, enjoying my fright—you know this feeling, Sergei? Vera? All too soon, my sled scraped across the sand put near the bottom of the slide, and I slowed to a halt.

"When I climbed from my sled, dodging around the others that were coming to rest as well, a smile broke across my face: for this, you see, was the first time I had been allowed to go down the slide all by myself; I couldn't have been more than seven or eight, as I've said. Always before, Mama had made me ride down on the sled with Papa. I had protested, of course, but Mama had insisted.

"But now, here I was at the end of my first solo ride, and I scanned the crowd for the faces of Mama and Papa and Mitya and Timosha, my little brothers. Accomplishments are always more affecting when shared with ones you love."

Vera suppressed a little smile.

"Not finding them, I wasted no time in waiting but raced around to mount the slide again.

"My nose was running, but I didn't want to take the time to search for a handkerchief and simply wiped it on the back of my mitten. A ragged white streak hardened along the length of the back of my hand—and now, I suppose you are thinking that this explains much about my careless manner of dress!"

Vera shook her head, bemused at this burst of ardor from Marya. Sergei politely avoided any commenting by sipping from his teacup. It hardly mattered to Marya what the other two did, so engaged with her story she had become.

"Once again," she went on, "I made the long climb up the stairs and was rewarded with finding Papa and the boys and Mama. When it came to the ice slide, even Mama must be a youth again.

"Papa was lifting Mitya onto Mama's lap when I called out to them all. Mitya and Mama shrieked as one when Papa gave them a gentle push onto the slope, but Mama turned to wave while Mitya clapped his mittened hands. I ran to stand beside Papa, who now climbed onto a sled himself, lifting little Timosha into his lap.

"'Good-bye, my Mashenka,' Papa said merrily, then whisked away. I rushed to hop aboard my own sled and join them in the auspicious descent. And right beside me came two peasant boys on their homely sled carved of a huge block of ice. They sat on a layer of hay inside the hollow carved there. Clutching the rope threaded through a hole in the ice, they hollered just as gleefully as if they were on the most brightly painted wooden sled on the slope.

"But, oh, now I've lost sight of my point and have slid willy-nilly into reminiscence! What I intend you pay heed to is the rough and obstinate nature of the child in my accounting—does she not live on in the adult you perceive before you?"

Marya held out her arms in a gesture inviting them to gaze on her.

"In our essence," she said, "we are everlastingly the same. These men who come each week—surely they were disagreeable even as small children!"

"Do you think, Marya, I haven't myself thought about this? I have a brother," Sergei said, "who could be the comrade of your other guests."

Marya tilted her head in question.

"Yes, my brother—Nikolai—he is in the Hussar Guard, stationed at Krasnoe Selo. But for that, I wouldn't be surprised to find he had, indeed, been among your guests some time or other! For he is fond of rye beer as well as vodka, of fat cigars and slender women—slender both in body and mind!—and of gambling at cards."

"*Your* brother?" Vera asked. "How can that be so?"

"Yes, but it *is* so. Nikolai wasn't always as he is today, is what I mean to say. I remember him as a boy. How wonderfully dear he was—oh, how he loved to hear Mamochka play the piano, and he would dance for us while she played. Of this I dare not remind him now!"

Sergei grimaced in mock fear.

"Another memory I hold close of Kolya as a boy—can this be the same person, I yet ask myself, whose face is now mustachioed and bearded?—when he was hardly more than a baby, perhaps three, I think, Papa had gone on a hunt with my Uncle Vanya and several of the neighboring men. I remember it so well because Papa had chastised me more soundly than usual for not joining the hunting party. But I've never had a taste for killing things. Instead, I stayed home, content to read to Kolya, who rested his head sweetly on my shoulder the while. When Papa came home, Kolya ran outside to greet everyone, excited Papa was back. I followed after, to make certain he didn't get too much underfoot. When Kolya saw the wolf they had shot, he ran up to it, tied atop a horse; I think he thought it was a dog, like our Kashtanka. He soon realized it was dead and began to cry before running off. I chased after him, and shortly found him in Mamochka's garden, picking flowers.

"'Kolya,' I cried out. 'What are you doing?'

"'I'm picking flowers to put on the grave of the dog Papa has brought us.'"

Sergei paused, cleared his throat, then went on.

"You may ask yourself, as I have countless times before, how it is such a gentle little boy could become the loutish man he is today. This I can't tell you. But surely then you can't blame the mother, for here am I before you—not the same at all as my brother!"

He threw his hands out to the side as if say, "Look."

"And what of your brothers, Marya—Timosha, was it, and …? What sort of men have they become?"

Vera's shoulders stiffened.

"Her broth—"

"No, Verochka—it's fine."

Marya wrapped her fingers around Vera's wrist.

"My brothers—Mitya and Timosha—they never had the opportunity to become men. They died as children, while I was here in Petersburg, at the Institute."

"Oh, dear God, Marya."

Sergei moved to the edge of his chair and reached toward Marya, then, perhaps thinking it too forward to touch her, put his hands on the arms of his chair.

"Forgive me. I had, of course, no thought of such a conclusion. I hope I haven't wounded you with my incautious question?"

His eyes searched Marya's face, sincerely concerned that he had inadvertently caused her distress.

"Please, Sergei. It was long ago now. I miss them still, and I, too, wonder how they might have fared as men. Yet it isn't with grief I look upon them mostly now, but with pleasant thoughts—how Mitya and I would pick mushrooms in the woods or pull Timosha on a sled. But perhaps this would be a good time to tell you also that my parents have perished as well. I wouldn't wish you to suffer this discomfort again."

"Uhf."

Seryozha sat back in his chair as if the wind had been knocked out of him.

"I was but nine when my mother died, and it was then Papa sent me away to the Institute. For a very long time I blamed my mother for this, for it's she who had always been so harsh with me, and to leave Khrupkaya Luna felt like banishment to me. I know now she loved me in her way, and if she was exacting, it was because she wanted what she felt was best for me. And yet so did Papa. They only but showed their wishes in a different manner."

Marya let herself linger over this insight before going on.

"Papa—he was a favored playmate of mine, when I was child, along with the peasant boys—he only recently died. I had not visited with him for years; and his work at Khrupkaya Luna kept him from visiting me in St. Petersburg. But my grief for him is profound. Before he sent me away, we were so close you couldn't have split us apart with water."

"How truly lucky I am, Marya," said Sergei, his voice quiet, thoughtful.

"Those I love," he continued, "they are still with me. If not in this city, at least in life. I can get letters from them, we can visit, they can—well, but, it's only rudeness on my part to tell such a one as you of my own good fortune. Forgive me yet again. You must think me an oaf, a stranger to the social graces. In truth, I'm not one for parties or for—"

"Sergei! You worry too much. Now come, it's late. I will have Ilyusha get your coat and summon a carriage."

"We will see you on Thursday, I hope?" added Vera.

"Yes. Yes—thank you. You are too kind."

His eyes rested on Marya in a way that unsettled her.

Perhaps sensing as much, Sergei turned then to Vera and said, "Both of you. Thank you. I leave here as ever, with a head stuffed with new thoughts, new ideas to consider. Always, your company is such a pleasure."

23
Grigorii

15 January 1876

Dear Masha,

How good to receive a letter from you after another long silence. I was pleased to hear this absence was occasioned by a surfeit of activity rather than its complete lack, as when a yawning melancholia immobilized you some months ago.

"Once burned by milk, you will blow on cold water," the saying goes, but I'm glad to hear you haven't been made so watchful by the departure of one friend that you've removed yourself from all commerce with others. (I recall you and Tanya at the Institute—"the inseparables"—and how wretched you were when she must return home.) It may be that the Alarchin courses have made compensation, in some small measure, for the lack of vision and substance with which the Ministry of Education imbues those lectures by providing you with excellent company. Vera sounds as if she may be a fine friend in the making, and a good friend is beyond all calculation. As well, I little doubt the women gathered at the meetings you attend have been taken aback by your breathtaking honesty and intelligence. The cause of women will be much enhanced by the infusion of your lively acuity.

Commendable, your desire to further the cause of women's educational opportunities, and perfectly within understanding. Yet I hope you don't set aside your pursuit of a future in mathematics for yourself. Do I offend, if I offer up a project for you to embark upon? If you should find, in some future trip to the Imperial Library, a more suitable endeavor to which to apply your talents, I, in turn, won't be offended at your not having embraced my suggestion. But in perusing those mathematical puzzles that have confounded the great minds of the past, I found one that seems most worthy of you.

The problem I have in mind for you involves Joseph-Louis Lagrange's model and that of Leonard Euler. Regarding Lagrange's model, think of a top in which the center of the top's mass is at its center—on the axis of rotation. Euler's model, in contrast, has the center of mass at the fixed point where the top rotates and not in the center of the top. Now. Here is the question: Can these two cases be expanded to include a top that isn't symmetrical? Imagine, if you like, a wooden top carved by a poor craftsman such that it's lopsided and inelegant, so when it spins its heaviest part isn't along the axis of rotation—is there, in other words, an equation that will describe the motion of such a body? To solve, in an analytic manner, such an equation of motion would insure you an everlasting place of glory in the history of mathematics. And there would be none, then, surely—between yourself and Sophia Kovalevskaya—who could deny women are more than capable of contributing to the field and deserve access to the same educational opportunities as men.

It may be you feel confident of success in such a venture, or it may be you feel, at my simply having set forth the problem, already defeated. But no matter: you must approach the task in like manner in either happenstance. Begin, first, with a review of Euler, and undertake to study Jacobi's work, if you haven't done so already. Lamé, Lagrange, Fuchs: the work of all these, too, may serve you. But you will find your own route into the matter, I feel certain.

I await with great excitement your first thoughts on the project I propose here. To be your sounding board as you begin such a problem—or one of your own choosing—brightens the prospect of walking these dull corridors each day on my way to try to fill the heads of silly schoolgirls with some thought other than making a proper match in marriage.

Friendship, and the intoxicating meetings you attend, will be a powerful distraction, but don't forget about our pact. It's enough for many to do nothing more than pound water in the mortar. But your mind is a treasure of which the world shouldn't be deprived. Others may find themselves enchanted by a coy laugh or the flutter of an eyelash, but for me, there is no match for bringing delight as an elegantly solved mathematical problem. Perhaps that's why I remain alone as a finger!

May the new year find you in exceptional intellectual form and may mathematics seduce you anew with its beauty!

Your champion,

Grisha

24
Lidia

Lidia Zhukova listened from the soft cave of her bedclothes as the wind grumbled past her windows like a symphony of bad-tempered bears. So primal, she thought, yet so melodic in its guttural crescendos and its sighing diminuendos. Lidia imagined herself its conductor, imagined she could control the intricate pattern of peaks and valleys, baton in hand. But the truth is, she wouldn't have had the strength to lift a baton if she'd had one, and the wind, like her body, wasn't something she could bend to her control. Her niece, Marya, however, proved surprisingly more tractable.

For more than a week, Lidia had been unable to leave her bed and she gave scant notice to the arrival and departure of her name day with scarcely a mention from any in her household (no one, it seemed, could muster the false joviality to imagine the day as festive, least of all herself). But always she waited eagerly to hear whether Sergei had continued to return. For each of his visits encouraged Lidia to believe that it might be possible to yoke his future to that of her niece's, as she fervently hoped. A great sense of relief washed over her each time she heard that Sergei had been the last to leave or had almost touched Marya's knee as he was making a point or that his eyes couldn't be torn from her niece even when Vera's teacup crashed to the floor.

One evening, late in January, Lidia had felt vigorous enough to be carried by Ilyusha to the chaise by the ceramic stove so she could once again take part in the gathering, albeit in limited fashion. She hoped her lungs would quiet themselves enough she wouldn't interrupt the assembled guests: she wanted to observe again for herself how it went with Masha and the man who seemed increasingly as though he might be her young charge's beau.

Only four young callers arrived at her apartments that evening, but one of them, thank goodness, was Sergei. None but Sergei lingered long, however, for they were hard put to distract Marya from the rapt attention she paid to the discussion between herself and Vera and Sergei. Lidia couldn't help but smile at this unlikely turn of events. She found herself in great sympathy, however, with the other gentlemen. The threesome's debate about whether the Imperial Library had indeed overcome its penchant for archaeologomania in favor of accumulating current scientific literature was a topic for only the most stouthearted—archaeologomania, they had disdainfully informed one of the other young men, was an inclination to buy rare books.

Had she the strength to call to one of the servants, likely she would have made her excuses as well, notwithstanding her interest in assessing the proceedings. In the meanwhile, she marveled at nature's wisdom, finding for every sturgeon in the sea another to love that most unusual face.

Lidia drowsed as comfortably as she ever did these days, warmed by the camaraderie of the three as much as by the birch logs crackling away in the ceramic stove near her feet. A delicate ruffling of feathers or the tap-tap of shifting feet from Zubilo's covered cage kept her company, too. When she would rouse herself from time to time, the three young people were as before: Masha and Vera, knee touching knee, and Sergei facing them, sitting at the edge of his seat, his hair and cravat slightly askew, while his teacup, perched precariously on one knee, rattled on its saucer as he gesticulated wildly with each point he made.

Lidia brazenly studied his lovely face, his blue eyes blazing with passion, then closed her own eyes again. As enjoyable as looking at him was, better still was savoring his voice, which though ardent was never strident and was imbued with a rich baritone timbre.

Since that heartening evening, however, Lidia hadn't been able to raise herself from her bed. Her body was wracked with such coughing she found herself wishing for the end. She had Nadya take away whatever mirrors were movable and cover whichever of those were not: she could no longer bear the sight of herself. Her cheeks were so hollow they were in perpetual shadow, and her eyes so sunken they seemed lost in the narrow sea of her face.

Yet she'd had, in all, she estimated, a good life. Her main regret—leaving aside never-quite-resolved issues regarding her long-ago friend Irina—was she likely wouldn't get to witness the culmination of Marya's story, or at least the part of it she so craved: to see her niece married—and, thus, safe. Safe from rumors and ridicule. Safe from speculation and spite. Little minds make much of nothing.

It was then she decided she must ensure the outcome would conclude suitably, and she waited impatiently for her niece's next visit so she could make clear to Masha what she must do.

Though Lidia's voice was so hoarse she could barely talk, she felt she must indeed speak. "Masha—Mashenka, my dove," she began, but the whispery croak that issued from her lips was so discordant, she wondered whether she should go on. Masha's earnest young face, etched with concern, was bent toward her to catch her words. There, but for the absence of some stubble, was Lidia's brother's face: the full red lips, peat-colored eyes, the long, straight nose dividing the oval of her face. Even the girl's hair, hued like a rook's feathers, reminded Lidia of Iuri—gone now (was it already) five years? The resemblance between father and daughter on this score, as Lidia saw it, was the more pronounced for the styling of her niece's hair: on the very day Marya graduated from the St. Petersburg Institute for Girls, she had cut off her beautiful hair and had continued to wear it short, as though she were one of those agitators for reform. *Nigilistka*, Lidia thought bitterly, not for the first time. She shook her head, mystified by the sort of discontent that seemed to seize so many young women these days—even those from good families. Nonetheless, Lidia had almost grown used to that *nigilistka* hair, for it sat on the head of one she had come to love.

Nearly overcome by a rush of emotions, Lidia charged on with her intended topic lest she be defeated all together by strong feeling. "I won't be of this earth much longer, little Masha, little lamb, to guide you. Shhh," she rasped over her niece's protestations. "Look at me, Masha. I'm a shadow. And shadows, my dear, aren't long around. A change in weather, the passage of time—pfft—they are gone. So now. We have important things to discuss. And we must discuss them straightaway, before this shadow fades."

Lidia let the intensity of her deep-set eyes bore into her niece.

"You must marry, Masha. As I am the last Zhukov of my generation, I've inherited all—the estate and all its income, these apartments. Because you will be the sole Zhukov left in line, you will next inherit them. You will be rolling, as it were, like cheese in butter. It isn't, therefore, your finances over which I worry, Masha. It's your state in life which troubles me. You mustn't end like me, a lonely, reviled spinster—you must marry."

"But—but, aunt, reviled? No, it's a great falsehood to say you are reviled. You are loved. By many. But regardless," Masha shook her head as though to clear it, "to the point: I don't wish to marry. I have no desire to … to … And I shan't be lonely—I have Verochka." She spoke quietly, as if she feared a raised voice might shatter her aunt's wasted body.

"Yes. Verochka." Lidia fanned her fingers up from the quilt in an approximation of waving away this argument. "I know you are quite fond of her. I'm old and I'm dying, but I'm neither blind nor a fool. But she will marry someday as well. She will leave this house as surely as will I." When a protest started to form on Marya's lips, Lidia raised her voice as best she could. "And even if she doesn't, what then? You are young and do not know how poisonous the talk of others may be. What they do not know themselves, they are not afraid to invent."

Lidia was seized with a coughing fit. Marya began to rise from her chair, not sure what she might do, yet unable to sit passively while her aunt coughed. But Lidia waved her fingers up and down, signaling that Marya do exactly that: sit. When the coughing had subsided, and her handkerchief was discreetly tucked away, Lidia continued.

"A husband allows you certain rights in this world, earns you a place of respectability and social acceptance a friend never will. You *need* a husband, Masha. Promise me—promise me, child, you will marry." Lidia reached her wasted arm across the bedclothes to clutch at her niece's wrist. "Sergei—he is smitten with you, Masha. I've seen how he looks at you. He is a good man, with a respectable position. You must marry him, Masha, if he will have you. A tomtit in the hand, Masha, is better than a crane in the sky."

As she spoke, Lidia pushed away the thought of what she might have done, had she been made to choose between Mikhail and Irina. But it was a foolish thought, a dying woman's thought. There could never be such a question. Now as then.

For a moment, Marya didn't speak, and Lidia watched thoughts move across her niece's face and behind her eyes almost as clearly as if they were in fact visible.

At last, Marya spoke.

"I will not let a spoonful of tar spoil a barrelful of honey, Aunt Lidia! What others may say of me does not come to bear on who I am. I care not what others may think! They can say they milk chickens, if they like—I know what is true. It's what *I* think that matters." Marya had risen from her chair and paced beside her aunt's bed, gesturing angrily with hands as she made each point.

But when Marya turned and caught sight of her aunt, who was naught but a husk with little memory of its fruit, she felt the color rise in her face.

"I ... I ... Forgive me, aunt. I meant no disrespect. But can you not see how ill-suited I am to take a husband?"

As she was speaking, Marya had knelt at the sick woman's bedside and taken her bony hand in her own.

"Please, aunt—do not ask this of me."

Lidia withdrew her hand, which shook as she lifted it to pat awkwardly at her niece's wrist.

"Masha, my dear. If you will not do this for yourself—and I tell you: you know nothing of what it is to be the target of everyone's guesswork and worst nature. But let that be. For you are too headstrong to believe an old woman like me might know something more of the world than you. Hush, now!"

Lidia spoke with surprising force to silence her niece, who had opened her mouth to utter some protest.

"If you will not do this thing I ask for yourself, then you must do it for your family name. Do you wish to be the one to bring shame and dishonor to the distinguished name of Zhukov? Think of your father, Masha! Would you bring disgrace down upon him when he is no longer even present to defend himself?"

At that, Marya's head snapped back a little, almost as though she had been slapped. To bring her beloved Papa into the argument—how unfair! But another look at her aunt, and she knew she could not argue further: the woman was disappearing before her eyes it seemed!

Marya closed her eyes, and with a sigh of resignation said, "Yes. Yes, fine, Aunt Lidia. As you wish. I will ... I will determine whether Seryozha is agreeable to this."

Lidia was suspicious her niece only *seemed* to comply. Because she was dying. "Promise me. Promise me, Mashenka!" Lidia's voice was a croak. She tightened her grip on Marya's wrist, though the change was almost imperceptible. Her gaze was trained on her niece's face.

"Yes!" Marya turned her face from her aunt as she spoke. "Yes, I promise, Aunt Lidia"—words spoken so softly, they were as lost in the small room as a kopek dropped in the Fontanka Canal.

25
Marya

The exhilaration that Marya felt after reading Grisha's letter was ground out by the conversation she had with aunt—especially the promise she had found herself making.

You need *a husband, Masha. Promise me—promise me, child, you will marry.*

The horrible croak of her aunt's voice would never leave either her dreams or her waking moments, Marya felt certain. And the bony press of Lidia's fingers on her wrist! How could she have said no? And yet, how could she say *yes*?

"I will determine whether Seryozha is agreeable to this." Marya's own words repeated in her head as well. "Yes! Yes, I promise, Aunt Lidia."

But were not promises broken all the time? And if her aunt were no longer present to see if the promise had been fulfilled ...

Yes, but the cat knows whose meat it has eaten, she reminded herself.

Part II

What we know is not much.
What we do not know is immense.

~ Pierre-Simon de Laplace ~

1
Vera's Journal

Tuesday, 8 February 1876

Lidia Zhukova died yesterday, 7 February 1876. Though she had wasted away to the feeblest of sparks, then guttered out like a candlewick drowned in wax, at least there was no violence. So often, among those with consumption, it's as if death were not content merely to carry off a life but must give a hint of the full extent of its power, pouring forth blood from one's mouth and nostrils to suffocate the poor soul with one's own essence. Mercifully, Lidia floated from us like a scrap of paper on the Moika.

Dr. Chlenov had come to look after Lidia earlier that day but said there was naught to be done except make her as comfortable as we might. Marya, Nadezhda, Ilya, and I kept watch at her bedside. When it seemed she might soon slip away, Masha sent Liudmilla to bring the priest.

"Quickly, Liuda. Quickly!" Masha spoke in a loud whisper. "I don't think she will be much longer with us. Bring Father Nikolai at once."

Liudmilla lifted her skirts to her ankle and ran from the room. Her heels could be heard pounding swiftly down the stairs.

When Father Nikolai arrived, we left the room so Lida might receive her last rites and confess her sins. Now she is gone, I try to imagine what sins she might have had to confess, she who worked her whole life to benefit the poor and unfortunate and who took me in, a stranger to her, and who took in

Marya, all but a stranger herself—and not a congenial one always, at that! But I remind myself Lida, too, was once young, open to all the folly that afflicts life's travelers. Perhaps there was a liaison for which she felt remorse, an illicit act committed in a moment of passion, a small theft—a thimble, or hair ribbon, or gold buttonhook—that has weighed upon her conscience these many years.

But while Father Nikolai remained with her, his ear, no doubt, pressed nearly to her lips so he might hear that wisp of voice, we stood silently at the end of the hall, each of us occupied with our own feelings of grief. Father Nikolai opened the door, then, and said, "She is ready to leave this world. You must come say your goodbyes. Quickly now." He motioned us in.

We were not long in returning to her bedchamber before her last breath shuddered forth. After Father Nikolai made the sign of the cross upon her forehead, chest, hands, and ankles, Masha dropped to her knees beside the bed and wept. If any present had not been moved to weep before this, the sight of Masha grieving in this way broke down our last reserves as we clothed Lida's body in a shroud. Nadya, who had been with Lida since before even myself or Masha had even been conceived, tenderly placed the icons in Lida's hands, and we wept anew.

Later, alone, Mashenka clutched me to her.

"Verochka! I have no one now, no one but you. Please! Please!"

"Yes, I am here, little Masha. I am here. I am here." I kissed her hair and held her tightly to me and at long last, she began to quiet. My darling Mashenka! She is now left without a soul in this world who shares her blood, her history. Thus I write, knowing all too well how it is to be an exile from one's own childhood. If I cry now for Lida and for Masha, I cry for myself, too, for the loss of poor hard-working Papa, dead now these ten or more years, and darling Mama, who is a wound not yet healed in my heart. Masha and I, we are alone in it now, together.

I helped her to undress and put on a nightgown. I pulled back the covers on the bed, and she let me lead her there. Soon after, I curled along behind her.

"So much loss you have suffered, my love. Grieve. Grieve, my Mashenka. It will do you well." Then I held to her while she pressed to her eyes the bedsheet she clutched in her hands. It seemed I could actually *feel* the sorrow in her body while she keened.

At last, the whisper of her sleep came to my ears like a soft, familiar music. I lay there a while. Then, yet quite awake myself, I breathed in the musky scent of her neck. To feel this kind of love for another woman, I could never have imagined. I did not dream of marriage, of a husband, as a young woman on Petrovsky Island. I cannot recall of what it was I did dream then, but of this—it was surely beyond what I could have imagined.

I tightly embraced Masha's waist so even in sleep she would sense I was there, tending her like the lost sheep she would never admit to being, playing shepherd as though it was the role I was born to.

2
Vera's Journal

Thursday, 10 February 1876

It's quiet in the house at last. The visitors are gone, and Masha has been given a small draught of laudanum to help her sleep. I am sitting at the small desk in our room, writing by the soft light of a single candle, waiting for sleep to call me; perhaps I should take some laudanum as well. But I will record the day's events first, and then perhaps sleep may come of its own accord.

Today we placed Lidia in a casket in the drawing room, her dear old face nestled in a pillow stuffed with birch leaves. When I bent to kiss her forehead, the clean, lemony smell of the crushed leaves was still faintly present. I tried to focus on that fleeting trace of freshness rather than the less-benevolent odors that had begun to inhabit the room.

Liuda and Nadya gathered candles to set around the casket, and Ilya lit them. We said our farewells to Lida, then, before friends began to gather. Lida's old friends Anna Karmazinova and Olga Levitskaya were first to arrive. Their faces drawn, they kissed Lidia on the cheek. As they stepped away from the casket, Olya looked as though she might faint, and Masha and I each grabbed an arm and helped her to a seat.

"Such a dear soul." Olya let out a deep sigh.

I patted her plump hand.

"Rest a moment; I will get you some tea."

Anya took a seat beside her and silently dabbed at the corners of her eyes.

"I shall get some tea for you as well," I called over my shoulder.

I handed each of them their tea and listened to their stories of Lida in the old days for a half hour or more. Marya, it seemed, was too distraught for these stories and had gone to sit on the other side of the room. When her grief has passed some, I thought, perhaps she will desire these moments captured from her aunt's life, and so I listened carefully as they reminisced.

While we chatted, a small brass orchestra, pressed uncomfortably into the hallway and partway up the stairs, softly played traditional funeral marches. Zubilo's punctuation of this musical phrase or that would have been merrymaking in different circumstances, and perhaps I should have removed him from the room. Despite his irreverence, though, it cheered me some to hear his lively song. As others came in—Sergei, Lida's other friends from her society work, several of Masha's former gentleman callers—they kissed Lidia's cheek and expressed their sympathies to Masha before finding a seat to await the arrival of Father Nikolai, who would be coming to say the blessing.

By the candles' end, all of the visitors had departed, and though it was time for dinner, none of us were much interested in that activity and contented ourselves with the few scraps of tea cake left upon the tray before going to our separate rooms in the apartments.

I let Masha cry for a while longer before I slipped away to find the laudanum in Lida's room. And when I suggested she consume a draught, Masha did not object.

Tomorrow will be a difficult day as well; we must take the casket to the gravesite at Lazarevskoye Cemetery for burial. The iron fence has already been seen to; I do not think Masha could bear it if the wild dogs began digging at the freshly restored dirt, so I made sure to ask Ilya today to see to the fencing. I must remember to speak with Nadya in the morning to be certain more candles are brought for our visit to the gravesite.

At first, I thought myself the worst kind of person, to ask these kind people, Ilya and Nadya, who have known Lidia and loved her these many years, to busy themselves with these tasks when surely they, too, must be grieving. But now I envy them the opportunity to occupy themselves and hold aside the sorrow, if only for some minutes at a time. If Masha did not need me so, I, too, would seek to divert myself from the pain.

My candle here is burning low, and Masha is stirring restlessly in her sleep. Enough recording of events for one day: I must try to get some rest. And maybe my familiar form beside Masha will vanquish some of her tormenting dreams.

3
Marya

As a young girl, there were so very many things Marya thought she might do—become a soldier, a wagon driver, a professor—but never did she suppose she might ask a man to marry her. Unquestionably, though, it made the utmost sense, given her nature, that if any asking were to be done, it would be Marya doing the asking.

Still, though they had buried Lidia and were done with the necessary paperwork, Marya could not yet bear to fulfill her promise to her aunt. To be sure, Marya was no stranger to grief, and so she thought she might take its presence for granted—pay it no more mind than one does the fat baron who can be spotted strolling, each and every day, in front of the Admiralty.

But grief took her by surprise. Hollowed her out, as a melon or a squash with its seeds scooped aside. For it was a complicated grief.

Hidden in it were the deaths of her parents and brothers, the loss of Katya, her anguish over being compelled to marry, the fear of living out the rest of her life quite alone. For though Vera seemed steadfast, Marya feared that by adding in Sergei, the two might cancel each other out as summarily as a positive integer added to its negative doppelganger.

Furthermore, guilt was lashed to her grief, like a cart piled high and towed in silence but for the occasional groan of protest by the wood for the extra load.

None of this, however, did she convey to Vera, who held Marya with the sort of caring one bestows upon an innocent. Marya kept silent about what she perceived as her darker self.

But soon, Marya fell to considering again how none save herself and Lidia knew of the promise she had made, and she sought to convince herself Lidia was not of sound mind when she extracted that oath from her. But if she were? As she'd told Lidia, she cared not at all for what others thought of her. Let them think her queer as the eight-legged lamb in Peter's kunstkammer. If that kept them away, so much the better!

It was then that she realized to excuse herself any longer from repaying her debt to Lidia was to risk never repaying it at all—a risk that meant betraying her aunt's trust in her—and more: betraying her father's legacy. For although reputation meant little to Marya, she would not, for all the world, sully her father's good name. He who had doted on her as a child—had he not earned the right to maintain his honor?

And so she made up her mind to press on with the vow she had made to her aunt. No sooner had she done so than she thought guiltily and with longing of Grisha's letter—past a month old, then—to which she had neither replied nor attended. The temptation to set aside her promise to Lidia in favor of losing herself in Grisha's math project nearly overwhelmed her resolve again.

It occurred to her, though, that to delay in fulfilling her promise would undoubtedly weigh upon her—a weight that would suppress her ability to make the leaps of thought needed to land upon a mathematical expression to describe the motion of Grisha's ungainly top. Once again, she determined to put aside her own wishes and desires.

And still she said nothing to Vera about her promise to Lidia, for Marya could not be certain until she had asked Sergei that she would, in fact, do so. If, in the end, she did not ask Sergei to marry her, why trouble Vera unnecessarily, she reasoned.

Furthermore, she must not only ask him but he must also agree. How likely was it a man would consent to marry a woman so bold as to propose the union herself? As unlikely as that seemed, it was even less likely, she supposed, he would agree to the terms she planned to set before him.

No, she saw no reason unduly to upset Vera.

Then, too, there was reason to fear Vera would not stay if the marriage was realized. Decent though Sergei seemed to be, what kind of life would

Vera imagine for herself, under such strange circumstances? Whatever promises Marya might make her, how would Vera ever feel secure in her fate when there was to be a legal husband in the household?

While Vera was off tutoring Pasha and Varya, Marya asked Ilyusha to carry a note to Sergei at the Imperial Library, feeling rather queasy about the whole operation.

In her note, Marya requested that Sergei join her for lunch two days hence at The Bear. The day of their meeting, Marya paced nervously in her room.

When she caught sight of herself in her mirror before departing for The Bear, her hands nervously kneading one another, she had to laugh at herself in spite of her discomfort, for this was perhaps the first time she had been made anxious owing to a man.

When Sergei entered the restaurant, he was, if anything, even more nervous than Marya.

"Marya. Is anything amiss? Let me tell you again how sorry I am about your aunt. Is there something I can help you with? I will be happy to do what I can. I do not have a great deal of money, but—"

"Please, Sergei!" Marya laughed. Sergei smiled shyly then and sat down at last.

"Forgive me, but I am afraid I am somewhat nervous. I am not in the habit of meeting beautiful young ladies for lunch. Or for any meal of the day, for that matter. Yes. I must be quiet now and see if there is some special purpose for your calling me here."

"You have sensed correctly. This is not an idle social occasion. I wanted to ask … That is, my aunt wanted me to … What I mean to say is—"

"Now I think it's you who are fretful! Please, Marya. You may ask me anything. Anything at all!"

He leaned forward and folded his hands on the table.

"I am afraid there is no way to ask but simply … to do so. So I inquire of you now, Sergei, whether you will consent to be my husband."

"Oh, dear. This is not at all what I might have expected! Though to be honest, I have entertained the thought of requesting the same of you, so it would be foolish—would it not?—for the answer to be anything but yes." He pulled a handkerchief from his pocket, then, and wiped his forehead.

"You must wait, Sergei, before you answer. There is—"

"I apologize, Marya: I am, as you might suspect, quite new at this."

"There's no cause to apologize. It's simply I mean to say if we are to marry, there will be some conditions to that."

"Of course."

He nodded, as though knowingly.

"But what are they, Marya?" he asked then, plainly realizing he did not know of such conditions after all.

"My aunt's apartments, which shall now be mine, are quite spacious and comfortable, and I would prefer to continue to live there."

"Yes, yes, of course! You have a lovely home. And in any case, my room would be much too small, really, for two us."

"Ah. And there is the other thing—the most important thing: there will be three of us, for Vera will stay on, I believe."

"Of course. She is a lovely person, and we get on well. This does not impress itself on me as a problem."

"Also, though, Sergei, there can be no sharing of a bed between you and me. You will have your own room, and a study as well, and I shall continue to share a room with Vera."

This he clearly was not expecting, for some shadow of dismay or regret or hesitation quickly passed across his face, but to this also he assented.

"Ah." He said. "Ah! Yes. Of course!"

Was his response overhearty?

"Like Vera Pavlovna," he went on, "and Dmitrii Lopukhov in Chernyshevsky's *What Is to Be Done?* Of course. It's the new way, is it not? How, one must ask oneself in this day, can a man of decency fail to act to right the inequities of our society! To become husband-in-name so that a woman may get the passport, for example, that would otherwise be denied her?"

Sergei paused and tapped his upper lip with a forefinger.

"With a husband, you would be able to move more freely in society."

His gaze grew distant and narrow. He sat and silently chewed his lip.

"Hmm," he said quietly, then lapsed into utter silence again.

At just the point when Marya thought she would not be able to withstand another fat minute of stillness and must jump to her feet and shout, *Enough, I withdraw my … my aunt's request,* he cleared his throat and said, "Yes, Marya. Yes, I shall do it: I shall become your husband."

4
Vera's Journal

Thursday, 17 February 1876

She tells me he means nothing more to her than a brother or a—a servant, she is only honoring Lidochka's dying request, I've nothing to be jealous of. Yet how does she think I must feel? Marya has agreed to marry Sergei.

"This will be the end of you and me, you must apprehend," I said to her. I struggled to make my tone seem angry, proud, when, in truth, I felt naught but fear. To think of life without Marya upended my stomach like a hay cart that has hit a boulder.

"No, my little dove. No, do not fret. All will remain as now."

She reached to embrace me, but I turned my back to her.

"Sergei has agreed to this," she continued. "It's a condition of our marriage. I promise you: this marriage will not interfere with you and me. You, Verochka, are my—"

"You promise!" I said. "It's not yours to promise, Marya. As for Sergei, a man will promise you anything for—"

"Verochka! That's just not so. Sergei is not like that. He is an honorable man, a man of his word. I am sure of it, Verochka."

"Then why, Masha, would he agree to marry you, if he does not have hopes for a marriage in more than name only?"

"Because he believes it's a man's duty to give women freedom, freedoms not allotted to women without husbands. He believes a chaste marriage is the purest form of love and respect!"

"Yes, this is the way many a man has tricked a woman into his bed. Perhaps you have heard of Liudmilla Radetskaya from Moscow? Her husband made the same promises of chastity to her, but soon he took her to his bed. Worse still, when that stinking commune of radicals they were at the center of began having financial troubles, that bastard, her husband, sent her out to prostitute herself. She became the mistress of a banker for him. Is that what you want for yourself, Marya?"

I was pacing by then.

"That's just soft-boiled boots, Verochka—nonsense, pure and simple. I cannot believe you would put such value in idle gossip, the poisonous outpourings of a gaggle of ill-educated women gathered round a samovar. Besides, that was nearly a decade ago. Things are different now. *Sergei* is different."

Marya's voice had taken on a hint of anger.

"Ah—so you *have* heard of her," I replied. "I don't believe her story is mere gossip, but even if it were, there are dozens of other women with that self-same story, women who believed some man had high ideals and a noble spirit. But they are all just alike. Mark my words, Sergei will split us like the rock beneath the miner's ax, Mashenka." My voice cracked at last. "And I cannot abide the thought."

At this, Masha folded me into her arms and kissed my neck and the tip of my ear.

"Shh, my darling. You must believe me. I would never do anything to endanger what is between you and me. I am convinced Sergei is a man of ethics, a virtuous man. And if he is not, so much the worse for him. He thinks me a strong, remarkable woman, or so he has told me, but if he does not honor his word to me, in any particular, he will see for the first time what a force to contend with I truly am."

I loosened Masha's embrace to look in her eyes. I saw but one thing: her love for me. Not a trace of Sergei could be seen in those dear eyes.

And that's how we leave things. She reassures me, yet I remain uneasy. I feel as though I am walking on a crust of snow, and if I am not careful, the surface will crack, and I shall slip through to the dense white depths below. A density so absolute it will admit no light.

5
Sergei

2 March 1876

My dearest brother Kolya,

You say, in your last letter to me, you are surprised to hear I am to marry. Well certainly no more surprised than me! A man of thirty-six, I have buried myself first in my studies, then in my work at the Library. I was able, somehow, to put off Mama—dear, meddlesome Mamochka!—and her ceaseless efforts to make a match for me during my university days. I, married to Sonya Ivanovna Filippova—can you imagine a more ridiculous pairing? How often I see her name, yet, in the society pages! (And should I chance not to, Mama is most quick to point it out.) With no prospects—not but a few months prior to this, really—I was preparing myself for life as a bachelor, happy to play uncle to whatever children you might someday father. Instead, here am I, about to be married myself.

You ask how I came to meet Marya Iuryevna Zhukova. Like you, I had not been acquainted with her family. Dora Vladimirevna (the wife of my section head at the Library) impressed into social service any who were neither yet married nor betrothed: we must attend a salon given by her friend who had a niece she wished to introduce into society.

There was no point in arguing with Dora, who would have enlisted the rank of her husband to hold sway over us. Though I went grudgingly, I found myself utterly captivated. Marya is very much a modern girl, Kolya. I'm not sure you will like her, though I hope it will be so; she is not one bit like Sonya Ivanovna or like any of the girls you court. She wears her curly brown hair cropped short and disdains the frivolity of brightly colored clothing. I have never heard from her such coquetry as a giggle, but on those occasions when she is given to laughter or when she smiles, her face enchants like the northern lights. But it's her mind which truly impresses. It's quicker and brighter than a flash of sulfur. One can almost forgive her impatience with the stupid and the vain as she holds forth on her two favorite topics, Dostoyevsky and mathematics.

I have read again my description and can see you might mistake her for an unattractive person. But then I have not done her justice, for, in truth, she is quite stunning, completely captivating. I was taken with her from the first, and came back, after that Thursday evening, to her Aunt Lidia's next salon on Tuesday. Long after the others had gone, Marya and I talked long into the night. She is never at an end of topics. She has read much and on many subjects, and I am an admirer of the thought she puts into the whole of it, no matter the area concerned. She has a dear friend—Vera Lvovna Dashkova—who is never far from her side, and together, the three of us have many lively discussions. We are quite a congenial threesome.

It was clear to me, after several visits (from which I was always the final guest to leave!), there was a true spark between Marya and me. I would, no doubt, have asked her myself, in the coming months, to join me in marriage had she not come to me shortly after her aunt's death and confided it was her aunt's dying wish we marry. You may think it bold of Marya to have come to me thus with such an admission, and I will allow I myself was astonished. But it would have been merely prideful and foolish had I turned her away when likely, as I say, I soon would have asked her myself to marry. So. I am to become a husband! How strange it feels to write that word in reference to myself.

As to her family, of them I know very little still, save they are all gone now; we spend so much of our time talking of more worldly and weighty themes we rarely share the more intimate aspects of our lives. I do know that her mother, Sonya, died when Marya was quite young. It was then she was sent off to the St. Petersburg Institute for Girls. Her young brothers then died while she was away at school, as did her much beloved Papa, of whom she speaks with reverence and affection. Her only other relative, her father's sister, has also died now, as I have here mentioned. What a sad life, eh, Kolya? I feel guilty sometimes with the riches of family I yet have: you, Mamochka, Papa, and dear cousin Filya. So little we know of death, Kolya. Can we fathom how it would feel to have its icy grip in our midst? No wonder Marya clings to her friend Vera.

Now we will be a family of three, Marya, Vera, and me—or rather, a family of four. For not only will Vera stay on indefinitely with us but also with her, a curious little bird with stout neck and portly body—a bullfinch, I think she said. (You know what resolute strangers nature and I are!) She captured the glossy-plumed creature at the Summer Gardens, I understand, as part of a lesson for her young pupils and will now keep him well-fed and warm until an open-armed spring welcomes his return to nature.

But you can imagine, perhaps, how frightening marriage would be to a young woman of Marya's age and what comfort having such familiar friends nearby might bring. Have I mentioned yet Marya's age? She is but nineteen. In some ways, she is much more mature than her years would suggest—but, then, this is not so very remarkable, perhaps, when one considers the hardships she has endured. Nevertheless, she is quite young, and marriage is something of which she has no experience. Nor I, of course, but the prospect of marital relations is not so frightening for a man, I think.

You see how I go on! For all my thirty-six years, I am as excited about this marriage as a schoolboy at holiday time. It's as if Marya were my own little orange to open up on Christmas morning.

I am pleased, Kolya, you have managed to take leave to attend our wedding, especially since it will be a small affair, with only ourselves, Mamochka, Papa, Ilya Bunin from the Imperial Library, and Lev Nekrasov, who surely you remember from back home at Svetliachie Gory. He, too, has remained in Petersburg, working in the Drawing Office of the Admiralty's Baltic Works. I used to see him quite often, over dinner or sometimes cards, though of late we seem to have drifted apart. I do hope Filya will be able to attend, but though I have not yet heard from him, I suspect it will be too arduous a journey from Italy for such a short celebration.

How long has it been since we've set eyes upon one another, dear brother? I hope you will not be too startled by how much I have aged. Though still rather blond, my hair is now streaked with gray, and I think you will find some wrinkles have taken root at the corners of my eyes. And you, Kolya, how does it go with you? Are you round as our Papa yet? At twenty and nine, let us hope not! When will there be a marriage of yours to attend? How is it *you* have managed to escape Mamochka's designs thus far? Perhaps with Mamochka under the enchantment of my marriage for now, you will have time to make a match of your own rather than consent to some woman whom Mama has selected for you. Sometimes, though, I think a mother knows better who is a good match for her son than the son knows himself. Not everyone, after all, can have my good fortune.

I am eager to see you again, especially under such auspicious circumstances. I hope you will find my Marya even more wonderful than I describe. I must go now and ready myself for bed; it will be a busy day at the Library tomorrow.

Until your arrival, my fondest good wishes,

Seryozha

6
Marya

Sometimes she found herself wondering whether it wasn't better that Lidia had died when she did.

"Though may I be struck dead if ever such is what I wished!" she would think, on those occasions.

Knowing with what love, with what desire to better her life, Lidia had consigned her niece to her fate, Marya could only imagine that the outcome would prove to be so extraordinarily different from what Lidia expected that surely she would have been wounded by how it all transpired.

In the weeks before the marriage, Vera lambasted Marya again and again.

Vera, Marya could plainly see, was troubled with doubt as they embarked on this journey, which was populated entirely with unknowns and unheard-ofs. And given the unusual nature of how their household would be formed, Marya understood that these were not the sort of doubts that could be shared with anyone but herself.

Marya found it the more difficult to defend an action she wholeheartedly wished she did not have to perform.

"Little dove," Marya would say, "you must believe: I could never love this man as more than a comrade, a brother, a friend."

Marya thought Vera foolish to worry about this marriage, though she did not say so out loud.

"Yes, Mashenka, I believe this is what you trust to be true. Yet what untold others have also thought thus, only to have their affections courted and won by the man in not more than a year's time!"

Marya found it all but impossible to argue with another's history or with one's own uncharted future.

Still, more than once, Marya found herself thinking: how little did Vera know her, to suppose Sergei could ever win her heart! Marya knew that never could she find herself cherishing Sergei as Vera feared.

Worse, though, Marya suspected that Vera was not being entirely candid, that there was more she would say on this subject, if she dared. For often, Vera seemed to redouble her sweetness for no reason Marya could discern. Flattery makes friends and truth makes enemies, Marya reminded herself—the whole while enjoying Vera's cooing overtures and tantalizing touch, just the same.

Or perhaps Vera meant but to seduce Marya from Sergei for good and all? And then Marya would deem such a thought absurd, for how could Vera fail to perceive it was alongside *her* that she bedded down each night—nights filled with more than chaste sleeping, what's more.

And yet Marya suspected that Vera might be withholding herself to some degree in their nocturnal twinings as well. Perhaps so she would have less to lose should Marya not hold steadfast to her vows to Vera?

Thus, on more than one occasion, fingers tangled in Vera's hair, Marya would bury her nose in Vera's cheek and speak not of love, per se, but of household arrangements—a curious form of wooing.

"Verochka."

Marya's heart ached at the breach she sensed had opened between them, and the ache gripped her voice so that she whispered.

"Seryozha—"

Marya paused, barely able to abide speaking his name in their bed.

"Seryozha knows it's with you I shall share a room—a bed, this bed." Marya's voice, though a whisper, was urgent. "I have told him."

Marya leaned on her elbow, then, so Vera could see her face and how thoroughly awash in sincerity she was.

"Verochka, I swear to you, he is resigned to—nay, in fact, is quite accepting of—having his own rooms in the house. Without benefit of my company. Save at the dinner table and at tea, where always you shall be with us, my darling, and may see for yourself whether there are any secret intimacies flourishing between him and me."

Marya studied her partner's face to see how her words had landed.

"Yes," Vera said. "Of course. Of course—how foolish of me!"

But Vera's reply fell short of the heartiness for which she seemed to be aiming.

"Verochka."

Marya kept her voice gentle, as if she were attempting to approach a rabbit in the forest.

"Think a moment of Chernyshevsky's tale, of Dmitrii Lopukhov's marriage to Vera Pavlovna and how he stepped aside when she fell in love with their best friend. Seryozha is Dmitrii Lopukhov made flesh."

"That's it exactly, though, Misha: the tale you describe is but fiction. And it's not to another man you shall give your love but to me. How can any of us predict the outcome of such a story?"

Marya wanted to lie back on the pillow and release her frustration—pound the bed with her fists, give out a scream of vexation—at being confronted yet again with an argument so quintessentially impossible to refute. And yet she knew that the least sigh from her would shoot fear into Vera's veins like water from the Gulf of Finland in winter.

Instead, Marya was careful to let no undue exhalation or word leave her lips but silently stroked Vera's soft cheek and her worried forehead. And she took comfort in Vera having called her Misha, an indication, to her mind, of the deep ties that yet bound them, for it was a name she had shared only with Vera—a name she trusted Vera alone to use with full knowledge of its significance.

For though Misha was a boy's name and had been used by Marya's schoolmates at the Institute to mock her and make fun of the boyish interests and mannerisms she'd brought along from her home in the country—from her beloved Khrupkaya Luna—Marya had secretly treasured the name for how it unwittingly promoted her to the rank of male.

She may have been only nine years old when she first arrived at the Institute, but already she'd learned much—primarily, that women were second-class citizens, regardless of one's place in society, unable to travel abroad without the consent of a man, unable to pursue a higher education. A woman in Russia could never be an explorer, a scientist, a banker, a soldier. What was left to women was the kitchen, the nursery, the needle and thread.

Marya, at nine, knew she wanted to be more than a spectator in life. They thought her a boy? So much the better for her aspirations!

As she grew older, of course, she became aware that to advance in life would take more than being given a boy's name of her own, yet she cherished that name and kept it in her heart like a talisman, a good luck charm, a reminder of her truest self. But given the level of disdain reserved for those who were careless of the latest women's fashions—like the nihilist girls (the *nigilistka*)—it was clear to Marya that her coveting this boyish name was unlikely to be met with approval. Consequently, it was not a piece of herself she readily shared.

When at last she had confessed the story of how she'd been taunted with the name Misha, and confessed also her well-guarded love of that name, she could not breathe for fear Vera would think her a freak, the sort of creature that, had it not thrived, might now be found among the jars in Peter's Kuntzkammer—albeit her deformity was not one that might be discerned with the eyes. An unfortunate to be pitied perhaps—if Vera did not outright revile her—but never to be loved.

Looking back, Marya could hardly believe she'd confessed all this to Vera—what astonishing things one says when passion marches one's brain before the tip of its saber! But the joy she felt when Vera told her "Misha" suited her, and how that suitability did not trouble her in the least, made the risk she'd taken feel doubled in value.

From then on, when no one else was around to hear, Vera often called Marya "Misha"—a name that gave each of them pleasure: Vera because it symbolized the trust Marya placed in her with the very sharing of this confidence, and Marya, that Vera did not find her repugnant for the importance she placed in claiming something so male for herself.

While Marya looked for comfort in these memories, Vera dropped into a shallow sleep as Marya continued to stroke the backs of her fingers across Vera's cheek—letting her know that she was still there, would always be there. As she let her hand slip lightly atop Vera's hair like a falling kerchief, she bent over and whispered:

"Only you, Verochka. Only with you do I share my innermost soul. You are my one desire."

A shadow of sorrow or grief or something dark as a cloud flickered over Vera's brow and she moaned softly in her sleep.

7
Sergei

8 March 1876

Dear Filya,

I was most saddened to hear you will not be able to attend my wedding, though not especially surprised, I confess. It would be a long journey for just a few short days of festivity. Perhaps, though, once Marya and I are wed, I can come for a visit.

Does it alarm you to hear me say, before I am even married, I will part from my bride for so long a time as a visit to Italy? I will tell you something I have not told even Kolya: Marya and I are to have a nihilist marriage. Do not be sad for me, though, Filya. I have undertaken this marriage of my own choosing. If I do not seem to fit the part to you, perhaps in some ways you are right. To begin, I have never been one for politics. Most days, I am far too lost in my books to even notice there is a world beyond. You, of all people, should know how I am. Remember at Svetliachie Gory how you would beg me for a game, and I would put you off, saying always, "Just one more page"?

Yet if you stopped to consider the injustice a woman like Marya must endure—a fine mind the world would as soon keep idle—you, too, would throw yourself upon the tenets of nihilism and rescue some like girl from a life of subservience and boredom! How will I rectify this injustice? you may ask. I have thought long on this, and one thing I can do for certain is help satisfy Marya's thirst for knowledge by selecting items from the Library's collection to bring home for her. She can come to the Imperial Library herself, of course, but so few women make their way to our doors at Nevsky Prospect and Sadovaya Street that those who do so feel rather unwelcome there. I will therefore see to it she has whatever book she might like. And if I have lived as a bachelor these thirty-six years, I can continue to live as such some years longer. For a nihilist marriage offers me some freedoms, too, Filya. I will not have to fear, like many husbands, being forced to endure round upon round of social engagements by a society wife. I will be free to study and expend my time as I choose.

But can you not see how Kolya would have little understanding of this arrangement? For a relatively young man, he is in many ways old-fashioned: smoking and gambling and I do not wish to think what else with his fellows in the Guard. And yet he is my brother, and so I cannot help but love him. I remember him, too, as a boy. How wonderfully dear he was—remember how he would dance when Mamochka played the piano? I dare not remind him of that now!

And what of you, Filya? Will you find me less a man now, as I enter this marriage, for not taking what a husband has a right by law to take? Of course I hope you will look beyond what is traditional in a marriage and see some nobility in what I commit myself to here; above all, however, I beg you to answer truthfully. I will be anxious, nonetheless, until I receive your reply. If I am convinced what I do is right—undertaking a marriage such as this—I ought steel myself and let it not matter what anyone thinks, even you, dear cousin. Yet I long to have at least one ally. Perhaps I yearn to be assured what I am about to embark on is not a naive mistake. But of course, if you do have any reservations, any cautions you wish to tender, by the time I receive your reply, it will be too late: the vows will have been taken and I will need to learn to live with what I will have done.

If only you were here, you could doubtless calm my fears. Remember how, when I was at the university and you were at the Academy of Fine Arts, we used to talk late into the night, firing up our conversation with strong tea or loosening our tongues with vodka? I do so miss our frank discussions. Why can you not paint the Russian landscape for a while instead? There are whole portions of your paintbox which I am sure lie all but unused! Yet what glorious sun-filled vistas you must see where you are. Can I blame you really for wanting to escape our cruel weather here in Petersburg? You have a chance to take your boots off well before May, and here I am trying to tell you to come back.

Well, *mon ami*, I must put an end to these nervous ramblings and get some sleep. I will await your reply with trepidation.

Your foolish cousin,

Seryozha

8
Vera's Journal

Saturday, 18 February 1876

The eve of the wedding. Marya and Sergei are entertaining his parents, Petr Vasilyevich and Liudmilla Pavlovna, who have arrived two days prior by train from their estate in the Crimea. They are staying here, as Seryozha's apartments are too small. They are nice enough people—Petr is large and robust and is entirely bald on the top of his head with thick wooly masses of white hair on either side, and Liudmilla, who one suspects is rather younger than her husband, is plain but with animated features; she has entertained us with delightful stories of her youth. Nikolai, Seryozha's brother is here as well from his post with His Majesty's Hussar Guards at Krasnoe Selo, as are Seryozha's friends Ilya Bunin and Lev Nekrasov.

Despite their congenial natures, I have excused myself from sitting with them after dinner this evening, pleading illness. Marya implored me with a look to stay longer there with them in the parlor, but I could not bear it. I am now in my nightgown, propped up on my pillows amid the blankets, writing by candlelight. For though my head does ache, I am far too full of apprehension to yet sleep. So I write about the wedding, which certainly will not quell my apprehension, yet it's what most occupies my thoughts just now.

Mashenka's dress is simple but altogether lovely: white silk with pearl trim at her wrists and at the hem. Tomorrow she will wear a long veil with a wreath of cherry blossoms and laurel. I am to help arrange her hair and dress her in the morning. What irony is there in that! Marya offered to excuse me from this task, not insensible to my feelings on the matter of this marriage. Though there are no kin who might assist her in her preparations, she assured me Nadezhda would willingly perform these duties. But is it not right my hands, my loving hands, fashion her into the bride? So I tell myself, but I am at odds to explain my own logic. I only know there is no occasion when I do not long to feel the heat of her. And there is the fear, of course, that the morning of the wedding may be the last opportunity to do so. Despite Misha's assurances, I remain wary about our future.

9
Vera's Journal

Sunday, 19 February 1876

I have paced and paced until I can do so no more. Now I sit and furiously scribble, before it's time to arrange Marya's hair and place the veil and wreath upon it. Misha—married. It's only a matter of hours now. I try to believe nothing will change, as she tells me over and again.

Misha has gone for her bath. I gave her a bundle of dried rosemary and lavender with which to scent the steam. I watched from a window across the hall as she traversed the courtyard to the wooden bathhouse, which Ilyusha had prepared, watched the steam billow out as Misha opened the door to go in, imagined the fragrance of wood and herbs and steam twined together. I ought to go bathe with her, savor the scented moist air and Mashenka, but I am too full of anxious thoughts to sit idle for so long and do not trust myself not to say something spiteful or self-pitying.

Last night, when Mashenka entered the room, I startled her, as I sat upright in the bed, book in hand.

"Verochka! I did not expect to find you wakeful. Are you well, my dove?"

"Yes, of course. Why should I not be well?"

"Your head—when you left us, your head—"

"Oh. Yes. It's much better. Thank you."

"Why are you not sleeping, though?"

She came and sat beside me on the bed.

"How can I sleep, when tomorrow you will become another's?"

"Ah, this weary refrain!"

She rose, lifted her arms in frustration, and paced a few steps. Then she came to sit beside me once more and spoke more tenderly.

"Vera, have I not made known to you how I hold you more dear than life? Have I not given my solemn promise that the sole reason for this union is to fulfill Lidochka's dying wish and naught else? Would you have me deprive a dying woman of her final request? Have I not affirmed to you, many times over, Sergei will be husband to me in name only?"

"Yes," I replied. "Yes! But can you not apprehend my fears? What safety have I—I with no legal claim to you or to anything? I am all adrift in this, with no precise place, no guidance on the proper way to conduct myself."

"Oh, Verochka. Would I could soothe your fears, kiss away your pain, but there is naught to do now but watch as our lives unfold."

She cupped my cheek with her palm and said, "You are my heart's delight, you know."

She got up then to undress for bed, and I watched, my head on the pillow.

She reached to the small of her back and undid the button there, letting the folds of the black wool skirt gather round her ankles like neat piles of soot. Then, her back to me, I watched her arms move as she undid the buttons of her blouse. She slipped it off and draped it across her desk chair. The curves of her shoulder blades stood like a summons above the soft material of her chemise. I bit my lip and closed my eyes. As always, I was undone by her beauty. She slipped her petticoats off, then, and gave a small shiver, for despite the lit stove, there was a chill yet in the room as winter stubbornly held us in its glacial reach. I savored the delicate arch of her foot as she stepped from the circle of her clothes to the polished floorboards, drank in the buttermilk tone of her skin, felt a knot of desire travel the length of my torso when she carelessly pushed a lock of hair from her face as she bent to pick up her clothing.

I wanted to believe her. I wanted to believe her love for me so strong it would rout all other claims on her heart. Trepidation, however, is bred by the unknown.

As Marya slipped into her sleeping gown, there was a commotion outside the door—much shushing and suppressed laughter. Masha was about to go to the door, when whoever was on the other side broke out in song: it was the servants, come to sing their customary pre-wedding epithalamium. When I realized they were singing a wedding song, I pulled the pillow over my head and tried not to hear.

After they had left and after Marya had herself fallen into a restless sleep, I tossed and turned and thought about Sergei. I remembered those first meetings with him, how gentle and respectful he seemed, compared with the others gathered at Lidochka's salons. I was struck by his sharp intelligence and his love of books, impressed by his status as a librarian at the Imperial Library, moved by his deference to Marya while at the same time not being vanquished by her fervent opinions. Unlike the other fops and fools, he did not take offense at Masha's vituperative discourse. Or if he did, he did not let it wound his pride and send him scurrying like his fellows. In truth, I was rather fond of him. Soft-spoken and kind, he was a pleasure to converse with. In this way, recalling my earliest sense of him, I hoped to calm my fears.

Why do I not trust him? I ask myself, after I have composed my litany of admirable traits. It's not Sergei I do not trust, I think, but, rather, this damnable union, which is meant to develop in a prescribed way—of expectations that go with marriage, there are a wagonload. While Masha would have it go another way, it seems easy for there to be misunderstandings, promises mistaken by one to be an agreement by another which that other never thought he was making. It troubles me yet, too, that Seryozha should agree to this marriage. I know it's the way of the time, that the platonic marriage is a tenet of nihilist practice, but Seryozha does not quite fit the picture of the nihilist. He is older than most of that type and does not adopt their coarse and rude ways. He is much too polite to be a nihilist! I believe he sincerely deplores authoritarian relationships (in this, he is nihilistic), and he is progressive in wishing autonomy for women, but, lord, he is no nihilist. His motives are, nonetheless, likely pure, but his heart—I am not sure his heart follows his head. I fell asleep at last, grudgingly admitting to myself that in all, though, Sergei is a good and decent man.

With the marriage only hours away now, however, it's hard to keep his goodness uppermost in my mind. I know there are sound reasons for this marriage. A marriage would lend an air of respectability to Masha and ease her way in the world. Yet her marriage does naught for me—shall I, then, marry as well?

Not even in a fit of ill temper or in jest can I say that! Likely I would never find someone to match Sergei in his kindness, his nobleness, his good nature. And even could I make a similar match, such would, without a doubt, put an end to Marya and me. No, there is naught to do now but wait out the future, as Masha herself has suggested. There is reason to hope all will be as she says, though the future, to be sure, is written as with a pitchfork on the water.

10
Marya

For the sake of Sergei's parents, Marya and Sergei did their best to observe the usual wedding customs. But since Marya's entire family had passed away, some adjustments needed to be made—starting with the performance of the blessing. With no father of the bride, who would fulfill that duty?

Marya would have been the first to declare that she did not care a fig about the wedding, with all of its foolish customs. For her, it was a way to bring Lidia peace where she lay in her grave and nothing more. Nevertheless, to have Sergei's father recite the blessing in her father's stead seemed to her a denial of her Papa, who's death yet rested like a stone on her heart. Still, what was to be done? Her father was indeed gone, and that was an end of it.

Thus, once all had gathered at the apartment at no. 112 on the Moika at eleven o'clock, she and Sergei knelt in the doorway before Sergei's father. He began by exhorting them to love one another always. When Marya glanced at Sergei, she was surprised to see him close his eyes as though moved by his father's words. This both puzzled and troubled Marya, but then she thought perhaps this was only part of an act to convince his parents that their liaison was genuine.

Sergei's father then charged him with providing rules for Marya to live by. Marya tried not to react but could not keep from narrowing her eyes at the thought of Sergei dictating how she ought conduct herself. Her soon-to-be father-in-law was oblivious to Marya's tamped down anger, though, and blithely continued, bending to kiss the bride and groom with great solemnity.

Then Sergei's mother, brother, and Verochka kissed each of them, after which Ilya and Nadezhda kissed them both on the shoulders while Liudmilla and the other servants stood and looked on.

Marya, seeing the blissful look on Sergei's face, again worried that he might be succumbing to the romance of the moment. But what did that matter? For whether he was or was not swayed more ardently toward her, he had made an agreement with her and was bound to abide by it.

When the wedding party arrived at the church, the vigil lights were flickering before the large icons of Christ, and the air was richly scented with the odor of burning oil and old incense. As they entered, each of them kissed the icon of the crucifixion on its stand, which stood in front of the royal doors—ornate and gilded as befit the emperor they were long ago designed for. Though Marya was no great believer, she nevertheless felt a chill run through her when she kissed the crucifix. The icon her father had given her when she was born was then placed on a small table nearby as though her father might somehow still bear witness to her marriage.

But she brushed aside this thought as nonsense and wondered briefly but bitterly whether, had her father not died, she would even be in this situation. Could not she and Vera have lived peacefully side by side at Khrupkaya Luna? Surely her father would have allowed her a dear companion.... But a nightingale, she reminded herself, can't be fed by fables or other flights of fancy.

Looking to shorten the ceremony wherever possible, Sergei and Marya chose not to have a choir or chanter to intone the liturgical responses, despite protests from Sergei's mother. The prospective spouses stood before Father Nikolai in his ecclesiastical vestments as he blessed and incensed them, along with Marya's icon. Father Nikolai then intoned several prayers with the deacon who had been assisting him.

So traditionally did the ceremony proceed, it would have been hard for anyone present to discern that the bride and groom were merely playacting for the benefit of others. This brought to Marya's mind the old adage, "all cats appear gray in the dark," and she was glad that Vera was not there, having pleaded illness again. As much as Marya had tried to shine light on every dark aspect of this arrangement with Sergei, Vera saw gray and only gray.

Consumed as she was by such dreary thoughts, Marya nonetheless soon found herself having to suppress a smile. Sergei's brother Nikolai and his friend Ilya had been selected to hold the heavy brass crowns over the heads of the bride and groom during the many prayers and readings, as well as during the procession that followed the wrapping of the priest's stole around Marya's and Sergei's joined hands.

But as they made the third turn around the lectern, the priest leading the couple by the cloth that symbolically bound them, Marya could see that their attendants were flagging. First Ilya's, then Nikolai's arms began to tremble. Mercifully for Nikolai and Ilya, Marya and Sergei exchanged their marriage pledges before the crowns could clatter to the floor.

As Marya and Sergei slipped their rings on one another's fingers, Marya released a small sigh of resignation. It was done. She had fulfilled her promise to her aunt. This meant to her only that soon she could return to her life with Vera. And she would make Vera see at last that they could not be split apart with so dull a wedge as a man.

With the ceremony at an end, the entire wedding party returned to the rooms on Moika and sat down to a long, leisurely dinner. Even Vera joined them, though she did so with some reluctance, not relishing the thought of looking on as all at the table reveled in the creation of a newly married couple. But she had grown weary of her own fears and suspicions and wanted to make a step toward trusting what her head—and Marya—told her to be true.

As for Marya, she found herself surprisingly relaxed, the free-flowing champagne no doubt aiding her ease. Among other things, she was relieved that Sergei had convinced his family that she was quite shy and so they shouldn't call out "Bitter! Bitter!" and expect the bride and groom to kiss "to sweeten the meal." To Marya's way of thinking, having this barbaric tradition out of the way meant they were nearly done with the worst of their charade. She began to celebrate.

Then Kolya nudged Sergei at the table, winked, and said, "So, will the next generation of book-loving scholars begin this very night?"

Marya had focused the greater part of her anxiety on the wedding itself and had pushed aside any thought of the wedding night. Had Sergei's family been staying elsewhere, there would have been no problem of course. But since they would be staying yet another night all together in the same apartment, it would be impossible for Sergei and Marya to sleep in separate quarters on what everyone assumed to be their first night together as man and wife!

The color drained from Marya's face, and she abruptly excused herself from the table. Vera rushed after her, with Sergei nearly on her heels.

"Kolya!" they heard Sergei's mother scold from where they stood in the next room. "You are not among your soldier friends now. Must you be so indelicate?"

"But Mama," Kolya began his protest.

Marya heard no more of her mother-in-law's reproach as she and Vera began to talk in heated whispers. Though Sergei had followed, he now held back, stopping just at the threshold, beyond their view. He knew his mother would have expected him to go after his distraught new bride, but he was far less certain of what Marya might want.

"Oh, Masha!" Vera's tone gave little clue as to whether she spoke in sympathy or reproach.

"Clearly, Verochka, I am not in the habit of taking a husband and sharing my home with his family on the wedding night! With the many other anxieties I suffered about this day, I had not thought about whether sharing a bed with him this night would be subject to scrutiny."

Vera turned away, then, but Marya couldn't tell whether it was in response to her words or because Sergei had stepped into the room.

"Marya, Vera." Sergei touched them each lightly on the arm, Vera's back still to them.

"Forgive me for not having thought more deeply about this complication. We should have planned a short journey to begin directly after the wedding to avoid this difficult situation."

After a pause, he said, "I know it's an awkward state of affairs, but it's for this one night only. I will enter the bedchamber with Marya at the hour we retire, and sleep fully clothed on the divan."

Vera turned then, her suspicion not at all hidden.

"We … we can make a curtain of bedding," Sergei stammered, "to better separate us, so … so that Marya can retain her modesty."

Vera chewed her lip, considering this offering from Sergei, wondering whether it was proof of goodness or merely a subterfuge to lull her—both herself and Marya—into a sense of trust. Not that it was hers to say. She felt again the weight of her outsider status.

"I don't doubt I can trust you, Sergei," said Marya. "And even if I cannot, I am not in the least worried about any advances you might think to make. I know my own mind. Even if I am called a pot, no one may put me in the oven."

Though the saying was an old one, it took on a lurid connotation in the current context, at least in Sergei's mind, and a blush seeped up through his beard.

"But I ask you again," Marya continued, seemingly unaware of the discomfort she'd caused, "of what import is it that the genuine nature of this marriage remain hidden from your family?"

Marya surreptitiously squeezed Vera's wrist, hoping to reassure her without drawing Sergei's notice.

"Please, Marya: well I know that, simply because I am your husband now, still I have no right to ask you to abide by my wishes. Such an archaic approach to the relations between men and women should, without doubt, be done away with."

He waved away his own introduction of this polemical discussion as not to the point.

"But … but please, Marya, if you have any small feeling for me at all, I ask this one kindness of you: that you respect my wish not to unburden our secret on my parents. They are old-fashioned in their beliefs and they would not understand our modern arrangement. Also, it would break their hearts to think I might not know the happiness they have known as man and wife.

"I know, of course," he continued, before Marya could raise any objection, "there is not but one path to happiness. For them, it's the binding ties of a conjugal relationship that are supposed to lead to happiness. While for us, it's the freedom within our union which makes us happy. But my parents … my parents," he stuttered, "they could not imagine an alliance such as ours. I could not bring them the great sadness of thinking their eldest son trapped into a loveless marriage."

"You feel trapped?" Marya smoothed the skirt of her gown, not looking at Sergei as she tried to contain her anger. He had, after all, agreed to the arrangement they'd made with full knowledge.

"No, no! You misunderstand! It's my parents who would think that. I … I have chosen freely, of my own will, out of the respect I have for you and your sex. My happiness does not lie in the prospect of making children with you or … or of satisfying the social habits of some imaginary circle of peers. Happiness for me lies in knowing I will make opportunities available to you, a single woman, which in our backward nation you could not ordinarily have. It lies in the rare opportunity I will have, in sharing your home, to discover the splendid mechanisms of your mind."

He paused then, a look of pleading on his countenance.

Vera had stepped away and put a finger between the bars of Zubilo's cage. The bullfinch—little bully, as Marya liked to think of him—hopped to a perch near her and was nuzzling her finger with his beak. When Marya turned back to Sergei, he was glancing nervously at his family, yet in the dining room.

Sergei continued, then, in an urgent whisper to Marya: "I know my wish to preserve my parents' belief about the conventional character of this marriage will cause us a certain amount of inconvenience, but it will only be for this one night. Can you not honor this last request of mine? Already you have honored my mother's wish for a typical ceremony, I know, but if you could just grant to me … to my … for my parents' sake …"

As Sergei's thought trailed off, Marya looked briefly to Vera for some guidance on how to respond but found none, in that the tense set of her shoulders had been almost ever-present since talk of the marriage first began.

Marya closed my eyes and sighed.

"Yes, Sergei," she said, "I will do as you ask. You are, after all, for whatever your reasons, binding yourself to me in this platonic coupling, so I shall honor this wish of yours. But what of Verochka? Part of what you and I have agreed upon is that Vera and I will continue to share quarters. How will we make that appear aright to your parents?"

"It's true I did agree to that, and I mean to abide by our agreement. But can we not make an exception for this one night? Can Vera not sleep elsewhere for this one night, while my parents are yet here? Again, I know I have no right to ask, but if in charity to me you could make this one exception, it would help greatly to maintain the facade—for my parents—that we are two young people very much in love."

A slight turn of Vera's head made it clear she knew her fate was being discussed. Her face burned in anger at not even being consulted.

Marya felt caught between two fires.

"Well," she said, then paused, still not wishing to make a choice. "Yes. Yes, I suppose it will do no harm for this one night only."

Marya did not wish to wound Vera, but the thing Sergei had asked of her seemed but small when of him she had asked so much, and for the entire span of his life.

Vera's view, however, was less expansive. She could not see beyond this one night, which felt to her like a confirmation of her fears and the beginning of an encroachment that might never end.

"Please," she said, her voice barely audible. "I'm not feeling well."

And with that, she pressed the back of a hand to her cheek, while with the other she lifted her skirts so she might fly more quickly from the room. Whatever impatience Marya had earlier felt with Vera's insecurity melted as she watched her ascend the stairs, tripping in her haste.

"Is she … I'm sorry if …" Sergei's face colored again, feeling he had transgressed but not entirely sure how, so chaste the plan seemed to him.

"I suspect it's nothing more than a headache," Marya said, "but let me go to her. Would you please make our excuses to your family? Tell them I will return to the table shortly, that I must check in on Vera, who has taken ill again. But do not let my absence interrupt the flow of the dinner more than it already has. Would you be so kind as to ask Nadezhda to bring the honey cake and glazed fruits?"

"Thank you, Marya!" Sergei said, his voice cracking with emotion, as he reached out to clasp Marya's hands. But so uncertain was he of what was acceptable behavior on his part in this uncharted passage that he let his hands drop dumbly to his sides.

Marya, however, did not give Sergei's awkward uncompleted gesture a second thought as she rushed to find Vera. For, even for the sake of her aunt, she would not be able to forgive herself were she to damage her relationship with the most precious being in her life.

Running headlong up the stairs, Marya thought to herself: *One night. If I can but convince her to allow me that, then I can convince her of the rest.* But she did not feel much confidence in her assertion. What she did feel confident of, though, was that never again, past this one night, would Sergei share her sleeping chambers.

11
Vera's Journal

Sunday evening, 19 March 1876

I meant not to act the role of egoist—I trust Misha; truly I do—but men, even Sergei … When did I come to think such base things of another human being? If it were not my own life hanging in the balance, surely I would be more generous in the assessment of his character. Yet I cannot seem to keep from speculating about what might happen, though I know I am but spitting at the ceiling.

And so here I sit, writing in the deepest part of the night, for there is no question of sleep, when my ear is tuned to listen for any small noise that might suggest he has torn aside the sheet that separates them or crept into her bed, invited or no.

When I close my eyes, the temporary transformation of our—Misha's—bedroom is quite vivid to me. For when Misha came to find me after consenting to Sergei's plan, she invited me to help her set up the room in a way that would make me feel comfortable. I knew she was sincere, was sincerely trying to set me at ease, and so I kept my uncharitable trepidations to myself for once and instead discussed, as genuinely as I was able, where we might string a rope from which to hang a sheet and where the divan on which he would sleep should be placed, and so on.

Then I went in search of Liudmilla and asked her to find a length of rope and several large sheets. I wondered what she must think of this request, but also, I was not much concerned. For what cared I about the servants' thoughts, when it was nothing of mine to hide? Though I tried not to think of the possibility that requests of any sort might not be mine to ask of this household's servants in the days and weeks to come.

As we waited in our—in Misha's—room for Liudmilla to bring the supplies I'd asked of her, Misha drew me to her.

"No," I said, pulling away. "Liudmilla might return at any moment to find us in an unseemly embrace."

"She is in my employ, Verochka. Not the other way around."

Her voice was placid as she pressed in close behind, her lips next to my ear.

I stepped away. I could not bear to be comforted by her, not tonight.

"Nevertheless, Marya, she's a servant, and servants are known to gossip. What will she think to find me here, in your arms on your wedding day?"

"She will think, my darling, that my dearest friend is wishing me well. Or she will think nothing of it at all—why concern myself over her thoughts? Whether she gossips? Another maid could easily take her place. Verochka, what is really—"

"Shhh," I said. "I think she is coming."

As if on cue, I heard her foot upon the stair.

"You see," I said.

"Verochka!" Misha said and took a step toward me, but I quickly stepped from the room to greet Liudmilla in the hallway and took the items she handed me.

"Did the Trepov family inquire at your bringing these things?"

"They did not see me, ma'am; I took the rear passage."

"Of course. How silly of me. Are they still at dinner?"

"Yes, ma'am. They are enjoying the glazed fruits and tea."

"Thank you, Liuda. You may go."

I could hear Misha pacing in the room behind me. Did she sense I was stalling?

I entered the room again with the sheets and rope. Misha looked at me and exhaled audibly.

"Here. Let me pull out this chair so you may stand and tie the end of the rope."

She pulled the chair from the desk beneath the window.

"I stand on it? Why should I be the one to tie the rope to the curtain rod?" I felt irritable and hoped it showed.

"Because you are the lighter of us and I can keep you from losing your footing while you fasten the rope. Whereas you should never be able to keep me from falling. And the way you are disposed toward me at the moment, I should not be surprised if you instead help me move toward rather than away from the window."

She poked me once or twice just above the small of my back, in hopes of eliciting a laugh. But I was not so easily jollied from my dismay.

"Yes. Fine then," I said, and I placed the sheets on the desk. I climbed upon the chair and held one end of the rope in my hand.

I leaned across the narrow desk toward the curtain rod and felt Misha's strong hands grasp me round the waist to steady me. I had little experience previously with the tying of ropes—I could not have told you one knot from the other—but I was determined our improvised curtain would hold and made do with a quantity of knots since I could do nothing to ensure their quality. As I began to settle back upon the chair from my toes, Marya gave me a playful squeeze on both sides above my waist.

"Marya!"

"Ah, yes," she said. "The servants might see."

Then I could feel her teeth seeking the flesh of my buttocks through my skirts and could not restrain a giggle. As I twisted from her hands, we both almost took a tumble, but she helped me safely from the chair.

I buried my face in her neck—ah, how feeble is my resolve!—and told her I loved her.

"And I you, my dove."

Then she lifted my chin and smothered my face in kisses.

"All will be well," she whispered. "You have my word. Now come. They will be wondering to where I have gone off. They will think you have gone into a faint and will be sending Ilyusha for the doctor if we do not hurry."

She lifted the chair to the opposite side of the room, and I tied the rope as tightly as I might to the bend in the sconce where a candle already burned.

Quickly, then, we pinned in place the sheets to form a wall before the bed, which, though without spaces between, was still quite insubstantial.

"There," I said when we had finished. "Go now."

I was anxious to be alone. Though my thoughts are a torment, I did not think I could continue to behave in a seemly fashion and could feel the hysteria rising within me. I turned to go to Lida's old bedroom down the hall where I would be spending my restless night alone.

"Verochka." Misha grabbed my arm, then, and turned me to her. "In the morning," she whispered and kissed each of my eyelids. "I will come for you down the hall and see how you have rested."

She held loosely to me, and I let my hand trail down her arm as I all but ran from the room, hoping she did not hear the small cry of fear that rose to my lips.

Will the morning never come? And is its arrival a thing for which I should wish? Perhaps the darkness ought be cherished.

12
Sergei

21 March 1876

Dear Filya, my cousin,

Some might think it passing strange a "true man" should take interest in the details of his wedding. (I think of Kolya, of course, who has the soul of a Cossack.) But I am confident you, an artist, relish the finest of details and seek out the smallest of nuances. If I am wrong about your character, I hope you will indulge me, nevertheless, as I find myself inexplicably but utterly sentimental over a wedding that's little more than a sham. Sometimes, when the substance is not there, one holds tight to the illusion—but in a sense, does that not describe precisely the business you are in?

But: the wedding.

Papa said the blessing as we kneeled in the entryway, since Marya's dear father is no longer among us to have performed that task. How Marya might react to this and every element of the proceedings concerned me greatly. What a strain it was to examine her like a specimen in a jar while trying to appear to the others as if I were gazing upon her with love! And to Masha, I must appear more indifferent to these rituals than a stranger come in off the street. For thus I believe she herself must have felt.

And yet a doubt: might she not have been moved by the solemnity of the occasion as I was? Might she not have found something of beauty in the rituals we performed? She is, all told, still a woman. Logical and inexorable though she may be, there must still beat inside her the sensitive heart of a woman. Do you not think so, Filya?

Let me tell you, though, often, I do not think Masha realizes how beautiful she is. Unlike most young women her age, she gives hardly any thought at all to her clothing and accessories, and yet in spite of herself, she is captivatingly lovely. Thus it was on our wedding day. She wore a simple gown of white silk with some appliqué. Her long veil was held in place with a wreath of cherry blossoms and laurel. Filya, she took my breath away. I will confess to you there were moments I forgot Mashenka and I were not going to be united as true husband and wife.

Tut! Do not lecture me, for I can almost hear you do so. It was naught but an evanescent faltering. You need not fear I have lost my head in this matter, nor my heart either. She and I are, as I've said, each of us bound by agreement. But let me return to safer ground and simply describe the ceremony.

The church was bright with candlelight, and after we kissed the icon of the crucifixion on its stand, we proceeded directly to the shortened service for which we had arranged, with no choir or chanter to intone the liturgical responses. Father Nikolai and a deacon intoned the prayers, we gave our marriage pledges, and returned to what soon would be our little home.

I would describe the wedding and dinner in greater detail, but I fear you already think me delaying a direct response to your most recent letter. So let me now address it without further postponement.

I would be less than honest, Filya, if I did not confess it saddens me you do not greet this marriage with the enthusiasm and encouragement for which I had hoped. Still, neither do you outright dismiss it. I thank you for that, Filya; you have proved me right to confide in you. And at least you do not chastise me for an endeavor some might see as foolhardy, nor do you laugh at me for acting the imbecile. I must tell you, though, your worries are unfounded. While you guess rightly that I do harbor a certain affection for Marya, I would not say I am in love with her. So let your concerns not trouble you: I go into this with my eyes fully open. I know what to expect and am as prepared as I can be. I am merely doing what any right-thinking man would do. I trust you would agree with me, Filya, though you did not offer your opinions, that it's a shame upon the Russian people the way we treat our women. We have freed the serfs, but what equality can there be when women are still so little valued they are not seen as separate from their fathers or husbands in the eyes of the law?

Someone who knows me less well than you might be suspicious of my motives, supposing I mean to take advantage of a young woman all alone in the world. But I know you will believe me when I say my intentions are naught but pure and honorable: I mean only to smooth her path in the world. Neither do I delude myself, though, she "needs" me in most of the usual senses of that word. I have never met anyone of her sex who is so capable. Were she allowed, I have no doubt she would provide for herself in every way without me. In the meantime, I feel pride at recognizing her situation and coming to her aid, asking nothing for myself but respect.

If she should come to love me someday, I cannot imagine I would be averse. But for now, I do not deceive myself she comes to me with the love in her heart of a wife for a husband. I tell you again, Filya, I am entirely aware of the true nature of our household-to-be and could not be happier. I will enjoy Masha's company, and that of Vera, and if it's not always Pancake Week for the cat, my life is fundamentally a good one. I ask nothing more. That Masha stirs me to my very depths with her striking looks is not a thing to be alarmed about, I think, but instead, just one thing more to sweeten what I am now on the threshold of entering.

I do so wish you could meet her. Painting is not her subject, nor mathematics yours, I fear, but I have no doubt the two of you would find common ground. In literature, perhaps—are you still a great reader, Filya? I remember our days at Svetliachie Gory, when you would come for a long summer visit, curling up together, one of us on each side of the couch, with one book or another from Papa's library, maybe Pushkin one day, Gogol the next. Kolya thought us strange; except when he was but a baby yet, he was never one to sit and read when he could be outside, hunting or wrestling with the other boys.

Tell me more, in your next letter, of Angelina and how your painting goes—let us not give my new life overmuch weight in our correspondence. I could write forever about Masha's charms—her sharp wit, the way her smile could make one cry because she leaves one feeling like one must earn it, her pleasing appearance—but then, when this letter has been blotted dry and sealed in the envelope, what of your life do I know? Tell me, dearest cousin, of your courtship. Do you find your beloved very different from a Russian girl? Have you mastered entirely, then, the Italian tongue? And I mean no pun there, dear Filya!

I would pay dearly for one of your landscapes, if only to see better in my mind the places you might stand or look out upon. Though you are far away, I have no doubt you know far more of the art scene here in Russia than I do, cousin, given that I am so often ensconced among the dusty books of the Library. If that's true, you probably know already that you and your kind—the ones who not only accepted their traveling scholarships from the Academy but chose not to return to Mother Russia—you are in ill favor with a certain group here known as "The Wanderers." But I say, let Kramskoy and the others have their Russian landscapes and their Russian peasants! While their impulse to capture the glory of Russia is a noble one, they go too far when they begin to restrict the subjects appropriate for art. I am no artist myself, but even I can see that to tell an artist what to paint is to ensure that what you have in the end is lifeless. For how can a man of the arts—a man of passion, after all—give life to what he does not love? In their own way, The Wanderers are nearly as bad as Tsar Nicholas I and his regimentation of the Academy of Fine Arts in the fifties.

I did not mean to drift so far afield here in my effort to say I am convinced any painting of yours, whatever the subject matter, is bound to be charming of its own accord. Can we arrange, somehow, for you to send a painting to me? I will have a studiolo of my own (to put it in the language of your new home!) in Lidia's apartments—I have not yet come to think of them as mine. A painting of yours to hang upon a wall there would give me a truer sense of belonging at no. 112 on the Moika. I will pay whatever you think a fair price, and I will arrange the shipping.

Please write soon, dear cousin—and let us make a bargain: your next letter to me will, in turn, be filled with nothing but you, no mention of me or my recent nuptials. If you do this, then we will be at a sort of equilibrium in our correspondence, neither too much of me nor too much of you, in the long measure. You may then tell me all the pretty singularities of your Angelina. (Will there be a wedding soon in Italy?) Be sure also to tell me what sum I should send for an original Filipp Ilyich Trepov!

I remain, your devoted cousin,

Seryozha

13
Grigorii

28 March 1876

My dear Marya,

Should I express joy at the news of your marriage? I know that's the typical response. But your measured words as you tell me of your husband, Sergei Trepov, seem to lack any particular ardor. Perhaps that's only the fault of the way the words simply loiter upon the page; were they to spring from your lips, it's possible my impression would be quite altered. I wish nothing more than your happiness, so if I withhold my congratulations, it's to be sure such gladness is yours.

I tell you, too, I am alarmed about what will become of your talents, worried the world has traded an extraordinary mind for an ordinary wife and mother. I give little regard to Pirogov and the others associated with the Ministry of Education—including D. A. Tolstoy, himself (Minister of Public Darkness, seems an apt nickname for him, I tell you!)—who feel the only reason to educate women is so they will make fit role models for their children. Bah! What nonsense. Women have contributions of their own to make to the world—and not just by bearing children! They are not, after all, simply incubators but thinking beings.

I rant. I rant, I know, but it's to persuade you of what you have to offer. Women, Masha, are making great strides. Just the other day, I read an article in *Crelle's Journal* by Sophia Kovalevskaya in which she proved a general theorem to the effect that a power series obtained from a partial differential equation in which only analytic functions occur would necessarily converge. Imagine! She has taken Cauchy's method of proof and simplified it greatly. She was not the first to try but has succeeded where all the men before her had failed. You must, Masha, you *must* find a copy of this article. Yes, you will find it interesting, but more, I fervently hope it will convince you there is reason to continue with your studies.

I have not the skill to coach you further in these matters, but you are bright enough to absorb much through your reading, and if Kovalevskaya could find a teacher and a champion, so, my dear former student, can you. There are men in Switzerland, in Germany, who know what women are capable of: go to them, Marya. Throw yourself upon their mercy and beg them to guide you. I will be your advocate—I will write to them of your facility with mathematical language.

Since you first entered my classroom, as a young girl of ten or eleven, I sensed your promise. Don't deny that promise, Marya.

With fondest regards,

Grisha

14
Vera's Journal

Friday, 31 March 1876

If ever I feel I must leave the city, must feel myself surrounded again by trees and grassy fields or I shall perish, I have found the antidote: a night at the ballet. It's a feast, a gluttonous feast, for the eyes and ears. Life in the country, when compared with a night at the ballet, is starvation. The stars, the open sky, the tousled heads of trees—I do not mean to say these are not without their own charms. But with the ballet, it's hard to compete for sheer beauty.

Last night, Sergei, Marya, and I went to see *Le Corsaire* at the Marinsky. When we had found our seats, I looked about and thought, as always I do when there, merely to sit in the theater would be pleasure enough. So expansive, so filled with color and artistic creation, so brimming with the world: Russians of every class (if you look high enough to the ceiling, at the seats that nearly meet it) and travelers from the continent over, and Americans as well. You could drown in the sea of voices. It gives me pleasure to close my eyes and give attention to one conversation at a time as the lot of them rise and fall around me. This is my singular custom to prevent getting lost in the immensity—but only after I have drunk to my fill the sight of the blue hangings bedecking the boxes, the gilt and white background of the theater's stalls and barriers, the cheery sparkle of the crystal chandeliers.

This evening last, I took off my gloves and pressed my palms to the blue velvet upholstery of my chair (still plush sixteen years from the day the theater was built!), breathed a sigh of contentment, and let my eyes drop closed.

I have been trying, in the two weeks since the wedding, to calm my fears about Sergei. In truth, seeing but little change in our lives has helped a great deal with the quelling of my worries. Sergei may now kiss Masha's hand when he takes his leave, but it's I who holds her as we travel sleep's path. It's I who knows not just the back of her hand but every centimeter of her soft skin. It's into my ear she whispers her most secret thoughts and desires. When I can hold tight to this thread, I have a magnanimous spirit toward Sergei and take pity on him or welcome him into our happiness as the mood strikes me. How ennobling it felt to include him in our excursion yesterday, to rise above my regrettably petty nature.

And thus it was with gaiety we three approached our outing—so great was my consequent equanimity I did not contrive to seat myself between Masha and Sergei and was content to close my eyes and listen to the babbling crowd with nary a fear of missing some transgression. My generosity was soon repaid with amiable banter between us as we waited for the curtain to rise, and with Masha's knee pressed close to mine when the lights had dimmed.

We watched with delight and awe as the story of the Barbary Coast pirates' shipwreck was told in mime and dance, called out "Bravo!" with the crowd when especially thrilling sequences were executed, and held our collective breaths as Medora was captured and recaptured by the slave trader.

After making our way through the throngs to the street, we sought a carriage. Masha would rather have walked, being not far at all from no. 112 on the Moika, but I had worn a yellow gown as an enticement to spring and could not bear to get it muddy walking through the thawing streets. So we fell in line with the other theatergoers to wait for a carriage. Sergei linked his arms through both mine and Misha's. Quite the proper escort, he, despite his pretensions to being a man of modern principles.

"I was captivated," said Masha as we waited, "by the seamless fusion of Petipa's choreography with Delibes's score in 'Le Jardin Animé.'"

I laughed.

"Why do you laugh?"

"I am only amused at how what you find most worthy of comment is a section approaching mathematical precision. So in character."

"Did you not find impressive," she said, her eyes narrowed to a squint, "how closely the music of movements matched the music of sounds?"

"Dear Marya! Do not take offense! I meant simply to note a telling reflection on your part. It delights me how thoroughly you have absorbed your course of study into every aspect of your life. I suspect you are right, though. Surely, 'Le Jardin Animé' will be viewed as a great achievement. So mesmerizing! My own preference, though, was for act 2 in the corsaire's cave. The energy! The variety! And you, Sergei?"

"Petipa is an artist, without doubt. I admire the way he directs the corps de ballet and the soloists as though he were a composer arranging the various instruments of the orchestra. Ekaterina Vazem was magnificent as Medora. A pas de eventails! I have never before seen such a thing. She takes pas of tremendous difficulty and makes them appear completely fluid and natural. Ballet never fails to give me a new appreciation of the human body."

"Why, Sergei!" I said.

"I meant … I did not mean …" He released our arms as though they'd suddenly caught fire. "What I intended to—"

"Really, dear. We know what you—"

"Verochka is merely feeling spirited tonight. We know you are not a wolf disguised in librarian's clothing."

Masha touched her hand to his wrist as emphasis.

Sergei stared down at Masha's hand as though it was of such rare beauty it had left him bereft of speech. Or perhaps I have put myself in his stead.

"Ah! A carriage." Masha lifted her hand from Sergei's arm. "Oh. It's spoken for already. Do you have prior knowledge of Petipa's work, Sergei?" Masha searched the street for a carriage, but every one of them seemed to have theatergoers already climbing aboard. "You speak as though you have more than a dilettante's interest."

"Ah. Yes." He fiddled with his cravat and cleared his throat. "A man unencumbered over these many years, I have been at liberty to choose my own entertainments. I have spent many nights in the company of Petipa, Madame Petipa, Vazem, Sokolova, Gerdt—though I expect I enjoyed their company a good deal more than they enjoyed mine since they in fact have never met me!

"I was especially pleased when this evening's divertissement was proposed as I have heard this may be Petipa's last appearance as a dancer. There is no one quite like him in terms of the expressive gesture. What a master of pantomime! Did you take note of how his—forgive me—passion—"

Sergei here gave a cough, as though the word might be stuck and need coaxing from his throat.

"—how it nearly exploded in the love scene with Medora? How readily he bespeaks the Byronic mood—

"But here: a carriage. Ladies?"

He took my hand and helped me to step inside, then Masha's, who must have been in an especially serene state, for she actually allowed him to do so. Sergei called out the address to the driver, climbed in, and shut the door.

"There is much to admire about Petipa," he continued, "but I most particularly appreciate his choreography, in which he mingles nuances with majestic style, technical flair with an awareness of the whole palette of the stage. I have heard the complaint that Petipa's choreography abstracts ballet to a dazzling ideal. I do not think this quite fair, however, since there are many facets to his style and an internal fluidity. If it's an abstraction, though, it's most certainly a beautiful one, capable of moving the audience with each moment of balletic grandeur. Is this not the purpose of art?"

"Well," said Masha. "I had no idea you were so well versed about ballet."

"Well, if you would—ah! A mist is stealing in from the Neva. I shall be glad of a hot stove tonight!"

He had turned to the window and peered out into the darkness.

I bit my lip and shook my head at how I'd someway managed to lose my way among three pines since the whole business of the marriage. Was it not painfully obvious that the man longed only for human company and had no ill intent?

I vowed, then, to perceive him with more charity. And to lose no time honoring that vow, I have retired early and left Masha and Sergei to converse as they will beside the warm stove in the drawing room. And, I might add, I have done so with great tranquility.

But now I look at the clock, it's apparent I have been writing for some time. I wonder of what they have talked so long—though Masha is seldom at a loss for words or topics.

Nonetheless, I do wish Masha would join me, now, in readying for bed. Should I go to her and ask? No, that would not do. She shall come when she is ready. All is fine, no doubt. Of course it is. I am merely being foolish. Still …

15
Sergei

4 April 1876

My beloved Kolya,

Thank you, dear brother, not only for taking leave to be present at my wedding but also for being an attendant. I trust you have recovered from the fit of palsy you had while holding the brass crown? Do not be affronted, dear brother—my teasing springs from a great affection, just as when we were boys you would make sport of me for burying my face in some book rather than roaming the woods with you. The woods! Such enchantment they held for you: you, lithely climbing a mizzenmast (when what I saw was the crusty trunk of an oak tree) and scanning the rolling waves of grain to the horizons for maidens in distress or pieces of eight or a pirate ship. But I have only imagined the adventure of clinging, in the wind, to the crow's nest of that oaken crown from my vantage point on the ground. For unlike you, who could scale a tree like a bear cub, I felt well the weight of earth pulling me to its open embrace and could never manage to transcend it. How different we have always been, my Kolya, yet how wonderful such differences, how rich they make our family when we unite as brothers, either at the altar or across the miles in a letter.

This reminds me, though, and I do not intend complaint, but it would be nice if for every letter of mine there were a letter from you to match. Often,

I must hear your news from Maman—and then I know such news as I get is abridged, as no doubt you withhold certain confidences from her.

It's not my wish, however, to chastise you; let us turn to more pleasant topics. Marya and I have settled in nicely together. We enjoy each other's company and a great life of the mind. Of the awkward moments of misunderstanding and hurt one so often hears tell of in new marriages, there have thus far been none. I know what you are thinking: you do not care one speck about a woman's intelligence as long as she is bright enough to know when to leave you to your own occupations; beyond that, it's her beauty and the passion of her embraces that count with you, am I not right?

But you must admit my Masha is comely in every respect. Tell me, if you would, I have judged aright—not, of course, that it matters how the world and you assess her beauty. Mashenka has an inner beauty that illumines her every feature, even during her cloudiest moments. No doubt this representation has put you in a state of amusement, and you perceive me the typical fool in love.

There is nothing, however, dear brother, typical about Masha and me, though you are too much the philistine to grasp the ways in which this is true. I say this knowing it will not offend you in the slightest, for you are the first to admit you like the meanest of pleasures: a good cigar, a Nordenskold vodka, brisk with shards of ice, a voluptuous woman eager to appear at the call of her name, and a serious game of cards. I am but your brother, and not in a position to sit in judgment of your aimless life. I merely hope you do not find yourself too often at the Lombard, trading your watch from Papa or your revolver for some quick cash. But here I go again, always playing the elder brother. You must think me insufferable. And yet I was so glad of your company at my wedding. Can you quite believe yet, Kolya: I, a married man? Nor can I.

It's a strange condition, marriage. In most ways, my life proceeds as ever it has: each day, I set to my work at the Imperial Library, which engages me as I doubt you, the quintessential soldier—never known to fall into a swoon about a printed page—could ever fully understand, and in the evening, I might go to the theater or the opera or a lecture, or join a friend in a discussion of philosophy or politics over a cup of tea. And yet I am bound to this woman, committed to share a life with her, a home, a—well, everything. You cannot imagine, Nikolai, the simple pleasure of sitting down to each meal with people who are dear to you. I, at least, never appreciated that when we were boys at Svetliachie Gory. But after years of eating a humble meal of cabbage soup and brown bread or a lonely piece of sturgeon and some kasha at a bare table by myself, I have come to value the unassuming felicity of a shared meal.

We lead a quiet life, in our small household, but the words we exchange over a meal or tea never fail to interest me. I repeat myself, I know, when I tell you Marya has one of the sharpest, most facinating minds I know, man or woman, but she continues to impress this singularity upon me with every interchange we share. There are men, I know, who would feel threatened by such a superior mind in what we have for so long declared the weaker sex. But I tell you, Kolya, I am too captivated by her insights, by her extraordinary way of seeing into the heart of some work of literature or some political matter, to notice I should feel threatened. What do I care if the thoughts most riveting to me are those of my wife? All the better, I say! It's like owning a coat which is not merely fashionable but warm as well.

Not that I fancy I own her. I don't think there's a man alive who would be capable of subjugating my wife. Why, were Masha ever to be captured by some savage tribe—Turks in great stinking kaftans or the Chinese with ribbons of mustache floating off their chins like holiday streamers—they would return her to the tsar himself and say, "Please, save us from the wicked lash of her tongue!" For she can be quite cutting when she encounters a mind wallowing in the shallows or condescending to her. Have I myself been bruised by the thrash of her words? Dear brother, I cannot even tell you. If I have been abused by her, I am in too much of a trance to even know it. It's the music of her utterances that puts me in her spell.

But you have never told me, Kolya, how you found Marya. Do not hold back to spare my feelings: give me your honest appraisal. But why do I even ask? Her charms would be obvious even to the most dull-witted fellow in your company. Perhaps my need is simply that of a brother thirsting for the approval of his kin.

And so I thirst, despite how little you really know her. Did you know, for instance, that she continues to educate herself, attending discussion groups? I have hinted it would please me to go with her on her journey of self-improvement—a sort of modest guide—but I think she hopes to surprise me with her newfound knowledge, for she wants only Vera as her companion on those evenings when she goes out to exercise her mind. She began attending the Alarchin courses before she and I met, and her dedication to making herself a commendable person is such that she continues to frequent the meetings that sprung up during the time of the Alarchin courses, even though the courses are now terminated.

The two of them—Vera and my Mashenka—are quite the pair. They are not all giggles and whispers like most young women of fashion these days. Nor, clearly, do they merely put on a show of serious conversation for me. For many is the time I will come upon them in the parlor, their heads bent together in quiet conversation. Just the other day, so lost in their shared thoughts were they, I startled them when I entered the room.

"Forgive me, Masha and Verochka: I did not mean to frighten you. What topic has made you so insensible of your surroundings?"

Vera blushed a little at being so absorbed as not to greet me upon my entering the room. But Marya, never one to be cowed by social conventions, replied they had been discussing the latest installment in *The Messenger* of Tolstoy's new novel, *Anna Karenina.*

"Ah!" I said. "Yes, as always, he begins a story that pulls you directly into the reality of the characters. May I join your discussion?"

I saw Marya quickly attempt to assess any feeling written in Vera's eyes. Perhaps the conversation between two women would muse upon different topics or in a manner dissimilar to when a man was present. But Verochka gave me the prettiest of little smiles and replied, "Of course, Sergei—please, come join us."

"So," I said, "what was it you were discussing when I interrupted?"

"Well," Verochka said. She knit her brow, then, and chewed her lip, confirming my suspicions they did not care to pursue their line of thought in my presence.

"We were deliberating about whether Pestsov was in favor of women's education," Marya said. "One minute, he is arguing it ought to be considered pernicious, the next moment, he seems in support of it, rightly assessing we are deprived of many rights because it's claimed we aren't educated enough and, by the same token, we are denied a suitable education because we don't have any real rights."

"Of course. Exactly!" I said, warming immediately to the topic. "I especially appreciated when he responded to the old Prince's suggestion that women are somehow feeble-minded by retorting this was how the Negroes were viewed before their emancipation. I would say this puts Pestsov firmly on the side of women."

"I feel the same," ventured Vera. "Pestsov speaks so passionately on behalf of women, in the end—shouting for women's right to independence and education—I can only believe Tolstoy means for us to see Pestsov as in support of women's education, in spite of at first describing such education as 'pernicious.'"

"Yes," Mashenka, replied thoughtfully. "I expect you're both right. But what really interests me is whether we can untangle which of the views in that argument represent Tolstoy's own. How shall we know?" Masha's entire face was engaged with the question.

"Oh," I said, taken aback. "One often wonders, of course, especially when a character's opinion is especially coarse or objectionable or macabre."

"Does it truly matter, though?" pondered Vera. "The important thing is such issues are raised in a form that can more readily be digested by a common population. The issues have been raised, and now, at least, they will be discussed, as we are discussing them, here in this parlor. Whether the author is for or against a matter will signify little in the discussion: each person will bring forth their own ideas because that's what means most to them."

"Yes, of course," said Marya. "But one always hopes the author is on one's side. It makes it so much easier to love his characters."

"But must we always love a book's characters?" I wondered aloud. "What of Raskalnikov?"

"No, of course not," conceded Masha. "Why, were I a character in somebody's book, I doubt I should be loved. Please," she said, silencing objections from me and Verochka. "Readers like a softer character, most typically. Women, at least. Men can be cruel—we have been raised to expect that—and still be loved. But a woman—a woman, whether a character on a page or standing before you, is expected to be sweet and pretty and compliant. I do not say it's not possible I should be loved; I who am many things that do not include a mostly tender disposition. But there would be much skepticism on the part of a reader that a woman of my character, of my temperament, could be deeply loved. It's all tied up, our expectations of women, with the issues of rights and education. Too many assumptions are made."

And so the conversation proceeded. I cannot remember every word of it, and were I able to, I trust you would soon put down this letter and turn to more entertaining pursuits. But for our little household, such conversation is entertainment enough.

Entertainment enough, I say, and in the main, this is true. This Thursday past, however, we found entertainment of the high-culture variety. Our little household took itself off to the Marinsky Theater to see Petipa dance the role of Conrad in *Le Corsaire.* He partnered with Vazem, and I tell you, dear brother, I think her beauty, her grace alone would have been enough to captivate you, if the story of shipwrecked pirates and slave trading did not accomplish this feat.

The music, too, was enchanting. There is a beautiful dream sequence, "Le Jardin Animé," which I understand is Petipa's own addition to Mazilier's Parisian version of the ballet. Petipa has outdone himself, Kolya. That sequence may be some of his best choreographic work to date. I think tomorrow, at the Library, I shall see if I cannot find a copy of Byron's poem on which the ballet was based to see if I cannot extend the pleasure of this excursion a bit longer.

And that's how it goes with me.

I plead now for word of your life. Is it true you still call on Elizaveta? How unexpected, if so. Could it be a woman has actually captured your heart? Or is this simply a romance you have invented to appease Maman, who yearns for both her sons to be out of her hair? I am aware asking you to compose a letter to your dreary older brother, the dull married man, is like throwing peas against the wall: either you will write or you will not; there is no point in asking. I will receive a letter from you, then, when I get one.

Until then, I will be

Your expectant brother,

Seryozha

16
Marya

In the moment, Marya did not remark any particular happenstances as harbingers, even though in the future she would look back and think to herself, "*There* was a sign. Ah: here was another!"

And though she would initially place the blame upon Sergei, feeling that surely it was his duty to have alerted her to aberrations of sentiment and intention, ultimately she came to realize they could share the blame and have sufficient to spare, knowing, too, that to rest blame on another's shoulders does little to lift one's own sorrow.

She suspected that the world, though, would find Sergei to be a man above reproach, deserving blame for naught: How many other husbands would take such interest in the life of a *woman*?

On one occasion, for instance, Sergei returned from the Library, his face alive with some secret pleasure.

"Good evening, Sergei," Marya said, amused at his effort to appear nonchalant. "You look like the cat who swallowed a bird...."

"I have brought you something."

"Have you?"

Under more usual circumstances of marriage, a woman in Marya's position might suppose he had brought a piece of jewelry or some other precious token. But as it stood, Marya could not conceive what he might have cause to bring her.

When he extended his hand to her, what she saw in it was a periodical.

"*Crelle's Journal*?" she said. "Is this the issue—"

"Yes, it's the—"

"Oh, Sergei! What a lovely surprise. How did you—?"

"I overheard you mentioning it to Vera. And I know how daunting the Library can be to those not well acquainted with it. As well, it's often frequented by those that make it an inhospitable environment for women. So I brought it here, for you to read at home."

She gave his shoulder a comradely squeeze.

"How very thoughtful. Please accept my thanks."

She turned, then, meaning to ascend the stairs so she might curl up in her room with this exquisite treat.

"There is … something else."

Marya twisted round to face Sergei. She cocked her head, unable to imagine what further there could be.

"You might … that is to say, I should not mind if you were to discuss with me more about your mathematical interests."

"Ah. Yes, to be sure. But I was not aware, Sergei, that you took an interest in mathematics."

"Well, yes. I mean, no, it's not my typical pursuit, but it might be that my interest would grow were I to know your passion … that is, I mean—I mean nothing untoward. What I intended to say is, were I to discover how this topic enchants you, perhaps my own appreciation would blossom."

A flush of red showed clearly on his scalp through the poor cover of his blond hair.

"Oh. Why, yes, of course. I shall take pains to include you in future musings on the topic."

"Thank …" He cleared his throat. "Thank you."

With that, he hurried off to his rooms behind the stairs.

On another occasion—perhaps the night of *Le Corsaire*, when Marya and Sergei had sat and chatted amiably after Verochka went off to bed—Sergei abruptly pushed up the sleeves of his coat and shirt, leaned forward to rest his bare forearms on his neat trousers, and pinned Marya with an earnest gaze.

"Tell me, Masha, of the substance of the meetings you attend with Vera. I have long been curious about what pulls you there, week upon week."

"How boring it would be for you, Sergei!"

Marya hoped that would be enough to dissuade him from further discussion.

"No, truly I should like to know. For undoubtedly, if it's of interest to you, I will find it of interest as well—is that not generally so?"

Marya sighed and wondered to herself how a quality that once inspired affection could become such a vexing trait. She was grateful, to be sure, that she did not have the sort of husband who felt within his rights to purloin her inheritance or rudely lay his hands upon her body. But could not Sergei find it in himself to muster up a modicum of indifference, like many another husband? Careful to do nothing more that might register her displeasure with him, she shortly offered a reply.

"But, of course. You are right, Sergei. It would appear I have not yet accustomed myself, despite our time together, to interacting with a man who wears enlightenment so comfortably."

Marya smiled in what she hoped was a convincing fashion, but the transitory frown that crossed his face suggested she had not quite succeeded.

"Come," she said, rising from her chair, "let's refresh our tea, and I shall attempt to capture for you the flavor of these meetings, Sergei."

"You must not be so formal with me always, Masha, or I shall feel like a stranger in these apartments. Please—call me Seryozha. I should like that."

He started to look away shyly, but then straightened his posture and looked her in the eye.

Marya cast her eyes down at her tea, momentarily embarrassed by his straightforwardness and feeling caught out for her earlier annoyance with him. When she spoke again, she sought for a hearty tone.

"Have I not been calling you just that, these months? Oh, surely you are mistaken, Serg—Seryozha. But come—you asked about the meetings. Let me tell you of them, though I assure you, they can often be tiresome in every respect. It's the same people, making the same arguments." Marya affected a stern tone, then, saying, "'Women must be allowed to enter our universities! That's where the fight is!'" And then, in an even gruffer voice, "'No: we must first work for the betterment of all society! What will we profit, as a people, if you and I can name each bone that lies within the body when so many in our cities and towns can see those very bones through the skin on their limbs for want of a decent meal?'"

"Oh, but, Masha! Such vital topics you address! These meetings—how stirring! Tell me: which side of the quarrel are you on?"

He edged forward on his seat, his arms again resting upon his thighs as he leaned into the conversation. He nakedly took in each detail of Marya's face, his eyes lively with excitement.

In the instant, Marya felt a flash of the fondness she had once felt for him. She hardened herself, though, and quickly put her affection aside, for fear of leading him to believe her feelings for him were other than those of sister or comrade.

"But of course!" He slapped his hands to his knees before Marya could speak. "You—you would be on the side of—. But no. You must tell me. It would be presumptuous to answer in your stead. So. Tell me."

Marya nearly smiled and thought, what a funny man, this Sergei Trepov. She felt a twinge of guilt then, that she, who had no use for his ardor, had been the one to put a lock upon it. And yet, she told herself, would there be, among women of more ordinary bent, one who would satisfy his desire for an equal in mind and spirit? Before she became more entangled in this snarl of thoughts than surely she already was, she spoke to his question.

"But Serg—Seryozha—there is no presumption involved: you know quite well I believe women must be allowed a true education, one worthy of their ambitions and intelligence. How can it be otherwise? To send women out among the people to better society now, with such a poverty of education, is like sending a workman to fix the runner of a troika with no tools. What little can be done is likely not to be done well."

"Absolutely! I agree entirely. And what do the men at these meetings say? What do they believe?"

"Men? There are no men at the meetings we attend. This, too, has been a topic of much discussion. Some of the women feel—but this I have told you already, have I not?"

"Yes, of course—how foolish of me. It was just I was so curious about what others of my sex might say—not dandies and sportsmen, like those I had sometimes met here in your aunt's parlor but enlightened men. I am not one to shout, 'To the people!' and I am no Narodnik nor even a nihilist, but

I cannot comprehend how so many of my fellows—and yes, women, too—cannot comprehend what seems quite obvious: women have much to offer."

He tugged pensively at his pale mustache.

"Perhaps, though," he continued, "I should seek out such a group of men. That is, men who are ill content to continue merely as our fathers had. Masha, would any of the women at your meetings know of a men's study group of which I might become a part? How I wish I might champion your cause, take up the banner for women's—"

"Seryozha. I know you mean well, but I do not wish your help."

"But Masha, the men at the Ministry of Education—there are other men who—"

"The battle standard is not meant for your hand, Seryozha."

"I don't mean to … I am not trying to … I am sorry, Masha. It's my enthusiasm: I only meant to help. To become enlightened. It's an issue about which I harbor great feeling. But if you do not wish for me to join the fight …"

"Thank you, Seryozha. I do not mean to be harsh, but this is a sound example of why many of us wish to keep the meetings for women alone: let a man come into the room, and always he will think he can accomplish a thing better."

"No—no, Masha! That's not my meaning. It's not my intention to take this struggle from your hands and make it my own; I simply wished to add another hand, an equal hand, in the skirmish. Truly, Masha, you wound me to think otherwise."

He pressed his fist upon his heart to accentuate the point.

"I know you mean well, Seryozha. I—" On the verge of reaching to pat his arm, Marya resisted the urge, fearful of his misunderstanding the gesture.

"If a study group is of interest to you, Seryozha, then of course you must join. Though I bear the name of wife, it's not my duty to direct your habits and your pastimes. And no doubt, to have men take up our cause will speak with greater force to those in charge than will our own voices, so often ignored. But let me not have cause," she added sternly, "to think of you as a husband looking after his wife."

She wished to scan his face to calculate the effect of her words, but he had turned aside his head and seemed to peer at the ceramic stove. He glanced at Marya, but then straightaway redirected his gaze to the dining room. Marya bit her lip. Twice he opened his mouth as if to speak, then said nothing. The ensuing silence was so uncomfortable that Marya would have ended it if she'd known what to say.

At last, speaking into his lap, Sergei said, "Yes. Yes, of course, Marya. Yes, of course. I understand. Of course. Yes."

He rose from his chair and wiped his palms along his thighs.

"I … I have some correspondence to which I must attend. Look at the hour," he said, as he pulled his watch from its pocket. "What can I have been thinking, to keep you here so long?"

"Seryozha! Wait." Marya called after he had stepped across the threshold, but with so little conviction he might not have heard her had he been yet in the room.

"Wait," she whispered, wondering what she might have said had he actually returned.

Well, she thought to herself. *Yes, you never fear to speak your mind, and this is what comes of it.*

17
Sergei

6 April 1876

Filya, my cousin,

I am cross with you. I distinctly remember asking that your next letter be about you and you alone, with no thought of me in your musings on paper, and yet you persist in addressing my situation. Very well. I will answer your questions as it seems you are sincere and not simply inclined toward courtesy.

Again you express fears my feelings for my wife are not merely platonic, those of a right-thinking, informed man of today. I am hesitant to protest, lest my protestations make me seem the more guilty of your charges. Yet should I say nothing, I shall look complicit as well. It seems I am caught between the sledgehammer and the anvil! Nonetheless, your questions interest me. I feel it's undeniably possible for a man to admire a woman for her beauty without feeling desire for her: a simple matter of aesthetics, much as I might admire in a painting the rich yellow color of a cheese or the voluptuousness of an apple without actually thinking to take a bite of either. To act on any desire I might feel for Marya would be as satisfying as biting into your painted apple, in any case, since she and I would not come together as equals. My analogy is flawed, of course, in that Mashenka is unequivocally real before me, whereas a painting lacks dimension and denies several senses. (And, as well, I must imagine entire the subject matter of your paintings as you have been woefully remiss in discussing your work with me, dear cousin.

Consider this not a chastisement but a plea: I yearn to hear of romance! The romance of the Italian countryside and of your fiancée as well.)

But to return to my original subject, if I were an artist like yourself, I should sketch Marya so you could witness the line and form—in a word, the art—of her face and experience the enchantment of it on your own. The description of my bride and the wedding ceremony, I concede, could be misconstrued as the ruminations of a man wholly taken with his subject matter. In a sense, quite frankly, I am, though not as you imagine.

If I document overly the details of that day, it's to say what a sham such ceremonies are—and I do not mean, now, simply that between Marya and myself. Ours, at least, was honest between the two of us. But others—others would make claims to a holy union or, in these more modern times, perhaps the union of hearts, when in fact they are alliances of power, agreements between two families to subjugate the daughter of one to the son of the other. If I examine the ceremony attentively, it's to expose it for what it rightly is—my warm tone notwithstanding.

There. Do I sound the nihilist now? I am not one, truly, but it's impossible to be a clear thinker and not find merit in much of what they petition for. And to watch Marya's mind going unappreciated by all but the small circle of our family is nothing short of a crime. If I long to take her hand, it's only to convey by my touch what words can never say: that I, despite my sex, understand what is in her heart, how she must hunger for an avenue for her vital mind.

And now you will remark my wish to take her hand—I nearly crossed it out, in anticipation of your critical eye. But I am all innocence, Filya. My feelings for Marya could not be more pure were she my sister. Not that I lack the proclivities of the male of our species, mind, but I am not an animal, unable to control my baser instincts.

I grow tired of this topic, though. Why is it I must always defend myself to you, cousin? Can you not trust I know my own heart? My heart, I tell you, does not harbor subterranean yearnings for my wife. She is my wife in name alone and thus, she will remain.

Still, it's difficult, some days, to take the good-natured banter of my fellows at the Library about married life, being the newest husband among them. Such a fraud I feel when I yield to their intimations, but what is to be done?—if I may quote Chernyshevsky. I could not stand their curious, disdainful stares were I to confess the truth. They would privately call me "auntie," for what sort of man but such a one as that lives with a woman in so chaste a state?

And what will I tell their wives, come next year and all those following, when Masha and I have no offspring to usher into the world? People will talk, Filya, mark my words. Not that *I* give a fig for what others say, mind. If I did, I should have traded in the lot of my Pushkins and Lermontovs for a hunting rifle many years past. But I worry for Marya's honor. An old-fashioned idea, perhaps, for a modern man such as myself, but we reside yet in an old-fashioned world, Filya. What do you advise on this matter?

I must go soon, but first I wish to tell you of my curious encounter with Lev Nekrasov. The mention of aunties is what has caused me now to think of it—though to be sure, for days after, I thought of little else. Let me take a deep breath and not start from the tail end of the tale. At the wedding, Lyova—who, as you may recall, served as one of my attendants. At the wedding, as I was saying, he and I vowed to take supper or attend the ballet together with greater frequency, for we found each missed the company of the other. Frankly, I wondered whether he had for some reason avoided my company, but as he greeted me so warmly at the church, my suspicions seemed foolish.

So. We were to meet last week for dinner, we decided. I first suggested Palkin Restaurant—at 47 Nevsky Prospect? do you know it?—where Tchaikovsky, I'd heard, and Mussorgsky and the like were known to gather. Rather like a schoolboy, longing to meet his heroes, I delighted in the thought of perhaps making their acquaintance. I wondered at the man who could create the majestic swells of the *Romeo and Juliet* fantasy-overture, marveled at he who could imagine into life *Eugene Onegin*, with all the passion and beauty of any of the most magnificent of operas. Surely I have romanticized them, but with what veneration I imagined setting eyes on them. Like gods they seemed to me, those for whom music flowed with no more spectacle than blood in the veins.

But Lyova ahemmed and spluttered and asked whether I wouldn't rather go elsewhere—"Shall we dine at Privato? I have a taste for Italian food. Would you mind terribly, Seryozha?"

"No, no—of course not," I lied, and we set off to Privato.

I had not had much experience with the fare of your new homeland and sought to make the best of my disappointment by embracing the adventure of a novel cuisine.

"Now," I thought, "I shall at last have a taste of my dear Filya's life!"

I sketched for him, as we dined, my life as a married man—in the broadest of strokes, mind you—and wondered aloud whether he had any luck in his own life finding a mate or whether he was yet, as I had so recently been, a habitual bachelor.

"Ah," he said, "ravioli!"

He pointed to a dish being carried past our table by a waiter.

"Like our piroshki," he instructed, "but smothered in a rich sauce. Perhaps that would be a good entrée into this cuisine for you?"

Thus he deftly steered the conversation from matters of love and followed with matters of the Drawing Office of the Admiralty's Baltic Works—an alteration of course on which I did not dwell, as I was eager to hear of his work, so very alien to a man of words like myself.

We chatted for some time about engineering and the Navy and about our days at Svetliachie Gory, and I resided for some time in nostalgia. When the Chianti—to what a different outlook its ruby red turns one than the crystalline vodka of the Russian people—when the Chianti, I say, had slowed our tongues and the minds behind them, my energy flagging in the warmth of our camaraderie, when capacious reflection had been lain to rest, I commented upon Lyova's beautiful red necktie.

A flush of matching color rose to his cheeks. He coughed.

"What? Oh, this. This—this. Yes, my tie," he stammered. "It's nothing."

He clumsily undid the knot and swiftly pulled the tie from his neck and stuffed it into a pocket.

"Lyova?"

"What? What? It's a crimson necktie, yes. You have found me out."

He drained the Chianti from his glass and looked away from me.

"Lyova? What on—"

"Do you think ill of me, Seryozha? Oh, please do not."

He leaned toward me, his red-rimmed eyes filled with pleading. "Tell me you are not repulsed, my dear friend of childhood."

"Lyova, dear, I have not the slightest idea what has upset you! But have I not always shown myself to be the most loyal of friends? Elaborate, if you choose (for I do not understand), or not, but it's beyond my imagining what you might tell me that could vanquish my love for you."

I grasped his elbows, where they yet leaned upon the table, and thus implored him to believe in my sincerity.

"Ah, you make sport of me."

He lowered his head.

"Lyova, no! I say to you in all honesty, I entertain no earthly idea what you fear I have discovered. All I have discovered is the depth of my feeling for you is yet as strong as when we were children."

Lyova scanned my features and judging them sincere, I suppose, began to speak, at last, of what was troubling him, though he directed his thoughts to the half-eaten scrap of bread lying yet upon his plate.

"I prefer … I prefer the company of men."

He looked fleetingly at me.

"Well, but—" I began, sensing he expected a response.

"Seryozha. Can you truly be such an innocent? I speak of gentlemen's mischief."

I knit my brow.

"Oh for godsake, Seryozha: I seek intimate relations with men."

Then he narrowed his gaze at me and waited for perception to dawn.

At last I grasped the truth.

"Oh! You are—. You engage in—"

"Yes, Seryozha. I am what is now termed 'a homosexual,'" he hissed softly. "I can see how this disgusts you."

"Oh, Lyova—no! No, it's only a momentary sadness has overtaken me that you have not trusted me enough to confide this before now."

Without a thought, I reached for his hand, and clasped it within my own to give strength to my words. And then, Filya—and I am ashamed to confess this—for an instant I wondered whether to touch him so might lead him to believe my intentions were other than friendship.

"Do not fret, brother, I have no designs on your virtue," he said, as if reading my mind. His mouth drooped in dismay. "Though if I may continue to be frank, I have sometimes wondered about your own inclinations."

"What! What I? Oh, no—no, I have always loved women, their soft skin, their—" I was positively spluttering, I tell you, Filya, in my anxiety to establish my true manhood. But at last I had enough sense to cease. I took a deep breath and recovered myself.

"Are you happy, Lyova? That's the only thing that concerns me."

"Not entirely, Seryozha—but not because of how I am! I have had done with the guilt and self-recriminations for quite a long time now. I am content with who I am. What leaves me short of absolute contentment is a wish for a—mate. Someone such as your Marya. Only, of course … a man."

His eyes burned with fervor.

And then, Filya, I nearly told him, nearly confessed all to him as I have to you: how my marriage is one of higher purpose, that it is not replete with tender embraces and wild passion, that there is no expectation of—as he might suppose, I mean. Let him see me as his ideal, as his own hope of love.

"But is that possible?" I said, struck by a thought. "Are there truly enduring partnerships between men? I have not heard of such a thing."

"It's not much talked about among the general populace, I'll grant, but yes, it's done, and it's somewhat tolerated, even, by men of our class. Prince Meshchersky and Burdukov, for example—Meshchersky, who publishes the newspaper *Grazhdanin*? Count Vladimir Lamsdorf (the diplomat—you have heard of him, perhaps?) and Prince Obolensky, who lives with him. If you frequented more society events—soirees and that sort of thing—the whispers of scandal would likely have made their way to you."

He paused, and we pursued our own reflections for a moment.

"I do not regret who I am, but I do yearn for the sort of domestic camaraderie of married life. Someone with whom to share meals, to select furnishings—to make a home."

"Now this, Lev, truly I can understand! How lonely is the solitary plate upon the table. Plates and mugs are meant to dwell in pairs with others of their kind." Then a thought struck me: "But how is it you can even hope to meet someone of your … who has your … that would be interested—"

"Oh, there are places. Discreet ways."

"Places? What sort of ways? Should I have met you on the street," I said, and loosened my tie in an uncomfortable flash of heat, "or here—that is, now—after nearly thirty years of friendship—I should never have guessed you were a … that you—"

"Ah, but now I have made you uncomfortable! Forgive me, dear friend. I will leave this instant." His chair scraped the floor as he rose.

"Stop!" There was more force in my plea than I had intended. "I mean, please do not leave, Lyova. It's not that I am … uncomfortable. I just do not know—this is a new subject for me, and I fear giving offense."

"If I promise you I will not take offense, will you promise in return to worry less about the words you choose? The questions you ask? If we are to remain friends (and I should like that very much), we cannot let my … proclivities form a wedge between us."

"Yes, I shall try. In short, let me say I would find it of the greatest interest to hear whatever more of your life you choose to share. I do not wish to seem like a voyeur, but Lyova, your life to me right now could not be more foreign than were you a sheik on his camel in the desert!"

"Dear Seryozha, I am not all that different! I yearn for love, for human contact, for food and drink much the same as you." He held up his hand then to silence my apology. "I take your meaning, though, my friend. I have withheld much from you since we have come to St. Petersburg and have kept some distance between us toward that end, for which I apologize. I should have trusted in your goodness. But even the best of people … But never mind. You asked how it is I can meet others like myself—or almost asked!"

His smile was brighter with this teasing than any I had seen for many a year upon his rugged face.

"But there are many places, signs, such as a red cravat—" Here he pulled his own partway from his pocket before thrusting it again away. He poured more Chianti into each of our glasses and ran his hand through his thinning hair. "Ah, where to start? It was all quite a muddle to me, when I first arrived here. I had long suspected where my true interest resided, and at boarding school, it was not hard to find others of a like mind. Surely, you yourself—no? Well, but of course your head would have been buried too far in a book to have noticed anything so worldly. But I … well, let me skip beyond all my childish searching and fumbling and tell you—and once I tell you, you will begin to see the city in a new light—tell you of the times and places where we seek out our kind.

"The Znamenskie Baths, the Passage (at Mikhailovskaia Square), public toilets (yes, I know—dreadfully degrading), Wednesdays at the Marinsky for ballet performances, Konnogvardeisky Boulevard—Palkin."

"But I've been to all those places!" I blurted out.

"Yes, of course you have, dear boy." Lyova gave a bemused smile.

"But how did I not … how do you—Palkin Restaurant? With the pipe organ and the stained-glass windows of Hugo's 'Notre Dame de Paris'? Where I had wished to dine tonight? *Palkin Restaurant*?"

I could not take it all in. And you, Filya—do you know all of this? Or is it only I who have remained so ignorant?

"Then why did we not go there tonight, if it's a place you like, where your … friends can be found?"

"Ah, but Seryozha: I worried my life, the hidden me, might be exposed to you—a careless comment from an acquaintance, a compromising caress on the shoulder …"

He shrugged and held his palms out. Then bitterness overtook him for a moment.

"Of course, I have stupidly exposed myself on my own—I am glad I did, however," he added.

"Palkin Restaurant," I said, and shook my head. "I cannot believe … The ballet? But. So tell me, Lyova—have you ever had … have you ever been in love?"

"You mean you think that I … you are not merely …?" I could not read his countenance as he pierced me with his gaze—anxiety? Gratitude? Relief? But he bested whatever had caused him to stammer and went on.

He sighed heavily and said, "Yes. After the time when I was a schoolboy (when often I became enamored of my classmates), there was once. Or at least I let myself believe it was something as noble as love.

"Mostly, the men I meet, the encounters are too … swift. Clandestine. For any wick to be lit. But … one Saturday, I took a stroll near the Cinizelli Circus, where young men who are … that will allow themselves to be hired—no, do not think me so sad, Seryozha. Do not judge me in such a way. It was not my regular habit. Only, the loneliness, it can sometimes be so …"

"Deafening? Like your head will explode between your ears if you do not hear some other voice than the one sighing so forcefully in the space of your skull?"

"Ah! You *do* understand, my old friend. Yes. In the main, I have learned to be content with my own thoughts, my own meager company. And then, at other times, I may perform unwise actions, like bargaining with apprentice boys for their company. Sometimes, I have bought them a ticket to the performance there, so that I might sit close beside another being and feel the press of a leg against mine, fingers looking for mine beneath a folded coat.

"One evening, however, several years past, there was a sweet-looking lad: Rodion Pavlovich. My darling Rodya. He looked even younger than his twenty-two years, with his creamy skin and a vivid bloom of rose to his cheeks. He had a crooked smile, his nails were bitten and dirty, but he was otherwise clean and nicely dressed. He asked if I would light his cigarette for him. 'No, I do not have a match. I am sorry.' 'It's nothing,' he replied. 'It's too expensive a habit for a man of my meager means, at any rate. Would you … care to buy me a ticket to the circus?'

"His manner was almost shy. Not quite so practiced as the other young men one so often encounters there. 'No,' I said. 'No, not tonight. I am too pensive for the noise of the circus.' 'Well,' said he, 'shall we walk along the Fontanka? The water lapping against the canal walls can be wonderfully soothing, I find—if you do not mind some company, that is.' Again that shyness. I looked him over once more. His ears a little large, his hair a ruffle of dark curls, carelessly combed and falling over his eyes, the color of rich, dark mud.

"'Why me?' I asked him.

"He shrugged. 'I see you are a good man.'

"'You were looking at me, then?'

"Again he shrugged. 'It pleased me to look at you.'

"'I please you a little then? You find me pleasing to your eye?'

"Already, we found ourselves leaning against the wall of the Fontanka. I stood apart from him, but he pressed closer and leaned his head against my shoulder. The moon was quite full and danced on the water. I felt a quickening in my belly. I knew I should not trust him who I found trolling the grounds before the circus, looking to hire himself for the pleasure of some strange man. Perhaps it's only because he needs the money, an act of desperation that he sells himself to strangers, I told myself. I took him home with me and we … In the morning, I pressed several rubles into his hand, feeling quite ashamed of myself in the light of day. I wished to be done with him, to wash my face and start the new day clean. Free.

"He refused the money. 'Did you think …? No!' he said, 'I am not like that, like the others.' If he had not already begun to dream of a life with me, he says, of going for walks, of improving himself with me, going to the theater, he should be cross with me for thinking of him in so base a way. And then he stood upon his toes, and kissed me. Just like that! Likely I should feel humiliated to tell you, Seryozha dear, how much this simple action enthralled me, how I flooded with pleasure. But so hungry for affection was I, willingly I believed he wished …

"For a month he shared my bed. 'My cousin from the country,' I told my landlady so as not to arouse suspicion. Happy? Yes, I was happier than I'd ever been. And when we had begun what might be—yes, it might be possible—for us to have a life together—" Lyova snapped his fingers.

"And then?" I was as breathless to learn the outcome to this as any love story.

"And then, my dear friend," said Lyova, pausing to consume a long swallow of Chianti, "and then, he simply disappeared."

"That's preposterous!" I told him. "A man does not simply disappear. Surely he gave you some inkling, some idea—"

"No, I swear to you: nothing. We parted company one morning in the courtyard to my apartment, with a plan to meet for dinner that evening, and from that night forward, I have dined alone." Lyova shrugged.

"But Lyova! Have you never sought him out?"

"Yes, for a time, I looked for him at the Cinizelli Circus and others of our haunts, but it broke my heart, each time, not to find him. And how much the worse, I cautioned myself, to find him, but in the company of another. So I stopped seeking for him."

"But are you not curious?"

"I was, to be sure. Did he find another … friend? Someone wealthier? Someone more to his liking? Did he meet with foul play? Had he found shame, at last, in setting up housekeeping with a man? I could see no method of inquiring after him that would safeguard the nature of our relationship and so in the end I set aside such useless pondering."

"And there has been no one … since?"

"I guard my heart more closely now, in my encounters. And they, the men, I … meet, they are guarded as well, and so we are like trains, clad in metal and heat, passing but for a short stretch on nearby tracks, then parting to different provinces."

"But how will you … how can you hope … with such an attitude—"

"How can I hope to find the sort of life that Meshchersky and the others have managed? Ah, there is the question! It's a question for which I have no answer at present but which I hope will one day make itself clear to me. Look at you! If an old man such as yourself could find love, surely there is hope for an old man like me as well."

"Yes, well," I started, but uncertain then how to continue.

"Come," said Lyova. "There is not discord in your marriage already? I do not mean to pry, though. Forgive my impertinence."

"No, no, do not worry. Nothing at all like that. Oh! Look at the time."

And with that I scraped my chair back from the table. As I gave him a hearty hug and a slap on the back, I hoped he had not noticed my abruptness. How could he not, of course, but I thanked him for confiding in me, wished him well, and kissed his cheeks, and we parted with a promise to dine again together soon.

As I walked down Bolshaya Morskaya Street, I shook my head in amazement of what I had learned. "Really," I muttered to myself, "I must take my eyes from the page now and again and see what flows through the undercurrents of Petersburg."

Am I truly so blind, Filya? I wished to discover whether I, alone, have been ignorant of such arrangements, but to whom could I speak of it, I wondered. Kolya, I think, surely would find such society worthy of denigration and would besides be unlikely to take interest in esoteric discussion. The man's curiosity runs less wide than the width of a kopek!

I supposed I might talk with my fellows at the Library. On thinking of it more, I realized I was loathe to invite either their mockery of my ignorance or future questions about my own private matters—best not to engage them so familiarly, I thought. And how like a gossip I should feel, besides! Even were I not to mention Lyova by name, the topic would seem all the more titillating, I suspect, for having been stripped of its particularity.

And Masha? How, Filya, how should I raise such a delicate topic with her, she who is a lady? Assuredly, she is no sheltered maiden, kept under glass like a rare specimen. No, she is a woman of the world, a woman who has met, no doubt, many a type of person, and though she might be less than shocked at the topic, I think I could not begin to speak, even were she a barmaid, with candor about something so … base.

So I must content myself to ponder this unexpected confession from Lyova with you alone. Letters, however, dear cousin, as without doubt you've realized, are a poor substitute for conversation, for the smooth exchange of ideas.

But how the time has flown here, as I struggled to recall each detail of my conversation with Lyova! I must go. As always, I have gone on much longer than I'd anticipated! Liudmilla will soon be here with tea.

She is one of the servants—do you remember I made mention of her in an earlier letter? What a charming young woman. Though her family is quite poor (from the outskirts of Kursk) and could not afford a proper education for her, she has an eager mind. I have promised to teach her to read, which she knows barely how to do. I feel at liberty to do so, since my absence will hardly be missed by my wife, who is busy at almost all times with our friend Vera. How am I to take up women's causes if I so little understand them, Filya? I only want to understand Marya. Such I have told Marya, but it's clear she does not believe me. No doubt she has good reason to ill trust those of our sex, Filya, but how is it she cannot see my interests are pure?

Well. Please, then, cousin, take my mind off my lack of insight into women, the one I share a home with in particular, and tell me of *your* life. When will you and Angelina be wed? And will you never come home, then, once you've given your heart entire to an Italian girl? Let me at least imagine your voice as you describe in writing your art, your love, your non-Russian life.

With a hint of melancholy for all that's lost,

Seryozha

18
Vera's Journal

Saturday, 15 April 1876

If my future were not at stake, I would find it rather droll that Sergei fashions himself as sensitive to the issues of women yet cannot see the issues he brings forth with his very presence to the women in this house! From the start, I have not encouraged his constancy in our lives—or not, certainly, such proximity as would come with his sharing our home! My worry has been that he would necessarily bring discord to Misha and myself, and look—she and I have had another disagreeable conversation.

Several days past, Sergei had asked Marya whether he might invite a guest to dinner some evening, a friend from the Library.

Masha, I remember, looked up from a book she was reading—some mathematical text, I think. Ever since she has begun a regular correspondence with Grisha, she has been immersing herself in mathematical readings of all manner. When I had beseeched her to continue her mathematical studies, she declined, but now, with Grisha's encouragement ...Though I sound what seems a bitter note, in truth I am glad, only, she is putting her mind to the work she so loves. No, that's not where our discord lies. It comes later in the account I mean to record here.

Absorbed in the text as she was, Misha did not notice that Sergei had spoken. It was the silence after that seemed to call her attention to the fact that something had been said.

"Forgive me, Seryozha, I was lost in my text. What is it you've said?"

"I was wondering, Masha, whether it might be agreeable to you if I were to invite Ilya Sergeyevich Bunin for dinner some night."

"Seryozha—really, you need not ask; this is your house as well. As long as Iulia knows for how many she must prepare dinner, there is no problem. Please: invite your friend to join us for dinner if you like."

At the first moment when Misha and I were alone in our rooms (and here is where the kernel of disharmony began its growth), I told her I suspected Sergei of hoping to—to distract me so he might contrive to steal time alone with her.

She gave a light laugh, but then seeing me serious, took me in her arms and said, "Verochka. Darling. You must turn away from these foolish thoughts. I will not tell you Seryozha irrefutably does not have warm feelings for me, for this I do not know, being careful never to provide an opportunity to find out. But I do not believe him to be the maker of schemes you think him. Why cannot it not be he simply grows bored or lonely here for lack of male company? Besides," she said, as she lifted my chin until our eyes met, "there is naught to fear in the presence of this visitor unless you find yourself in accord with him—perhaps it's I who should be nervous?"

She spoke sternly, but a slight twitch in her lip told me she meant to make a joke.

"Marya!" I said. "Don't be foolish!"

I tried to give her a playful slap upon her arm but she ducked aside, and with more pursuit and dodging between us, we soon discovered ourselves fallen upon the bed.

But there was little in the way of amusement, I found, when Ilya came to dinner, for his attentions were sufficiently directed at me to make me feel discomfited, and this directly upon his arrival.

He drew my hand to his lips, in the French manner, upon entering our door, and murmured, "Bon soir, Mademoiselle Vera."

I felt a knot of anger take form—not for him but for Sergei, who had put him up to this, I was certain. True, Ilya greeted Masha in like manner, but his lips did not linger so long upon her hand as upon mine.

Then he seated me at the dinner table, taking care to help me with my chair. Noticing Sergei had not done the same for Masha, he chastised him.

"Sergei! You were too long a bachelor. Do you not know it's the duty of every gentleman to help his lady to seat herself at table? Come! Where are your manners?"

"But Ilyusha—what an old-fashioned custom. We care not, in our agreeable household, for the sort of tradition that implies women are a less capable sex."

"Nonsense! This is not a case of weaker or stronger but of good manners. Is that not so, Vera?"

"I do not mean to be contrary, Monsieur Bunin, but I am afraid I agree with Sergei on this point."

"Monsieur Bunin? And not Ilya? You need not be so formal, Vera. We have not known each other for any great length of time, to be sure, but I have known Seryozha for some years now and so, by proxy, you and I are as old friends as well."

"As you wish, Ilya." I knew my tone was curt, but I did not care. I turned from him, then, in a none-too-subtle attempt to redirect the conversation.

"Masha—has the latest issue of the *Russian Messenger* arrived yet with the next installment of *Anna Karenina*?"

"Ah! Lev Tolstoy," Ilya said. "Is his writing not masterful? In his hands, the Russian countryside nearly blossoms from the page right before your eyes. But in writing, what I most delight in is satire. Have you read, ever, 'The Lovers of Learning' by Grigorii Eliseev?" He looked from Masha to myself. "Surely, Seryozha, you must have read this second sketch of his in *Spark*, some ten or fifteen years ago?"

"Yes, yes. Of course. What sort of librarian should I be had I not read this story? No doubt each of us at the Imperial Library has read it. Except possibly the Germans—Val'ter and Dorn and the rest. They, I think, are the sort that inspired Eliseev to write such a parody of civil service at the outset. Nevertheless, Eliseev hardly compares with Saltykov-Shchedrin when it comes to satire, would you not agree?"

"No—you are absolutely right. But the library theme of Eliseev does entice those of our profession, just the same. That flash of recognition—so seductive. It's the difference, say, between a novel by George Sand and that of Lev Tolstoy—to return to Tolstoy. Sand is undeniably a fine writer, but Tolstoy—ah, Tolstoy! Here is writing that speaks to the heart."

At this, he pounded the left side of his chest.

"Surely this is why, Vera, you so eagerly await the next edition of the *Russian Messenger* with its next installment of *Anna Karenina*. It's the way Tolstoy captures the Russian spirit, the soul of our women, our men, the very soil."

"You do not mean, of course, to speak for me, do you Ilya?" I said. "You do not know me well enough to know why it is I might look for this latest work of our countryman. It could be I mean to write a review for the *Book Herald* or the *Historical Messenger*. Perhaps this work means nothing more to me than a ruble or two or a quest for advancement."

"Oh … but I … are you …? I didn't mean to—what I meant was—"

I would have enjoyed seeing him dangle some time longer, but Sergei took pity on his friend and quickly changed the subject.

"George Sand! That reminds me. I once heard a story of a woman just outside of Petersburg, some ten years or more ago, who was sitting in her garden when a bear appeared and startled her. Have you heard this story? And do you know how she frightened the beast away? She threw a volume of George Sand at his head!"

Masha laughed.

"Yes," she said, "I've always suspected it was a copy of *Jacques* she threw."

"Now how do you come to find fault with *Jacques*?" Sergei asked. "Does not the entanglement of Octave, Fernande, and Jacques aggrieve you? Sand so adroitly sketches their confused emotion, their pain—I do not see how any could fail to be moved by the inevitable tragedy that awaits them."

"How sentimental you are, Seryozha! I remember you saying quite nearly the same thing," Masha said, "when we spoke, some months ago, about Dostoyevsky's *The Idiot*. Perhaps the cataloging of books day in and day out turns one's emotions inward—is that so, Ilya? Do you find you are more prone to deep feeling from communicating only with books all day long?"

"Sentimental? No more than the next man, I think. On the issue of *Jacques*, at least, I find myself aligned with you. With a kind of fury, I read on about Jacques's misplaced nobleness, his leaving of Fernande to that scoundrel Octave. What sort of man leaves his wife to another? He should have fought to retain her, I say! Do you not agree, mademoiselle?"

He tipped his head toward me in a sanctimonious fashion, and I could sense my face begin to flush to the roots of my hair. Had Sergei said something to him of our arrangement?

"N-n-no," I said, recovering myself. "No, I most certainly do not. What barbarism! A woman is not a man's property, to be fought over like a … like a plot of ground or the … the last chop on the plate."

I held up the platter on the table, and the absurdity of this act, of equating a tract of land with a small cut of meat, made me suspect I might be overreacting, but I could not contain myself.

"A woman is a being with emotions—emotions over which she cannot exact complete control. I find Jacques to have acted quite honorably," I concluded.

"Yes, yet this story—it's but a fiction. People do not behave so gallantly in life. Intentions often give way to the primitive: anger, fear, jealousy. Life is much more untidy, I am afraid. Certainly you must have observed this yourself, Vera, being a worldly woman."

"Fiction it may be, but is not fiction often based on life? And my life, Monsieur Bunin, is far from disordered. Again, I think you presume too much. We have only just met this one time since the wed—since a month or more ago now."

"Yes! Well!" interjected Sergei. "Discussions of literature do tend to evoke much passion, do they not? And what of mathematics, Marya? Surely it's a topic less fraught with emotions?"

"For those not of a numerate bent, perhaps. But among those of us who hold the pursuit of mathematical truth dear …"

"Truly!" Ilya said, with a murmur of wonder.

"Yes, truly, Monsieur Bunin. To those not in tune with the wonders and mysteries of such truths, the world of numbers may seem dry and as constant as the Urals. But irrefutably, this permanence is an illusion. As the practice of mathematics evolves, earlier mathematical 'truths' are called into question, and heated debate will ensue within mathematical societies and in the pages of those periodicals devoted to the discoveries of this science."

"Discoveries, you say?" put in the contemptible Bunin. "It has been my impression that the stuff of mathematics is all air and phantasm."

"Ah, but that's a mistaken impression, sir. Mathematical structures are not, as you believe, simply imaginary creations of the human mind but, rather, are as natural and real as the formulations other scientists create to explain the world around us. We may not measure, always, a thing you can see—like how long it takes for this spoon to drop to the floor—" and here she let a spoon fall from the table to make her words come to life, "but where our imaginations fly is tethered by the need for what we formulate to connect with all the other parts of the mathematical hemisphere. Much like a link in a chain."

Masha made circles of the forefinger and thumb of each hand, then, and linked them.

"And one or more of the links connect with the real world," she continued. "So you may see some links that appear to float off into space, but every mathematical entity is in effect tied to a tie you can know with your senses."

"Oh dear," said Sergei. "I daresay if we tarry on this topic much longer, you shall lose the lot of us! Though I don't presume, of course, to speak for anyone but myself," he added and cast a glance at me.

At this I felt a flush of satisfaction that I had put him on notice I was not to be taken for granted or to have someone speak in my stead.

"I take no offense should you wish to redirect the conversation, Sergei. The steps of logic I so easily ascend will leave the unaccustomed breathless. Like anything, it's all about practice, though aptitude of course plays some role."

"Yes ...," said Ilya thoughtfully.

"But Ilyusha," Sergei continued, after a pause, "I meant to ask you whether you had read Stasov's latest notes on cataloging. Not a theoretician myself, I am quite in awe of his ability to distill librarians' organization problems into near overriding principles."

"Indeed, he has a mind that can pare away all the excess as if it were a potato—and still find something useful to do with the peelings, such as make of it a vodka!"

And so the conversation shifted to talk of the Library—though this did not stop him from putting his eyes all over my person like a moist palm. My skin recoils yet to think of it.

When at last he stood, ready to depart, he bent to lie his lips upon my hand again, but I grasped the hand he placed beneath my own and shook it firmly, then quickly released him.

"Good evening, Ilya."

"It has been a happiness, mademoiselle. I hope I may have the pleasure of your company again?"

"Yes. Perhaps if Sergei invites you to dine another time, I shall see you at table. Again, I bid you good evening, sir. Now I must retire."

And with that I made my exit.

Soon thereafter Marya joined me in our room.

"Do you now believe me?" I said.

"I believe in nothing else, my love."

She wrapped her arms around my waist and swayed me to and fro.

"I am serious, Masha!"

I pushed her arms from me and held her hands so she might not grasp me again.

"Did you not witness Sergei's machinations at work this evening?"

"I don't know what you—ah! I thought you had forgotten that silly notion."

"There is nothing the least silly about it. It's quite serious—he hopes, Marya, to force a wedge between us, and if he cannot be that wedge, he will find another to do the driving apart, and in Ilya he has found a willing partner."

"Now I know you must be speaking in jest, my dove! Seryozha is quite brilliant in his own way but clever as all that? And Ilya was naught but a gentleman. A bit of a fop, perhaps, but—"

"I swear by the icon of Saint Vera I have not fabricated his attentions!" I threw my hands up in exasperation. "Truth! 'Vera' means truth, at the root."

"My darling! What importance you lend to this insignificant evening of chops and chatter! But I do not doubt your perception that—"

"Perception. Perception? By perception you mean not a thing of facts? I tell you for a fact his eyes lingered over my person just as his lips lingered over the back of my hand."

"Then let us believe your facts—what do they matter? Whether Seryozha is at the root or Ilya is merely smitten or—well, it matters not. For my fact—let me offer it now to you—is that I am steadfast in my love. The only wedge that can split us is you."

"You would accuse me of being disloyal?"

Even as I said it, I felt I misconceived her words to a purpose, but the evening and my fear of Sergei's intentions had left me at a pitch of peevishness from which I could not climb down.

"Verochka. Please. You are but torturing yourself. You know very well what I mean. I do not presume to speak for any save myself, and for myself I can say assuredly there is naught that could tear us asunder, lest you wish it."

"Now you mock me! Throwing my words to Monsieur Bunin back in my face. 'You do not presume.' You do nothing but presume! Recall how you first came to touch my hand, undo my skirt ..."

"I? But never once did you—ack! I do not wish to quarrel, my beloved. We are both tired. Always things look better in the light of day."

She reached for my hand, but I snatched it away, too angry to allow myself to be mollified by her tenderness. We readied for bed in silence then, with awkward pauses in which we took care to keep ourselves from touching. In bed, I lay rigid, in want of Masha's body pressed to mine but uncertain how to respond when she had done so.

Were I to let go of my anger, my anxiety, so quickly it would all seem a playact, so I held it dear until at last I could hear her breath take on the rhythm of sleep. When she rolled aside, I slid from beneath the covers and crept away here to the closet, where I sit folded on the floor, and scribble out my anger by the light of this diminishing candle. But my feet are quite chilled now, and my passion is all but exhausted, as am I, and so I must blow out my poor torch and hope to find peace in sleep.

19
Sergei

20 April 1876

Darling Kolya,

How do the lengthening days find you, my dearest brother? I confess I find myself longing for more welcoming weather, for the opportunity to stretch my legs more and be about. The long winter holds the heart still, like a chrysalis. All in its time, of course, brother, but I swear by the beard of the tsar, I am ready to burst free of such shelter as that static state affords! It's all well to entertain at home, to spend time with loved ones in the comfort of the stove's blazing fire, but does not a restlessness overtake you? Bah! Take notice of whom I ask this question! You are restlessness itself. But even I, your sedentary kin, can grow weary of confinement.

And so, I have recently dined with Lev at Privato, at Grand Morskaya no. 36, not too far from the Café de Paris. Have you yet tried the food of Italy? Since the time Filya has been in that far country, I have longed to have a taste of it, so I might share in his world. Lyova is a great proponent of that country's cuisine, and I think I begin to see its merits. I especially enjoy the pasta dishes, with their rich, flavorful sauces, though it takes some getting used to, those long strings of noodle!

Lyova, something of an expert now, had shown me how to wind the noodles around the fork using a spoon to hold it all in place, but I am yet quite clumsy at it, and I'm afraid the sauce flies about as indecorously as bird droppings. Though no doubt the proprietor would shudder to hear such a comparison.

Lyova and I talked for some time about our lives, about childhood days—when his family would come for long summer visits—do you remember, Kolya? And then we talked a while of his work. I swear to you, Kolya, seated beside either Lyova or Masha, I begin to feel like a gymnasium student again! How complicated their minds. It's no secret, to be sure, that I have no pronounced aptitude for mathematics. Woe to me, then, for asking of him on what it was he worked, for here, as best I remember, is his reply:

"Ah! How busy we are now. I am engaged in preparing drawings, as at all times, based on the engineers' specifications. What has made our days unusually hectic, these past months, is work we are doing on a special project: the building of the *Petr Veliky*. It will be the first armor-clad ship in Russia's Navy. A heavy vessel, thus the tolerances are especially critical, and drawings are checked many times before they are released to the shipbuilders. You cannot begin to imagine how many pieces there are in a ship of this size! From the tiniest bearings to propellers taller than a man by half, we must draw each piece that the engineers design. At the same time, we have begun work on the first steam engine, which will have 5300 horsepower when we are done. Work on the special projects—"

"Wait! Wait!" I told him. "Armor clad?"

"Yes. You see, during the Crimean War (how is it you do not know this, Seryozha? for shame!), Russia's wooden sailing ships were not equal to the speed, the power, brought to bear on them by the steamships Turkey's allies supplied. Our Baltic Works, in fact, grew out of a need to address that problem. A merchant of the first class and a naval architect—oh, well, you do not wish to know the entire history! Adequate to your needs to say Baltic Works' primary mission from the start has been to create warships. The armored gunboat *Opyt*, Russia's first metal ship, was built there in 1862, and early in 1866, the frigate *Admiral Lazarev*, a coast defense vessel, was launched. Now we are creating vessels one and two steps beyond, able to withstand enemy fire and outrun their ships, both in pursuit and retreat."

"So it is warships—only warships? You do no other work?"

How disquieting, I thought, to create works whose only purpose was to destroy. Perhaps it's indelicate to confess this to one's brother when said brother is a soldier! It cannot come as a surprise to you, however, that my nature is a peaceful one. So.

"Well, no …," Lyova said. "Such ships are our glory, though. And to be candid, this facet of our work is what others ordinarily find most interesting—though I should have known this would not be the case with you, my gentle friend."

"Yes, I can see where such would be a fascination—for tsar and country and all. Here, here!" I raised my glass in mock toast. "My tastes, however, as you allude, run in a different path—more toward the fundamental, such as the drawing itself—your tools, paper, and so on. I have told you, no doubt, Filipp is painting in Italy?"

"Why, yes.… But you know, Seryozha, the kind of drawing I do is not—"

"Of course, of course! I have my head all day buried in cataloging, but I am not so cut adrift from the world I am unaware of how mechanical drawing differs from fine art."

"Oh. Forgive me, Seryozha. I did not mean—"

"Do not worry, old friend! I have not taken offense. I am, rather, amused. No, I meant not to draw a parallel between your work and Filya's. Only to say why I find myself more captivated by your mechanics than by the end result."

"Right. Of course. How foolish of me!" He struck a palm to his forehead.

"Please, Lyova! There is no need to do yourself bodily harm on my account."

"Tools, you are interested in, you say? Here they are before you."

And with that, he emptied the contents of a small satchel onto the table: pencils, a penknife, compass, straightedge ruler. It was then the waiter came to bring our food, and after Lyova returned his things back to the satchel, we talked again of boyhood and the unambiguous bucolic life.

Talking with him about our childhood days has put me in a fit of nostalgia, and for the moment I long to be far from St. Petersburg, inhaling the peculiar sweetness that comes of the mingled smells of summer flowers, new mown hay, and the nearby pine trees. What a glorious smell! Even our great Peter's Summer Garden, with all its flowers in bloom, cannot rival Svetliachie Gory for its wonderfully unique fragrance.

It's not merely summer that I yearn for moreover, as you may think. For, despite my short outburst at the start of this correspondence, I long as well for the brilliant colors that winter evenings cast upon the snow at our boyhood home. Do you remember? There is nothing quite like it here in St.

Petersburg, the snow being disrupted at regular intervals by buildings and wagons and here and there piles of refuse.

Do you remember how the sunset painted a kaleidoscope on our winter landscape? At one moment, the hillocks of snow might be tinted crimson or rose, with the long shadows they cast dyed a delicate green. Or when the rosy light soon becomes orange, and all of the shadows transform to purest blue? How long we would sit, by the frosty window, repeatedly clearing a place in the rime so we might see the sun sink lower and lower until finally it dropped below the horizon and flooded the sky, and the snow beneath it, with a golden light, while the shadows quivered among ever-changing shades of violet. When I was a young boy, I thought it was a sort of magic. To tell you the truth, Kolya, I am not entirely dissuaded it is not. Masha, no doubt, could offer the science behind the altering hues, but I think I rather prefer the enchantment.

All day today, among my stacks of books at the Library, images of that early life have been floating to the surface. Remember how Maman, after we had dined on summer afternoons, could be found dozing in an armchair in the sitting room with a handkerchief spread across her face? We would come in from the garden, where we had been talking or playing with our tin soldiers, and you could see the edge of that tattered cloth fluttering with each exhalation. Or how Grandmère would chastise us each time we spoke Russian? "*En français*!" she would say, and crack our knuckles with her fan. "So vulgar, Russian. I must have a word with that nurse of yours. Teaching you the language of peasants and serfs!"

But I meant to tell you of dinner with Lyova, and off I go into memories of another time. It's a tired notion, to be certain, but I cannot help myself from noting how much simpler those days were. In my youth, such simplicity seemed a bane. Now I would greet it as a boon. Forgive me if I have the aspect of weariness. It's only disappointment I have not, at the age of thirty-six, made comprehensible all of life, or in any event, all of *my* life. Likely you do not give it a thought when your life does not fall neatly in line, but I am a man of order, of reason—as well as a man of passion (do not laugh! I have my passions). It's no good telling me I worry too much: it's my disposition, and I am resigned to it.

One more reminiscence, though, before I close. Lyova and I laughed like schoolboys to remember how Papa, on one occasion, dressed himself as a mummer and led a performing bear around the room (do you remember?)—and the bear was in fact Viktor Evgenyevich, the gardener, costumed in a raccoon coat! And Papa would call out, "Come along, Misha, do, for us, a dance! Show us how cook falls upon the ice. Show us how the girls primp before the mirror." And the bear danced and fell down on the floor and fluffed its hair and fought with Papa. Ah, but do you see what I mean about simpler times? How easily we were entertained!

Perhaps when the sun stays longer with each visit and the air feels less like a razor across the face I will put aside the past for a little bit and live fully in the present!

Bah! You will say I am far too young for nostalgia, and you are right. I have no rationale for this near melancholy turn. A brisk walk will perhaps restore my spirits.

Your foolish brother,

Seryozha

20
Grigorii

25 April 1876

Dearest Masha!

We must make a plan! Can we meet? Shall we talk? Forgive my mania—surely, though, if any might understand my passion, it's you.

I am delighted, of course, at how Kovalevskaya's article in *Crelle's Journal* has sparked a desire to pursue your intended course and, as well, that you have taken an interest in the problem I proposed. For I believe our Almighty Father has a purpose for each of us; your purpose is to do great things in the field of mathematics. And mine? Surely it's not to stand before a bunch of silly schoolgirls and drone on about the Pythagorean Theorem or a handful of logarithms. No, surely it's my destiny, instead, to lead you to yours. And so at last we are at our true crossroad, where you and I meet, each to fulfill his destiny. It does not matter whether you share my faith in the Lord; it matters only you place your faith in me—not because I am almighty but because though I am no mathematical genius I know enough to recognize such genius in others. It's no secret I see that genius in you. So most important of all, you must have faith in yourself, in your abilities, which are a great deal more than negligible.

So here is what I think we must do: my father has a childhood friend who is acquainted with Strannoliubsky. I shall ask for a letter introducing me and see if he will take you on as a private pupil. That's but a first step, to prepare you for when the universities begin to admit women. And they will. Any fool can see it's inevitable. So you must be prepared. I do not know whether we have but a year till then or ten years, but we must begin.

Are you agreed to this plan? I shall not begin until I receive your permission, though I dare say I shall not be able to stop myself from drafting, in anticipation, the letters we will need! You will ask, no doubt, about the cost of hiring a teacher such as Strannoliubsky. We must hope he will be captivated by your ability and find the challenges and joys of a student such as yourself payment enough, much as Kovalevskaya charmed Weierstrass to undertake mentoring her those years she spent in Germany. (Again, it's father's connections that bring me this poor gossip of mathematicians.)

And if Strannoliubsky is not thus captivated, what then? This is not my question—I do not see this outcome—but, rather, this is what I anticipate will concern *you*. But just in case—then what? Then I shall call upon those right-thinking friends of my mother's and father's who will want to bring an important mind to flower. I can hear you laugh to think of yourself as a flower. But I do not mean some tender thing to wilt at the first raw wind or furious rain. But a flower you are, just the same, a Maltese cross, I think—by which I do not mean, of course, the inert white cross on the tunic of some graduate of the Corps of Pages. No: I mean the burst of scarlet that so startles the eye in some garden. This suits you perfectly—I'm afraid there is no point in arguing—since it's the pride of our Russian soil and its name among scientists, *Lynchis*, is Greek for "lamp" for its fiery red flowers. And you are that lamp, just waiting to be set ablaze.

Excuse my romantic comparisons, which are but a product of my enthusiasm for your talents and of little poetic merit, I'm sure, for I am no poet. (How often have I heard it said, however, the poet and mathematician share much in common. Both care a great deal—do they not?—for pattern, repetition, symmetry.)

But why do I let myself wander like this, when I mean only to say I am anxious to serve you in the goal of reaching the height of your true talents in whatever way you deem right to use me.

Your faithful servant,

Grisha

(I have read again my mad scribblings here and were one to come upon them without foreknowledge of our correspondence, they might suppose this a love letter! And in a way perhaps it is: a love letter to the pursuit of education. Go with God, Marya, my friend.)

21
Marya

Strannoliubsky!

Each time she thought of the possibility of working with him, Marya felt a current run through her. The energy made her feel like a child on her name day, anticipating a bit of honey cake or a chocolate or two. She paced by the door, the afternoon she got Grisha's letter, waiting for Vera to arrive home from tutoring. Barely was Vera in the door than Marya grabbed her by the hand and pulled her along up the stairs.

"Masha! Masha—wait."

Marya just turned and grinned at her.

"What's happened? What is it? Masha!"

"The most wonderful thing, Verochka."

Vera had never seen Marya so ebullient. She couldn't imagine what might have put Marya in such an amazing mood. She wanted to pummel Marya until the news, whatever it might be, had spilled out. But she didn't want to do anything either to spoil the moment, so simply clambered up the stairs in Marya's wake as best she could.

Once inside their room, Marya pulled Vera to her and began covering her neck and face in kisses.

"Masha! What is—"

Marya cut Vera off, covering Vera's mouth with her own. Marya pulled away and took Vera's face in her hands.

Vera gasped.

"Oh, Masha! But I haven't even had time to take off my overco—"

A swift twirl by Marya, who had taken Vera around the waist by one hand, again cut her short.

They twirled until they were dizzy and toppled, as if in slow motion, to the floor.

Vera lifted herself onto her elbows, blew aside a tuft of hairs that had fallen across her face, and said, "Now truly, Masha, what has come over you? I am delighted. But one can't help wond—"

Marya swept her torso up from the floor, grabbed Vera, and pulled her on top of her.

"Strannoliubsky," she whispered in Vera's ear.

"Masha! That tickles. Now be serious."

Vera wrested herself from Marya's grasp, got to her knees, and pulled Marya to a seated position."

"Now tell me."

"I shouldn't be so excited, Verochka. Nothing may come of it. I feel foolish now, acting like a silly schoolgirl, but truly I am energized simply by the thought."

"The thought of what?" Vera took Marya by the shoulders and shook her in mock seriousness.

"Grisha only said he would try."

"Masha, darling, your words are flowing like a Möbius strip, going round and round but never getting anywhere. What? Don't look so surprised—I know a math term or two. Calm yourself and tell me from the beginning."

Marya took a deep breath, took Vera's hands into her own, and recounted what she could remember from Grisha's letter—which was quite a lot since she had read it perhaps a dozen times since its arrival while awaiting Vera's homecoming.

"Oh, but darling, that *is* wonderful."

Vera leaned forward on her knees and kissed Marya on the forehead.

"And I won't even be cross with you," she said, as she sat back on her heels, "that so often I encouraged you to pursue your studies and only now, with Grisha's urging, have you done it."

"Vera! You needn't be cross. It wasn't that I disregarded your council—only that I saw no way forward. Now, with Grisha's intercession, it seems like there may be some way. I know you have always and only wanted what is best for me."

Marya stood up and helped Vera to her feet as well, then unbuttoned Vera's overcoat for her, letting her hands slide under the coat, when she'd finished, to Vera's back.

"Masha, love, if we continue thus, we will never make it to dinner tonight. Sergei will wonder—"

"Let him wonder!"

"Masha?"

"It's nothing, Vera. Seryozha has just been irritating me with his attentions."

"Really?"

A small smile formed on Vera's face as she turned toward the dressing table to find a comb.

Having raised the specter of Seryozha, Marya fell to brooding about him. He had, of late, come to kiss Marya's hand, in greeting and on taking his leave, as any husband might. And on occasion when he would find Marya alone, crossing the room, he might call out, half in jest, "Ah, my wife!" and take her by the waist and attempt to pull her into a waltz or gavotte, much as she had just done with Vera moments ago. Or, when he might chance upon her, sitting at her studies, he let his hand rest upon her shoulder or gently touch her cheek. At such times, Marya could scarce contain a shudder. "Sergei. Please."

She had begun to feel that, with each day, her former good, pure, sacred feeling of friendship for him was vanishing. His caresses, tender looks, courtesy, concern—all this enraged and irritated her to an unreasonable extent. And yet, she was not so heartless as to fail to notice his crushed manner each time she rebuffed him. She regretted his suffering—he would become stiff and detached with any unkind word or action from her—and she longed to cry out "Forgive me—forgive me, Seryozha," and lay her hand upon his arm.

But she knew instinctively that to speak so tenderly would only inflame the situation. She felt at wit's end, at moments nearly frantic with a desire to escape the horrible, hopeless situation in which she found herself. She began to misplace things: a stocking, a glove, a box of matches—small odds and ends here and there.

After one such particularly distressing encounter with Sergei, a week or two prior, she had curled up at Vera's feet, where she sat at the side of the bed, and put her head on Vera's knees.

"Verochka, are you not weary of St. Petersburg? Let us run off somewhere together! Just you and me. Perhaps Paris. Or London—Lidia loved London. Or—oh, I know—Zurich. Remember how you once encouraged me to go to Zurich so I might study mathematics?"

Vera had lifted Marya's chin and said, "What ever has come over you? You know I have not the means for that class of travel! And you—you know you cannot go abroad without first getting leave from Sergei. I wonder whether he would grant that. Whether smitten with you or no, he seems genuinely fond to have you in his life."

"Smitten! Who has said smitten? I simply wish to see the world with the woman I love. And as for money—"

"Please, Misha. Enough of spinning fantasies for today. I must prepare my lessons for tomorrow."

Some nights following that, while settling under their bed covers, Marya tried a new tack.

"Verochka, darling, do you never tire of these crowded streets, the noise, the mud? Let us go to Khrupkaya Luna. There you might find a dozen friends for Zubilo! We could tramp through the woods, like regular naturalists, gather berries and mushrooms to eat, leaves and flowers to draw and study. Come. Shall we do it? Let's!"

"I am surprised, of late, by this romantic vein you seem to have found. What an agreeable thought, my love. There are reasons enough, though, why this is not a topic we should entertain further."

"Reasons? What reasons? You shall tender your resignation with the Solovyovs, I shall pack my books and my propelling pencil, and off we shall go."

"Your brain has become addled with too many numbers and equations," Vera said, then, tapped her finger against Marya's forehead.

"My reasoning is sound!" Marya protested.

"Is it? What of the law that requires you to live in the same household as your husband? And even if we might find a way to circumvent that, there is the matter of the house at Khrupkaya Luna being let to Count Muraviev and his family."

"We could—"

"Hush," she said, and put her fingers on Marya's lips. "Do you wish to tell me what has inspired this recent desire to be away from here?"

Marya considered, then, and again now in the current moment, telling Vera of the true extent of her revulsion for Sergei, of the way her flesh responded to his touch—his touch, which somehow no longer seemed simple, clear, and all innocence.

She did not wish to keep from Vera so much as a thought or feeling yet felt certain that her own doubts about Sergei's intentions would only redouble Vera's. And since Vera was right—that Marya's plans for the two of them alone were foolhardy—they would find themselves still in the same household, the same situation, only in worsened straits for knowing that something in their triune household had begun to turn. So she vowed, for the time, to keep to herself the level of despair she felt about finding a resolution to the situation with Sergei, which was growing increasingly wretched.

22
Vera's Journal

Thursday, 27 April 1876

While Mashenka loses herself to a world populated by integers and the ghosts of philosophers of science, I have begun to work with Zubilo. My *Girl's Own Treasury* provides instructions on how I might go about training him, and therefore I have undertaken to do so, though it's a fool's mission. Why teach him to fly to my hand at the sound of a bell or retrieve his water in a miniature bucket if I am to let him go in a matter of weeks, as Kaigorodov recommends?

Why indeed. Shall I be honest with myself and say that perhaps I do not intend to let him go? Or, that if I do, it's with the hope that he shall return, as the *Treasury* says he might: "A bullfinch that has been thus trained may with tolerable safety be allowed to fly out the window, if there be no wood close at hand." There are too many leave-takings already. First Lidia, and who knows but that Masha may follow, albeit not in such everlasting fashion. If I wish to make of Zubilo a companion, should I be reproached? For the nonce, I set aside my motives and relish the challenge of shaping another being according to my will.

I began by placing, within his cage, a small bag of seed and a thimble of water, to each of which I attached a bell such that he might not take either without causing the bell to sound. At first, the tinkling of the bell did naught but scare him, and he flew about the cage seeking egress. I stayed near to him, during this stage, so that when he had accustomed himself to the thin music of his sustenance, I might be near and thus grow as familiar to him as the rapeseed on which he supped.

A week hence, and I can now entice him to alight on my hand when I ring the bell. For he knows I will have for him a bit of hemp, which he seems to find quite a delicacy. He is beginning, I think, to become fairly fond of me. Several times now, with no signal to prompt him, he has perched upon my shoulder. And now, as I write, he stands upon my writing table and cocks his head at me. With his stout little body and short neck, he reminds me of our Ilya. I wonder whether Ilyusha would be flattered by the comparison? He is a peculiar enough fellow that he well might be.

Of course, with Zubilo sitting before me, a question implicit in the tilt of his tiny head, he is foremost in my mind just now. But there is another reason I sat to record my thoughts: today, Pasha, Varya, and I had a stimulating history lesson. We have talked of the tsars, the Crimean War, and the creation of zemstvos so that rural districts and large towns might have a hand in their own government (ah, always the teacher—even in my notes to myself here!). We talked not only about Russia, of course, but of events elsewhere in the world, too.

Lately, we have talked of the United States, of its forming and general history and customs. Today we started our lesson by taking notice of the practice of slavery there. The children were fascinated by the thought that one human being might own another and wanted to know how this might come to pass.

To capitalize on their interest, I asked, "And what had we here in Russia that bore a resemblance to slavery?"

Varya screwed up her face in thought and tipped her head (rather like Zubilo, actually!) and Pasha tugged at his hair, a habit he has when he concentrates especially hard, as if by this effort he might physically wrest the thoughts from his mind.

"Nothing?" he said.

"Have you ever heard of serfs?" I asked.

"Yes!" said Varya.

"And what is a serf?"

"A kind of peasant?" Pasha tried.

"Well, yes—in a way. But serfs, like slaves, were peasant families that were bound, by a decree from Tsar Alexis in 1649, to a particular landlord. They could not marry without the landlord's permission and they had no rights of any kind and must endure whatever their owners subjected them to."

Pasha eyed me with suspicion, as if I might be attempting to test his gullibility.

"Do we have any serfs?" Varya asked. "Are you a serf? Mama tells you what to do ofttimes."

"Don't be stupid! Mademoiselle Dashkova may come and go as she wishes."

Varya pouted, but Pasha ignored her and continued.

"But do we? Have any serfs?"

"No, little one. The serfs were freed five years before you were born. Tsar Alexander emancipated them by proclamation on 17 March 1861."

"What is me-mancipate?" Varya asked.

I kissed the top of her head.

"*E*-mancipate. It means to give someone their freedom."

"Were the serfs from … from Africa?"

"No: they were Russians. Just like you and me. There were other differences between slaves and serfs as well. Serfs, unlike slaves, all owned a piece of land that they might till once they had completed all the tasks their lord had given them. And they might sell the extra things they grew on their land and keep the money for it. Also, serfs and lords did not always keep separate, in the way slaves must not frequent the same places as their masters. Often, here, a serf and his lord might be found worshipping in the same church, one beside the other."

"So all Russians are now free?"

"Well …," I said, debating the wisdom of what I was about to say. "Not entirely. Women are subject to their husbands' wishes and are not free to move about as they choose. A wife must live with her husband and she cannot get a passport separate from her husband that she might travel of her own will. Women cannot seek employment without their husbands' permission and they do not have a right to a university education."

"So … since you do not have a husband, you are free?"

"Ah, but now we have hit upon a topic that's too complex to address truly. And it's not within the subject of history." And there we ended the day's lesson.

True, I suffered a loss of courage to press my point. Vasily Solovyov and his wife, though, I say to myself, engaged me as tutor to their children, and not as a propagandizer. The values I am entrusted to pass along to them are nothing more controversial than honesty, diligence, respect for their tsar, their country, their parents. It's not my sense, from Evdokia Solovyova, that she wishes her children to embrace progressive ideals.

Still, perhaps a seed has been planted that will germinate and mature.

23
Sergei

2 May 1876

Dear, dear Filya!

At last! A sketch of yours. And how much the sweeter it is of your Angelina. But you must let me send you ten or twelve rubles. I hope that rate is not an insult: I am not a man accustomed to buying art. What money I have usually goes to books, or perhaps for theater tickets. But I am telling you nothing you mightn't have guessed. When you tell me what sum would be fair compensation for the pleasure of gazing on your lovely Angelina, perhaps you can tell me as well where I could best go to have this fine work framed. Though you are long gone from Russia, you no doubt still know better than I where I will find the best craftsman for framing, for it simply will not do to tack your sketch upon the wall in my quarters like a schoolboy, to let the edges curl and fray.

But the sketch, if I have not quite said as much yet, is exquisite. You were skilled when you left Petersburg, but the subtlety of your touch here is enough to make a grown man weep. How proud of you I am, Filya. And your Angelina, too, is lovely unto herself. Such delicate features. If that countenance does not belie a foul temper or simpering attitude, then you are as lucky a man as you seem, cousin.

And I, I am lucky, too, for Masha is a wonder. I only wish I could re-create her on paper for you as you have created your beloved for me. And now you will again read between the lines to tell me I have intimated love for Marya. This once I shall not argue, cousin. For if you were not right in this assumption ere now, you may be so this time. I have begun to notice an alteration in myself.

There is—and there is no other accounting for this—an ache in my heart at every chance encounter in the parlor with her or when I catch an unexpected glimpse of her through the doorway of my study. I long to take her up in my arms and hold her to me, but of course to do so would be to break my promise to her. And there is little hope she would return my affections, for she pays me barely more mind than the servants, save at dinner or over tea when we continue to have the most stimulating conversations about literature and the newspapers and everything under this cold Russian sun.

Worst of all—and I can scarce believe I mean to confess this—I have spirited away a glove of hers so I might hold it before my nose at night in my bedchamber and breathe a while her scent. Far from curing me, this puts me in greater agony. Twice now, I have risen from bed and, in a fever of passion, headed for her door, thinking to confess my change of heart. But the chill of the air has so far brought me to my senses before I might feel the chill of her rejection.

I am in an agony of desire, Filipp. You will wonder, no doubt, I did not see this coming, since you seemed so certain of it yourself. But I tell you I felt sure my convictions about the rightness of this sort of marriage would save me from the dumbness of my all-too-human heart. I ought find it noble, I suppose, to suffer for such an honorable cause. My gratification should come in knowing I have helped bring a woman some freedom from her enslavement to men in our backward nation. I tell myself these things again and again, and also, she and I have made an agreement, which I, as a man of honor, must respect. I am a sane man at the Library, where I learn much from Stasov every day about his new theories of cataloging, but I enter these apartments as if walking into a tormenting dream. It's no use, either, telling me you might have predicted so—in fact, told me as much. Now I am here, what shall I do?

Before I fill reams in this delirious fashion, I will force my pen to some other subject, a subject less agitating to my spirit. Of what can I write? Ah: let me tell you of Liudmilla. Do you recall I was to undertake teaching her to read? We are progressing quite nicely. She has a quick mind and is eager to learn. She has overcome some of her initial shyness with me—always before when I spoke, she would blush and could never bring herself to look me in the eye for longer than the flicker of a firefly—and now, along with our reading lessons, we often have warm conversations. She is a sweet girl, though she does not have Mashenka's brilliance, of course. Only Liudmilla, though, of all our household, lets her eyes linger on my face with affection, for she often expresses gratitude for the time I take with her, a poor serving girl.

We generally meet for lessons in my study, when Marya and Vera have gone off to one of their meetings. We began with a simple child's primer, but I think it embarrassed her to be reading such childish things, so we moved rather quickly to Pushkin. And to Lermontov:

By hot noon in a vale in Daghestan
Lifeless, a bullet in my breast, I lay:
Smoke rose from a deep wound, and my blood ran
Out of me, drop by drop, and ebbed away.

But perhaps "The Dream" is too stirring for a young woman of fragile sensibilities: no sooner had we read this passage than Liudmilla began softly to weep.

"What is it?" I leaned toward her in my alarm.

"I am terribly sorry, Sergei. Forgive me. You have not the time to listen to a silly girl like me weep. It was, after all, only a dream."

And then, fool I am, I made it worse: "Well, that's the title of the poem," I said to her, all self-important in my knowledge, "but Lermontov did, in fact, die in just such a manner, in a duel at age twenty-seven. It's uncanny—is it not?—that he should have predicted his own death."

At this she burst into tears anew and turned her face from me.

"Liudmilla?"

Was it indelicate to have mentioned these facts?

She waved me away with her handkerchief. In a moment, after she had brought herself in control, she whispered, "It's just … how very sad."

I began to reach for her hand, to comfort her, but that seemed somehow improper, and I did not want her to feel I made advances.

"Should we … do you want to continue with the lesson?" I stuttered instead. "Or should we end here this evening and continue some other night?" Without waiting for an answer, I said, "Perhaps it would be best if we ended here."

And I awkwardly escorted her from the room. But then I wondered if I hadn't given her a bad impression. I did not wish her to believe she has done something amiss in her display of tender feeling. It's I who should be ashamed, having dismissed her so rudely. Filya, I understand less and less my own behavior.

But when we met again, the lesson was much less stormy and now all seems aright. I did not dare ask about her outburst but inquired instead of her family. I assumed that a safe topic, but then worried a moment she had lost someone dear in a duel. If that's the case, she did not deem to mention it, but told me, instead, she had seen her father only the other day, as he was a fireman for one of the railroads and so sometimes would call on her when he was in Petersburg. Two young brothers and a sister are at home with her mother, while one brother, Timofei, has taken work in Moscow. She has met my family, of course, when they stayed here for the wedding, and she kindly asked after them.

Well, I am quite past tired and have paused repeatedly to rub my weary eyes. Lonely though it may be in my bed, it's time I go there. Good night, my cousin.

I will await your advice about Mashenka quite anxiously.

Your foolish cousin,

Seryozha

24
Vera's Journal

Monday, 8 May 1876

What a lovely day we had yesterday! I enjoyed even Sergei's company—more than I have for some many weeks now. Aleksandra Kobiakova joined our little household for tea and met Sergei for the first time. Over cracknels and jam, we talked of literature and rumors of the revival of the old Land and Freedom organization. Sasha had heard that, though it had disbanded more than a decade ago, owing to lack of support among students for their revolutionary propagandizing, new leaders were starting it again with new aims.

"I had heard those rumors," Sergei said, "but one hears many things whispered among the clientele at the Library. I did not think it true."

"Yes, it's true," said Sasha, who was far more involved in the discussion groups than Masha and I have been. "There is to be a 'disorganizing section' that will fight the police directly, I've heard, and protect the movement against disloyalty. Their aims, though, in the main, will be less about promoting revolution among the peasants and more about sending teachers and others among them to uplift their lives."

"That may be," said Masha, "but from all I have heard at the meetings we attend, I don't think there will be peace for long. On so many fronts, there seems to be a growing dissatisfaction. I want an education but not at the cost of lives!"

"I hope you don't mean to give up on our work, Marya." Sasha leaned from her chair toward Masha so that she might grip her hand. "We need minds like yours. Your kind of strength."

"So you, too, have come under her spell?" Sergei said. "I have been amazed by her from the first time I met her."

I felt a slight twitch.

"Shall we go for a walk?" I suggested, before we should go on, all speaking our admiration for Masha (which though deserved I could not bear to hear more of from Sergei). "The sun is shining, and I am quite anxious to quit the familiarity of these rooms after so long a winter."

Masha looked at me with raised eyebrow, wondering, no doubt, at this sudden fervor for the out-of-doors.

"What a lovely idea!" Sasha seemed genuinely enthusiastic about taking a stroll.

"Well then," said Sergei, "let us be on our way! I shall go find Ilyusha and ask him to bring our outdoor garments."

After a flurry of putting on coats and wrapping mufflers about our necks, we stepped out into the bright sunlight, made especially brilliant as it reflected off the last vestiges of snow. Everywhere there was the sound of dripping water as the snow melted from windowsills, gutters, rooftops, and branches. Birdsong filled the air as well, and I felt a pang of guilt over harboring Zubilo yet. *Next week*, I told myself. *There may yet be a cold snap.*

We strolled along the Moika, headed toward the Kryukov Canal. The trees on Novaya Gollandia were only just beginning to bud, and one could make out, behind the high walls, a few of the oddly shaped buildings used by the navy. As we neared the southern tip of the island, Sasha turned to face us and skipped backward a few paces.

"Which way shall we go?" she asked.

Sergei and I looked to Masha who, with little hesitation, said, "Let us turn along the Kryukov and head to the Neva."

With that, Sasha faced forward, and we all fell in step with one another, linking arms. There was something about the smell of thawing earth under an insistent sun that would hear of no state but cheerfulness.

We chatted gaily as we walked toward the river and reminisced about winter when we were children, far from St. Petersburg.

"I remember one year," said Sergei, "the snowfall was so heavy, roads needed to be cut to the stables and to the winter kitchen, there beneath the house. We all joined in: Papa, Kolya (though he was not much use, being but a very small boy yet—he insisted, though, he be allowed to join), the serfs, and Fyodor Nekrasov, who was visiting. All around us rose walls of snow, and it reminded me of the Esquimaux, about whom I'd recently read. It was both frightening and lovely."

"Yes," said Sasha. "Winter can certainly be deadly if one does not pay her the proper respect. When I was a child, I recall having heard of a peasant who had been found frozen to death alongside the road."

The three of us gasped as one, which synchronicity caused us a small chuckle.

"He had been drinking in a neighboring village and either he lost his way or stumbled and could not get up, drunk as he was."

"Oh, dear," I said, which hardly seemed adequate, but I did not know what other response to make.

"We also had wolves once, who crept one night into our courtyard looking for food, I suppose, one very harsh winter," said Sergei. "They were met with the sharp teeth of our watchdogs, and the snow, in the morning, was dotted with blood."

"Did any of the dogs die?" I asked, not certain I wished an answer.

"No, but several definitely needed mending. One, Zhuchka, had a long rip in his skin and one of the serfs somehow knew to mend it with needle and thread."

"I always wanted to hunt wolves," said Masha, a note of wistfulness in her voice. And then she laughed.

We all turned to her.

"No, no—it's not the wolves I find funny. I was thinking about how once we had a visitor from England and Nikolenka, our coachman, winked at Papa when we took the Englishman for his first sledge ride. The wink was to let Papa know that the sledge would 'accidentally' take a spill, sending us flying off into the snow. The look on that man's face! I am quite sure he thought he would die or at least break a limb, and it was with great surprise he found himself dumped into something akin to a feather bed. He could not suppress a smile as he dusted the snow, dry as salt, from his coat. There was one time, too, when Nikolenka forgot to cover the horses' hindquarters with the net of woolen cords, and we were all pelted with a volley of snowballs sent flying from the horses' hooves as we got underway. I thought it was a tremendous lark. Mama, however, expressed her displeasure with Nikolenka's forgetfulness in no uncertain terms."

By that time, we had reached the river, where the breeze was brisker, and we pulled up our collars and our scarves. The river was beginning to show signs its icy coat would soon be shed and left to float out to sea. Great cracks in the ice resounded like gunshots from time to time, and we were silent in our awe. As we approached Senate Square, I broke the silence.

"This summer, shall we hire a boat and make an excursion to the point of Elagin Island to hear the concerts given by the military bands? Or we could simply tour the branches of the Neva and stop to watch the sun as it dips toward the horizon. I love the glimmer of lights from the fishing villages and the dachas, and everywhere the sound of tambourines and horns and reed pipes played by the boatmen."

"Yes, let's," said Masha. Her face softened, and I felt a brief quickening in my heartbeat. *How does she do that to me?* I wondered.

Then we stood before the bronze horseman. I felt quite small next to it, the clear sky enhancing the feeling that his raised hand might touch the sun.

"Upon a shore of desolate waves / Stood he, with lofty musings grave, / And gazed afar," Sasha began to recite. "Before him spreading / Rolled the broad river, empty save / For one lone skiff stream-downward heading."

"Strewn on the marshy, moss-grown bank, / Rare huts, the Finn's poor shelter," joined in Masha, "shrank, / Black smudges—"

"—from the fog protruding." Sergei and I added our voices. "Beyond, dark forest ramparts drank / The shrouded sun's rays and stood brooding / And murmuring all about. / He thought, 'Here, Swede, beware—soon our labor / Here a new city shall be wrought, / Defiance to the haughty neighbor.'"

When as we all paused for a breath, as if on cue, we burst into laughter that we should all stand here, on a sunny May day, reciting Pushkin together.

"How I love that poem," said Sasha. She pulled a strand of hair from her mouth that the wind had ripped free from the bun atop her head. She tucked it behind her ear, though it did not long stay there.

"I cannot imagine this stretch of land devoid of buildings." Sergei cast his gaze from St. Isaac's Cathedral eastward toward the Admiralty, his hands stuffed deep into his coat pockets.

"Nor I." I linked my arm with his, feeling tenderly toward him in that moment. He started at my touch, but on seeing it was me beside him, smiled sadly, I thought, and patted my hand before plunging his own back in his pocket again.

"I love, thee, Peter's own creation," shouted Masha, her arms thrown out, her head back. "I love thy stern and comely face, / Neva's majestic perfluctation, / Her embankments' granite carapace, / The patterns laced by iron railing." She raised her voice above the resolute breeze and continued to recite. "And of thy meditative night / The lucent dusk, the moonless paling; / When in my room I read and write / Lampless, and street on street stand dreaming."

"Yes!" said Sasha, ignoring the few passersby who had stopped for Masha's "performance."

"How I love that section," said Masha. "What a master, Pushkin."

"Can there be any doubt?" Sergei took his hands from his pockets, releasing my arm, and held them out in question.

"What a *glor*-ious day!" I could not contain myself from whirling about a time or two, arms outstretched to heaven.

And with the warm camaraderie of schoolchildren, we headed homeward. With Sasha and Sergei walking ahead of us, getting better acquainted, I dared let my head rest against Masha's shoulder. It's easy to believe in a bright, untroubled future when the sun embraces you after a long, hard winter. And I believe.

25
Marya

Between the coming of spring and Grisha's encouragement, a kind of giddiness came over Masha. Grisha's optimism and his recommendations for reading caused her fire for mathematical pursuit to burn more strongly than ever.

Sophia Kovalevskaya, Marya thought to herself, *does not even know I breathe, and still she has become the torch that lights my way.*

Too, Grisha's enthusiasm—and his unwavering belief in her—made her suppose a life in mathematics was possible for a woman. She knew well it would not be an easy road, but she wanted so much to make the journey that she discounted the perils.

She was further bolstered by Vera's cheering on, and she appreciated well that Vera did not deride her for pressing on with her studies only when Grisha had intervened. It was not because Vera's faith in Marya had so little worth to her—meaningless as a block of ice to a citizen of Siberia in winter. Vera's belief in Marya, rather, was what let her fall more deeply in love with her, in those early days, when she was still so damaged from having lost Katya in her life and was afraid to let herself love anyone else again. At the same time, though, Marya was skeptical of Vera's verve for pushing her back onto the path of mathematical pursuit, given that Vera's love for her likely made her unmindful of the obstacles confronting a woman with a passion for mathematics in a way Grisha was not, and so in this one thing his opinion might bear more weight than that of Vera.

As he'd proposed in his letter, Grisha came for tea one day, the afternoon of his day off, in order that he and Marya might plan for her further mathematical education.

When Marya found him in the foyer, after Ilyusha had announced his arrival, he was holding a ridiculously large hat in his left hand.

"Marya—Masha!" He held his arms out as in a prelude to an embrace. "How lovely you have grown."

Marya approached, and he kissed each of her cheeks.

"And you, Grisha, dusted with chalk as ever."

Marya brushed the white powder from his lapel.

"Is today not your day off? How come you to have chalk on you today as well?"

"I believe after all these years, it now simply seeps from my pores," he said, shrugging.

The smell of chalk dust brought a shiver of memory to Marya of schoolgirl days—a memory, and a sneeze. He took over the brushing of his own lapel.

"Has Ilyusha forgotten to take your hat? Ilyu—"

"Please, Marya: no." He lightly touched her wrist. "I prefer to keep it with me. So seldom do I get to leave the halls of the Institute that I, well …"

He blushed again.

"Well come then," she said. "We shall put your hat on the table among the tea things, like a centerpiece." She noticed him lightly bite his lip. "Or you may keep it on your lap, if you wish."

Marya gave a light laugh, enjoying a side of him she had never had opportunity to see as his student.

"You must think me foolish." He looked down, when the two stood before the chairs in the parlor, and ran his fingers lovingly over the stiff brim.

"Oh, no, Grisha! I could never think that of you. I find it charming, that's all. Please—sit. It's a lovely hat."

"Do you think so?" He leaned forward in his chair. "I bought it at Nicholls & Plincke's English shop. I thought about getting—. Oh, but you do not care about my hat! You are merely being polite."

"No, truly, Grisha—it delights me to see this side of you."

"But of course. As a student, you and I would never have spoken of such things—especially, as I've said, since there is so little need of a hat when one teaches at the Institute. It was not a wise expenditure."

He again let his fingers trail lightly over the crown of the hat.

"If it hurts no one and it gives you pleasure, Grisha, it was not unwise. Would you like some tea?"

Nadezhda suddenly appeared, anticipating Masha's needs as at all times, it seemed, and poured the two of them a cup of tea. She set several sugar cubes along the edge of each saucer.

She gave a slight curtsy, then, and asked: "Might I get you anything else, Marya?"

"No. Thank you, Nadya. Thank you. You may go. Cracknel?"

Marya pointed to the plate on the table after Nadya had left, and they helped themselves to some food before resuming conversation.

"So tell me again," he said, "how you enjoyed Kovalevskaya's article in *Crelle's*. Was it not simplicity itself, the sort of thing which sets you to wondering why no one before has hit upon the solution?"

The two talked a while, then, about Cauchy's theorem and Abelian integrals and the like, which had both of them sitting on the edges of their seats and speaking with great animation, until several servants peeked their heads into the room to see if something was amiss.

Marya smiled a little to herself, realizing that most would consider their delight peculiar. But there they were, absolutely blissful, each of them, to have someone with whom to share their academic ardor. From time to time, one or the other of them might rise and go to the samovar for more tea, but they did not otherwise move from their seats for some hour or more, talking on uninterrupted.

At last, as darkness began to steal up the windowpanes, Grisha turned to the true reason for his visit.

"So. I must ask: Shall I implore Papa to approach his old friend for a letter of introduction?"

Marya sighed.

"In truth, I have thought of little else since receiving your letter. And you know I do not tend toward modesty. But—"

Marya paused a moment, distracted by the bright grin upon Grisha's face.

"But I feel modest about approaching such a man as Strannoliubsky. Can we not find someone of lesser stature with whom I might learn? I simply, that is, I think—"

"No, you mustn't think that way! And who else would we find? Me? But you see from our conversation just now you already outstrip me in the quickness of your perception. There is no one more deserving of working personally with Strannoliubsky than you. Or so, at any rate, you must convince yourself. For it will not do to approach this endeavor with timidity. You must strive to be like that young ruffian who once so often turned Madame Riasonovsky's characteristic pallor red as a cherry."

The two of them grinned at the thought of how she'd once vexed the headmistress at the St. Petersburg Institute for Girls.

"The floors of the Institute have been woefully less clean since you graduated," he said, referring to how often she had been made to get down on her hands and knees with a scrub brush and bucket in punishment for some infraction or other.

"Well." Marya said, still uncertain.

Grisha reached across the table and gave Marya's hand a quick squeeze.

"Yes," Marya said, then, "yes, have your father see if he can secure a letter of introduction so we might approach Strannoliubsky."

"Oh, Marya."

Grisha rose from his chair in one buoyant movement, and let his hat fall to the floor unnoticed. He took Marya's hands in his own as she also rose.

"How happy you have made me," he said.

As Masha turned to retrieve Grisha's hat, from where it had rolled behind her, she noticed that Sergei had stopped abruptly just outside the parlor door.

"Seryozha! You must—"

"Good day," he said nodding toward Grisha. "I do not mean to interrupt."

"No, Seryozha, you are not interrupting. Come: meet Grigor …" Marya trailed off as Sergei's rigidly upright back receded down the hallway to his room at the back of the apartment.

Marya turned back to Grisha and handed him his hat.

"That was my husband. Sergei Trepov. I had hoped to introduce you. He is a … a remarkable man."

Grisha's eyebrow rose but he politely refrained from speaking any misgivings.

"I must go," he said, then, shifting seamlessly from their moment of awkwardness. "But I shall write soon to let you know how it goes with father's friend and with Strannoliubsky. Oh dear. Oh dear me." He pressed his hat to his chest, over his heart. "This is *quite* exciting."

Then he kissed Marya's cheeks and was gone, while Marya was left to puzzle over Sergei's strange rudeness.

26
Sergei

16 May 1876

Dear god, Filya, what have I done? I have kissed Liudmilla. Not in polite greeting, but as a man kisses his wife. Or no—less tenderly than that.

Masha. Oh, my Masha! I have dishonored you in your own home. Need I tell you Masha is all I think of, cousin? Now especially, when I have reason to fear there may be another in her life. I saw them together when I returned from the Library two evenings prior. I suspect it was that Rostovtsev fellow with whom she professes to discuss mathematics by letter. But I saw the two of them together, Filya: his face bore far more joy than would result from a discussion of mathematics, of that I am certain.

I have not slept or eaten well for days now, so tormented am I by my love for Marya, and now, with the arrival of this apparent new rival … And yet it's Liudmilla whom I have grabbed in such base manner and pressed to me, forcing my lips upon hers like some loutish beast. Had not Vera and Nadezhda passed outside my door in conversation, I swear, Filya, I don't know what I might have done. I have disgraced the name of my father. I am too distraught right now to continue this missive. I must think—THINK—what it is I must do now. I fear all is lost, Filya. I am a cad, a coward, a fool!

Seryozha

27
Marya

There was no ignoring that shortly after Grisha's visit a change had come over Sergei. Even Marya could see he seemed haggard. Distracted.

The first time Marya noticed this, she, Vera, and Sergei were sitting over their evening meal. Sergei was particularly quiet, more than had been his custom. He seemed in ill humor, would not look at anything but his plate, on which the food sat growing cold.

Marya exchanged a look with Vera, who gave a shrug. Marya thought about asking him if something troubled him but she could not bring herself to do so, fearing his answer.

Her nervousness prompted a longing to talk—about anything, anything at all that might come into her head. But nothing did, and she felt the silence around the dinner table press in on her. At last, a carriage passing along the Moika suggested a topic to her.

"Did you have horses at Svetliachie Gory, Seryozha? Yes, of course you did," she said, not pausing for a response, "for you have told us about your father going hunting. Did you know I, too, used to go hunting?"

Marya paused for his response and when she got none, she continued as though she only need tell a bit of her story yet to rouse him. And if not, she reasoned, at least there would not be this horrible silence.

"It was Papa's idea; Mama did not at all approve. How strange it seems now, in a large apartment in the sprawling city of St. Petersburg, to think of myself hunting. In truth, it seems like another life, and of course it was, though strangely still my own somehow. Do you know," Marya said, turning to Sergei, "I sometimes wonder if I would even remember now what it is to mount a horse or fire a gun."

He glanced at her but said nothing. His eyes seemed dull and vacant, and Marya shuddered at the sight.

"Of course you would, Mashenka." Vera, too, was striving for a sense of normalcy. "I don't think those are the sorts of things one forgets. A name, perhaps, you might forget, but the body remembers things the mind does not."

With Sergei's chin now cradled in his palm and his eyes still directed down, Vera risked a raised eyebrow at Marya, but Marya merely frowned at her and continued.

"In truth, I loved Papa most of all for this—that he took me hunting like a son. Mitya was too small, you see, still clinging to Mama's skirts, and darling Timosha was only a baby. So Papa asked me to come along, even though he needn't have, of course. I felt terribly grown-up, I remember, when Papa and I went hunting. The first time I went with him is as sharp yet in my mind as the events of yesterday, though it was fourteen or fifteen years ago now.

"It was early in May, the time of year when woodcocks are most prevalent. Dusk had just begun to lay its gray filter over everything when Papa said we should ready ourselves to go. Dusk, he said, was the best time to hunt woodcocks. Papa and Nikolenka saddled the horses. My Uncle Sasha was visiting and came along too. The dogs, who knew without anyone saying so that we were about to go out for a hunt, began to pace restlessly in the yard. As for me, my senses were so alive with anticipation my skin tingled.

"At last, we were ready to go. Papa on Syvka, Uncle Sasha on his Ryzhik, and I on Tumasha, we rode to the marsh. Along the way, a gentle breeze whispered through the rye and wrapped itself around our limbs. The last slice of red from the sun slipped between the birch and aspens, and larks sang from pure joy, it seemed, at the coming of spring. Overhead, in the deepening blue, geese called out to each other as they flew in their orderly formation, back from their winter vacation. The dogs loped alongside us, their wet black noses pulling in all of the smells the warm night air had to offer."

"You are quite the poet, Marya," interrupted Vera. "What a lovely picture you paint with your words."

"I have had quite a long time to think about that moment," Marya replied. "Remembering those pleasant times was one of the ways I got myself through those lonely first years at the Institute. Though remembering also made me sad. Such an odd thing, how the same exact memory can make you both happy and sad.

"But in any case, we were all three of us, Papa, and my uncle, and me, awed by the majesty around us. It was I who first dared break the silence.

"'Papa?' I said.

"'What is it, Mashenka?' I remember how handsome Papa looked in his black leather riding boots and how his lean frame towered high above the ground up on Syvka. I could not see his dark eyes in the fading light, but I could tell by his gentle tone they looked on me kindly, as most always they did.

"'Papa, when will we hunt wolves?' I could not disguise the excitement in my voice, I remember, and my heart beat harder at just the thought of the sharp fangs and menacing yellow eyes of a snarling wolf."

Sergei looked up, but when he saw Marya's eyes on him, he quickly lowered his gaze.

"Papa and Uncle Sasha looked at one another and chuckled.

"'Ah, Mashenka! Let us first learn to shoot woodcocks, then perhaps rabbits before we go out to look for wolves.' And they chuckled again.

"But I did not mind their laughing at me, as you might think I would. What I heard was that someday I would indeed hunt wolves.

"We trotted along in silence, then, and listened to the music of the crickets and the steady rhythm of hooves on packed earth, while we watched the sun slip farther from the sky.

"When at last we reached the marsh, we climbed off the horses and lightly tethered them to a tree. The dogs—Buyanka and Druzhok, spectacularly beautiful borzois—how I miss, here in the city, having the company of a great, large dog! The dogs, as I was saying, moved in restless looping patterns around us while they waited for the signal to flush out the birds. I watched reverently as Papa loaded a gun for me.

"First he rested the butt of the gun on the ground with its barrels pointed up like the horses' flared nostrils—isn't that a strange image to recall? Then he poured gunpowder into each barrel. The powder had a fine acrid smell that caused my mouth to water. After the powder, he put in little wads of felt and tamped these down with a ramrod. The ramrod, when it struck the felt, bounced up, clanging, but Papa continued to tamp until the ramrod jumped right out of the muzzle. Then he loaded the shot into the barrels, which he tamped down too.

"'Hyah!' he called to the dogs. 'Hyah! Buyanka, Druzhok—to the birds.'

"The sky, then, was a light purple, and the dogs, as they ran out toward the marsh, had no color of their own. My heart beat with such fervor it masked the frogs' throaty songs and the goodnight calls of peewits. I scanned the sky, afraid I would miss the first urgent flurry of feathers when the dogs flushed out the woodcocks. When the woodcocks began to climb into the sky, dark spots in the dim light, I wanted to be ready. I put the butt of the gun up against my shoulder as I had seen Papa do and practiced taking aim along the barrel.

"'No, Mashenka,' he said kindly and took the gun from me. 'First you will watch,' he said. He carefully handed the gun back to me, and just as he did so, there was a flurry of wings and the frantic cries of woodcocks taking flight. Papa quickly took aim and fired, but he did not hit any. I bit my lip, feeling responsible for his missed shot. He gave an unhappy sigh, and I looked at him, hoping for absolution.

"'It's fine, Mashenka. There will be more birds. Come. Let us go meet the dogs.' Uncle Sasha chewed pensively on the end of his mustache as we waded through the tall, damp grass. Uncle Sasha, who had not endured the same distractions as Papa, had been luckier and had downed a bird. We looked to see who would bring it back, Buyanka or Druzhok. Secretly, I hoped it was Buyanka, who was my favorite. One wonders, as a grown woman, why such a thing should matter, but it did."

"I understand perfectly!" Vera's hand was poised with a morsel of fish speared on her fork. "I often worried, as a girl, that my favorite goat—do not laugh! Yes, I had a favorite goat. We kept, always, one or two that we might have the milk whenever we liked, and sometimes the meat. Papa said he much preferred goat milk to that of a cow."

"Truly?" Marya said. "I have always found goat's milk to have a curious taste." Marya wrinkled her nose. "But your goat—tell us of your goat. Did you dress it in petticoats?" Marya said in a teasing way, trying to block Sergei's pained-looking face from her sight.

"No more than you did Buyanka," she retorted. "Besides, my favorite goat was male. At any rate, I worried my goat did not get as much of the food scraps as the other goats and I would try to chase them away."

"Did it work?"

"No, but he was as fat as anything, so I think he was doing just fine without me! But was it Buyanka who brought back the bird?"

Marya felt increasingly uneasy, the longer Sergei remained silent, but she felt she was too far into the story simply to abandon it and so pressed on.

"No, of course not: you know it was Druzhok who trotted over with the drooping bird dangling in her mouth, as you've heard this story before."

"Yes, but I do not wish you to skip any of the story. And next?"

"Then Papa patted Druzhok on the head and told her she was a good girl. When she dropped the bird at his feet, I picked it up and handed it to Uncle Sasha to put in the leather pouch he wore at his side. 'Hyah!' Papa shouted with no ceremony, and the dogs were off again.

"'Now. Mashenka,' he instructed, 'you must put the gun so,' and he positioned the butt against my right shoulder and placed my left hand at the base of the barrel. 'Use these two fingers to pull the trigger,' he said. 'When you are older and stronger, you will need only the first finger. Use the end of the gun to line up the bird. Follow it a bit until you are sure you have it in your sight and so you can better guess at its path of flight. Then, when you are ready, pull the trigger. But above all, Mashenka, relax. If your shoulder is too tight when you fire, it will hurt all the more when the gun kicks back.' Uncle Sasha nodded his assent to this advice, still chewing on his mustache. 'You will do fine, little one,' he said and clapped me lightly on the shoulder. He had noticed, I suppose, my nervousness.

"Then we all turned our attention to the deeply muted sky in hopes of at least one more shot at the birds, though no one hoped more fervently than me. But alas, while birds did rise again and we watched as three of them dropped like stones into the field, not one of them had dropped because of a shot of mine."

Sergei had leaned forward, his forehead resting on the heels of his hands, his fingers gripping at his hair. Masha felt like it would be awkward, at best, to continue and deeply suspected it was altogether thoughtless. She wondered whether she should stop. But if she did, would they all, then, just sit in grave silence? Just as she was trying to screw up her courage and ask Sergei what was troubling him, Vera spoke up.

"Go on." She leaned forward, her chin upon her hands, with great affection evident in her eyes, which only increased Marya's discomfort. She wondered whether Vera was insensible to Sergei's apparent anguish or whether she was, possibly, enjoying it. But no, Vera, too, must be confounded by his strangeness and yearning for some sense of regularity, reasoned Marya. At any rate, Marya had set a path from which she did not quite know how to depart with any grace.

"Papa said I should not be concerned as it was only my first time and I would do better next time. Nevertheless, I was disappointed: when we had set out that evening, I was confident I would bring home at least one bird. I was cocksure of myself in those days."

"Unlike now, of course," said Vera. Her comical interjections made Marya feel yet sorrier for Seryozha, so she did not engage in her banter.

"Papa whistled for the dogs," Marya continued, even as she wondered, yet again, at the wisdom of having undertaken this long story. She had begun to wonder, as well, whether Seryozha would even notice if she simply stopped.

"When we … when they barked, we made our way toward them to collect the rest of the birds.

"We walked back to the horses, then, the dogs running out ahead of us, and Papa draped his arm over my shoulder, and I let my head lean on his hip. I could not tell if I was tired or sad—do you know what I mean?"

Marya had been about to turn toward Sergei, but quickly aborted that inclination. She felt herself flush, and pondered why she could not bring herself to address him directly, to express concern over his obvious ill state.

"But this is how it went for some time or two more," Marya said, eager to be done with this story. "I fretted constantly at my inability to hit anything, but Papa was patient and continued to make small adjustments in my stance, the way I followed the trajectory of the bird, how I positioned my eye, and so on. With each shot, my eyes watered from the smoking powder.

"At last I downed a bird," Marya plunged on, grateful to finally be bringing this torture to an end. She spoke rapidly, almost as if by rote.

"I wanted to jump up and down and shout, but I recall thinking that did not seem very grown-up, so I contained myself to a smile. I looked over at Papa, who nodded approvingly.

"But when Buyanka dropped the blood-caked bird at my feet and I picked the lifeless body out of the mud, my joy, for a moment, was diminished at the realization those brown-speckled wings would never enrich the night sky again. I cradled the slack form in my arms. Its long bill rested near my left elbow, and I stroked its downy head.

"Then Papa tousled my hair. 'That's my girl, Mashenka. Well done,' and I was once again filled with pride. I held the bird out to Papa to put in his bag and formed a grin on my face before Papa could notice my weakness and think me soft and not fit to be a hunter. Can you imagine? I so wanted to be a boy at that age."

Sergei remained disconsolate, and Marya could no longer bear to ignore his wretched state.

"Seryozha … Are you—" She spoke softly, as if fearful of startling a nervous horse, and still he reacted badly.

"What?" he replied impatiently. "Am I what?"

His chair scraped the floor as he abruptly stood up.

"I have work to do in my study."

Then, just as he was about to turn down the hallway, he paused briefly in the doorway, and Marya saw his shoulders sag. He turned toward the two women, then, but his eyes were focused on the sideboard.

"Forgive me." His voice was so faint, they could barely hear him. "I … I have been tired," he said, then left the room.

28
Vera's Journal

Friday, 19 May 1876

Really, given the events of the day, I ought be sleeping right here where I sit. But in fact, I find myself altogether invigorated, for though the day was a long one, it was rousing.

And yet I must be tired, still, for in what peculiar fashion have I set out to record a day's events! My thoughts are clearly in a muddle, in need of sorting. I shall try, hence, to present the passing of the day in its proper order.

In the morning, I gave Varya the task of copying a passage from *Eugene Onegin* so she might practice her penmanship, while Pasha and I worked on recitation:

His hair cut in the latest mode;
He dined, he danced, he fenced, he rode.
In French he could converse politely,
As well as write; and how he bowed!
In the mazurka, 'twas allowed
No partner ever was so sprightly.
What more is asked? The world is warm
In praise of so much wit and charm.

We passed the afternoon with some dreary lessons on religion, I'm afraid, with which I had difficulty holding the children's attention. Or it may be the coming celebration proved too much distraction. Suffice it to say, there was much squirming in their seats and some squabbling between them.

At last, however, the dinner hour had come, and as I was invited to join in the marking of Varya's name day, we gathered in the dining room, which was gaily lighted with candles and lamps, and the chandelier was festooned with colorful ribbons. Varya jumped up and down and clapped together her hands when we entered, then ran to her mother and hugged her about the waist.

"Thank you for remaining with us for the festivities this evening, Vera," said Evdokia. "Varya fairly adores you." At which, my young pupil buried her face in her mother's skirts.

"Varya has an eager mind. She is a pleasure to teach. As is Pasha. I am honored to be included among your guests this evening."

Shortly, then, other guests—cousins, business associates of the children's father, aunts, and uncles—began to arrive and we sat down to a feast. After, Varya received her gifts, and then I apologized for taking my leave so early, but I was to join Marya at a meeting.

I took a carriage to the Vyborg District, where many of the women enrolled in the Courses for Learned Obstetricians lived. I do not think I could have their dedication, to direct all of my financial resources into my education so that I must live in the most impoverished section of the city. It had been years since I had been to the Vyborg, but I knew that my poor boarding house of last year, after my parents were both gone, would likely seem sumptuous by comparison. And our apartments on the Moika? A veritable palace!

With a degree of guilt taking root, I watched the demeanor of the city's face change as the carriage bumped along. When we passed the Hay Market, I saw peasants packing up the wares they had brought to sell—butter, vegetables, milk, fish—and winced to see the pigs, frozen, leaned against a wall, having been pulled from a cellar somewhere, its melting blocks of ice harvested from the Neva in December or January, I expect, running pink, now, with porcine blood. I shuddered to think of it. There before me, however, with no imagining required: a brigade of a hundred pigs, all set upon their hind legs to make the best use of space. It's a sight not to be matched for grisliness, the heads lolling to the side where throats were cut at the start of winter, the eyes staring blankly from the masks of their faces, each giving poignant expression to the sorrows of this life. I turned my face from the city, then, and my thoughts to my destination.

Marya was eager to attend tonight's meeting—which was held in the cramped room of one of the school's students—as she had heard these students were not eager to pursue revolutionary roads to their ideals. With so many activists now held in prison by the authorities, neither Masha nor I desire to test the limits of their repressionist zeal. Masha, despite her impatience with all manner of stupidity and her tendency to flare, is at heart a peaceful person. As for me, I do not wish to martyr myself for a cause that gives no notice to the issues of women in its visions of the future and expects women will once again sacrifice themselves for the good of all. In this, the revolutionaries differ little from their conservative counterparts!

When I stepped from the carriage, I was struck by how dismal the street was, with buildings cramped together like toes in a shoe too small and air dank with sewage and decay. I nearly called out to the driver not to depart without me. A woman approached from the other direction, then, and was greeted by whistles and shouts of "Hey, vivisectionist!" "Disemboweled any corpses lately?" The laughter following this wittiness hit me like a slap, but the woman in the medical school uniform at whom the comments were directed affected to pay them no mind. I hoped Masha had not been detained: I did not relish leaving this district at a late hour unescorted.

The stairwell was dark, with only one lamp lit on a landing several floors up. I followed the student up the sloping stairs and tried not to focus on the thick odor of overcooked cabbage and misery. We stopped at the doorway on the right on the fourth floor.

"You are coming to the meeting?" She gestured with her thumb toward the door.

I nodded yes.

"Iulia Kviatkovskaia," she said.

"Vera—" I cleared my throat. "Excuse me. Vera Dashkova. I am pleased to make your acquaintance."

"Come," she said, "we are at the room of my friend, Varvara." She gave the door two sharp raps, then opened it without waiting for a response.

When a view of the room was before me, I took it in quickly, for there was little to take in: a sagging bed, a stool with a cracked seat, a wooden chair with half the back broken off, and a dented samovar on a crudely built shelf nailed to the wall. Against the wall leaned several other women, many also in medical school uniforms. Others gathered in small groups and spoke quietly, though one group was difficult to distinguish from another given that the room was of such modest size there was scant space between any of us. The room, as I'd come to expect, was thick with cigarette smoke, but not so dense that I was prevented from noticing the rapid scurrying of several cockroaches along the wall below the shelf.

"Verochka!" Masha pressed her way through the crowd toward me, placed her familiar hands upon my arms and thrice kissed my cheeks. "You have arrived! We are nearly to begin. Did Varya enjoy her celebration?"

She steered me to an unoccupied square of floor space. Before I could respond in any fashion, there was the scrape upon the floor of a wooden box at the back of the room, and the woman with whom I had shared the stairwell climbed upon it.

"My friends," she said. Her voice carried with ease throughout the tiny room. "I know many of you here and know that you, like me, do not wish to provide the school authorities with any pretext for closing the courses. In spite of those who disdain us for remaining, as they say, on the margin of the movement, I know that we are in support of the cause."

"Here, here!" A soft cheer rose among several of those gathered.

"I mean not only ideologically but materially as well, when the means are available to us. My brothers Timofei and Aleksander have dedicated their lives to the movement. Some of you have seen them here or in my room the next floor up, come to store such documents as those with which the authorities find fault or to meet out of sight with others in the movement. You, too, perhaps have your own story of providing some small refuge without actually becoming plainly involved in the movement. I see you nod."

She pointed her finger at first one then another and another of the women.

"Then you will be pleased, especially, to welcome our visitor, Marya Subbotina, newly released from her imprisonment for distributing illegal literature to the workers at the textile factory in Ivanovo-Voznesensk. Marya, though near death from time spent in a punishment cell beside an unbearably hot stove, has taken no time to recover and is instead here tonight to solicit our help. I introduce her to you now."

Iulia Kviatkovskaia's head disappeared among the sea of others to make available the box to Marya Subbotina, who was barely visible, even so, above the other heads. She had the same hollow cheeks that Lidia did during the time I had known her, and indeed the effort of climbing atop the box was enough to cause her to begin coughing. Too, her face was badly scarred. I heard later that she had tried to burn herself alive, so desperate was her situation while in prison.

Once she had stopped coughing, though, her voice was surprisingly strong: rich and mellow.

"Thank you, fellow fighters for truth and freedom, for hearing me out. I have come to beg your help on behalf of those who have not been so lucky as to be released from prison yet. It has not been me alone on whom the rank prison conditions have exacted a profound toll. Beta Kaminskaia—poor Beta! She was, it's true, released into her father's custody—but only after a period of confinement in a mental hospital. Anna Torporkova tried to poison herself by eating matches. And one of the men, Georgievsky—his desire to escape the dreadful conditions under which they hold us was so strong that he hit his head against the wall repeatedly in an effort to find freedom in death!

"Friends, I beg of you: please join me in easing their plight in whatever small ways we can. I have been making bed linens for them, and I also have as a goal to collect books to help them turn aside their most desperate thoughts and mon—" here she paused to cough, "and to collect money for extra rations of food or small items they might need." She pulled a handkerchief from her sleeve and wiped tears from her cheeks. "The students among you especially, I know, are far from rich, but if you have anything to spare ..."

Several women, among them Masha, pulled rubles from their pockets or purses and handed them forward. Someone had found a china cup, and the clink of coins could be heard as it was passed around the room. I began to weep for all the injustice and, at the same time, for all the kindness in our dear Russia. Masha put her arm around my waist and pulled me close. I blew my nose loudly with no care for demureness.

"Thank you. I thank you for your generosity," said Marya Subbotina, the chipped cup in her hands overflowing with coins. "Books! Yes," she said, in response to a question from someone. "If you have books to contribute, you may send them here to Iulia Kviatkovskaia's room above; she will see they are sent to me.

"If we do not all agree on the best route to help the people, nor, perhaps, even on what our goals should be, whether to alleviate the plight of the poor or to improve the lot of women, we are in agreement, at least, that change must come. And we will work toward it in the fashion best suited to our temperaments. I am not here to challenge your way but encourage you to continue to engage in the struggle.

"There are those who feel chastened—frightened, even—by the large number of us who were arrested and locked away. And for what are we locked away? For trying to educate the worker about the conditions of their employment. Is this a crime, I ask you, to seek betterment?"

Murmurs and shouts of no.

"Your tsar and his minions think so! But we know it's not so. We all have a right to decent wages and living and working conditions. You, standing before me, may be right to feel little can be done to further the cause when one's actions result in captivity within a prison's walls. Fine, then. Let us regroup, strategize, work within the system, if you deem that best. And support those who may yet give their lives."

She raised the cup of coins over her head, and several spilled out as she stepped down.

"Bless you, Marya Subbotina!" someone shouted.

"Thank you."

"Da svidanya!"

"Such a noble warrior."

The crowd erupted in cries of gratitude. I leaned heavily into Masha, glad for her corporeal reassurance.

The extravagant pain and sacrifice of these women, when I think of it now as I write, makes me all the less sympathetic to Sergei's troubles, whatever they are, for surely he has made them himself.

29
Sergei

20 May 1876

Dear Kolya,

I thank you for your letter. I feared I had been too harsh with you. Now I know I have.

Masha, since you ask, is quite well. She stays busy with women's meetings—not philanthropic groups, like Maman, of course, but more educational, maybe even political. Since I have never myself gone, I cannot say with certainty.

I am most happy to hear you and Elizaveta are getting on well. But no talk of a wedding date? I fear I begin to sound like Mamochka, but, really, Nikolai, do you not think it's time for you to settle down? This is one time I beg you not to procrastinate, brother, as is your usual habit: to keep your love at bay is not a prudent thing.

I'm afraid this will be but a note, Kolya, and a short one at that. I have not been getting enough sleep of late. You may grin at this, if you like, but I am too drained to protect my dear wife's honor.

I will write again soon, for I fear I have repaid badly your time and thoughtfulness in writing so graciously to me.

Your undeserving brother,

Seryozha

30
Grigorii

22 May 1876

Masha, my dearest protégée,

Our adventure begins! Papa has heard me out, and though he is himself no scholar of mathematics, he trusts my estimation of your talents: he promised to begin a letter to Vassily Strannoliubsky as soon as I had departed. If we are in luck, if Strannoliubsky is not abroad and is in a charitable frame of mind, perhaps we will hear news as soon as a few weeks from now.

It will be all I can do, now, to keep from watching the time during each class every day to see how long till I may check for mail. And if my students have paled beside your considerable light, never more so than as we consider where your journey will take us as teacher and former pupil. I should feel shame, for I fear I may give my present students short shrift when it comes to the care with which I deliver my lessons, but I tell myself all will be worth it, when you, dear friend, work at the side of a true mathematical genius and I may stand nearby to catch what of your gleanings may trickle down my way. Then someday I may pass along to my students this golden knowledge.

My mother, since you ask, is quite well. You needn't feel untoward for venturing to inquire after my family, which you have worried might be taking liberties. I sense the rapport we have achieved and the correspondence we have shared have allowed us some additional intimacy. The Institute, as you know, can be a lonely place—and this is so even for a teacher—away so long from one's family and with such a closed circle in which to discover friends. This is why your letters, with those from my sister Elizaveta and my young brother, at the Alexander Lyceum (Nikolai is his name), are such a joy in my life. Liza has a new baby, and I yearn to watch the children grow and flourish. There is nothing to be done about it as long as I remain here at the Institute, though I am grateful for the long summer months in which I can join Liza and her husband Alexei and the children in Rybinsk.

Since we are finding a new place for confidences in our relationship, you and me, I should like to confide there is some unexpected compensation, at last, for my time here at the Institute—besides your own bright light, of course. I have become acquainted with the new teacher of French, Mademoiselle Tatiana Pavlovna Verstovskaia. I am, to tell the truth, quite smitten. She has a voice like smoke, eyes that flash like fire, and red-gold hair that shines like the sun. (Do you thank the heavens, for the hundredth time, that I do not pretend to poetry?) She is lithe of frame and nimble of mind. I have told her of my prize pupil (that's you, in the event you are not confident of my meaning), and she hopes to meet you someday. What a delight, were two of the most radiant women I know to become acquainted!

And what of you? Is your husband well? He did not seem so when he arrived at your apartments the day of my visit, and it has caused me some consternation on your behalf. He is not of a violent nature, is he? It eases my concern to know whatever his nature you have an ally there in Vera. I wish I had had an opportunity to encounter her. I know she must be of robust character to withstand the stormy nature of my Marya!

I must go. I have an assignation with Mademoiselle Verstovskaia beneath the ash tree in the courtyard, where we hope to enjoy the improved weather while we walk and exchange pleasantries.

Please write and tell me all is well with you; I wish to hear no tales of an ill-tempered husband. I also wish for a report of any progress you may have made on your project.

Eagerly,

Grisha

31
Sergei

24 May 1876

Filya, my cousin, why do I not receive a post from you?

I am sentient of the verity that though an eternity seems to have passed, since last I wrote, it's naught but a week—scarce enough time for a letter to reach you in that southern clime, for you to pen a reply (especially to a message so deranged as one I sent you), and for that reply to reach my doorstep here. And yet I yearn for your counsel, for I am in a stew of regrets and passions, Filya, and I am made nearly immobile with my storm of emotions. Liudmilla and I have broken off lessons. I have written her a formal note of apology for my misbehavior. I am not unmindful of the irony that, had I not been teaching her to read and write, she likely would not be able to decipher my note. At any rate, I am quite sure I have offended her—of course I have!—for she avoids my eyes. Or maybe it's my eyes who avoid hers. At any rate, we contrive to pass one another as quickly as our feet will carry us when we chance to meet. And now I am a truly lonely man, Filya.

For in my shame, I excuse myself from dinner early, when I am home, but mostly I stay for long hours at the Library, then wander the streets of Petersburg, a tormented man, insensible often to the elements or my basic needs. Some evenings, a twinge of hunger has broken through the haze of my thoughts and feelings, and so I have stopped at Leiner's for some Black Sea oysters and pickled mushrooms or, most often, I have bought only tea from this street vendor and boiled eggs and sausages from that one, standing in the very street and eating them from the scratched plate and with the fork provided by the vendor. I cannot be a pleasure to watch, for I take no pleasure in the eating.

Of all my wishes now, and I have many, I wish, dear Filya, you were here to proffer advice to me, put your hand on my shoulder to steady me, or slap my haggard face to loosen the tangle of thoughts behind it. This problem of mine, with its twin fangs, causes me to beat against the ice like a fish. It's useless to hope for a good resolution, I am convinced. And yet I must do *something*. And soon: for even Marya has made note of my restive demeanor.

"Your eyes!" she said in alarm, the other night at dinner. "They are swollen and red. Shall I call the doctor, Sergei? Are you ill? You have been working long hours at the Imperial Library—perhaps you have exhausted yourself. Verochka—have Ilya send for the doctor."

"No!"

I jumped from the table, overcome by this small kindness on her part and not wanting a doctor to visit, since he would discover my only ailment to be one of the soul.

"I am a grown man, Marya, and wife though you may be, I will attend to my own health."

I cast her a glance, then, meant to be imploring of her understanding but I fear it conveyed, instead, malevolence, for she leaned back in a kind of horror. I turned then and left the room.

I went to lie upon my bed, though I expected no rest. And none did I get. I tore open my shirt collar, for I felt I could scarce breathe, and the button torn from it gave an emphatic ring against the porcelain pitcher. I ran my fingers through my hair like a madman, pulled at it, wishing to wrench the anguish from my brain. Then, Filya (does a man admit this to another man? I am too demoralized to care), I began to weep. Not soft tears, running poetically down my coarse cheeks, but deep wrenching sobs, so I buried my face in a pillow lest the women or the servants hear.

If you were here to guide me, I am sure you would give me good advice, for even as a very young man, you gave me advice wise beyond your years. Desperate to unburden myself to someone, to find advice and solace, I bethought myself to meet with Lyova for dinner. I asked to meet at Palkin's, not contemplating at all what famous composer I might chance to see there or which of Lyova's compatriots might espy his red tie. My only thought was that the organ music might cover any weeping to which I might succumb.

From the minute I saw him, though, I felt my mission would end in failure. How might I confess that my marriage, which seemed to offer some measure of comfort to him in the name of love sought and kept, was naught but a sham? And even were I to do so, would he, with such different sensibilities, even understand? But in truth, it's the shame I feel at my corrupt nature, my weakness, that kept me all but mum.

I picked at the smoked goose, the radishes, the dried sturgeon, but scarce had they touched my lips than I returned them to the plate. My spoon sat like a lost anchor at the bottom of the bowl when the fish soup was served. And though I thirsted, I could not swallow a drop of my Kalinkinski Pale Ale with its clean, pure taste. Purity and I have no business together these days.

Poor Lyova! He endeavored to cheer me, to inquire after my health, to extract my thoughts. But I could do no more than utter a groan here, a tortured squeak there.

"Seryozha—tell me what is wrong with you or I shall go mad with worry!" he said at last and put his hand upon my shoulder in a brotherly fashion.

The tenderness of his concern was too much for me to bear.

"I must go," I said, in a half sob, threw some rubles on the table, scraped my chair across the floor, gathered quickly my things, and careened my way to the door like a man crazed.

I walked toward the Moika in a daze, half fearing, half hoping I would throw myself across the embankment into the canal's icy water. But coward that I am, I merely returned home, slinking in like a thief, a criminal, which surely I am, for I am as nefarious as any who have broken some law.

So in the end, I remain utterly alone here, in my dilemma as in my life, and my decisions must be my own, though surely they will be flawed as my character—how could they be else?

I am coming to a resolution, Filya, that even in my delirium of passions I know you will say is mad, but I see no superior course, and perhaps it could have a better outcome than we expect. Of course it will not, but I must hope. And what I must do, Filipp, is I must confess. I must confess all to Marya: my love for her, my sleepless nights dreaming of her touch, my indiscretion with Liudmilla in the lunacy of my desire for her, for Mashenka alone. A tender embrace from her, Filya, or even a kind word could put my racing thoughts to rest. I crave her love, it's clear even now to me, but perhaps her understanding and forgiveness will allow, at least, some peace within my tortured soul.

This is no way to live. Why did I not listen to you, Filya? I am naught but a fool.

I will seal up this letter, which bears witness either to my saving or to my folly, and fetch Ilya to see to its posting. Then I will throw myself on Marya's mercy. Wish me well, fair cousin.

With more feeling than reason,

Seryozha

32
Vera's Journal

Wednesday, 24 May 1876

When Sergei was but a visitor to Lidia's parlor, I found him charming, sweet—quite lovely for a man. Now he is resident in Marya's home, it's another matter entire. For I remain firm in my opinion that, were he given the choice, Sergei would prefer to be sole resident of Masha's heart.

Though he is lately but a dismal version of himself, I have guarded against a softening of my feelings for him—some one of us must remain mindful of the secret yearning I am persuaded he harbors. And so, while Masha expresses her concern over his debility, I have withheld my sympathy. At dinner, I have tried to counter the somber mood, but Masha feigns not to notice my entreaties to engage in banter or, worse, gives me a look of irritation.

"Can you not show the man a bit of compassion?" she has asked when we are alone in our quarters.

No, I cannot, I want to call out, for I suspect what he harbors in his heart is anything but honorable. Yet I remain silent. Sullen.

However, tonight not even I could keep my heart shut against Sergei. When he joined us at table his eyes were red rimmed, his hair untidy, his shoulders sloped like those of a condemned man. He stirred his soup despondently, and though he several times brought the spoon near to his dry lips, he could not seem to bring himself to take the sustenance. His breathing was labored. (How well I know every shade of breath, having shared a home with a consumptive!)

Nadya came to clear the soup things.

"Are you done, sir?" she asked of Sergei.

Receiving no response, she said, "Sir?"

"What?" He raised his head to look at her. "Yes," he said then. "Yes, please: take it away."

He pushed the bowl toward her, closed his eyes, and then sighed, as though it were the hardest work he had ever had to do. Nadya knit her brows and silently cleared away his bowl.

Marya seemed about to speak, but I was unable to refrain from blurting out, "Sergei! Truly something is amiss. Shall I—do you want us to—"

The forbidding glare he turned upon me made me cease. I turned with pleading eyes to Masha. She placed a finger to her lips.

"Sergei—Seryozha."

Her voice had a soothing tone. She reached across the corner of the table toward his hand, which was lying there, inert. Never had I seen such sadness expressed in a *hand*. As Misha's fingers were about to close about his own, she suddenly withdrew. I saw it too: there was a look in his eyes like that of a starved dog sighting a few scraps of meat on a bone. Masha cleared her throat.

"Seryozha—are you … ill? Do you need a doctor? I don't mean to pry or to … to … Shall I send Ilyusha for Dr. Chlenov?"

"A doctor?" He sat stiffly upright in his chair, his fists balled on the table. "A doctor? Ask again, if you must." He spoke in a loud snarl, and Nadya, who had been about to begin bringing the main course, turned about and shooed back Liudmilla as well. The aroma of buttered caraway potatoes drifted into the room in her wake. "A doctor!"

"Seryozha—calm yourself. We—Verochka—Vera and I—we are just concerned for you. You look … you look … you appear to be … not quite—yourself."

"A doctor!"

He repeated this single word again as he rose from his seat. He rested his knuckles on the table and leaned forward.

"You know nothing. A doctor! A doctor cannot help me."

Then he shoved back his chair so quickly it toppled over, but he seemed unaware of the loud crash that drew the servants in from the kitchen.

As he left the dining room, he raised his hands and face skyward and said, in a strangled voice, "Let God help me, if he can."

His hands balled into fists, and he raked the knuckles down his face. And then he was gone.

When the servants saw the toppled chair and Misha frozen, halfway out of her seat, Nadya held her arms out to her sides and began to back all of the assembled servants through the doorway from which they'd entered. Marya thumped down in her seat.

"Nadya," she called, just as the door was about to close behind her. "Nadya, please: if you could serve the rest of the dinner now."

I rose and set Sergei's chair aright.

"Monsieur … Monsieur … what of Monsieur Sergei?"

"It's fine, Nadya. He is only a bit ill at the moment; do not trouble yourself. He will not be eating with us tonight, however. But if you please, could you now bring dinner for Vera and myself?"

We could scarcely eat, of course. And we dared not discuss what had happened lest he reenter. The silence was hollow and disagreeable. Once or twice we tried to break it—are not the potatoes delicious? do you think it will storm tonight?—but we could not sustain it, and at last we set aside our napkins and utensils and retired to our room, too distressed even to consider attending tonight's women's meeting, though it was a decision we came to wordlessly.

When we were closed in our room, I turned at once to Masha.

"Mashenka—I am frightened: What is amiss with Sergei?"

"I don't know, Verochka, yet it's something, clearly. But you need not be frightened, little dove."

She smoothed away a stray hair or two that had fallen onto my forehead.

"It's true," she continued, "we have never before heard him raise his voice. But Verochka: it's Sergei. Sergei Trepov! He is no more capable of doing harm than are you, my darling."

She cupped my cheek in her hand, and absentmindedly left it there, her eyes focused on some distant point.

"Except perhaps …?" Her voice trailed away, barely above a whisper.

"Oh, Masha! How can I have thought him capable of meanness?" After a pause, I added what I might have realized earlier: "I could have been kinder to him."

I turned quickly aside lest Misha see my eyes well up.

"As could I," she said. I could feel the soft caress of her breath on my ear as she leaned in behind me. She put her arms about me and nestled her face into the angle of my shoulder and neck. My guilt spilt out, then, and tried to wash itself away with tears. We did not speak a word, but she made tighter her hold upon me, at which my guilt and sadness washed over me the more.

At last she kissed me on the cheek and, yet behind me, gave my hips a gentle squeeze.

"Come. Let us ready ourselves for bed. The morning is wiser than the evening. Perhaps we will see more clearly what must be done when we reach the other side of the night."

After we had washed our faces and put on our night things, we climbed beneath the covers. Masha covered my face with a dozen kisses light as the brush of a rose petal.

"In the morning," she said. "Things will most certainly look less somber."

She drew back, then, and gazed upon my face. In the dull flickering light of a single candle, I could just see her eyes, which seemed to drink in my every feature until I felt myself flush and turned aside. Gently, she turned me toward her again and held my face there with the curve of her palm. The wind outside, wishing to deliver a storm, knocked upon the window, but I barely noticed, for Masha held me in a kind of trance.

"You are my heart," she murmured and kissed me firmly upon the lips. "This is but another adversity we shall pass through as one. I promise you, Vera Dashkova."

She looked into my eyes again, then pressed her lips resolutely to mine and tasted from them, until our two mouths were joined as one and each tongue could not be distinguished from the other. I pulled aside then and gasped from a familiarly pleasant ache.

"But Misha—Seryozha."

"We will not allay his problem in this room tonight, no matter how long we might talk of it, whether we sleep or stir, whether my lips savor the sweetness of your neck or feel only the breath of my own slumber. There is but one thing I know without doubt, and it is I love you, Verochka mine. Is it so wrong that I seek, in you, an antidote to Seryozha's poisonous outburst? My heart is breaking for him: Will you not mend it?"

She nibbled hotly at my ear, then, and I moaned as though a purring cat. She pressed me to the bed and let her legs rest astride me while savoring my neck and shoulder. My hands hungered to know her for not a dream and coursed the hard wings of her shoulder blades, the fleshiness of her buttocks, and up again to just below the pits of her arms.

"Misha," I said, as if only just now had I determined who she was. "My darling."

I raised my head and let my lips wander from her neck to her chest. As they found her breast, her back arched in a kind of rapture, and through the cloth of her gown, my teeth played upon her nipple. She clutched my shoulders tightly with her hands and gave a small cry, and then another.

Thunder cracked, and as if it were a signal, we neatly turned so I was atop, with Mashenka's familiar shape below. I kissed her neck and cheek and ear with the abandon of a beast, Sergei's difficulty long since rudely pushed aside. The added guilt of our nocturnal selfishness here, this night, might ambush us at a later hour, but at that moment, I had little care for anything but my own ardor.

Masha rolled me from her. As she lifted the hem of my gown, I thrilled to the slightest brush of her fingers on my skin, and I squirmed in a kind of agony. She took my hands in her own and placed her lips upon where I dare not speak and nuzzled.

"Oh," I said. And, "oh," again. "Masha!"

The covers were bunched at our feet, but I don't think I felt the cold. I let go her hands and clutched the sheets, my eyes closed, as I let myself be lifted, my back arched like a ballerina in flight. Thunder clapped again, and lightning shown like a lantern before my shut eyelids.

"Masha?" I said, and she laid her head upon my thigh. "Masha—did you hear something?"

"The thunder?" She lifted her head to look at me. "Was there thunder? I could not hear it above your cries."

I reached to give the crown of her head a good-humored rap, but she spun aside and grasped my legs behind the knees, and we played at fighting until we had once again fallen into heated embraces and ardent kisses.

Misha fell into a heavy sleep, then, but guilt found me again and would not let me pass into blissful repose. I pulled my arm from beneath her and crawled inside this clothes cupboard to write down all of my terrible secrets as if this pure white paper were a confessor. At first I worried I would set the clothing alight with the lightly leaping flame of my candle, but as my scribbling grew more furious, my worry over the candle simply ceased.

The storm is quieting at least, and sleep seems finally wishing to pay me a visit, so I will snuff out the candle and find my way to our bed.

33
Sergei

24 May 1876, yet

Filya, oh Filya!

I have not been above imagining myself a fool, but I find I am now beyond my own imagining: what I have witnessed puts all in a new and garish light. Who could imagine such a thing? Even you, I dare say—even you, with all of your good sense and caution and insight—could not have imagined what I have seen. Do I rave? It's well I rave, for while I rave here to you, I can do no harm. What I have only just now witnessed, never before could I have supposed to be possible.

But if you are to understand me, I must impose some order on my chaotic emotions, which thrash about among my thoughts and disorder them. I went to Masha's room, as earlier today I wrote I would, and I knocked upon the door. Too impatient or too insensible to wait for a response, I threw it open, intent on my confession. I think I spoke her name, Mashenka, I said, or I think I did, but I cannot be certain for what met my eyes has blotted all else from memory: there, upon the bed, a sheet slipping from their nearly naked bodies, were Marya and Vera in the throes of passion, whispering one another's names and letting forth crude, wild noises. Friends? They are not dear friends, as I have believed, but lovers—as man and wife! And to think, after everything Lyova has—but never mind: two women together, in such a way—who could conceive such a thing?

"My God!" I wished to cry. "My God! What are you doing?"

But maybe I said nothing. I turned and ran from the room, I remember, and came straightaway here, where I have paced and smoldered and wept this past hour before writing to you of the night's events. I am sickened, Filya. Not by what I saw, though certainly it was shocking, but by the knowledge there can be no doubt now all hope is lost: I can never expect Masha's love.

What will I do, I ask myself, come morning? Might I petition for divorce? Such a petition would never be granted, for with what complaint would I bring the petition forth? The truth would be at once unbelievable and scandalous—damaging to me, to the woman I yet love (despite her perfidy), to the good names of our families. The fault would likely be seen as mine, and is it not, in some way? And anyway, divorce, in Mother Russia, is harder to come by than a home without a samovar.

Yet how can I face this new knowledge in the blinding light of day? This night, its blackness so suffocating and heavy, might seem like it will never end, but surely a new day will come. I will see their faces, as ever I have seen them before—but no, their faces will be disfigured for me by what I know. I know what they are. Who they are. Surely, I am less than nothing to them, to Marya—how can I possibly … I don't know, Filya. I don't know. Am I failed by my inability to conceive a happy outcome? I am failed. It has failed me, my imagination. I am a failure. Was ever the pain of sentiment so crippling?

34
Marya

How mistaken is the notion that, were something dreadful to happen, there would be some warning or at least a sense of foreboding. To be sure, that morning—oh, that terrible morning—the sun shone brightly, and the sky was brilliant, with a few small clouds looking like bare spots where the night's storm had scrubbed the sky's fabric clean through. It was the sort of morning that made one feel like life had begun all over again: fresh. And new.

Neither Verochka nor Marya wanted to lessen the intoxicating effect, and wordlessly conspired not to speak of Seryozha. At least ... not right off. They ate a hearty breakfast of boiled eggs and black bread, sipped at their tea, and gave passionate opinions about where Tolstoy intended to take them next in his story of *Anna Karenina* and wished the latest issue of the *Russian Messenger* would arrive so they could consult it to determine who might be correct.

But when the merriment had ebbed a moment, Marya looked at Vera and knew they were both thinking the same thing.

"Do you suppose we should go see to Seryozha?" Marya said. "It's unlike him to take breakfast so late. He is due at the Library in but an hour."

"Oh, but Marya—he grew so angry at us yesterday when we tried to intervene. Perhaps he would rather keep his own counsel?"

"In truth, Verochka, I don't know what is the best path. I wonder whether he is his own best adviser now."

The two fell silent a moment while they considered.

"Perhaps we will learn more if we enter the house through the servant's door, in a manner of speaking," Marya said.

Vera inclined her head in an attitude of listening and waited for Marya to go on.

"Let us not address directly the matter of what may be concerning him. Shall we invite him, instead, to the theater this evening? It may be enough for him to get out among others and divert his attention from his own travails."

"What a splendid idea, Misha. We will show our concern for him without calling undue attention. I shall go find him and tell him, shall I?"

"Yes, why don't you?"

As Marya walked over to the samovar to get more tea, she heard Vera knock on Sergei's door, just beyond, and call out, "Seryozha? Seryozha, are you there? We would like to invite you to join us at the theater this evening. Seryozha?"

Marya heard another knock, and then, after a pause at the door of his study: "Seryozha? Are you—"

Then Vera let forth a piercing scream, a scream unlike any Marya had ever before heard.

35
Sergei

~~24~~ 25 May
(midnight has passed: it's another day)

Dear Mama, Papa, and Kolya,

I have been failed by my power to imagine. I have been failed by my desire to bring about a betterment of our world. I have failed, in short, to abide by my own convictions. Failure is in my every breath, but I don't think I shall fail in my intentions this night, and so you shall receive these mad scribblings when my body is cold and bereft of life, as I am bereft now of a reason to continue along this decaying boulevard of existence.

You will not understand why I have done you the dishonor of taking my own life, and I cannot explain to you why it's a necessary act, so you must trust only I do not mean to hurt you. Even now, I think with a fond ache in my heart of my idyllic childhood, of the love and care you have shown me all my days, and I cannot believe, looking back at the wheel rut of my life's progress, that it's here I was destined to go. But there does not now seem to be any turn in the road, only this one way forward, to take my own life, so I can salvage something yet that's noble, though it may not seem so to you. But please, Mamochka, dear Papa, and darling Kolya, believe me when I tell you there is no other way.

If my hand seems shaky in the setting down of these words, do not think it's fear or indecision that mars their flow: I am resolved this course will be best for all. You will be shocked, for I have given you no hint of my melancholy. You may blame me for this lack of candor, but would it have been better to weigh you down, in letter after letter, with my sadness and failings? No, I think it's better if you receive it all at once, and so the dailiness of your lives heretofore will have been spared.

Why? you may ask. Why does an eldest son, a beloved brother, end his life before its time? But it's my time, of this I am convinced, though there is no explaining why this is so in a letter that can open but never close a conversation. Or rather, this letter *is* the close of a conversation for which I never found an opening with you. Any flaw here, however, is my own. Though I am ill-positioned to beg favors, I beg of you that you tell Filya that I love him and that I should have listened to him from the start; he will know what I mean.

I beg of you, too, that you not blame Marya: what I set out to do here is without her knowledge or her blessing; she is as blameless as you. She has enriched my life in countless ways, during the time of our brief marriage, and deserved a better reward than to find her husband dead, his blood staining the carpets of her ancestors. If you were to look in on her from time to time and provide for her, if need be, I know I shall rest more comfortably in my grave. She is and remains an extraordinary woman. What makes a man believe he can simply put on an ordinary pair of shoes to walk to heaven and pluck a star there for his own treasure?

I love you all.

Seryozha

36
Sergei

25 May, not yet morning

My most precious darling Mashenka,

Forgive me, first, if I take liberties, speaking to you so intimately, here at the threshold of my life's end, in a way I never dared when I was squarely in this life. Forgive me also for leaving you this way, but it has lately become plain my happiness here, with you, is impossible; it's so as not to interfere with yours that I depart.

You have made life both astonishing and full of torment. In the end, the latter has won out. Though not a breath of air may remain in the inert body you see before you, know my every pore is yet filled with admiration and love for you.

Can this truly have been God's plan? I am not so brazen as to guess at what He might have wanted, but my entire life repudiates the notion there was ever anything so grand as a design directing it.

Your devoted husband,

Sergei Trepov

37
Marya

The blood! You cannot imagine the blood. It had leapt to the walls in dark specks, and the carpet—there was naught they could do but dispose of it. Even a week and more later, there remained a dark stain in the wood of the floor that resisted every manner of cleansing.

But the blood was not what Marya saw at the outset. What greeted her first, when she'd heard Vera's scream and ran to determine the cause of it, was Vera herself, crumpled to the floor just in the hallway beside the door to Sergei's study. Marya dropped to her knees and pulled Vera's lolling head into her lap.

"Verochka," Marya whispered. "Vera, what is it? Please say you have not—"

Marya couldn't finish her thought, but instead touched her fingers, with trembling hand, to the place on Vera's neck that kept a measure of her life. With deep relief Marya closed her eyes in an involuntary prayer of thanks.

Still not looking beyond the woman she so loved, Marya tightened her hold on Vera's jaw as though she might yet slip away. Then she lightly tapped Vera's cheek.

"Verochka," she whispered. "Verochka. Tell me what has happened. Verochka—please: rouse yourself, my darling."

Marya's eyes stung as she worried the danger to Vera was perhaps more than slight.

"Verochka," she called more firmly.

Nadya could be heard racing in from the kitchen, her skirts and apron swishing loudly.

"Mademoiselle," she said, somewhat out of breath, "Marya shall I send for—" She stopped abruptly, nearly crashing into Marya and Vera, still sprawled before the doorway, and let out a gasp. She covered her face with her hands and turned toward the corner, away from Sergei's study.

"Nadya?"

With one hand still cradling Vera's head in place, Marya turned to where the maid stood.

"Nadya? Are you—"

Marya could see that Nadya was trembling.

Nadya let her hands fall from her face, then, and took the hem of her apron and swiped it across her eyes and held it to her mouth.

She had started to turn toward Marya, but quickly averted her gaze to the wall.

"Do you not see?" Nadya sounded angry. Or incredulous. Or perhaps both. "It's Sergei, Mademoiselle. Your husband."

Then she released a corner of her apron so that she might point, though not looking herself where she pointed.

Reluctantly, Marya slowly lowered Vera to the floor and let her head rest there, then rose.

"Seryozha?" she said, as she peered for the first time round the doorframe into his study, her heart beating swiftly as a borzoi giving chase.

"Dear God!"

She felt her boiled eggs and tea heave threateningly in her stomach and her knees began to buckle.

"Seryozha."

She steadied her voice as best she could and steeled herself to enter the room and see if he yet lived, though the dark pool about his head made it seem unlikely. She bent down, thinking to seek out his pulse as she had done with Vera, but she could not do it.

"Tell me you have not done this thing, Seryozha," she whispered to his lifeless body."

She stood quickly, then, and hoping against hope said, "Nadya. Send for Dr. Chlenov. Quickly now. Hurry—in case he yet lives."

Dazed, she stooped again to set aright the chair that had toppled when, apparently, Sergei's body had tumbled from it. It was then she noticed the two white envelopes on the desk, one with her name written in a trembling hand. She reached for it slowly, not certain she really dared open it.

"And the inspector," Marya called after Nadya, as she took the envelope between finger and thumb.

"Tell him there's been … there's been an accident."

She stared a moment at her name. Her eyes darted to the other envelope, which she now saw was addressed to Sergei's parents and brother. She took that envelope in her other hand and gazed at their two white faces with dread. With his inert body lying but a foot or two from her, she could imagine with what outpourings of pain they must be filled.

As if in a trance, she stepped from the room and sat with her back pressed to the wall. She set the envelopes on her thighs. Though she once again rested her hand alongside Vera's face, her palm cupping it, she could not tear her eyes from the envelopes.

Vera stirred, and Marya glanced her way but immediately looked back at the envelopes. Her hands trembling, she took the one with her name, carefully tore open the wax seal, and read. She let the letter drift to the floor and her head fell back against the wall again.

"Seryozha, oh Seryozha: What have you done?"

Her voice was barely above a whisper.

"No. No: it's my fault. I know it full well. For I thought I had been truthful, but I was not truthful enough. I should have made you see …"

A low moan came from Vera, and Marya turned her attention to her.

"Verochka."

Marya lightly patted her cheek, and Vera's eyes fluttered open. For a moment, she seemed to try to comprehend where she was, but then it was clear that the full memory had returned to her.

"Oh my God, Misha. Oh my God."

She pulled herself up to a sitting position and wrapped her arms around Marya, burying her head against Marya's shoulder.

Marya stroked her hair, which had come unpinned in several places. The second envelope crinkled beneath Vera's hip, and Marya reached to wrest it out. As she did so, the seal came loose.

Curiosity and fear of denouncement at Sergei's hand caused her to set aside concerns about trespassing, and though she could not still herself enough to read the letter from beginning to end, phrases leapt from the page to her eye: "the dishonor of taking my own life," "I cannot believe … that it's here I was destined to go," "not blame Marya."

She winced with a pain that was almost physical and brought her hand to rest on the floor, still clutching the letter.

"No, no." Marya whispered through the ache in my throat.

Vera tightened her grip on Marya, who closed her eyes and focused on simply breathing. Her limbs felt heavy as logs.

"Hurry—hurry—in here, inspector." Ilyusha's voice carried through the halls to the women's ears.

Marya found herself fervently wishing she was a girl again, with her Papa there to take care of everything. For the first time in a long while, she yearned to feel the scratchiness of his cheek scrape across hers in embrace, to smell the sweet odor of his pipe tobacco lingering in his clothes. She thought of how he had shaped her spirit, of how he taught her to hunt, to love learning, to tell the poisonous mushroom from the good. She saw in her mind, as if in a photograph, his study at Khrupkaya Luna, the saber that hung above his desk, the floor-to-ceiling bookcase filled with Lermontov and Pushkin and Gogol, the small round table where he sometimes received visitors. She thought of how the moon may be carved away to nothing yet always it returns.

"Come," Marya said to Vera. "The inspector is here."

And as Marya stood, she gathered Sergei's last words into her hand.

Epilogue

Recriminations, grief, and trepidation in many shades have weighed upon us in the year since Seryozha took his life, and still, I do not find satisfaction in their examination. Add them up, and what have I? Sadness beyond belief.

It occurs to me, of course, that human interaction may not be sorted, quantified, and resolved in the same way numbers can. Which disadvantages me in that realm, for I have little patience for what cannot be scribbled on paper and manipulated into sense.

And so we begin to set aside the burdens of these twelve months. Verochka and I have come out whole on the other side through what function I do not know, but it must be based in love, of which we have an abundance. I have, at last, taken up Grisha's project again, and though he protests understanding of my situation, it may be that we have lost our chance to connect with Strannoliubsky. I am less dismayed by this than I might have thought. I have come to realize my attention need be distributed more to those in my life who take human form—Verochka, most certainly, but also Sasha Kobiakova and her small circle, with whom friendship has taken root and begins to grow—and less to the cold, clean comfort of mathematics. I have come to realize as well, nimble though I may be with numbers, I likely do not share Sofia Kovalevskaya's genius. Or perhaps my love for Vera, and the tragedy we have borne, has made me too soft for the trials of a woman who yearns to pursue mathematical study in this time and place.

Verochka's love and a cleansing letter from Seryozha's cousin Filya, in which he absolves me of certain guilts and clarifies the progress of Seryozha's turmoil, have helped to ferry me across this river of trials. For Verochka, the guilt has been especially fierce, for she is of an intensely tender nature and berates herself for being more callous toward Seryozha than she would've been had she not been so fearful on her own account. Perhaps my assurances of exculpation have been of some consequence, but it may be that setting free Zubilo shortly after Seryozha left us provided her some release, as though little bully, little Zubilo, had tucked her cares beneath his wings and carried them away.

THE END

Acknowledgments

Portions of chapters 5, 10, and 10.5 were published as the short story "Vector" by the online periodical *Escape into Life.*

Infraction is based on a true story, recounted in Laura Engelstein's "Archives: Lesbian Vignettes: A Russian Triptych from the 1890s" (*Signs: Journal of Women in Culture and Society* 15, no. 4 [1990]: 813–31). Engelstein's research opened a whole world to me, which I now hope to open for many others. The historical details that augment the twelve-page account given in Engelstein come from numerous sources. Key among them are Barbara Alpern Engel, *Mothers and Daughters: Women of the Intelligentsia in Nineteenth-Century Russia* (Cambridge: Cambridge University of Press, 1983); Dan Healey, *Homosexual Desire in Revolutionary Russia* (Chicago: University of Chicago Press, 2001), including judicious borrowing from the writings of Mikhail Kuzmin cited therein; Suzanne Massie, *Land of the Firebird: The Beauty of Old Russia* (New York: Simon & Schuster, 1980); and Mary Stuart's work on librarianship at the Imperial Public Library. In the main, I have endeavored to adhere to the chronology of women's activism as set out by Engel, but I have condensed some of this history in order to include more aspects of the movement within the time frame of the novel. I have also taken liberties with the timing of Maurice Petipa's ballet *Le Corsaire*, which would have, in fact, taken place some eight years earlier than the events of the story, and with references to the Cinizelli Circus, the first stationary edifice for which was not built until a year after our story.

Historians Dianne E. Farrell, Barbara Alpern Engel, and Adele Lindenmeyr generously provided guidance on research questions even though I was previously unknown to them. I offer thanks for this kindness, especially to Adele Lindenmeyr, who also took the time to read and comment on the manuscript. I thank Jane Costlow for information on bird keeping in Russia, and Gitta Hammarberg for sharing with me her article "Dogs and Doggerel: Gogol's Eighteenth-Century Roots" prior to its publication.

Thanks are due as well to the Ragdale and Hedgebrook Foundations, where portions of the work on this book were completed; to Jack and Nancy Forde for partially funding a research trip to St. Petersburg, Russia; to Mikhail Iossel and the Summer Literary Seminars for providing the framework for that trip and for a small fellowship to help make it possible; and to the faculty and students of Vermont College's MFA in Writing

Program, from whom I received valuable comments on the book in its most primitive stages; I particularly thank VC's Walter Wetherell and Diane Lefer for their in-depth critiques of an early draft and Sydney Lea for encouragement, advice, and friendship.

I also owe a debt of gratitude to friends and family members for the many forms of assistance they provided: to Erik Carlson, for being my personal Russian translator and go-to guy on all things Russian; to Mary Kay Zuravleff for information on the Russian Orthodox faith and for taking me seriously as a writer; to Daniel Jaffe for his guidance on pronouncing Russian names and places; to Jane Lichty, Joe Parson, and Maia Rigas for providing me with important reference materials; to Emily Williams for detailing the particulars of her passion for math; to Lisa Brackbill, Linda Bubon, Erik Carlson, Deborah DeManno, Erin DeWitt, Renate Gokl, Eleanor Mayer, Mollie McQuillan, Julie Penn, Rovana Popoff, and Emily Williams for helping me fine-tune the manuscript at various stages; to Gregg Shapiro for sending me to Rattling Good Yarns Press; to Sukie de la Croix and Ian Henzel of the aforementioned press for finding merit in the tale I've spun here; and to Barbara Karant for being a charter member with me of Artists Anonymous, though I doubt we'll ever kick the addiction.

And in a category all her own is Kathy Forde, whose contributions are more than I can count, though certainly among them have been her creative efforts to manufacture writing time for me, suggestions for improvements to characters and scenes in the novel, her tough-love pep talks, and the constancy of her affections.

About the Author

Yvonne Zipter is the author of two nonfiction books (*Ransacking the Closet* and *Diamonds Are a Dyke's Best Friend*), three poetry collections (*Kissing the Long Face of the Greyhound, The Patience of Metal,* and *Like Some Bookie God*), and a number of short stories, including "Günther's Wife," which won first place in LitPot ezine eclectic's Flash Fiction Contest, and "Third Date," which was selected for *Best Lesbian Love Stories 2005*. She was also the author of the syndicated humor column "Inside Out," on lesbian life, which ran for ten years in newspapers from Washington, DC, to Oklahoma City to San Diego after its debut in Chicago's *Windy City Times*. She is one of the founders of *Hot Wire: A Journal of Women's Music and Culture* and a 1995 inductee into the Chicago LGBT Hall of Fame. In 2020, she appeared briefly in the documentary *A Secret Love* and provided some of the narration. Her published poems are currently being sold in two poetry-vending machines in Chicago, the proceeds from which are donated to a nonprofit arts organization called Arts Alive Chicago. She holds an MFA in Fiction Writing from Vermont College. She recently retired from being a manuscript editor at the University of Chicago Press. She lives in Chicago with her wife Kathy Forde and retired racing greyhound Gracie—their fifth since 1999.